THE KEEPER'S
CUP

KEN FRY

www.booksbykenfry.com

Join Ken Fry's Circle of Readers and Get Free eBooks
http://bit.ly/circleofreaders

Edited by Eeva Lancaster

Cover Design and Formatting by The Book Khaleesi
www.thebookkhaleesi.com

BOOKS by KEN FRY

AUDIOBOOKS

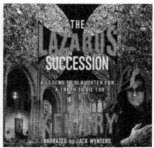
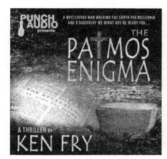

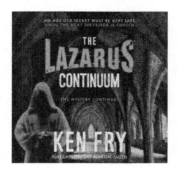

~ Available on Audible and iTunes ~

Glastonbury Tor

GLOSSARY

Glastonbury Tor - is a hill near Glastonbury in the English county of Somerset, topped by the roofless St Michael's Tower. The entire site is managed by the National Trust and has been designated a scheduled monument. The Tor is mentioned in Celtic mythology, particularly in myths linked to King Arthur, and has several other enduring mythological and spiritual associations.

The Tor seems to have been called *Ynys yr Afalon* (meaning "The Isle of Avalon") by the Britons and is believed by some, including the 12th and 13th century writer Gerald of Wales, to be the Avalon of Arthurian legend. The Tor has been associated with the name Avalon, and identified with King Arthur, since the alleged discovery of his and Queen Guinevere's neatly labelled coffins in 1191, recounted by Gerald of Wales. Author Christopher L. Hodapp asserts in his book The Templar Code for Dummies that Glastonbury Tor is one of the possible locations of the Holy Grail, because it is close to the monastery that housed the Nanteos Cup.

Santa Alleanza - The Vatican's Intelligence Service

Celtiberians - a group of Celts and Celticized peoples inhabiting the central-eastern Iberian Peninsula during the final centuries BC.

The Botoritta Plaques - Four bronze plaques discovered in Botorrita near Saragossa, Spain, dating to the early 1st century

BC, labelled Botorrita I, II, III and IV

Botorrita II is in the Latin language, but Botorrita I, III and IV, inscribed in the Celtiberian script, constitute the main part of the Celtiberian corpus.

Aramaic - Semitic language of the Northern Central, or Northwestern, group that was originally spoken by the ancient Middle Eastern people known as Aramaeans. It was most closely related to Hebrew, Syriac, and Phoenician and was written in a script derived from the Phoenician alphabet.

Aramaic dialects survived into Roman times, however, particularly in Palestine and Syria. Aramaic had replaced Hebrew as the language of the Jews as early as the 6th century BCE. Certain portions of the Bible—i.e., the books of Daniel and Ezra — are written in Aramaic, as are the Babylonian and Jerusalem Talmuds.

Among the Jews, Aramaic was used by the common people, while Hebrew remained the language of religion and government and of the upper class. Jesus and the Apostles are believed to have spoken Aramaic, and Aramaic-language translations (Targums) of the Old Testament circulated. Aramaic continued in wide use until about 650 CE, when it was supplanted by Arabic.

Tomb of Jesus Ossuary - A burial box, or ossuary, with the inscription "Judah son of Jesus," found in the East Talpiot district of East Jerusalem.

Fata Morgana - A Fata Morgana (Italian: [ˈfaːta morˈɡaːna]) is a complex form of superior mirage that is seen in a narrow band right above the horizon. It is an Italian term named after the Arthurian sorceress Morgan le Fay, from a belief that these mirages, often seen in the Strait of Messina, were fairy castles in the air or false land created by her witchcraft to lure sailors to their deaths.[citation needed] Although the term Fata Morgana sometimes is applied to other more common kinds of mirages, true Fata Morgana is different from both an ordinary superior mirage and an inferior mirage.

Hanged, drawn and quartered - To be hanged, drawn and quartered was a punishment in England used for men found guilty of high treason.

The full punishment was made up of the following: The victim was:

Dragged, usually by a horse, on a wooden frame to the place where he was to be publicly put to death. This is one possible meaning of drawn.

[1] A more likely meaning of drawn is the removal of the inner organs.

[2] Hanged by the neck for a short time or until almost dead (hanged).

Removed from hanging and placed on a table. Still alive, the victim was cut open in the abdomen and his intestines and sex organs removed (this is another meaning of drawn—see the reference to the Oxford English Dictionary below). The removed organs were burned in a flame, prepared close to the prisoner.

[3] The victim's head was cut off, and the rest of the body hacked into four parts or quarters (quartered).

LiDAR - or *Light Detection and Ranging,* is a popular remote sensing method used for measuring the exact distance of an object on the earth's surface. Even though it was first used in the 1960s when laser scanners were mounted to aeroplanes, LiDAR didn't get the popularity it deserved until twenty years later. It was only during the 1980s after the introduction of GPS that it became a popular method for calculating accurate geospatial measurements.

LiDAR uses a pulsed laser to calculate an object's variable distances from the earth surface. These light pulses — put together with the information collected by the airborne system — generate accurate 3D information about the earth surface and the target object.

The Gospel of Thomas - was discovered near Nag Hammadi, Egypt, in December 1945 among a group of books known as the Nag Hammadi library. Scholars speculate that the works were buried in response to a letter from Bishop Athanasius declaring a strict canon of Christian scripture. Scholars have proposed dates of composition as early as AD 60 and as late as AD 140.

The Coptic-language text, the second of seven contained in what modern-day scholars have designated as Codex II, is composed of 114 sayings attributed to Jesus. Almost two thirds of these sayings resemble those found in the canonical gospels and its editio minor counts more than 80% of parallels, while it is speculated that the other sayings were added from Gnostic tradition.

The Gospel of Thomas is very different in tone and structure from other New Testament apocrypha and the four Canonical Gospels. Unlike the canonical Gospels, it is not a narrative account of the life of Jesus; instead, it consists of logia (sayings) attributed to Jesus, sometimes stand-alone, sometimes embedded in short dialogues or parables.

The Gospel of Philip - is one of the Gnostic Gospels, a text of New Testament apocrypha, dated to around the 3rd century but lost in medieval times until rediscovered by accident, buried with other texts near Nag Hammadi in Egypt, in 1945.

As in other texts often associated with what has been referred to as "Gnosticism," such as the Gospel of Thomas and Gospel of Mary, the Gospel of Philip defends a tradition that gives Mary Magdalene a special relationship and insight into Jesus' teaching.

Valentinian Theology - Valentinus and his followers believed that God, the supreme Father is "uncontained, incomprehensible and cannot be seen or heard" (Against Heresies 1:2:5). Therefore he defies accurate description. He is infinite, without beginning or end and is the ultimate origin of all things. He encompasses all things without being encompassed (Ep5:3, Gospel of Truth 18:34, Valentinian Exposition 22:27-28, Against Heresies 2:2:2). Everything including the world lies within the Father and continues to be part of him. God manifests himself through a process of self-unfolding in the subsequent multiplicity of being while maintaining his unity.

All Valentinians agree that God incorporates both masculine and feminine characteristics. This is in opposition to traditional Jewish and orthodox Christian descriptions of God in exclusively masculine terms. According to most sources, the Father (or Parent) can be understood as a male-female dyad. This is related to the notion that God provides the universe with both form and substance.

AUTHOR'S NOTE

Is there a different truth behind the greatest story ever told?

What if everything you know about Jesus and Mary Magdalene is wrong?

What if there's a story that goes deeper... a story that when revealed, could threaten the faith of billions of people around the world?

What will powerful factions do to get hold of this information?

I suspect that The Keeper's Cup will upset some people of various religious denominations. This was never my intent, but I don't doubt there will be reaction. I can't help that nor make apology. At all times, I have attempted to show loving kindness and respect.

Pre-Constantine Christianity had much to say before, but with a large swipe of his brush, much of the early writings of the Essenes and others, were doomed to the bin by the Emperor, (who only became a Christian on his deathbed). Including the writings of both disciples, Thomas and Philip.

Since there was no mention of miracles or Christ's crucifixion, their words were deemed not worthy.

Through history, The Magdalene has been portrayed as a prostitute. The amounting evidence that she was a woman of huge spiritual dimension contradicted the patriarchal dimensions of men as superior. Hence, the appellation. That has now been refuted.

The canonical Gospels themselves fail to agree on certain

points. So... what can be trusted?

The entire issue has fascinated me for many years. I would love to know if it was true or not, but the evidence always appeared shaky to me.

Because of that, my story attempts to place a new perspective on events. I'm aware that at times that can be clumsy, but it was written with hope and joy.

How did Christianity appear in England long before the early saints arrived?

That, I think, is an intriguing question. Don't you agree?

That factor alone made my story worth writing about. Highly speculative, it is. Though, no more so than people walking on water or changing water into wine.

At the end of the day, it is a story... nothing else. I don't ask you to believe it. It's not about that. It's about a deep love of humanity, and the cruelties that entwine that concept.

~ Ken Fry
Surrey, UK
July 2020

CHAPTER 1

C RACK! The splattering noise groaned loud from splintered timber. Its torturous sound penetrated and fractured the surrounding silence.

Wood split. Blood flowed.

Red stained hands held hard onto metal grips, grabbing at the cruel nail that pinned both heels and ankles together to the wood in a tormented embrace.

Tug… tug… pull… twist… gently turn.

The rivet began to loosen.

Joseph of Arimathea, with bent and aching body, strained gently on the impaled spike and started easing it away from the wooden structure.

Bone splinters fell away, along with flesh and more blood.

A low moan came from the impaled man, followed by a soft whisper. "Gently, brother. Gently, I pray you, as yet I live…"

Joseph, shocked to hear the whisper, ensured his endeavours became more delicate as he wielded the pincers once more.

With a few more gentle tugs, the nail loosened and released one heel, and then the other, until at last, he eased the nail out and freed the blood-encrusted feet.

He placed the nail in the leather pouch tied to his waist.

The figure became unconscious and his head rolled downwards to his lacerated and gore-streaked chest.

On the man's side, the spear of the Roman Centurion, Longinus, had performed its task. A chest wound lay open, dripping blood.

A woman with long, red hair hanging from her shoulders, her face creased in sorrow and anguish, held a wooden cup close to the wound. Its seal was wedged open as the woman called The Magdalene filled it to the brim. Afterwards, she held it tightly to her bosom.

Why she had done this, she knew not. She only felt a compulsion to do so. For a reason she could not understand, it was of importance. She had heard Joseph's tortured whisper. *He lives! He lives! Jehovah be praised!*

As she heard those words, the woman's body started to shake. Joseph too, found it difficult to concentrate. His pale lips began to quiver... but there was more to do. The man lived but his heart beat an erratic rhythm.

Close by, the man's mother, whose name was Mary, wept aloud. Tears of disbelief ran down her lined face. *This is my son. He harmed nobody, nor did he steal or murder, and yet... this they have done to him.*

Joseph, with gentle urgency, reached the wrists and moved firstly to the right one. Once more, he used his metal tongs to grasp the head of the offensive nail. Again, he began the delicate extraction process.

The spike had missed vital arteries. The Romans knew how to make a death slow and painful.

As he went about the painstaking process of freeing the man's wrists, Joseph could see the man lapsing in and out of consciousness. *It was a miracle that he was even still alive!*

Using his own body to prop up the impaled figure, he wasted no time in freeing the right wrist. With another small tug, it was free.

"AAAH!"

Joseph stared at a crimson hole pumping out blood. With haste, he moved to the left and repeated the process until both wrists were free.

From the blistered and raw lips of the crucified man came a plea, almost inaudible. "For the love of God, water, water."

Joseph knew he could not honour the request. He moved closer to the man's ear and whispered, "You are not to be seen alive. Quiet, Master, I beg you. Please bear the pain a while longer and water will arrive once we are gone from here."

He placed the two blood-soaked nails into his pouch with the first, looked across to Mary, ran his stained arm through his white hair, and nodded.

There was a deathlike pallor to the man's face. A tomblike pastiness bathed the naked figure, made more so by the inter-section of crimson streaks of sweat-imbued blood. He lapsed into unconsciousness once more.

Mary leant forward and stroked the face. "Yeshua, my son, my adorable son. What have they done to you? You spoke only of love and kindness, and this is how they repay you." She produced a shroud, and along with the Magdalene and Joseph, they lowered the sticky, mutilated, inert body from the cross and into it. With care, Mary wrapped the shroud around her son.

He continued to breathe.

Just.

A sparrow fluttered and hovered close by, a sad lament from his beak.

Joseph had commandeered a donkey with a small, low cart. They eased the unconscious, covered body onto it. When it was done and they began moving away, it looked like any other funeral cart.

The sparrow followed.

Above, the sky surrendered to thick, black, and ever darkening clouds. Afternoon light was turning into sudden night. Beneath them, they felt the ground around begin to tremble.

All was not well in heaven or on earth.

CHAPTER 2

Three years later...
North West Gaul
Burdigala, now called Bordeaux

The gaunt figure pulled his robe tightly across his body as a gusting wind blew in from the sea. His long, dark hair moved without protest or defence across his weary face. The air was rich with the smell of the ocean and tasted of salt. He'd been walking since the sun arose. His gait was unsteady and the pains in his feet and arms were never far away. It had been that way since the nails had been pulled from his flesh and bones those three years gone.

His mind continued to flick through all possibilities. Decisions had been made. He had assembled his tools and they were packed and ready for the journey. Nearby, and moored, was the fully equipped fishing boat given by his sympathetic followers. News had reached him that Joseph ben Caiaphas, the Jewish High Priest, had learnt of his survival, his escape, and his whereabouts. He was now being hunted. The death sentence had to be fulfilled.

For Yeshua, it was time to leave. The avenging hand of authority was reaching out for him. If it grasped him, this time, there would be no escape from the cruelties of crucifixion. To accompany him was his ageing mother, Mary, also The Magdalene Mary, and their young beloved son, Judah. The Magdalene was carrying her unborn child of two months.

Everything they needed – tools, coins, clothing, fishing nets and various other items – were on board. They intended to make frequent stops in various ports.

"Where do you think we shall be going?" asked Magdalene as she twirled the ends of her red hair.

Pointing across the sea, Yeshua replied, "I had a dream last night. My heavenly Parent told me it was now time to leave Gaul. It is no longer safe. I was told that there is an island to the north that some are calling Britannia. It is to there we must direct our boat. The journey will take many months at sea, but with fair winds, we may reach it before our child is due. God will protect us. But we must away now before knowledge of what we intend is discovered. Come, all of you."

"One moment," Magdalene said. "There is something we must do. Do as I do, please." Gathering her shawl and robe around, she knelt gently to the ground, her long hair billowing out and partially obscuring her face. "Let us hold hands."

She reached out for his mother's and Yeshua's. Judah smiled. He was being an adult and held his small arms out and they each held a hand.

She spoke softly but her words were carried across land

and sea. "Let us thank this land of Gaul for giving us safety and protection. It is now a blessed place and its soil is holy. We are about to depart and wish its people health, prosperity, and faithfulness to God, our Parent, forever. May our blessings cleanse you of all wrongdoings and sins. Amen."

They all uttered, "So be it."

Within the hour, the shoreline had vanished, and they followed the coastline northwards. The people left behind would miss her healing powers.

* * *

Eighteen months later...
Ynis Wydryn, The Isle of Glass
Known now as Glastonbury Tor

Judah loved his new sister, named Sarah. Both Mary and the Magdalene had similar affections for her. There seemed to be an aura around her that was indefinable. Born in close proximity and in the shadow of the Tor, Yeshua felt that his Parent had chosen this place for a special reason. Its significance could not be denied.

More remarkable, they had eluded the Roman search squads and the far-reaching grasp of Caiaphas. It had not taken long for his family to be accepted by the local tribe. Yeshua's words and woodworking skills were in demand and respected.

For this, he was given assistance in building a roundhouse made of wattle and daub. It was vastly different from the stone home he once had in Judea. The roundhouse roof made of straw and mud had a hole at the very top of it to allow smoke to escape. All cooking was done on a central fire

7

inside. The ground was covered in a mixture of reeds and straw with thicker piles for bedding.

He made small bowls and utensils for the community, or whatever they wanted him to make. When asked, he would talk of a God, invisible and greater than their pagan druidic forces. He argued that the forces they revered were part of God's plan and creation. To many, his words made sense… but to others, they were a threat to the established hierarchy. He gathered many followers as the years advanced and amongst these were the tribal chieftain, Arthwys and his wife, Brianna.

Arthwys was a strong and intelligent man – tall and with a sturdy build. His face expressed the hardships of his life with scars and blemishes, but from his brown eyes shone a kindly but firm expression. He was also brave and had proven himself in battles many times. He was taller than most and his long blond hair hung thickly around his shoulders. Fixed around his neck was a decorative gold and silver torc. This was the emblem of a tribal chieftain and leader. He wore a fur tunic, and thick woollen trousers, and around his waist hung a short sword. His wife, Brianna, was dressed in a flowing woollen skirt and fitted doublet.

It had not taken him long to develop a fondness for Yeshua and his family. They had added a new dimension to the community, not only with their skills, but also with their intriguing words of their God.

Judah and Sarah had come to regard them as their second mother and father. There was great love between them all and they shared frequent kindnesses with small and often unexpected gifts.

Without being aware of it, the community and others around had begun the silent, almost stealthy process of change.

* * *

That morning was wet, cold and with much rain and wind. Yeshua was working on a small table he hoped to barter for supplies. Previous examples had proved popular. He paused to rest. His old wounds were always there to give a painful reminder of his role in God's grand scheme of things. There were frequent short, sharp stabs of pain in his feet and simultaneously followed by others in his wrists and hands. When this happened, he understood, accepted, and gave thanks to God.

His mother, Mary, and Magda, as she was called in their community, were preparing bread and meats for their next meal. The roundhouse filled with warmth and smoke, mingled with the delicious aroma of breads baking.

A dark shadow filled the entrance. Both women looked up, startled. It was Arthwys. He was dressed in furs and decorated robes. The expression on his weathered face was grim.

Magda gave a quick look at Mary who looked worried.

"What ails you, Arthwys?" Mary asked.

His voice was urgent. "Come quick! It is Brianna. She has been taken with a sudden sickness and cannot walk. Our Druid cannot cure her. I have been to our water well and implored our Druid Great God Nodens to exercise his healing powers, but he has not answered. I fear she may be dying. I have seen and heard how you and Magda have healed others. Is there anything you know of that may help Brianna live?"

The Magdalene looked across to Yeshua who had stopped working. For a moment, he closed his eyes as if in prayer. On opening them, he looked across to her. "You know enough, sweet wife. Go to her. You know what you must do." He turned to Arthwys. "You are a good man, Arthwys, and it

9

shall be done, and when you see, you will believe in our Good Parent, as you have heard us speak the name of God. Of that, I am certain.

Magda bowed her head. "Wait, Arthwys." She went to the darkest part of the large room and uncovered a leather pouch. "It is here still." She picked it up and signalled for him to return to his own dwelling. "I shall follow you."

He looked puzzled. "What is that you carry?"

"It is not for you to know or to be concerned about. She will be better and live."

A small knot of people had gathered around the entrance to his roundhouse. News of Brianna's plight had reached everyone in the community. They stood in a huddle around the entrance to his dwelling.

Arthwys pushed them to one side and strode into the room. Brianna lay on a rough covering of straw. She was bent in two in a foetal position. Her hands and fingers had gone white and had locked into a claw-like state. She was unable to move and soft moans came from her mouth, which was flecked in dribble and drool.

She appeared paralysed.

Arthwys spoke softly to her, "Brianna, my poor wife. Magda may be able to help. She is here for you." He summoned her over. Brianna made no sound or sign of recognition.

Magda stood over her. She raised her eyes skywards and offered up a low prayer. "In the name of God our Parent, and the Christ, I ask that this woman Brianna may be healed, and allowed back to her people. I pray that she may also be able to follow you and spread your word to all."

The onlookers went silent. From the central fire, smoke drifted lazily upwards to the hole in the roof. Nobody moved.

The Magdalene knelt down beside Brianna and opened the pouch before lifting up a wooden cup. She lifted the tight lid to reveal its brim which was full of bright red and watery liquid. It had not changed and had remained in the same condition as when it had been collected that dreadful day years ago on the hill of Calvary. Time had not diminished it.

With care, she turned Brianna's head around. Now, Magda was again locked in silent prayer as she poured the blood and water into the open mouth.

Liquid poured from the cup to Brianna's mouth, but the cup did not empty... nor did its level diminish. The onlookers did not see this.

Almost at once, Brianna's body began to shake.

Arthwys looked alarmed. "What have you done to her? What was that you gave her?" He shouted with a look of incredulity across his broad face.

"Wait and you will see," Magda replied.

Everyone looked aghast. No sooner had they done so when Brianna's body went limp as all tension left it. Her hands and fingers straightened. A few moments passed before she lifted her head with a smile on her face, that had now returned to its usual colour and complexion. "Where have I been?" She looked around at them all. "I must have fallen asleep."

"You have been in the care of our Parent, and now you are healed." Magda embraced her. "Give thanks to God."

In awe, every person present sank to their knees, uncertain, but certain in many other ways, that what they had witnessed was something beyond their understanding. Of that there remained not a doubt.

CHAPTER 3

Vatican City
The Present Day

T he bishop wished he was back at his favourite church close to Soho in London. Our Lady of the Assumption and St. Gregory had a quiet spirituality he adored. He had never enjoyed the pace and the crowds who flocked around the Vatican almost every day of the year. Surrounded by the suffocating presence of ancient Roman culture, an overbearingly hot sun, plus the aroma of coffee and pasta cooking, did little to improve Bishop Vincent Fisher's mood. Wearing his bishop's cassock and the purple sash adorned with a gold pectoral crucifix, he stood close to St. Peter's Basilica and its permanent queue of the faithful and the curious.

"Monsignor," a voice called loudly to him.

The bishop adjusted his sunglasses and turned around.

Walking swiftly towards him and waving his arm was a short, overweight man, whose face was drenched in sweat.

Not certain how to respond, he simply replied, *"Si?"*

"Monsignor, *Buon giorno.* I do speak English. I am Father Vincenzo."

Only then did the bishop notice the priest's half covered collar. "Have we met before Father Vincenzo? How may I help you?" He shook the extended hand.

"Forgive me, Monsignor. I have recently been appointed to the Dicastery for Communications, headed by Palo Ruffini, our prefect. As such, we knew of your visit here. I recognised you from the photographs we have. You're here to meet with Cardinal Nicholas who will introduce you to our Holy Father, Pope Adrian, yes?"

Why is he telling me all this? A feeling of annoyance rippled through the bishop as he twirled his gold and purple ring, part of a bishop's attire. *How on earth do they get all this information on me? Is there nothing secret anymore?* "You're well informed." He snapped with a sour tone.

"It is my job, Monsignor. I am told that you are to discuss excavations connected to certain legends back in your country?"

"Whatever I'm here to discuss will be between me and the pope, not the cardinal and certainly not you."

The bishop's frank annoyance did not deter the priest, even as the bishop's pace noticeably quickened across the square. He persisted. "I understand that earlier this year, in your country, an eminent archaeologist, Dr. Helen Newbury, God rest her soul, was found dead at the bottom of a cliff where she had been digging. The police said it was an accident. There was no sign of foul play. It was rumoured that she, on your behalf, was looking for a holy relic, purported to be connected with Jesus himself. Can you verify that, Bishop Fisher? Who has taken over from her?"

Bishop Fisher had an uncomfortable thought. *I don't believe this man. Something is not right about him.* "I have nothing more to say to you, Father. Look, I am not at liberty to speak about anything. Why don't you contact Cardinal Nicholas directly, as you are so interested? I have reached my rooms and I bid you goodbye."

Father Vincenzo's expression hardened. "It's been a pleasure to meet you, my bishop."

"Thank you, Father."

"There's one more thing, Bishop Fisher."

"Don't you ever give up? Watch out! Careful now." He raised his voice as a large, black delivery van screeched to a halt beside the priest.

"It's fine, Monsignor, it is for you."

"What? Now listen …"

He did not finish his sentence. Vincenzo, with strength beyond his flabby frame, seized the bishop by the shoulders and lapel, spun him around and pushed him hard into the open side door of the vehicle. The bishop fell to the floor and another man waiting inside kicked him hard in the ribs and then followed up by sitting on him and bending his arm in a painful lock. Before he could shout out, another blow struck his head and he went senseless.

* * *

Bishop Fisher struggled to open his eyes to see where he was. With great effort, they opened, but he was unable to move. He was in a small, bare room and tied to a wooden chair. A wet leather gag was bound around his mouth. Two Italian looking men stood in opposite corners next to him.

Fear gripped his pounding heart and racing mind. In his entire life, he had never experienced terror on this scale, even when as a small child, he had tumbled into a deep and dark well and was undiscovered for two days. He now feared for his life.

Turning his head, he could see the dubious priest, Vincenzo, sitting close by and filing his fingernails.

Bishop Fisher made an effort to speak but only succeeded in producing a muffled, gulping sound from behind his gag. Nobody looked at him. The sound of a door opening caused him to look across his other shoulder. His eyes widened with astonishment. The tall figure of a gaunt looking, skeletal man, with a prominent limp, walked in. He wore a cassock, and the trademark red *zucchetto* of a cardinal was perched firmly on the thinning hair of his head.

The bishop, in a state of shock, fought to find his breath. He recognised the man immediately. It was Cardinal Nicholas.

The cardinal limped around him, and with desolate grey eyes devoid of compassion, he carefully scrutinized the prisoner. As he did so, he opened his solid, silver cigarette case, lit a Davidoff cigarette, inhaled deeply, and without care, blew a lungful of smoke through the nostrils of his hooked Roman nose in the direction of his captive.

"Greetings, Bishop Fisher." His voice resonated like an off-tune funeral bell. "Welcome to Rome and to Vatican City. We are sorry that we have to meet in this manner, but really there was no other option." More blue-tinged smoke drifted through the air. He nodded to one of the men who walked over and savagely tore the gag off the bishop's mouth. The cardinal managed a tight-lipped smile. He gave a crooked smirk revealing cracked and yellow teeth, inhaled deeply, before blowing another lungful in the direction of the bishop's face. "Now, I'm sure that will allow you to speak more freely."

Fisher gulped in several mouthfuls of much needed air and gasped out. "What is the meaning of this? What do you want from me? This is an outrage! You'll never get away with it."

The cardinal looked amused. "Oh, but we will. The last place the *carabinieri* will come looking for your dead body will be here – a stone's throw from the pontiff's palace."

Fisher experienced another injection of terror. "Dead body! What are you on about? I don't understand any of this!"

"Bishop, it doesn't have to be a fatal outcome." He lied. "I have some questions for you, and if you answer these truthfully, you may live. I need to know what you are about to tell our pope. My informants have told me the most interesting of rumours. What exactly are you looking for in your excavations? What have they found so far and where are you looking exactly? I also understand a false operation has been underway to keep others off the trail of your true goal. Who is in charge and where does your funding come from? I want answers to all these questions and maybe… I'll let you live."

"My information is for the pope only. I have nothing to say to you." As soon as he had said these words, Bishop Fisher had a certainty that his life was not going to be long, and he may never reach the pope. How could he be let free now?

"As you wish, my good bishop. I shall leave you now and when I return, I hope you have changed your mind. There is no reason why we can't work together." He turned to leave, but before he did so, he nodded at the men in the room.

With the cardinal gone, a silence descended on the room

like the bishop's church on an early Monday morning.

It didn't last long.

He felt a sharp blow across his neck, which sent his head lurching sideways. The leather around his mouth was replaced and the new gag cut into his mouth, muffling his screams. His head went one way then another, time after time.

There was no respite until Vincenzo held up his hand and the beating ceased. Blood dripped from Bishop Fisher's mouth, nose, and temples.

"Bishop, we have not yet finished. This is just a sample of what could get very much worse for you." He turned to his men. "Strip him."

His clothes were ripped and cut from him. When that was done, Vincenzo lobbed a bottle of watery oil to one of the men. "Lubricate him well."

The man dripped oil over the bishop's entire body and smoothed it in with a large cloth. When that was done, Vincenzo produced two electrodes from behind a table, wired up to the main system. He clipped one to the bishop's nipple and the other to the back of his hand. Before Fisher could react, Vincenzo threw the switch, and turned the voltage control handle.

There was an immediate crackling explosion of static electrical sound as hundreds of volts zapped into the Bishop's chest and arm.

His torso arched and his head lurched backwards with eyes full of agonised dread. The electrodes were switched off.

"You will talk now? If you do not, this will go on for hours, even days and nights."

"You will perish in hell." The bishop's agonised response was laughed off.

"So sorry for this, Bishop." Vincenzo threw the switch

and cranked the handle again.

The screams went on for over two hours until the pain-shot, twitching and convulsing body of the bishop could take no more. "Enough! Enough! I will tell you."

Bishop Fisher nodded his head. The gag was removed and with a voice racked with pain and terror, he proceeded to tell them everything they had asked to know.

The secret mission was now no longer so.

* * *

Five days later...

Cardinal Nicholas gave a wry smile of satisfaction. In his hands, he held a copy of the Vatican newspaper, *L'Ossevatore Romano*. Like most other Italian newspapers, it carried reports of the discovery of the body of the missing English bishop. He had never arrived at a prearranged meeting with Pope Adrian. Nobody had an explanation.

His ravaged remains had been discovered in the *Parco Regionale dell'Appia Antica,* Europe's largest park, and barely three miles from the city centre of Rome. It was being said that he had been attacked by a small pack of wolves that had been terrorising the city outskirts of late. The wounds were consistent with such an attack.

He settled down for lunch with a glass of fine *Carmignano* red wine and read and reread the wolves' attack report several times. All had gone better than expected. He now knew everything that the pope knew and his involvement. The cardinal was going to ensure that once his own secret operation was in place, the pope would not know much more either.

For the next stage of his operations, a visit to the UK

would be required.

CHAPTER 4

Six months previously…
Wookey Hole Caves (Seven miles from Glastonbury)
Somerset, England

The Grade Two listed Victorian Church of Mary Magdalene, designed by Benjamin Ferrey and built in 1874, overlooked the car park. It was an entrance into the mysterious and impressive labyrinth of caves, which stretched for miles underground. They are called 'solutional' caves. Weathering, and the natural acid from groundwater, which over time had dissolved the rocks, formed them. Explorers and the scientific community knew with certainty that there were as many undiscovered as had been found. Attempting to reveal their true extent was dangerous and difficult work. It required highly experienced scuba divers who were prepared to take treacherous and potentially life-threatening endeavours.

Up to twenty-five chambers spanning a mile in extent had been revealed, with differing depths of water down from shallow to as much as five hundred feet. All were sourced by the River Axe which flowed through the cave system. Technology had taken over and the water level was kept artificially high. The waters formed a continuous network of lakes and pools. Umpteen fossils and human remains indicated that the caves had been lived in for over forty-five thousand years. Certainly, the Celts, two thousand years ago, made use of them. There was an abundance of evidence that had been discovered around the stalactites that grew like pointed daggers from the roof of the cave, and the flat or round tip stalagmites that grew from the floor beneath them. When the two meet, they are known as a pillar. The stalactites formed the stalagmites beneath them. Water, containing calcium bicarbonates derived from the limestone rocks, found its way back into the limestone to form a tiny ring. This began a slow drip that took hundreds of thousands of years to form.

It was a spectacle that had enthralled millions of visitors.

That afternoon, Dr. Miriam Sinclair, standing at five feet eight inches and possessed of a shock of thick, auburn hair and haunting deep brown eyes, surveyed the surrounding rocks and cliffs. She was fluent in several ancient and modern languages – a marine and terra archaeologist. In her hands, she held meticulous cave maps which had taken years to put together. She had nothing important in mind, albeit a short recreational dive. Sections of the caves were closed to visitors and taped off. As a site of Special Scientific Interest (SSSI), accessibility to these areas was given only to those with permits. She had a permanent pass.

Since she was a young girl, the entire landscape of caves

from Cheddar Gorge through to Wookey Hole and onto Glastonbury had exercised an enormous pull on her psyche. For some reason, she thought the village church was aptly named. Of late, her feelings and attraction to the place had grown. She felt she knew everybody in the area, and they seemed to know her in return. That, she dismissed as fanciful nonsense.

She stepped from her motorhome, having changed into a neoprene dive suit. Her lustrous hair was pinned in small plaits to accommodate the tight-fitting hood. At thirty years of age, there wasn't an ounce of surplus flesh to be seen. Fitness had always been part of her life.

She carried all the necessary equipment required for a short dive – lamps and compressed air cylinders. They were not going to depths requiring trimix gas.

Waiting patiently by his own vehicle, and similarly clad, stood her diving partner, university professor, Fergal Lars Christi – known otherwise as Fergy. He was born of Danish and Scottish parents. His main areas of scholarship lay in philosophy, metaphysics, and logic. He was in his late thirties, also a keen diver, and a marathon runner. He stood at the same height as her and had thick, long, dark hair. His expression was one forever questioning, yet open. Small creases in the corner of his grey eyes gave him, she thought, an added attraction. She often thought there was a retro appeal about him. People had remarked that they looked and seemed similar in so many ways.

Bending her head at a slight angle, she flashed her dark brown eyes at him. "You ready then, Mr. Fergal?"

"Let's just say, Miriam," he replied in the gravelly voice he was well known for, "I've been ready and standing here like a potted plant for the last fifteen minutes." He gave a hearty grin in case she thought he was being difficult.

She playfully slapped his arm. "The sunshine will make you grow." As always, she gave him stick over his height, but he never took it seriously.

"What chambers do you want to look at today?" he asked.

"I'm going for nine and three again, and possibly four. Some ancient tools and bones were found around the waters there a month ago and if my hunch is right, there might just be a few more."

"I heard that too. I heard another story as well."

"What?"

"You know I'm National Coordinator for The Society of Ancient Discoveries, don't you?"

She laughed. "Don't I just! A bunch of screwballs who keep claiming to find hidden and lost, so called biblical secrets."

"That's not fair. Didn't we find those gold rings and silver goblets buried within yards of the tomb of Lazarus near Jerusalem last year? They were carbon dated to over two thousand years old. We do useful work."

"Well okay, I'll grant you that. So, what is it you want to tell me before I swim away from you?" She couldn't help smiling. She secretly loved his schoolboy enthusiasm and his amazing drive and tenacity whenever they're working on a project.

"Sit down for a minute or two. This might take a while." Taking a deep breath, he began. "Two nights ago, I had a visit from a Roman Catholic Bishop. Bishop Vincent Fisher. He told me an intriguing story, one I'd never heard before, but he had heard whispers of it for many years." He paused.

"Well, go on then. We don't have all day." Miriam gave an exaggerated sigh.

"The bishop told me that in what was known as Judea,

now modern-day Israel, there has been another unreported discovery of a small number of scrolls. They were located not far from where the Dead Sea Scrolls were originally found at Qumran.

"An obscure group known as the Society of Truth in Archaeology achieved the unearthing. They're a breakaway group from the Vatican's Pontifical Academy of Archaeology whom they accuse of cover-ups and suppression when the facts don't suit or threaten their dogma. Some of the scrolls were in a fairly battered condition and will take many months for the Israelis and the dig team to piece together, even using the latest technology. Two or three scrolls, however, remained in remarkable condition. Although, what you archaeologists call *good*, most people would bin!"

Miriam's interest was piqued. The dive seemed of less importance now. "Go on. This is getting fascinating."

"It gets better. The bishop said, what was found appeared to be fragments related to the writings of both Philip and Thomas, whose gospels were rejected by the early church. Around seventy AD, the time the temple of Jerusalem was sacked by the Romans, an unknown person or persons wrote down their words. They may be copies of earlier renderings." He paused again and appeared to be deep in thought. "It's not difficult to understand why the church rejected their original works. The new scrolls implied that Jesus did not die on the cross but survived the ordeal. Joseph of Arimathea did not collect the blood and water from the wound caused by Longinus's spear thrust – rather, it was collected by Mary Magdalene who carried it with her at all times after Joseph dismantled the nails from the cross and from Christ's body. Still breathing, he was taken away, and when he was capable of mobility, Jesus, the Magdalene, and Mary eventually fled to

Egypt. There, they had a child named Judah. Then, to escape further capture and punishment, the family made a long and perilous journey to France. This time, both Philip and Thomas accompanied them."

"Whoa there, Fergy, this is getting hard to believe. The entire Christian world has been brought up on the four gospels and the crucifixion. This is never going to be accepted."

"I know that, and the bishop was clearly a worried man. He told me more. What was further written was that later, they settled in France in the city we now know as Marseille, before moving on to Nantes and then northwards to a town called Burdigala. We know this today as Bordeaux. They did this to escape both the Jewish and Roman authorities who they learnt had heard of his survival and were looking for him. From there, leaving the two disciples behind, they procured a fishing vessel and headed for the land that was being referred to as Britannia, our very own country. It was written that the Magdalene was pregnant again."

Miriam, with a look of disbelief, creased up her face. "I can't see that this story will ever be accepted. If Jesus landed here, where did he go and of how can that ever be proven? As an archaeologist, I know that there has never been a shred of evidence, ever, that such an event occurred."

"That may be so," Fergy nodded. "You've heard numerous tales of the Holy Grail, but this one is not about that. What both Philip and Thomas wrote in those scrolls was that Jesus lived and that his blood was collected by the Magdalene in her wooden cruet or goblet, and not by Joseph of Arimathea. The cup, both Philip and Thomas state, were seen to be used in the healing of many sick people. Whether it is John Hardyng's so called *Sang Real* or as we know it, the Holy Grail, can never be known. The records conflict." He stood up and started pacing. "The astonishing part of the tale was that no matter how many times she used it to heal, it never emptied. Both these disciples travelled throughout France with the Magdalene and Jesus and wrote down what they saw. Get that, eh! Now, the bishop is not short of friends in important circles. He had checked out all references to such an object. He himself referred to Frazer's renowned work, 'The Golden Bough.' Using information gathered from his contacts and what he picked up from Frazer's work, it led him to Druidic practices whereupon he found references to various names from the ancient Celtic past. The Druids barely left any evidence of their history. The Romans destroyed what they found and what was left of their tradition was predominately oral – passed on from one adherent to another across the ages. He discovered something that got him excited. It was passed down in the Middle Ages and then seemed to vanish and has not been seen since."

"What was that?" Miriam's interest had risen by many notches.

"There was a written record that accounted for some remarkable healing performed by a woman from one of the Brythonic Celtic tribes. The legend concerned a woman called Magda, and her man known as Jah. It was said they came from a tribe around these parts, possibly the Dumnonii or Durotriges two thousand years back. I don't have to tell you the significance of those short names, do I?"

"Fergal, hold it right there, will you? You're treading in my territory. I'm the archaeologist around here. Of course I know about the tribes and their domains. I also know that the names Jah and Magda are not Celtic. They must come from elsewhere. Yes, I agree, the names are uncannily biblical."

"Yep, I thought that'd get your interest. Before you say

anything else... listen. The bishop went further, almost into a complex fantasy. Frankly, even I find it hard to believe. He said that in some of the burial mounds around these parts, ancient artefacts, and inscribed stone tablets, presumably Druidic, gave reference to Jah and Magda and a wondrous healing cup that cured all manner of illness. She was known as 'The Cup Keeper,' or 'Keeper of the Cup.' What became of the pair is not known apart from the reference of two children they had, a boy and a girl. The bishop said it had direct connection to the story of Jesus coming to this land. If true, it dispels stories of him being here in his younger, earlier years. So in one sense, if this story were true, Britain could be a holy land. What he was telling me was that much of this information had found its way into the newly discovered scrolls. How it got there remains a mystery."

Miriam smacked her forehead. "Stop! Stop!" Her voice was accelerating. "This is doing my brain in. Are you suggesting that somewhere around these parts are artefacts and God knows what else that may have belonged to Christ and the Magdalene, not forgetting his mother, Mary?"

The professor leant forward with a serious 'trust me I'm a professor' expression. "If the story is true then it is more than possible. It is known that the southern part of our country became Christian well before many others. Two gold crosses found not long ago lay on the eyelids of an ancient Celtic king or prince in a burial chamber discovered in the town of Southend in Essex. They were estimated to be sixteen hundred to two thousand years old. Well before Augustine and others. How did they get there, eh?"

"Why are you telling me all this?" Miriam's expression was now puzzled.

"Our names, activities, and interests somehow found

their way to the bishop. He said our knowledge of the caves and mounds in this part of the country, our archaeology and diving skills, were exactly what he was looking for. To get to the point, he wants us to start a clandestine expedition and create a team if needed. The objective is to undertake and find out what we can. He said that anything buried around here would sooner or later be dug up and found."

"Should we accept? How on earth can he fund such a proposition?"

"That was my question to him. Are you ready to hear this?"

"Oh, do go on. I'm all ears."

"His funds are virtually unlimited. They come from the secret purse of the pontiff himself, Pope Adrian." Fergal paused to enjoy her look of astonishment.

"What!" Miriam gasped. "That can't be true." Her eyes had opened wide and matched the drop of her jaw.

"But it is. I was as astonished as you. It seems the bishop is highly influential and a secret supporter of the breakaway group, *Society of Truth in Archaeology*. The pope funds their activities and those funds were instrumental in discovering the latest batch of scrolls. What's more, the pope it seems is no Catholic die-hard. He has a liberal agenda, which if revealed and implemented, could rip the Catholic Church and all its dogmas apart."

Miriam blew out a large lungful of air. "Let's say we forget the dive today and get into my wheels and talk about this some more. It's hard to believe and raises many questions."

"I agree. Let's go."

CHAPTER 5

The Present Day
The Vatican

Pope Adrian VIII, a Dutchman like the first Pope Adrian, arose from off his podgy knees as he finished praying in the confines of his sparse bedroom. Devoid of paintings, art, and decoration of any form, the only recognisable symbol of his grace was the large crucifix bearing the body of the crucified Christ. It was as tall as he and affixed to the wall overlooking his bed. There was no need for anything more. The grace of Christ was all that would ever be needed. In his early sixties, he was not atypical in age. Most popes had been in their seventieth year or more. The youngest, however, was Pope John XII, who was astonishingly a mere twenty years of age in 955 AD or thereabouts. The election of the current Pope Adrian had not been without dissent. His liberal views were well known and had caused a minor upheaval in the ranks of cardinals.

His prayers had not dispelled his anxieties. He was aware that many people hotly opposed his radical agenda for the Catholic Church. He remembered the death of Pope John Paul 1 which was surrounded in conspiracy theories. This gave him cause to wonder what his own future might be. He didn't doubt that amongst the Cardinal College, there were dangerous elements.

In the most secret compartments of his heart, he never doubted the necessity of the church to guide the spiritual welfare of his worldwide flock. Yet times, values, and perceptions had changed. In many ways, the planet was in grave danger of over population. Those changes only went further in reinforcing his most secret doubts. It had been almost impossible to keep these to himself. He believed the church needed a drastic examination of its core dogmas and be willing to accept changes.

Amazingly, he had never truly believed in the virgin birth story. He had been reading the well-researched works of James D Taylor, and the likes of Simcha Jacobovici, and they only seemed to reinforce his doubts. There were too many accounts of Jesus surviving the crucifixion ordeal, or of it even happening, and his marriage to Mary the Magdalene and their subsequent children. He was in a quandary. He hoped that he was wrong as he regarded the story of Christ as the most inspirational of his sixty odd years of life. In that respect, it mattered little who Jesus's parents were.

Such sacred relics as The Shroud of Turin, Veronica's Veil, and The Holy Prepuce, the circumcised foreskin of Christ, had never been substantially proven. Faith alone was all that was needed to believe such items. That type of faith, he knew, was monumentally important to the welfare of mankind. But he himself never believed in the authenticity of holy relics. There were too many fakes and enough wood from the true cross to build a football field full of immense barns.

He couldn't avoid dilemmas like the overpopulated world and its threat to Earth's ecology. But the causes of birth had to be controlled somehow. Control was not a sin.

These were views not acceptable to many of the conclave. He believed that a return to a simpler way of life had to begin. Headed by Christ in a realistic manner with full awareness of all possible problems. God, he thought, would not want his creation to suffer so.

His faith in God remained unshakeable.

One way or the other, he desperately needed evidence about the whole episodes around the life of Jesus. What was being discovered lately was rendering the biblical accounts as more than a little shaky.

In what he thought of as being in the utmost secrecy, he began funding a clandestine circle which comprised of a handful of like-minded seekers. They were known as the *Society of Truth in Archaeology* – or SOTA for short

What he hadn't understood, was that even the most closely guarded of secrets have a way of being uncovered. SOTA was no exception.

Cutting through these thoughts came disturbing reports concerning the mysterious death of his trusted conduit, Bishop Vincent Fisher. He had never attended the private meeting they were supposed to have last week. Now, it was being said that his mutilated remains were the work of a small pack of wolves terrorising the outskirts of Rome.

He didn't believe it.

In his mind, he was unable to dismiss the idea that in

some way, the bishop's role in the group had been compromised, and therefore, if so, the entire edifice could be in peril.

What he was thankful for was the large and top-secret portfolio he had received earlier from the bishop. That portfolio was to have been the subject of their meeting. It contained every location – from Israel, France, and Great Britain – where the Christ was alleged to have been. It also contained details concerning everybody the bishop had had contact with. It was substantial. Accompanying it was a transcript of what had been found and translated so far.

* * *

Later that evening, seated in a large, winged back chair, Pope Adrian was alone and had left instructions that he was not to be disturbed no matter who it was.

Apart from God.

On his table lay the fruits of Bishop Fisher's endeavours. They were extensive and startling, even to a doubter like he sometimes considered himself. He noted that the bishop had copied in only one other person – a Professor Fergal Lars Christi in the UK who could be heading up the operation. It came with photographs of him and his second, Dr. Miriam Sinclair. The professor would have to be informed of developments and the death of Bishop Fisher. It was now vital to set up a trusted link between the professor and the Vatican.

Who?

What the transcripts contained was explosive, likely to cause controversy and outrage. It seemed that the centre of the perceived controversy was England. If proof could be found, it would overturn every other dissident theory and cause either an upsurge in belief or a mass exodus. That revelation was a decision he alone could make and in the utmost secrecy. The Israeli authorities had agreed to keep the entire project under wraps and buried behind closed doors. They too were fearful of a backlash in their own beliefs and religious structures.

If the hub of activity was to be centred around sites and areas of England's mystic past, then the person who will lead the way and liaise with him should know and understood the country and its people.

There were several perturbing anomalies. A form of Christianity was known to have appeared in Midwest and Eastern Britain long before St. Alban and Augustine and others had arrived. How was that to be explained? There was one glaring possibility, but Pope Adrian dared not dwell on that until he knew more.

He didn't know who to trust. If he opened up to somebody else, that was another brick in the wall of secrecy removed.

But it had to be done.

There's only one real contender. The English Cardinal, Nicholas, who knows the country and its customs well. Yet, he has the weight of his duties as director of our investigative arm, the Congregation for the Causes of Saints. As such, he is already responsible for verifying stories that might be of interest to the Church and newly discovered relics.

Most he had discounted as forgeries. But there were a few, very few, that seemed authentic. This could be one.

He would need an assistant… another hole in the wall.

Pope Adrian decided he would have to devise a smokescreen to disguise the real reason for the clandestine operation. The cardinal would not be given all the facts.

It was time to summon him personally.

CHAPTER 6

Harry's Café Bar
Piccadilly, London

Wearing a midnight blue, tailored mohair suit of some elegance, together with a gleaming white open necked shirt, a tall man walking with an obvious limp strode in. His walking cane beat a rhythmic tattoo on the stylish flooring. It seemed that the very walls and tiling, in all their sophisticated splendour, opened up to welcome Cardinal Nicholas. The bar glasses gleamed, shining like jewels in a black box.

Alongside, expectant, and subservient, stood rows of enticingly labelled bottles waiting to be poured. The cardinal had left his cassock and *zucchetto* back in his hotel room. His meeting needed slick, modern handling. Priestly robes would not do. He found himself enjoying the glossy image he was projecting. He couldn't see his contact yet.

Time for a quick drink.

In the last twenty-four hours, he had mused upon the chain of events that had led him here. What had shocked him and confirmed his convictions, was that Pope Adrian was the sponsor of the now not-so-secret breakaway archaeology group, SOTA.

Unexpectedly, back in Rome, he had received an urgent and secret summons from the pope himself. He had not expected that. News of the bishop's death had swept through Rome, and of course, the Vatican. At first, he had wondered whether his plans had been discovered... and he was prepared for trouble. His own conservative and rigid orthodox approach to Catholic dogma was becoming more widely known, and not just to an inner select few. It was spreading.

The elite formed the foundations of his group, *Ordinis Sancti et Sanctae Crucis et Gladio,* – the Order of the Holy Cross and Sword. They were opposed to any liberalisation or loosening of strict observances and behaviour. Even *Opus Dei* was not immune from their surveillance of the creeping hand of sin and immorality, subtly disguised by the hand of Satan. The use of the *cilice* and self-flagellation did not go far enough.

As an orphan, stricken with poliomyelitis, he was left with a permanent leg disability. Raised in the East End of London, he had known little of love, tolerance, or compassion... only rejection and disdain. But he had survived. He understood brutality, unremitting hardness, and how that quickly got him what he wanted. Attracted by the mysticism and rituals of the Catholic faith, he became a priest after training. He had a hard and inflexible view on the way the tenets of his faith should be carried out. Such was his devotion and intellectual grasp of doctrine and its requirements. He quickly rose through the ranks. As the years passed, he began to despair of the too, too liberal path the faith had begun to tread. It was surrendering to the Prince of Evil.

The cardinal had a unique way of spearheading his agendas. He knew he would kill and had done so to maintain the precious God-given standards of the true faith. What lengths, lies, deceits and deceptions were required to maintain them, he was, by the Almighty Father prepared to do so. He was convinced that he was an Angel of God, sent to preserve the one true faith in its most severe form. St. Peter himself had said that Satan was going around like a roaring lion, seeking whom he might devour. Popes were on the menu. He was increasingly convinced that this pope had become part of that circle.

Christ was sent into this world that he might defeat Satan and all his works. If his suspicions are true, and the pope thought it untrue, then Christ's mission on this earth had no meaning. Anything or anybody – other sects, religions, science included – that opposed the one real truth, by actions, deeds, words, or thoughts, were enemies of Christ and his Holy Father. Their wicked souls would burn for eternity in the deepest hell. It would be their deserved reward.

At their meeting, what the Pope had attempted to confide in him, he already knew. That amused him. He had that information beaten out of the stupid bishop. The pope told him that he didn't want rumours of Jesus having survived the crucifixion spreading, or of him being married to Mary Magdalene. The bishop had told him another story in between his screams. The truth was just the opposite. The pope wanted it to be true.

Pope Adrian was the Antichrist, of that he was certain. What the pope really wanted was for these scandalous heresies to be broadcasted far and wide. He wanted to change the one true faith into a sinful, liberal dog's dinner of soft and sloppy edicts, fit only for God's darkest hells. There wasn't a doubt in Cardinal Nicholas's mind about it. Pope Adrian had to go.

Firstly, the meddling archaeologists in the UK and whoever was working for them had to be eliminated. Once accomplished, his own covert and surreptitious order could easily gain control within the glorious Vatican. A global upheaval would then begin in God's name. It would be a worldwide crusade.

A smile spread across Cardinal Nicholas's face. He could almost see it coming to pass.

Then, another tantalising thought entered his mind. What if this cup of life is to be found? Could that be possible? It had certainly gripped the bishop and also the pope, enough for him to fund an expensive search operation. What power that would give him and his new order. It would be beyond anything imaginable. Medical science would be rocked!

He had another comforting thought. To fund the project, the pope had given him a briefcase with a million dollars in bearer bonds, drawn on The Institute for the Works of Religion, a private bank otherwise known as the Vatican Bank, situated in Vatican City.

* * *

The bar was empty, so he sat and ordered a strawberry daiquiri cocktail. This was a favorite indulgence when away from the eyes of other priests and cardinals.

It was then he spotted him. The man he was expecting to meet, sitting in a secluded corner of the bar. He was reading a copy of the catholic publication *The Tablet*, as had been arranged. Clutching his drink, the cardinal moved toward the man.

Cardinal Nicholas spoke first with a prearranged code. "Interesting title. Do tablets cure all ills?"

The man looked up. He had a shaven head, facial features resembling a bag of spanners, and the look of a man who had spent time in jail. His hands were as bulky as a bunch of bananas. His voice was as heavy as a ball and chain. He replied, "Mostly. Even placebos can work."

It was the agreed response. The cardinal extended his hand. "I'm Nicholas. Who are you?"

The man grasped it with a steely grip that gave the cardinal cause to wince. "My name is Cracker, Daniel Cracker. That's what I'm known as." The man assessed him with a boldness bordering on rude. "So, you are Nicholas. Nicholas what or who? "

"That's all you need to know, Mr. Cracker."

Cracker smirked. "Suits me. Our mutual friend called. So you want some work done, I understand?"

Nicholas pulled out a chair and sat opposite. "Let me get you another drink. What is it to be?"

"Peroni."

The cardinal ordered the beer and placed his large portfolio on the table. It was a condensed and censored duplicate of the folder the pope had given him. "In here, you will find all the information you need. I have also attached a separate fee structure. I hope you can read?"

Cracker leant forward with a face aglow with menace. "Patronise me again, sunshine, and the deal's off, but before that, I might possibly smash your face in. Just so you know, I have a master's degree from the University of Life. Do you get my meaning?"

The cardinal blanched. Nobody, since he had been a young schoolboy, had spoken to him so. "My apologies, Mr. Cracker, and yes... I understand you perfectly." He continued. "Within, you will find photographs of a few individuals, all of whom may have to be dealt with later, in whatever manner you think suitable. If they find things, they are to be delivered to my assistant, who you will protect if needed. You will need to let them do their work and see what they find. My assistant will tell you what and when."

Cracker zipped open the portfolio. A silence descended between the two men. Cracker was the first to speak. "Hot stuff, Nicky boy. So you are a cardinal, eh? Hot stuff. I'm not religious, but I see what this is all about. Dealing with a bunch of nammy pammy dirt diggers, with a little persuasion if necessary, shouldn't be difficult." He paused and opened a secondary envelope which he studied intently. "Like the fees. Most generous, too. Anything found – documents or hard evidence – will be handed over to your assistant. Now who might your assistant be?"

The cardinal swung around to see the glass door being opened. Striding across the oak panelled, art deco interior, he could see Father Giuseppe Vincenzo making his way towards them. Almost as if to add some drama to the meeting, he was dressed in black, complete with his Roman collar and a crucifix hanging from his chest.

CHAPTER 7

Somewhere near Glastonbury, England
Present times…

T he Keeper of the Cup held her small vessel aloft and walked among the wounded and dying warriors of her tribe. The battle had been short and fierce, and the price had been paid. Her man, his grey hair blowing in the wind, was by her side. His lips moved as if in prayer before she administered to those who needed it. The wounded recovered. They lived to fight another day and their sacred rites and new beliefs were mirrored by the miracle of her cup.

Kelvin's daydream vanished as a soft breeze steered him back into reality.

The Grove of Taranus had always been dear to him. Here, he felt the healing power of nature, which empowered him in so many different ways. It was a sacred place. The grove was little known and those that knew of it he counted as his followers. It was secluded – a natural creation surrounded by mighty oaks and elder trees. Above, an open blue sky gazed down, giving patches of light, which perfectly complemented the darker areas. It had been that way for hundreds of years. Close by was a small clear lake, not blue but grey, from which it forever gave a good view of *Ynis Wydrn*, The Isle of Glass – the Tor of Glastonbury. Its ancient name was what his exclusive sect of Druids preferred to use.

Saint Michael's Tower was built on top of Glastonbury Tor in Somerset. This mystical hill, with seven deep terraces sat in the heart of Summerland Meadows, within the Somerset Levels. Myths still existed of the Neolithic labyrinth of tunnels below the Tor, running all the way to the Abbey in Glastonbury. It was said to be haunted by Druids and some even said – fairies. The ancient Britons named this magical spot *Ynys yr Afalon* or the Isle of Avalon – the centre of the legend of King Arthur.

Kelvin Stallybrass preferred to use his ancient name, Iseldir. He stood at six feet in height, was heavily muscular, and people often said that his countenance was one of wisdom and mystery. He was an impressive figure at forty-four years of age. Jet-black hair, with the odd patches of grey and white, hung loosely on his shoulders. On his chest he had a tattoo of the Cretan Maze that made up the Tor of Glastonbury. For many women, he was an attractive proposition.

Iseldir believed that ancient men, Celts, and Druids, shaped the Tor with ridges into a maze formation.

As a druid, he had broken away from the modernised, sanitized, respectful form of druidism that was now the acceptable image of the movement. He had reverted to the old practices, which he thought was the true way of nature. Julius Caesar had written that the practice of the letting of blood and the sacrifice of animals were part of their rituals. That part of the ancient rites, he was not prepared to do.

Iseldir, in his edicts, encouraged a dislike of Christianity – particularly the Roman Catholic Church. He saw them as responsible, in distant times past, for butchering and burning many Druids. The church had never apologised. They were an affront to nature.

He was alone in the grove. He needed to muse over certain events and things he had been hearing. The grove was the perfect place. Quiet and free of people. Its history was one of complete naturalness. It was here that he could sense and be in touch with the ancients and all their wisdom. Their song and the atmosphere vibrated through his entire mind and body.

Dotted around the clearing and forming a rough circle were a number of upright and flat stones – far older than the trees and must have been part of the original grove, formed in Celtic times. He sat on a centrally placed and flat-topped stone. From here, he could recognise what remained of the Ogham tree runes carvings. Most had been erased by time, and what remained were referred to as 'The Sweet Cauldron of the Five Trees'.

A - Ail: signifying birth is everywhere
O - Ohn: Initiation upon hills and dolmens

U - Ur: The love-goddess
E - Eadha: The repose of the warrior
I - Iodha: Death and hope's gateway

He knew where to look, but it took a trained eye to spot them. Their shapes were based on natural lines, and their meanings needed layers of understanding. He saw both the runes indicating the grove, the mistletoe, the various trees around, and oddly... there was a small crucifix carved beneath. What seemed to be two names written in the Ogham script had melded into the ancient stone over time, rendering any interpretation as useless.

The more he gazed at them the deeper his meditation became. It was at moments like these, which were rare, that he thought he could discern the name Jah and Magda. They were woven around a small cup.

Of late, the writings had figured in his dreams. He did not know what his vision meant. Could it be what the legends spoke of was carved into this stone?

Iseldir was proud but never arrogant. He believed he could trace his lineage back to the days when the local tribes of the Dumnonii and the Durotriges held sway. A man, Arthwys, and his woman, Brianna, had led one of the tribes. Their names had been passed down through the ages. In this way, they still lived within the stories passed on to their people.

Iseldir often dreamt of this man and of the druid masters across the ages. He believed he descended from them. He had no written proof, but such was his intuition, he needed no other proof. The feeling was so powerful it consumed his twenty-first century life. Intuitive wisdom was part of a druid's life and it had never failed him. It was a talent that was, in some mysterious way, handed down through time – from druid to druid. It had not passed him by.

What he had heard around and seen in dreams gave him cause to be angry and dismayed. It was told that a man, whom many believed as Jesus the Christ, also known as Yeshua, had somehow survived his crucifixion and the thrust of the Roman centurion's spear. That he had fled to Britain, together with his mother and his woman, Mary the Magdalene. With them was her son and later their daughter. The legend said that the Magdalene possessed a healing cup filled with water and the blood from the wounds of Christ on the cross.

Was that what my daydream was about?

It was said that the cup had more powerful healing properties than the plants used by the Druids – *selago* and *samulos*. Their potions healed many, but it was nothing compared to the supposed cup, which never emptied no matter how many times it was used.

Passed down through Iseldir's tradition, and of late, figuring powerfully in his dreams, this story was wrapped in the secret tradition of his order, known only by the Chief Druid, never to be revealed to anyone else.

Upon his ordination as Iseldir, the Chief Druid of his Order, he became a recipient of that secret. Whether the story was true or not, one thing Iseldir knew for certain… if such a cup existed, it belonged to nobody else apart from the Druids, the guardians of the secret.

He felt the hairs on his arms rise. *What if the story was true?*

What dismayed and angered him of late, was the news that archaeologists would be digging amid the hills and caves around the sacred lands of Cheddar, Wookey and Glastonbury.

It appeared that the secret was not his alone. Others knew

also.

He felt that the timing of his dreams was not a coincidence. *Was he meant to protect whatever is hidden?*

If this cup existed, and then removed from its resting place, it would amount to nothing less than rape.

Rumour has it that the Roman Catholic Church was backing the venture. That, he found hard to believe. The last thing they would want is proof that the Christian messiah did not die, and instead... lived here... with his wife and children!

Iseldir had intimate knowledge of the caves and had spent much of his life exploring and diving in them. He knew them more than any man alive. He could be of use to such a search. He could volunteer to guide them and in so doing, prevent any attempt to remove whatever they find – if anything could ever be found.

If such a miraculous cup existed, it would offer a range of possibilities for humanity... a longer and more balanced life, free of disease. But he also understood that whoever possessed such an artefact could have enough power to rule the world.

And that's what he feared the most.

He reached into his leather bag, one that he had made himself, and pulled from it an object wrapped in gold cloth. He had found it years back while diving in the shallow waters of the Wookey Hole cave structures.

It was a rectangular tablet.

Made of metal, it seems, the tablet bore three rows of letters or markings of some sort. He had never been able to decipher them.

With that in mind, Iseldir decided it was time to approach the archaeologists. The plaque would surely pique their interest. *A good bargaining tool.* He knew where they were supposed to stay – at the local hotel where he worked as a barman.

It was hard to keep secrets in a small community. The receptionist had told him earlier, before he went on duty, that two academics with a stack of diving gear had booked in. Later, they were visited by two other men – whom she thought were Catholic priests. They wore prominent crucifixes.

Priests! That's all I need!

The two academics had made an open-ended reservation. It seemed that the rumours could be true. He needed to find out.

Catholic priests! That shook Iseldir. *What were they doing here?*

Robbery and even the destruction of artefacts that were not theirs, was all he could think of.

CHAPTER 8

Through his middle-aged personal assistant, Francesca De Luca, he established contact with the professor. Eyebrows had been raised at her appointment, but for him, she was discreet, spoke fluent English, had an Oxford University education, and a passionate Catholic. She ticked all of Cardinal Nicholas's boxes.

She confirmed the professor's meeting with the cardinal, via email and a letter bearing the cardinal's personal seal. The meeting would be in five days at their hotel, which has been paid for as long as it was required. Other details would be discussed by the cardinal himself.

* * *

The professor and Miriam were alone in the bar area of the modest Ancient Gatehouse Hotel in the city of Wells.

Francesca De Luca had confirmed media reports of the circumstances surrounding Bishop Fisher's shocking death.

"I find it hard to believe," Fergy spoke quietly. "He was a likeable and enthusiastic person. Wolves roaming around Rome and killing people is a story beyond belief."

"I never met him, but he sounded like the sort of person I would have liked. When are we due to meet his replacement? A cardinal, no less. Cardinal Nicholas." Miriam looked around as if he expected him to walk in."

"Another half hour yet and he may have an intermediary with him. A priest by the name of Father Vincenzo."

"We're dealing with a lot of priests nowadays." Miriam sighed.

"While we're waiting, I'll order another round. I don't expect our cardinal will want one."

They didn't have to wait long. Twenty minutes later, the cardinal strode in. He was wearing his mohair suit and looking more like a stock exchange dealer. Alongside him walked Vincenzo, but this time in casual attire.

Fergy stood, recognising them both from the photographs Francesca De Luca had sent him. *Great God, they look like something out of Hollywood central casting.* "Cardinal Nicholas?"

"Yes, that is me," the cardinal replied. "You must be Professor Christi?"

"Yes, I am, and this is my colleague, Dr. Miriam Sinclair. We're pleased to meet you."

The cardinal introduced Vincenzo and they shook hands before sitting. "I can see from your faces," Nicholas began, "that we are not what you expected. You must forgive us. We rarely have the chance to live outside our cassocks, collars, and hats. What you see is rare and does not happen often."

"No problem," Fergal replied, but couldn't help thinking

that Vincenzo resembled an Italian used car salesman.

Both priests ordered coffee and declined Fergal's offer to pay for them.

The first point was the death of the bishop. "I find it hard to believe that in sight of Rome, a man like him gets mauled to death by a pack of wolves," Fergal said, shaking his head.

The cardinal tightened his thin, leathery lips, and without seeming to open his mouth, responded with a tinny tone of voice. "The bishop had been careless and indiscreet. That attitude contributed to his death, I suspect. God rest his soul."

Miriam shot a glance at Fergy and sensed his reaction. He, like herself, had taken an instant dislike to the cardinal. The milk of human kindness does not seem to be with him. She gave her partner a brief nod. He would know what that meant. He always did.

"I find that a bit harsh, Cardinal. He seemed affable, intelligent, well-informed, and highly efficient."

The cardinal's reply startled them both.

"Satan has a way of manipulating people. I fear the bishop had been one of them."

Miriam quickly interjected. This was not what they were here for. "Let's get off the subject, shall we? Cardinal Nicholas, I suspect you know far more than we do about religious sensibilities. They have nothing to do with us." She carefully avoided bringing Pope Adrian into the discussion. "I suspect there's more to your story then we are being told. Frankly, we are not interested in Catholic politics. We are here to perform a service."

That was a small lie.

"We have expertise that you need and you're here to purchase our knowledge in diving and archaeology. We've read the original brief from Bishop Fisher and I presume it remains unchanged. What we understand is that you are asking us to investigate the degree of Christianity that was found here, and if possible, locate from our Celtic past, any evidence that Jesus had survived his crucifixion, lived amongst us, and possibly had a family. Correct?" She did not mention the cup.

"Correct."

"What we further understand is that details of further gospels allegedly written by Philip and Thomas are the keystone to these stories. The Israelis are holding them in secret, although the bishop had been given full access. In his investigations, it appeared that Mary Magdalene was the dominant force and had supposedly possessed healing abilities. That the Magdalene had two children, and that to this day, their descendants might exist somewhere."

The cardinal remained as expressionless as a stone carving. "I do what I am asked to do. What I believe in this matter is of no concern."

Fergal's look was one of scepticism.

Cardinal Nicholas continued, "Let's discuss your plan of action and how we will communicate. Father Vincenzo will be your point of contact. Due to my duties, I would be unable to oversee your search at all times."

Thank God for that, Fergy thought.

"Father Vincenzo will contact you frequently and visit your areas of investigations."

Vincenzo leant forward and in moderate, accentuated English, spoke. "I am staying nearby but may go away at times. This is the number of my hotel." He handed over a slip of paper. "I wish to accompany you in the first few days so I may get some understanding of what you are planning. *Grazie molto.*"

"Understood. Miriam, dig out our schedule and itinerary.

We need to discuss this now."

"There is one other point," the cardinal interrupted. "At times, you may observe another man in your vicinity. He is Father Vincenzo's helper and guard. He will also help guarantee your safety – from others we know of who might try and interfere with this project." The cardinal had never been averse to telling lies.

"What a load of rubbish!" Fergy snapped. "I thought this was a secret project. The last thing we want is some sort of guard tramping around our archaeological digs."

"It is a secret mission, but I'm sure you will agree, professor... it is better to be safe than sorry. He will be totally discreet, and rest assured, you will not see him every day. If you wish, you will be introduced later."

They spent the next hour sorting out points of reference and ensuring both the cardinal and Vincenzo understood locations and references. They agreed to meet Vincenzo in three days' time when the mission commenced at the Wookey Hole caves.

The priests arose and gave their farewells. The cardinal's smile appeared as friendly as a wet Monday morning.

They were finally alone.

"What a pair of creeps," Miriam hissed.

"Too right. If it weren't for the intrigue and of course the money, I wouldn't want to know." He gave a deep sigh. "After all that, I could do with a stiff drink. How about you?"

"Yes, a large Shiraz would go down well." She grinned.

Fergal got up and went to the bar to place the order. The barman, wearing a chic, white tunic and black bow tie, began pouring the wine. The professor noticed the barman's name tag. *Strange name, that... Kelvin Stallybrass.*

The barman gave him a polite nod. He had heard every

word of their discussion.

"On holiday here, sir?" he asked politely.

"Not really," Fergy replied. "We're here to do some diving around the caves. We're part of a scientific exploration. What we hope to find, God only knows."

"Well, what d'you know?" Kelvin feigned surprise. "I used to dive these caves years back, before they got taped off for SSSI."

It was Fergal's turn to look surprised. "You've dived in the caves around here?"

"Frequently. It's a hobby of mine. I've a current BSCA advanced open water diving certificate, plus underwater photography certificates with cavern diving techniques."

"Hey! Hold it right there, Mr. Stallybrass." The professor turned to Miriam. "Miriam, over here... quick."

Sensing his excited tone, she made for the bar counter.

He quickly made the introductions and repeated what Kelvin had told him.

"Looks like our man, Prof."

"Sure does." He turned to Kelvin. "Fancy some cave work, Kelvin? It's well paid and if we plan it properly, you may not have to give up the day job." Fergal went on to explain that the mission was an attempt to discover if Christianity reached the Celts long before any of the so-called saints arrived to spread the word. He refrained from mentioning the never-empty, miraculous cup, or of Jesus or Mary Magdalene.

He would have been surprised to know that Kelvin was fully aware of what they were hoping to locate.

They discussed it further and both Miriam and Fergal quizzed him about diving. His answers were correct.

"Do you know what, Kelvin?" Miriam said, smiling. "I've a feeling you know more about diving than we do. So... will you join us?"

"Without a doubt," Kelvin's reply was positive and eager. "Let me just say, it's long been an idea of mine that there could be more than meets the eye around this area and the caves."

"Let's hope so." Fergy said, relieved. "I think we could make a great team."

CHAPTER 9

The Vatican...

Pope Adrian sat alone in his private chamber. Earlier, he had cast his thoughts back to his early life. His father had been a boatman in the idyllic village of Giethoorn, in northwest Holland. It was called the Venice of the Netherlands, owing to its numerous waterways and bridges. Both his parents had been devout Catholics, and had raised him so, before he left to join the priesthood.

He remembered the heady days as a seminarian, and how inspired and driven he had been. That drive had led him to become the leader of the Catholic Church. It seemed like a fairy tale.

His drive had been shaped by a powerful spiritual experience. While on a silent retreat, he had heard a voice whispering to him in the Dolomite mountains. It wasn't Christ or

God. No, it was The Magdalene telling him that she was the instrument of Jesus – the Sophia, the embodiment of Holy Wisdom, who had been present with God during the creation.

Since then, the vision had stayed with him, changing him forever. He had revealed it to nobody, knowing it would be rejected by his peers and he would be shunned.

He believed that one day, that truth would be revealed and patriarchy would falter. The true light of the world would then shine across the entire planet and humanity would finally know the truth.

The ancient Hebrew word for God was YHWH or Yahweh. It was said that the name had been revealed to Moses and YAH, the first part of the name is feminine. Indeed, he had found that in the books of Proverbs, Genesis, Exodus and others, there were certain clues given which reinforced this vision.

He had read the gnostic beliefs and the Gospel of Philip which maintained, via the Valentinian Theology, that God was *SYZYGY*. In one sense, God was unknowable and androgynous – depicted as a male and female dyad. There can be no concept of maleness without femaleness, just as there can be no darkness without light. The division into opposites was ultimately an illusion. God was Sophia. She was the *SYZYGY*, the divine female twin, and the Holy Spirit of the Trinity.

These were thoughts and ideas that had forever bothered him and caused long bouts of doubt. It was his abiding secret. The God he loved was neither female nor male. God was of spirit, an amorphous element.

Adrian frequently reminded himself that in recent years, the Episcopal Church had dropped all references to God as male – such *as He, Father, Lord, and King. 'Our Father who art in* heaven' has been replaced by *Our Parent who art in heaven.* He smiled at the thought. This may seem strange to most people, having been taught the former version. He wondered about their tolerance of gay sexuality and their willingness to integrate with other faiths. Indeed, he contemplated the impact of that to his church and faith if such principles were ever adopted by the Catholic faith.

It was these thoughts, coupled with his early vision, that had prompted him to secretly fund the Society of Truth in Archaeology. If they could uncover something buried in the past, then it would go a considerable way to alleviate or confirm his doubts. He knew that he was not alone with these thoughts.

It had been a disturbing day for him. He had prepared himself for bed but was guessing he would not sleep easily. Beside him was a detailed report handed to him by the office of the *Santa Alleanza* – also known as *L'Entità*. Its motto, *Cum Cruce et Gladio* – "With the Cross and Sword" – was highly indicative of its intent. Established in 1566 by Pope St. Pius V, the office represented part of the Vatican's highly sophisticated intelligence agency.

They had received the report directly from the *Dirigente Superiore* of the *Polizia di Stato*. The report concerned the death of Bishop Fisher and the circumstance surrounding it.

The document contained several factors that eliminated the wolf attack reports.

The bishop's DNA, taken from his blood, hair, and saliva, were consistent as his. There were two other examples that were clearly not his, nor were they from an animal, but from some other people. There was no record of them on the police database, so these were noted and placed on the appropriate files for future reference.

Earlier examination had revealed that the bishop's skull had been fractured. Deeper analysis revealed no animal DNA, no fur, nor any recognisable teeth or claw marks. This was inconsistent with an animal attack. They concluded that the torn clothing and flesh were not caused by a wolf as initially claimed.

Forensics had revealed microscopic traces of metal and wood. The team indicated that hooks and spikes likely caused the mutilations. The park was a busy place during the day and many people passed through it on a regular basis. Microbial forensics revealed that the body had been dead for at least forty-eight hours prior to being discovered. The conclusion was that it had been dumped there.

The pope offered up a silent prayer for the soul of the dead bishop.

My suspicions were correct. I never believed that news report. Clearly, he was murdered. I now have no doubts it's connected to the work he was doing for SOTA. Someone had discovered its existence – and that means they know of my part in it. Cardinal Nicholas could be in grave danger, as could I.

He is due back here soon. I must talk to him. The archaeologists could also be in peril.

He bit his bottom lip, an old childhood anxiety trait. He wondered if God was punishing him for his secret doubts about much of the Bible – anxieties which had grown of late.

Above all else, he was determined that the church should not fall into the hands of the ultra-hard-line cardinals and priests. He knew they were many.

Adrian bowed his head and asked for guidance. For once in his life, he felt powerless.

CHAPTER 10

Wells, Somerset, England

Vincenzo sprawled his portly body across the hotel bed. He was making sure his compact Vektor CP1 ceramic handgun was working correctly. He didn't wish to use it, but with the cardinal and Cracker about, the stakes had been raised. It didn't seem a bad idea. He was pleased with the trust the cardinal had placed in him. His own reputation back in Rome was that of a rogue priest. He was aware of the name other priests called him behind his back – *Il Cacciavite Cardinali* – 'The Cardinal's Screwdriver.' When the going got hard, he would keep on turning. He was what the English referred to as a 'rough diamond.' Rough he may be, but he was in total agreement with the cardinal and his extreme vision of the church's role on the planet. He had no problem with extreme tactics and the use of weapons to uphold the word of God. It was his duty, as was that of the Crusaders of old. In his secret heart, he found he enjoyed that aspect of his work.

The sound of the phone ringing startled him. He grabbed at it. "*Si?*"

"Hello. Father Vincenzo?"

The sound of Professor Fergal Lars Christi's voice reminded him he was in England. "Ah, yes I am. You are the professor, no?"

"Correct, Father. We are preparing to go to the caves. Please meet us there in thirty minutes. We will wait for you."

"*Si,* I will be there." He hung up.

For a few moments, he allowed himself to revel in a sense of gratitude toward the cardinal. Many years back, it was Cardinal Nicholas who had persuaded him to embrace the religious life. At that time, he was but a homeless drug addict living in the many parks that adorn and surround the city of Firenze, Florence. He had little money, was unwashed, and faced a bleak future. He had one talent. He was tough, and when aroused, what he was capable of knew no boundaries.

One time, a gang of three minor criminals who were determined to rob anybody of anything they could find had confronted the cardinal, who had been a bishop at the time. For some reason, Vincenzo went to his rescue and set about the men with considerable ferocity. They took a heavy beating and fled. The then bishop, Nicholas, took pity on him and offered him shelter and food. They had understood each other.

Vincenzo had realised the advantages of a priestly life – especially under the now cardinal's all-embracing wing – and had entered the seminary. In no time, he learned the ways of the religious.

The life offered hauled him from the gutter, and he was

forever grateful to Cardinal Nicholas. Vincenzo would do anything the cardinal asked of him. Everyone knew this and he soon became known and feared. Who would have believed his progress? Now, here he was in England helping to safeguard a top-secret assignment,

He would do whatever the cardinal required. Bloodletting in God's name was perfectly acceptable. Cardinal Nicholas had convinced him of that.

* * *

Dr. Miriam Sinclair and the professor, both in their neoprene dry suits, began checking their equipment for their expected dive. It would also be their chance to see how well Kelvin could perform. He said he would be bringing his own equipment. Their checks were routine and one they knew by heart. They made sure they had two of everything, in case of any equipment malfunction. They had about fifteen items listed, and these included essentials like oxygen tanks, fins, flashlights, underwater cameras, knives, pressure regulators and timers.

The plan was to examine the shallower depths. They knew that in the past, near the water's edge, items had been found. They'd start there before going further.

Whilst doing a double check, the tall figure of Kelvin Stallybrass appeared. He looked similarly attired and complete with identical equipment.

"Greetings." His loud voice echoed around the cave entrance. "I'm all ready. How about you two?"

"Yep," Fergy replied. "Nice to see you, Kelvin." He stood up. "So here's what we're going to do. On the first dive, we will allocate a shallow section not far from the water's edges.

There's no need for a buddy system until we go deeper… if indeed that is necessary at this stage. Lake three should be ideal for our first dive since it's not far from the entrance." The others nodded in agreement. "All we have to do now is wait for our tubby priest."

They didn't have to wait long. There was an almighty over revving engine noise as a red and black pick-up truck screeched to a stop yards from them in a cloud of dust. It ignored the parking signs. The door swung open as Father Vincenzo, with a hefty Canon DSLR camera slung around his neck, jumped from the cab with surprising agility. He was dressed in an incongruous, black track suit bearing the logo of the *Athletica Vaticana* – part of the Vatican Sports Association. On his feet, he wore an expensive pair of Nike trainers. Vincenzo had thought the outfit made him look fit and sporty.

His smile is as sincere as a funeral director's over a pauper's coffin, Fergy thought.

"*Buongiorno, figli miei.*"

"Hi Father, let me introduce you to our other member, Kelvin. He's a seasoned diver with years of experience around these parts," Fergy said.

The two men shook hands. Fergy gave the priest a brief overview of their dive. before they set off into the caves and beyond the taped off SSSI area.

The air was cool and remained at a constant temperature of eleven degrees centigrade. Vincenzo immediately began taking pictures of the interior and of the crewmembers. It was clear he had precise instructions to photograph their every action.

Once their equipment was assembled, correctly fitted, and checked, the three divers took up positions at the agreed points. When they reached their diving stations, Vincenzo shouted out, *"Un momento, por favor. Un'altra fotografia."* He swiftly moved between them and blasted off three camera shots. These, like the others, would find their way into the cardinal's files. "How long will you be?"

Miriam answered. "Forty minutes max unless we find something of interest."

"Okay," Father Vincenzo replied. One could see he was shivering. *"Fa freddo,* I'll go outside before I freeze to death here." He turned and disappeared from view.

"Thank God for that. He just bloody annoys me," the professor snapped.

"Me too," Miriam said.

"Religions like his are an affront to nature," Kelvin responded.

Fergy looked across at Miriam and from behind his mask, she saw his eyebrow rise.

At that point, he raised his arm and gave the agreed signal. Their timers were all set, and as he lowered his arm, all three divers slid silently into the cold waters.

* * *

Rome…

Cardinal Nicholas opened his eyes after dozing off for thirty minutes. He was seated in the business class section of an Alitalia flight into Rome's Leonardo da Vinci International Airport, situated in Fiumicino. Behind him, he could hear the soft reassuring whine of the A321 Airbus's twin jet engines. He stretched out his misshapen, sinewy leg and felt a glow of inner satisfaction.

It had been an eventful day. As expected, he had received

a call from the pope's aide requesting he attend an audience with the Holy Father. All seemed to be falling into place, and what the professor and his small team could accomplish would only add to his good fortune. They seemed to know what they were doing, and all he could hope for were results. Vincenzo, he knew, would stop at nothing to make certain all was going to plan. The man wouldn't hesitate. That thought was comforting.

The intercom announced there was thirty minutes of flight time remaining before they touched down at the airport.

Later, after clearing Rome's airport, in a room with an astonishing view of the Vatican, he had conducted several round table meetings with his senior fellow sympathizers. They formed the core of the *Ordinis Sancti et Sanctae Crucis et Gladio* – The Order of the Holy Cross and Sword. There were eight senior members in total, although there are members whose identity can only be found in the cardinal's encrypted database.

In these meetings, he had outlined to a shocked gathering, the depths of the Antichrist's hidden agenda, and his transparent attempts to hide the real reason for the existence of SOTA. He had also explained the real truth behind the pope's efforts. Truths that he had beaten from the now dead Bishop Vincent Fisher.

"How do you know that?" another cardinal asked upon hearing what Nicholas had said about the pope's reasons for supporting SOTA.

"The very man organising SOTA's activities had mistakenly confided in me. This may come as a shock to you all, but our now belated brother, Bishop Fisher, told me. He was acting for our Antichrist who is currently ensconced in luxury in the palace before you." He pointed through the window. "God rest the bishop's soul." To emphasise his supposed concern, the cardinal stood and made the sign of the cross. His face remained as a sharpened flint.

There followed gasps of astonishment. "Where do we go from here?" a voice shouted.

The cardinal felt his chest heave as he took a deep breath. "Have no fear. I have the pope's trust, the poor fool. I am now in charge of operations and all finds will be reported and handed over to me. He will see only what I want him to see. This pope will not get away with undermining our true faith, given by Saint Peter through Christ and our Blessed Virgin Mary. If I have to rot in hell to prevent such a disgrace, I would willingly do so." As he spoke the words, he wasn't quite sure if that was true.

He glanced at his watch before ending the meeting. "I have a meeting with His Holiness in twenty minutes. That should be interesting. I wonder how many more lies he will try to spoon out. If anything new transpires, I will, of course, let you know. *Buon pomeriggio, signori.*"

He turned and exited through a side door into a large courtyard, which led to the pope's private quarters. Thoughts ran through his mind. Pope Adrian had not mentioned the story or legend about a healing cup that contained water and blood from Christ's crucifixion wounds. The cup that supposedly remained full and was never empty. He had first heard of it in the newly discovered written words of Philip and Thomas. Superficially, it seemed like a phoney legend. However, the fact that the pope was so intent on discovering the so-called truth of Christ's survival and such a miraculous cup, added a degree of cadence to the story. The history of the

Celts in Britain and even any surviving Druid records would surely mention the artefact and the events surrounding it, if it had existed

* * *

Pope Adrian gazed around his room, at the sumptuous art of old masters hanging from the walls. He made a mental decision that they would have to go. They had an aura of decadence, of overindulgence, unseemly for a person attempting to improve the lot and concerns of suffering humanity. In many ways, he longed for the simplicity of his rooms back at the seminary all those years ago. *There is far too much unjustifiable gold and splendour in attendance. Yes, they should be disposed of soon.*

Overriding these thoughts, he was anxious to hear a report from Cardinal Nicholas, although he realised it was still early days. Such expeditions have been known to extend into years. The bishop's untimely death had led to a hiatus in the mission, but now events were moving along once more.

A buzz on his desk-mounted CCTV screen revealed the expected arrival of Cardinal Nicholas. The pope operated the entry system and the door swung open, allowing the cardinal to enter, but not before the cardinal had adjusted his *zucchetto* and brushed down his cassock.

Cardinal Nicholas genuflected and was offered the Piscatory or Ring of the Fisherman to kiss. Once done, he was shown to a seat.

The Pope spoke. "I trust all is well with you, Cardinal Nicholas?"

"Couldn't be finer, Most Holy Father."

"What news on our SOTA project?"

"Holy Father, it is underway once more. Father Vincenzo, my aide, is attending to the project. As we speak, he's on site at the team's first dive. We anticipate there will be digging involved in due time. There has to be Celtic evidence on how Christianity seemed to arrive there before our saints." He paused, and a sly gleam came from his eyes. "I personally do not believe the nonsensical stories that Jesus was not crucified, or another that he was, but survived the ordeal. That he had then moved around Europe and ended up in England... These things are of course absurdities manufactured by Satan's agents."

Pope Adrian's face froze. He didn't blink or change his expression. *Now, where did he hear all that? I only told him we wanted to know how and when our faith arrived in Britain.*

He decided not to give too much away. Bishop Fisher, he trusted totally. But for a reason he was unable to fathom, the same did not apply to the cardinal sitting in front of him. But no matter... the die was cast.

"Cardinal, please tell me the location and any history attached that may have a bearing on our conversation."

"Most Holy Father, they are in a cave system in South West England, around a series of intricately linked cave systems known as Cheddar, Wookey Hole and Glastonbury. The area was and still known today as a stronghold of Celtic culture. If anything is to be found... it must be there."

"Let us hope so, Cardinal."

"I am preparing a file for you, Your Holiness, complete with the photographs Father Vincenzo is assembling." *You will be seeing only those I choose you to see.*

"I look forward to that, Cardinal. Is your aide, Father Vincenzo, efficient and capable of understanding what we are attempting to discover here? Above all, is he trustworthy?"

"Most certainly, Holy Father. It was I who introduced him into the priesthood years ago. I trust him with my life."

"I hope it need not come to that, Cardinal. It is good to hear of your trust in him. This mission is of utmost importance to our faith and would need to be handled with extreme discretion. Now if you please, I have some matters to attend to. I will contact you again soon. Keep me informed of your movements, please." Pope Adrian rose.

"Most certainly, Holy Father." Nicholas again genuflected, before turning and leaving the room. What he didn't realise was that the entire encounter had been recorded and videoed.

Once alone, what Pope Adrian did next was unprecedented in the chronicles of papal history.

CHAPTER 11

Kelvin hadn't forgotten his Druid name, Iseldir, or its importance. As he slipped under the cool waters of the cave, he offered up an ancient Druid prayer, but not before he had deposited a small Lemurian crystal into the clear waters. He mentally recited:

Hear you, these sacred waters,
It is I, Iseldir.
Our quest is pure. Our quest is holy.
We pray for healing blessings from your waters.
We pray for healing blessings from the sea.
We pray for healing blessings in these waters.
That they might shine in crystal purity.
May we find, with your blessings, what we seek.

When that was said and done, he felt a warm glow of spiritual satisfaction. The search could commence.

The waters around him were as of daylight. He could see

around him clearly. Pottery fragments had been discovered on the shore edge. He was now down to the agreed limit of thirty feet, a fraction over nine metres. Just below him was a flat outcrop of rock covered in stones and flint.

He peered long and hard at the bulging rocks. *If that doesn't hold something of interest, I'm a nanny goat's mother.* Kelvin swiftly swum down and opened his specimen collection bag. Scanning around quickly, he saw something that looked promising, but he would have to get them into daylight to find out what they were. His time limit was now almost up. With swift movements, he gathered up what he could and deposited them into the open bag. He then struck out to the surface. On surfacing, he could see the other two had also done the same. Removing his mask and mouthpiece, he yelled out. "Did you find anything?"

"Not sure yet. Let's get to the bank and check." Miriam gave a cheery wave.

"Just a load of shale and flinty bits." Fergy waved his bag at them. "Let's see what we have."

Minutes later, they were emptying their bag's contents. Miriam got excited at some brown coloured pottery fragments that were clearly ancient, although a cursory examination gave no clue of age. They were, due to the stillness and constant temperature, remarkably well preserved.

"We'll have to examine and analyse them some more back at the lab. What about you, Fergy?"

The professor scuffed, dragging his hand through the gravelly stones and then peering hard at his find. "Nothing that you couldn't find on Chesil's famous beach in Dorset. Anything interesting there, Kelvin?"

Kelvin did not say a word. His lips seemed to be moving in silent prayer.

"What have you got there, Kelvin?" Miriam pointed to the large, flat rock he had in his hand.

For a moment, he didn't respond. His eyes were glazed over. Then he snapped out of his trance and exclaimed, "I can't believe I found this on my first dive. Look!" He held it up.

"It's a triskelion."

"What's that?"

"An ancient Celtic, Druidic and even Christian symbol, reflecting the belief that all things come in threes. It's based on Archimedean principles. As you can see, it's a rounded spiral with three arms radiating from a central point, turning counterclockwise. It stands for any one of hundreds of Celtic and Druidic Triads found in their literature. Part of the foundation of their ancient cosmology, which stands for land, sea and sky."

"The three in one. The Father, Son and Holy Spirit," Fergy quipped. "Hey, how do you know all this? I thought that was my field. I may have a rival here!" He laughed out loud. He knew the myths and legends but never took them seriously.

Kelvin remained serious. His silent prayer had been answered and shown only to him. He knew there could only be one other discovery to complete the three-fold lore. Had he not previously been led to discover that mysterious plaque?

He had yet to show that to them. He gave a short prayer of thanks to the elements. He ignored Fergal's question.

Miriam gave Fergy an enquiring look. There was more to Kelvin than he had let on. "What are we going to do with it?"

"We will have to catalogue it, complete with photographs, location and other details. I expect our minder out there will need to be told, although there's nothing particularly Christian about the find. No doubt his boss will have the final say. After all, they are paying for all this."

Kelvin looked up. "They have enough artefacts in their vaults. Why would they want this?" His voice was laced with anger.

"You may be right, Kelvin. This could belong to a museum, but I don't think our rotund friend would care for that. Do we tell what we've found so far?"

Kelvin took a deep breath. "Let's wait and see. Later, I'll show you something else I found awhile back. You may be able to tell me what it is."

"Look forward to that, Kelvin. Let's look around a bit more. It won't do any harm to keep our fat minder waiting longer… and we say nothing for now, okay?"

* * *

Later that evening, having found nothing further, the professor sat resting in his armchair. He had boiled water and was spooning the Assam tea into the glass teapot he had brought with him. He never used tea bags. They never tasted quite the same. Fergy stirred the brew with care, enjoying the subtle aroma that came straight from a section of heaven.

He jumped when there was a rap on the door. It was Miriam. She had booked a room down the corridor from him. As she frequently did, she had been thinking of the project they had embarked upon. There was more talking to be done, especially about their new friend, Kelvin. He had turned out to be a man of mystery. After their dive, they realised there was more to him, and they needed to find out what.

Many people imagined, because of their closeness, that she and Fergy were an item – lovers at least. It had never been that way. As children, they had grown up together and lived just a stone's throw away. Their parents had been close friends, and their lives closely entwined.

Miriam's father had been a roof thatcher until a stroke prevented him from climbing up ladders ever again. It eventually killed him. Her mother was living in a care home and unable to function on her own. Miriam went to see her every week, but dementia was getting a grip on her and she often couldn't recognise her own daughter.

She and Fergy often talked about their odd relationship, but never once did either of them overstep the invisible line. She had often wondered, and still did, if they would ever be romantic. Neither had current relationships with others, although in the past, that had not been the case. They adored each other, holding high respect for each other's respective ways of life and achievements. They were a perfect match. Some even said they were like brother and sister.

After her knock, the door opened and he stood there holding the teapot.

"You timed that well. Come in."

Just then his mobile began to ring. "Oh bugger. Who can that be?" The screen showed an international caller. It was not unusual. He frequently received them from colleagues and enquirers.

"Hi, Professor Christi speaking. How can I help you?"

The voice at the other end sounded soft, almost South African in its intonation.

"Hello, Professor. Good to reach you. Please do not be startled by this call. It's from Rome. The Vatican, to be precise."

There was a pause. "The Vatican. Is this some sort of joke?" He swung a wild look at Miriam who looked startled. "If so, you better get off the line right now."

"No joke, Professor. My common name was Jayden Van Cleef. You know me more as Pope Adrian." He paused as he heard gasps from the other end of the line. "So now, do I have your attention?"

Fergy gulped and switched to loudspeaker for Miriam to hear. "Now just a minute, whoever you are..." He was interrupted.

"Stop right there, Professor." The voice remained soft and calm. "This call is being made in utmost secrecy. My trusted friend and spiritual brother, the late Bishop Vincent Fisher, God rest his blessed soul, had included your name in his research for the Society of Truth in Archaeology, known as SOTA. Correct?"

Without thinking, Fergy replied, "Correct..."

Pope Adrian continued, "The project is now in the hands of Cardinal Nicholas and his aide, Father Vincenzo – who has reached you, yes?"

"That information is known only to the smallest group of people," Fergy replied, his doubts fading fast. It *is* the pope! *How do I address him?* "Holy Father, as you may imagine, this is difficult to believe. If you are who you say you are, what can I do for you?"

"Professor, you are in a privileged position that only I know of. My representative, Cardinal Nicholas, will be sending me information and photographs on anything you may find in support of these newly found writings of Philip and Thomas. Yes?"

"Yes."

"Let me say, just between ourselves, I need double clarification. I have a strong feeling that I may be misled. So, what I am asking is, will you please send your own report, details and photographs and your opinion about anything you find, directly to me using my private mailbox address? If you agree, you will do this without the cardinal's knowledge."

"What on earth!" Fergy exclaimed and looked across at Miriam who had puffed out her cheeks with a rush of exhaled air.

"Yes, indeed. What on earth..." The pope's kindly tone softened Fergy's amazement.

"How do I know you're really the pope himself?"

"You don't, Professor. But like you, only the truth interests me, and when faith shows it to be real then I know it's God's work. Before his death, the bishop informed me of certain facts. You have a Shetland Sheepdog named Dickens, after the author you greatly admire. You are also the National Coordinator for the Society of Ancient Discoveries and have a lifelong close colleague, Doctor Miriam Sinclair. Our intelligence network, the *Santa Alleanza*, is very thorough and have checked out all these details. You have no cause for concern. The skills you possess are well suited to our requirements."

Fergy gasped and turned to Miriam who merely shrugged.

"In heaven's name..."

"Yes, indeed. We are doing this in heaven's name, Professor," Pope Adrian interrupted. "Are you agreeable to what I have asked?"

Fergy looked over to Miriam. This time she nodded.

"We agree."

The pope's voice maintained its gentle timbre. "I prayed you would. Go to your computer right now and punch out this code." He gave a combination of eight letters and numbers. "This is changed every day. Now enter, what do you see?"

Fergy read it out…

For the Servant of God (Only)
Box 69 Saint Martha House
00120 Città del Vaticano

"Perfect. That code no longer works now except for you, and this is the only address you will use." There came a short pause. "Computers are too easily hacked. Old-fashioned postal procedures still have their uses. I thank you for your help, Professor, and I apologise for what must seem to be a most strange thing for you to hear. Without your help, I fear truth could be buried forever. Bishop Vincent told me he had trust in you. I sense he was correct."

Fergy felt any doubts he had vanishing. The caller was indeed Pope Adrian.

"This is my very private and personal phone number." He gave out a series of numbers – 0112358132134558. "Your numbers are also registered on it. All the time you have been talking to me, it has been employing a voice recognition system on you. If it fails to recognise you, it will disconnect you from my phone immediately. Such measures are necessary in these times. There are currently only six people who have this number. You are now the seventh."

Fergy had no words. He was scrambling to note down the

phone number given by the pope.

"Professor, I must leave you now and I look forward to receiving details of your progress." Before the phone went dead, the pope's last sentence was in Italian. *"Buonanotte, professore. Dio ti benedica."*

After the call, a silent Fergy walked slowly to a chair and slumped down. He looked across to Miriam. "Wow… that was amazing! The pope, no less, and he has concerns about Cardinal Nicholas. I don't think we can all be wrong in that aspect. What do you think about all that?"

"Surreal. What are we getting into?" She found a seat and sat facing him. They had much to discuss.

"I don't know, but there's something going on and it seems it has a lot to do with religious politics. They're hoping we'll find something that will further their own cause. I'm sure of it." Fergy was staring hard at the pope's number when he suddenly sat straight. He bent closer and blew out a lungful of air. "Hey, just a moment…" His voice was charged. "I recognise this sequence. It can't be a coincidence."

"What can't be a coincidence? What do you see?"

"His phone number… it's the first part of the Fibonacci sequence. You know? Each number is the sum of the previous two. At first glance, it looks like a random series of numbers but when you look closely – 0112358132134558." Fergy rapped the paper with his pen. "0+1=1… 1+1=2… 2+1=3… 3+2=5… 5+3=8… and so on. It's amazing! Our pope appears to be a learned man. This sequence can be found throughout the natural world – the leaves on a stem, the seeds in the centre of a sunflower, and spiral galaxies, just to name a few. And it's the pope's phone number!" He laughed at the incredulity of it all.

"You're crazy! Can't see what's so important about that."

Miriam shrugged.

Before he could reply, the hotel phone rang with a shrill tone that startled them both. Fergy picked up. The reception-ist told him he had a visitor. A Mr. Kelvin Stallybrass.

CHAPTER 12

He looked apprehensive as he walked in, declining a drink. "I'm not thirsty, thanks." Kelvin sat down on a spare chair. "I just wanted to say I enjoyed the dive today and finding that triskelion. You seem to know your stuff okay." He paused and shifted his gaze to something only he could see.

Fergy waited, not really appreciating the surprise visit.

After a few seconds, Kelvin said, "I was wondering... I have something you may be able to help me with."

"What's that, Kelvin?"

"I mentioned it to you earlier. It's something I found a year or two ago when I was trying to find a decent pool to dive in not one taped off by the SSSI signs. It's this." He reached into the briefcase he was carrying. "It was lodged between two cracks and looked as if it was solid rock. That's why previous digs must have missed it." He pulled out an A5 sized tablet. "It's inscribed and I can't work out what it is." He handed it over to Fergy with care. "Finding that triskelion earlier prompted me to show this to you."

Fergy looked at the tablet. It could be made of bronze. "It reminds me of the *Botoritta Plaques* discovered in nineteen seventy-nine. Here, have a look Miriam."

She took the tablet, produced a lens, and began to peer hard at the writing.

As she examined the object, she shared her opinion. "The longest, extant Celtiberian inscriptions are those written on four bronze plaques from Botorrita near Zargoza in Spain, dating back to the early first century BC. Sadly, this is not Celtiberian." She gave a teasing smirk. "It's something more exciting. You found it in a cave around here, Kelvin?"

"That's correct, in Wookey. Should I have handed it in? What is it?"

"I can't believe what I'm looking at. I'm glad you didn't hand it in."

"Well? Come on, Miss Linguistics. What is it?" Fergy asked, his interest awakened.

"It's Aramaic. The language Jesus spoke."

"Holy Mothers!" Fergy's eyes widened and he felt the hairs on the back of his neck stand. "Can you read it?"

"Give me a while or two, and pen and paper, please."

The room went quiet as she began to write letters with a soft mumble coming from her moving lips. Fergy looked across to Kelvin who could only shrug.

The tea was forgotten. Fergal poured more drinks, and all that could be heard was the ticking of the clock and Miriam's soft murmurings. Forty minutes passed and Fergy was getting impatient.

"Is there a problem?" he asked with more than a tinge of

irritation. "First the pope and now, a startling Aramaic tablet."

"Shhh!" she snapped. "Be quiet, will you? I'm trying to put this into some sort of order so that you numbskulls can understand it. It's not easy."

Another thirty-five minutes later, Miriam put down her pen and looked up. "I've written it down in verse form. This is what it says." Slowly she began to read out loud.

Before my Parent you can only kneel
From whose eternal cup you may heal
Then seek the glass beneath the skies
The grave wherein the hidden secret lies.

"It's a riddle!" Miriam explained.

"How can this be happening? How can this tablet be connected to our search?" Fergy stood up and started pacing the room. It was then he realized he hadn't given Kelvin the whole story. He turned to Miriam and knew she was thinking the same thing.

She gave a quick nod. It was time to tell Kelvin the full extent of their mission.

He turned to Kelvin. "Kelvin, there's more to our search than we have let on."

Kelvin held up his hands. "I guessed as much, and a tablet written in Aramaic has confirmed my notion. The healing cup that can never empty is what you're looking for. It's been a secret story amongst my people for two thousand years."

"What? You know of this? Who are your people?" Fergy exclaimed.

"I am a Druid. The Chief Druid of my particular Order. I am called Iseldir."

"Well, that explains how you knew so much about your find this morning."

Kelvin nodded. "So, are you going to tell me more? Maybe we can help each other."

"All I can tell you at this point is that you're working on a secret mission funded by the Vatican. There isn't much more to tell yet. Our minders are the two men you saw us talking to the other day. You should know that we don't entirely trust them, but for no particular reason. It's just a feeling. Don't mention or show them your plaque. I'll take a photo of it, but you'd better hold on to it. Keep it out of sight, whatever you do." Fergy slapped his thighs and stood up to stretch. "Hey, it's been quite a day. A call from a pope with a Fibonacci phone number, a secret address, and an Aramaic plaque complete with a mystic verse. What's next, I wonder?" He noticed Kelvin's face becoming more confused. "There's much we need to think about. Who inscribed that plaque and what is it referring to? Our quest has suddenly taken a giant leap."

* * *

Cracker positioned himself where he could see exactly what the three researchers took in and out of the caves. As yet, they had nothing to report. It was proving to be a boring task.

Vincenzo kept a watch on everyone. He was thankful for Cracker's presence. By the look of him, he could be most useful when the going got rough. It was time for him to make another visit.

Carrying his flashlight and camera, he set out on foot. When the skies opened up with terrific flashes of lightning and enormous claps of thunder, he was forced into a run. The waters could rise and rush in wild torrents through the cave structures.

Dripping wet, he lurched into the cave area as already the waters had begun to rise. Ducking under the protective tape, he saw there was nobody around. *They must be diving.* His flashlight revealed three backpacks in a tidy row. *These could be interesting.* He began unzipping the first one. The name on the label was Kelvin Stallybrass. Lifting up the flap, at first he could see nothing. Then he saw something that got his attention. He was staring down at an old bronze plaque. He gasped. *Where did that come from and why hasn't it been declared?* He didn't need to be an expert to understand that whatever it was, it was incredibly old indeed. Within seconds, he was taking pictures of it. The cardinal would be pleased to see them. He would know what to do.

The sound of someone surfacing from the water forced him to stop. It was Stallybrass, who at once saw that his pack was open.

He tore off his facemask. "What the hell do you think you're doing?" He bellowed at the priest.

"*Mi dispiace.* This is yours? I am so sorry. I wondered why it was left here. I did not know it was yours."

Kelvin's face stretched in anger as he moved it within inches of Vincenzo's. "So now you know. Don't bloody touch it again. Understood?"

Vincenzo gave a look of mock apology. He would like nothing better than for Stallybrass to take a swing at him. If he did, he would be in for a big surprise. His Vektor CP1 was resting snugly in his concealed shoulder holster. "So sorry, Mr. Stallybrass. Now please, take your face away from mine."

Kelvin did not fail to notice the underlying warning in the priest's words. *There's something about this priest I can't work out.*

Both the professor and Miriam emerged from the waters. The tension was noticeable.

Fergal pulled off his facemask. "All okay here?" he asked with an element of concern. Miriam stood next to him.

Kelvin snapped his reply. "It is now. I found Father Vincenzo snooping through my backpack."

"No snoop. It was an accident, believe me." The priest, spreading out his arms and hands, affected an apologetic expression.

The professor paused. "Easy now… easy. I'm sure it's only a misunderstanding, Kelvin." In his mind, he thought… *I don't think it was.* "Let's forget it."

"*Si.* Let us forget it. I shake your hand." Vincenzo responded in a singsong Italian way, and with a rigid smile that barely concealed his rage, thrust out his hand to Kelvin.

Kelvin looked unhappy. It was obvious he didn't believe the priest's story. What he had in his backpack could be the most astonishing artefact discovered in the UK. *He must have seen it and photographed it and it'll end up God knows where. It belongs to the ancient people of this land and not the Roman Catholic Church.*

Kelvin, mindful of the sensitivity of the mission, and with a look that was as sour as a rotten lemon, held out his hand. He said no more, turned his back on the priest once the shake was done, picked up his pack and moved back behind the other two.

"*Grazie mille.*" Without another word, Vincenzo turned and headed out. He had decided to contact Cracker. After that episode things, the situation could begin to heat up. Whatever that tablet was there was a deliberate attempt to hide it. That was against the rules. His photographs would be on their way to the cardinal that evening.

CHAPTER 13

The grounds of *Domos Sanctae Marthae* – Saint Martha House – were silent. A silence broken only by a soft wind easing through gaps in the modern structure. The Domus Sanctae Marthae stood adjacent to St. Peter's Basilica in Vatican City. completed in 1996, the building functioned as a guesthouse for clergies who had business with the Holy See and a temporary lodging for cardinals participating in a papal conclave. Pope Leo XIII had the St. Martha Hospice built on the site in 1891, and in 1996, it was rebuilt into the structure it is now.

The full moon proffered a soft glow around the structure, reflecting its presence off the glass door entrance. A figure of a cowled man could be seen approaching the doors. It was as if he did not wish to be recognised. At his approach, the doors swung open and he continued inside. Moving across to the furthest wall, he approached an illuminated box with a built-in plasma screen. He moved up close so that his face touched it. It was a retinal scanner for access control. It captured the pattern of the retina's blood vessels inside the physical eye. If it was not recognised by the database, entry would be refused, and a security alert would be activated. It didn't. The man whose eye it was scanning had had it installed.

Pope Adrian stepped backwards, and to the left of him, a hidden partition silently slid open. He stepped inside as the wall closed softly behind him. He was in a long corridor with other corridors on each side, numbering from one up to twenty. The corridor he wanted was on his right and numbered six. He swung into it and was confronted with row upon row of secured lockers, each holding extremely sensitive Vatican notes, discoveries procedures and a host of other topics. The cabinet he wanted was number nine – known as 69 – that is, Row 6… Box 9.

The soft hum of the air conditioning and the occasional clicks of an encrypted code being remotely entered elsewhere, broke the funereal silence of the chamber.

Every move of anybody in this area was heavily monitored by an array of CCTV cameras with a triple back up system.

He had personally watched through this system a trio of high-ranking Swiss Guard activate an encrypted code they had. They carried a postal package, which would have passed all tests for bombs, gases, viruses, and anything that could be harmful. There were three codes and pins. They had only one. When activated, it revealed a hidden slot sixty centimetres in length and with a width of five centimetres. Its purpose was to allow posts that had passed security testing to be placed in its aperture. It would remain open for ten seconds and then slam shut, concealed and inoperable for forty-eight hours –

even if nothing had been placed in it. For that time period, it would be inaccessible. Any attempt to illegally open the steel box would automatically destroy the contents inside and the entire security system and the Vatican's Corp of Gendarmerie would be alerted.

Using his smartphone, the pope activated the coded pin number, which he did three times as required. There came from the grey coloured box a soft whine, a buzz, and then the front dropped down as if on a spring. He reached in and pulled out a C4 sized envelope and he knew without looking who it was from. The bronze coloured label confirmed it: *Professor Fergal Lars Christi* together with his address stared up at him. The professor was living up to his promise. Pope Adrian smiled as he reactivated the automatic system to seal the box once more.

He walked back the way he had come, through concealed portals and into the night air. He had a mild feeling of reassurance. His uneasiness regarding the cardinal was assuaged by the thought that he had an ally in the professor. He could hardly wait to open the package. He was like a child waking up on Christmas day to see what he got.

* * *

Walking into his private chambers, Pope Adrian gave the guards instructions that under no circumstances was he to be disturbed. Once in, he activated the electric curtains and his desk lamps. From his pocket, he produced and switched on his portable anti-bugging device. The device searched for any hidden cameras or listening devices. He panned the room twice. The screen remained clear. It was safe. Reaching into his desk drawer, he produced a bottle of fine Hennessey

Cognac and a brandy glass. It had been there for months, and he rarely imbibed. Right now, it seemed appropriate. Tonight, he sensed a gathering pressure around SOTA, and that very much involved him.

He poured a moderate measure of the Cognac and reached across his desk for his gold and silver letter opener, complete with the papal seal embossed on the handle. For a moment, he paused, took a large gulp on the drink, allowing its hot flush to spread through his chest and stomach

He carefully inserted the silver blade into the top end of the envelope and slit it from end to end. Once fully open, he pulled out a blue coloured file secured with a large paper clip. Opening, it he saw an introductory note plus a Word document prepared by Professor Christi, together with three coloured photographs. He read through the document first. It stated exactly what they had been doing, the pottery they had found and the way the mission was proceeding. Mention was also made of the Druid's find of the triskelion. It described their meeting with the cardinal and Father Vincenzo and what they'd discussed.

What he read next caused him to take another large gulp on the brandy. The cardinal had seen fit, without saying a word of it, to employ heavy muscle to oversee the project. *What is he doing? It's bad enough that Vincenzo is involved. I can't tell him I know. He might suspect I have someone spying on him.*

He read further. The professor had outlined the episode between Stallybrass and Vincenzo and considered that the backpack was being searched. Christi went on to describe the tablet and where it was found and how old they suspected it was.

What caught his attention was the professor's note that the inscription was in Aramaic. Dr Sinclair's translation and rendering into verse form were also there.

> *Before my Parent you can only kneel*
> *From whose eternal cup you may heal*
> *Then seek the glass beneath the starry skies*
> *The grave wherein the hidden secret lies.*

Pope Adrian jumped out of his chair. His eyes were riveted to the photographs and the translation. His hands and legs were shaking.

"But how can it be?" he cried out aloud. "That's impossible! Oh Great God, it's the language of Jesus!"

He read and reread it many times, his mind whirling with a myriad of possibilities. He had never felt so excited.

Aramaic.... in England!

He took another drink and punched both his fists to the skies.

CHAPTER 14

S he lay locked in a deep dream of peace. The sands beckoned to
her, as a zephyr in its wake whipped particles into a whirl.
They, in unison, beckoned to her as they began their magical
dance across the vast empty desert.

Her hand reached out as she stirred beneath heaven's moon to
follow the enchantment. Across spaces of forest and of towns and
villages, they spun across an ocean of blue and sparkling waters. A
land lay before them and she knew that she, whom she sought, would
be there.

Her mother waited beneath the diamond sky. The nightingales
in the branches sang before their unknown flight began.

"Tarry, child, tarry. Thy cup I still do carry."

Their arms reached out for each other across the welcome grass
and she handed her daughter the never empty cup.

Miriam woke with a start, her arms outstretched. She shouted out one word, *"Mother!"* Her hand went across her mouth. She took stock and realised she was alone in her bed. Her breath came in short, sharp gasps.

That was so real. I can still feel it in my mind and blood. She took a deep breath and shook her head. Whispering to herself, she said, "That was like a separate reality or some sort of entanglement. First in one place and then instantly in another, and all at the same time." She thought back to what she had learnt from her researches. *One of the strangest aspects of quantum physics is entanglement. If you observe a particle in one place, another particle – even one light years away – will instantly change its properties, as if the two are connected by a mysterious communication channel.*

"Damn it! It was so bloody real." Her mind revolved on the compelling and gripping aspects of her dream. She thought back to earlier years when she, as a lapsed Catholic, had formally rejected all religions. Yet that dream had cast a mysterious shadow over the interlinking of science, mysticism, and religion.

Miriam accepted that both science and religion sought the truth, yet both used different approaches. Science was free of dogma and unprovable beliefs, although there were often dissenting voices concerning any theory until it was proven. Even legendary scientists like the mighty Isaac Newton were known to be tied up in alchemy, dreams, and Freemasonry.

She was a scientist and researcher. That dream intruded on all her tightly held scientific paradigms. *No more thoughts, it was time to get up.*

Jumping into the shower, she turned the heater up and stood motionless under the steamy torrent. How many minutes she remained like that, she didn't know. Her mind was full of that dream. She attempted to forget it and think about the day ahead. There was to be a meeting between them all. She and Fergal wanted more details on where Kelvin had found the tablet. It could be a useful research point.

It didn't completely work.

* * *

A pallor of Davidoff cigarette smoke drifted in lazy swirls around the room. Putting the lighted cigarette to his mouth, he took another deep lungful into his skinny chest and leaned back into his leather, swivel office chair. In his hands, Cardinal Nicholas held a downloaded printout of Vincenzo's photographs, suitably enlarged so the script could clearly be seen. There was an accompanying note. It stated how he found the tablet and his suspicions that the team were trying to conceal the artefact. It further stated that the tablet was in the rucksack of Stallybrass and not the professor or the doctor.

His observations are interesting but not proof enough. How this could have been found there, without causing any excitement, is unusual. Using an eyepiece, he bent closer to examine the script. He could make neither head nor tail of it. He decided he would have to get a linguist to check it out and then he would have a clearer picture of what it might be.

The photographs are excellent. The tablet is interesting. *But what is it? What does it say?* If he took an educated guess, he'd say it was either Ancient Hebrew or even Aramaic. He chose Aramaic. He wanted to avoid any political or religious difficulties, so offering it up to Israel or the Middle Eastern countries was borderline. Instead, after some Internet research, he chose a Swedish Aramaic newspaper. He found it hard to believe, but it existed – called <u>Bahro Suryoyo</u> or The Syriac Light. It was published in five languages and available online. It championed the Aramaic language and the Syriac ideals and culture.

Perfect. He immediately set about drafting an email to the editor, complete with attachments. In it, he outlined who he was and what had been found, without saying where. He would be honoured, he said, if they could reply and confirm if the script was Aramaic, and if so, what might it say?

Once completed, he read it through. He checked the attachments and clicked 'Send.' It was done. Now all he had to do was sit and wait. If the results were what he suspected, it was unlikely he would be sending them to Pope Adrian.

He sat back to finish his cigarette before making a call to Vincenzo. It was time to tell him to get Cracker active. That might have a sobering effect on their attitudes.

* * *

Later that morning, both Fergy and Kelvin walked across the car park to the open doorway of Miriam's LV 6.8 luxury motorhome. Inside, it was big enough to hold a conference. She had obtained it with the money from the sale of her deceased parent's property, knowing that she would be constantly travelling in remote and distant areas. It had proved invaluable to her lifestyle. She adored it.

Having cleaned up the various files and paperwork into orderly piles, she stood at the door waiting for them. They were on time.

"Welcome aboard, you two." She had prepared an enormous spread of coffee and biscuits.

Kelvin spoke first as soon as they sat down. There was an angry look in his eye. "I'm not going to waste time about this. I need to say, I don't like that priest and he was definitely photographing the tablet."

"Don't worry, nor do we," Fergy said. "If that was what he was doing, then his shots are on their way to the cardinal for certain."

"What's he going to do with them?" Miriam said as she poured coffee into their cups. "If the pope is funding this enterprise, then I guess they will be reaching him too."

"That doesn't matter," Fergy said. "As he requested, I've sent him all the details of our mission, including finding the tablet. I've even added your verse translation, Miriam. He doesn't entirely trust the cardinal. In this respect, he is one jump ahead of him, whether the cardinal shares our finds to him or not."

"This is a recipe for a total mishap. Religion once again screwing up everything." Kelvin thumped his fist on the table. "The Druids look like the real saints in these matters, caring for the environment and all that supports it. I believe in dreams and I had a dream that clearly showed me this is the way I should be treading. I never thought that it would be full of intrigue and suspicion."

Miriam looked up sharply. "You believe in dreams, Kelvin?"

"Mainly when I can follow them through. Yes."

The professor interrupted. "Stop. We're not here to discuss metaphysics, dreams, synchronicity, or clairvoyants. Kelvin, I'll get to the point." Leaning forward towards him, he looked him squarely in the eyes. "We need to know where you found that plaque. Believe me, it could prove vitally important. Will you tell and show us, please? Whether you like it or not, you have become part of this quest."

Kelvin sipped his coffee. He stared hard at the tabletop and the outline of his jaw visibly hardened.

Miriam placed her hand upon his arm. She knew his mind was turning. "Kelvin, you were meant to be here, as is Fergy and myself. I too have had a dream about this whole thing. It defies explanation in real terms, but in unreal terms it seems so true. Ask yourself this… how is it possible that we met you and you have that tablet which is startling evidence that what we seek could be true? Kelvin, it was meant to be."

She paused and realised her approach was non-scientific, but with Kelvin, it was more than necessary.

He shut his eyes and lowered his head. Miriam glanced over at Fergy. He nodded at her. It had been the right approach. Her hand remained on his arm.

She saw his fingers quivering on the table. Without looking up, and with his eyes still closed, he spoke. "Thank you. I am a Druid, the Chief Druid, Iseldir of The Clan Taran, and have been so for many years. "What I found was resting amidst our grove and in its sacred waters. It is little known, and in many ways… it is secret. As such, its secrets belong to us and nobody else, least of all the Catholic Church. I have come to like and respect you both but am concerned about many things. Yes, I will show you, but if anything else is found, it is ours and not to be placed into non-Druid hands. That will include you both." He lifted his head and opened his eyes, aglow and staring at them both with an intense fervency.

The strength of it caused them both to take a sharp, inward breath. Iseldir had unknown strengths and depths, that they would never have suspected of the barman, Kelvin. The man was transformed.

"Kelvin," Fergy began. "We respect what you say and of course, anything found, no matter how remote its druidic connections are, you will decide what to do with it."

94

Kelvin looked deep into their eyes, searching. At that moment, his grey eyes gave him an unusual, solemn, reverential persona.

Standing, he opened his arms. "Thank you. You are honourable."

Fergy and Miriam exchanged glances. Then, they too stood up and the trio embraced.

Thirty minutes later, the group was seated in the Land Rover Defender, complete with their diving gear. Miriam was driving and following Kelvin's detailed instructions.

"Hey," she announced. "We didn't tell Vincenzo where we're going."

"Shouldn't worry about that too much. Look in your mirror." Fergy tapped at the rear-view mirror.

She did. Behind them, a red and black pickup truck had been following their every turn, remaining at a discreet distance. It could only be the priest.

After a few more miles, Kelvin asked her to stop. To their right, they could see a dense mix of overgrown undergrowth, bushes, and trees. Miriam pulled over.

Kelvin was the first to get off. "Follow me and take care."

They made no attempt to see what the priest was doing. That was entirely up to him.

Kelvin pushed into the undergrowth and marched at a swift pace. Miriam and the professor attempted to keep up with him but were constantly stung by nettles and got caught up in thorny brambles. Kelvin seemed to have no such problems. They managed to keep sight of him, and after fifteen minutes of fast pace walking, they saw him come to a halt.

"Thank god for that. My legs are killing me." Fergy sounded breathless as he approached Kelvin.

Miriam scurried in behind, hanging on to Fergy's shirt-tail. Her arms were scratched.

"This is it." Kelvin's voice had become quiet and respectful, as if he were in a church.

Miriam took quick stock. They stood in some sort of glade, hidden away from any casual observers or hikers. Surrounding them was an encompassment of oak and ash trees which formed an uncanny, natural circle. Dotted around to form a smaller ring, was a circle of very ancient looking, flat-topped stones. They had the brush of antiquity about them and must have been put there a very long time ago. They bore no resemblance to any other rocks or stones found in the region.

Fergal looked upward to the canopy and the natural, circular shape it formed over the grove. He began to take pictures of it and of the glade and its stones. Kelvin said nothing. He knelt on one knee with his head bowed. His lips appeared to be moving in prayer.

Miriam gave Fergy a sharp glance and he stopped taking photographs. She was glad of that. For some reason, it didn't seem to be quite the right thing to be doing.

Kelvin stood. "This is my place. I call it the Grove of Taranus. This has been here for thousands of years. It is tri-formed of oaks. The middle tree is Taranus, the Bull, who is a divine strength and inspiration." He pointed. "The branch to the right signifies Beli, the sun. To the left, the branch represents Esus, the being who inhabits the very tree. Look around here at the stones. Esus has been carved here amongst others, emerging from the tree and representing completed man. The root of the grove, directly at a point due South, represents the All-Mother, Ana – the proper manifestation of fire and water. The entire place is full of our symbolism, which would take hours to explain and explore. But trust me. Look ahead."

They followed the direction of his pointing arm. What they could see was a small, crystal clear lake, glistening in the noonday sun. "That is where I found the tablet, buried close to the water's edge. Directly North of the tree... what do you see?

Miriam shielded her eyes. "Wow, you can see Glastonbury Tor in the distance."

The mystical outline dominated the area for miles around. It seemed to Fergy that it was completely understandable why so much mystical energy seemed to be part of the place. "Kelvin, I appreciate what you are doing, but I'm not into the druid thing. However, I can't deny this place makes the hairs on the back of my neck stand up. Can you show me the exact spot where you found the plaque?"

"Walk forward twenty yards and you will be right there."

Fergal mentally counted out twenty yards as he walked. "Is this it?"

"That's it."

The professor looked down. The water was lapping close to his feet. The ground was of a sandstone and shale mix. He crouched low and scraped at the soil with a small trowel.

"You won't find anything, Professor. I've done that a thousand times."

He looked up. "I accept that. How deep is that lake?"

Kelvin shrugged. "I don't know exactly, but it's about thirty to fifty feet."

"Have you dived it?"

"Not for years. It's pretty uninteresting if I remember."

There was a loud crashing noise behind them, and they turned to see two men pushing through the brambles and undergrowth. It was Vincenzo, wearing his Vatican sweat suit.

The other man with him looked like a bald, granite block, but wearing a zip-up bomber jacket and dressed in a pink T-shirt and denim jeans.

"Father Vincenzo!" Miriam blurted out. "What are you doing here?" She wasn't entirely surprised. She was certain now that they were the one following behind them in the pickup truck.

He seemed out of breath and trickles of sweat ran down his blue-veined and throbbing temples. With his accentuated English, he replied, "I ask you the same question. You are to tell me where, when, and what you do. *Si*, no?"

"Nothing of the sort, Father. This has nothing to do with our excavation. Kelvin is showing us his favourite location around these parts and its view of Glastonbury Tor. Look." Fergy pointed northwards to the hazy image of the Tor. He turned to regard the other man. "And who's this with you?"

The man didn't say a word but stood there with folded arms, his face wearing the look of a blacksmith's anvil – hard and expressionless.

Before he could reply, Kelvin beat him to it, and added in sour terms. "Come to take more pictures then, *Father*?" His emphasis on the last word was laced with sarcasm.

It didn't go unnoticed.

"You can't forget, eh? Not to worry. This man is Signor Cracker. Please meet my helper. He is expert in many things." Vincenzo's last comment had a sinister ring to it.

"Why do you need a helper, Father?" Miriam didn't fail to notice Cracker's sullen air of menace, and the unmistakeable bulge of a weapon around his shoulder. She'd seen his kind many times in the Middle East. *He's like something from the movies. This is going from bad to worse.*

Vincenzo shrugged. He looked nonplussed.

The professor broke the oncoming deadlock. "We're about to go back to base, Father. Sorry you've had a wasted journey. We will contact you soon with our next location and plans." He had an afterthought. *He won't know about it. I'll get the others up at daybreak before this tub of lard is even awake.*

With a grunt, Vincenzo swung around to leave. "*Fammi sapere molto presto tuoi piani!*" He gave a jerk of his thick neck and with a scowl on their faces, he and Cracker headed back the way they came.

"He wants our plans very soon," Miriam said. "Have we got any?"

"I've an idea about coming back here but without him knowing," Fergy replied.

"Well, how did he know about us earlier? He wasn't about and made no calls to us. Could someone be watching us?" Miriam felt a tinge of fear creep in.

"I've no idea. It's possible." Fergy simply shrugged.

"I think I know the answer." Kelvin looked positive as he tweaked his ear with an exaggerated gesture."

"You do? What's that then?" The gesture with the ear didn't go unnoticed.

"The man's a spy. He's a funnel for the creepy cardinal. I think, somewhere, we've been bugged."

For a few seconds, Fergy was silent. "I don't see how he or the cardinal could possibly do that. I don't believe it, Kelvin. You're making this whole thing look like some TV thriller series. Look, I suggest that if we make plans, we'll only let him know what we want him to know and take it from there. But I agree about one thing... we have to be extra vigilant. Agreed?"

They nodded their assent.

Miriam was somber as she spoke. "Fergy, Kelvin may have

a point though. One thing I noticed, and we should bear it in mind, is that the muscle-bound, beef burger he brought along with him as a helper was carrying a gun in a shoulder holster."

"Jesus!" Kelvin gawped.

"You certain of that, Miriam?"

"I've seen enough of them on my travels. As sure as eggs are eggs, I'd almost guarantee it."

"That shifts the perspective a bit," Fergy responded. "I can't imagine so called men of God – priests and high-ranking cardinals – doing such things."

"Start believing it then," Kelvin said. "This is the Vatican we are dealing with. If they can string dodgy papal bankers up under London bridges, or be rumoured to have poisoned a liberal pope a month after taking office, then they can do practically anything they wish. Bugging us would be child's play."

The grove went eerily silent. Not a breeze blew, nor a bird called.

CHAPTER 15

Gathering daylight, a primrose sky stretched its long fingers across the surface of the water and the infant sun shone upon it as a radiant jewel. The air smelled of fresh leaves wrapped in the mystery of the grove. The silence was broken only by the remote call of a curlew. In the distance, the Tor cast a shadow across its surrounds like black velvet.

"It's not yet fully light," Fergy said. "I'll need a flashlight, most likely. I can see the waters clearing, though."

"You sure you want to do this alone?" Kelvin asked.

"Yep," he nodded. "I need some peace and quiet. I work better that way. This mission is turning into *impossible*." He laughed at his own quip. He then slipped into his full diving kit and apparatus.

Miriam helped him with his tank while he adjusted his face mask. "I'm looking forward to this!"

Behind them, Kelvin was staring upwards at the clearing skies. His lips were moving, and his arms opened wide.

Hark O Grove. It is I, Iseldir
Forgive us our respectful throng
The distant subject of the druid's song,
We seek to find that which beneath these waters lie
Once more a tribute to the Gods from our sky.

Miriam stopped what she was doing. The words Kelvin was saying was being carried toward her by the wind. Without understanding why, she bowed her head. She knew the words by heart.

"What are you doing?" Fergy barked at her.

"Sssh! Be quiet for once, will you?" She pointed toward Kelvin.

Fergy shrugged. *She's having one of her moments.* He gave her the thumbs up sign and slipped into the lake, swam out for a bit, and then dived down and was out of sight.

"Wait!" Miriam shouted after him. It was too late. He was gone and beneath the waters. She was going to give him her customary cheek kiss when he dived alone. *Oh well. Another time.*

Kelvin's prayers had ceased, and he had moved to stand alongside her.

"Reckon he'll find anything?"

"Well, let's hope so. The professor knows what he's doing. In his world, he's become a bit of a legend, and he's better than most at finding hidden things. Did you know? He found an ancient Chinese box, still sealed, dating back to the Shang Dynasty. It contained scripts and pictograms of that era. Guess where he found it? If you don't know, you'll be amazed. It opens up numerous possibilities, just like your tablet does."

"Wow. I've no idea. Where?"

"Caballo Lake in New Mexico, USA!"

"Holy shit! How did it get there? That's extraordinary."

"So, I'm reckoning if there's anything to be found, he will find it." She shifted her gaze to where he disappeared.

* * *

The first thing he noticed was how peaceful the lake appeared to be underwater. He'd done countless dives over the years, and the silence imbued into this one was striking. The early sunrays were beginning to penetrate, and the waters were becoming clearer by the minute. In front of him, as he struck out and downwards, he could see the firm sand and shale walls. With his flashlight strapped to his arm and his headlamp, he had no trouble surveying his surroundings. He swam from one width and followed the banking downward.

It looks like Kelvin was right. This entire lake looks barren. I can't even see any marine life.

The lake was not huge. Checking his chronometer, he gauged how much time he had left and began exploring. A few more downward kicks and he touched the bottom. It was about forty-five feet to fifty feet in depth. The area was strewn with minute pebbles and stones of varying sizes. A few water plants clung precariously amongst the stones, many of which were strangely flat in shape. Using his knife, he unearthed a few and placed them in the pouch strapped to his waist. He spent another fifteen minutes attempting to find anything of interest.

Tugging at one rock, it refused to budge. *Odd,* he thought. Using his knife in one hand and the small trowel in the other, he began to clear the silt and sediment around it. *This should come out easily, but it's not even moving.* As he struck harder, the rock began to loosen. Then he saw what was causing it to be so obstinate. Part of it was jammed by something else. *What's that?* He saw the edge of something that could only be a rectangular or square construction. He lost interest in the rock and began a careful clearing of the rest of the sediment around it. *This is man-made. There could be no doubt about it.*

More scraping, prodding, tugging…

His heart rate increased whenever he found something that he sensed could be of importance. Right now, he felt alive and on the verge of making a discovery. The feeling flooded through him. *How long has this been here?*

It looked remarkably well preserved – due to being submerged for God knows how long. What ever its original colour was, it had now changed to a brownish, yellow hue. With more knife and trowel work, he finally released the object from its watery grave.

It seemed to be a box of some sort. A quick measurement and he ascertained it to be thirty centimetres long by thirty centimetres wide and fifteen centimetres deep. Intriguingly, it appeared to be sealed.

A familiar rush of archaeologist's adrenaline surged through him. It had been some time since that happened. He dug and trowelled around the area some more, but there was nothing else to find. He placed the box into the side net tied around his waist *Must get this to the others. This could be important. Let's hope so.*

The discovery was not heavy, and he powered his way up to the surface where he saw Kelvin and Miriam looking out for him. He gave a wave and struck out towards the banking.

Once there, he stood up, removed his tank, facemask, and fins, and gave his two colleagues a grin.

"Well? You look happy. Did you find anything?" Kelvin asked with more than a degree of eagerness.

Miriam nodded. "Of course he did. I know that grin. I've seen it countless times when he's on to something. C'mon, show us."

The professor reached into his bag and produced the flat, time-worn stones. "There you are." He handed one to each of them.

"You've got to be kidding." Kelvin looked at the stones in his hand. "These are stones I've seen many times."

"Of course he is." Miriam laughed. "I know him of old. C'mon now. Show us what you really have."

"You have to let an old man have his fun." Fergy smiled as he pulled out the box from the netting and held it aloft. "Behold!" He announced with some drama.

"What is that?" Kelvin demanded with an annoyed edge to his voice.

"Don't worry, Kelvin." Fergy replied, sensing the druid's irritation. "Remember? Whatever we find here is ultimately yours."

"True," he nodded. "But it's annoying that the first time you come here, you find that."

"Well, I'm not here for some sort of debate, Kelvin. This is what I do." Fergy started putting the box in his rucksack. "Let's get this back to the university laboratory and have a good look at it. I can see it's sealed, but I have no idea how old it is. The sealant appears to be bitumen, also known as asphaltum or tar. That, we can confirm in the lab. If so, it's an oily form of petroleum, made from ancient by-products of decomposed plants. Whoever threw this into the lake knew what they were doing. The stuff's naturally waterproof, and here's the clincher, it has been used for tools, sealants, and a range of tasks for at least forty-thousand years!"

The others could feel his excitement. It was infecting them both.

Fergy dressed up in a hurry. "That little beauty has been nesting down there for God knows how long. What it is and what's inside it, we will soon discover. Let's get going."

In a rush, they gathered up their gear and headed back to the Land Rover.

CHAPTER 16

Ynis Wydryn, The Isle of Glass

She pointed to the thorn which had begun its slow blossoming. "My husband, look! The hawthorn seed we planted from Joseph begins to show its beauty." A wind caused her to brush the grey hair from her eyes as she gently held a burgeoning petal. Above them, the winter's sun had initiated its watery descent to herald in the approaching dusk.

He reached out with his scarred wrists and hands, now with the wrinkles and blemishes of age, announcing the decline of flesh and blood. The dreadful scars remained as fresh as they were on the day it happened. He reached out to touch the flowering. "They have a wonder of their own and will be a reminder to humanity of our Parent, and what we can achieve if we care to look and seek. It will take time to come to fruition. Many, many thousands of years, I fear."

They stared at the joyous sight before them, as a common feeling of intuition passed between them both.

"Let us talk, Mary, in the warmth of our roundhouse. I have been feeling much of late that our time is nigh."

"Yes, beloved. It is almost time. I have felt this, too."

Once inside, away from the eyes of villagers, they embraced and held each other closely.

They knew.

Mutual understanding, acceptance, and a lack of fear wrapped around them and into every sinew and atom of their bodies.

Smoke drifted lazily from the central fire, up and through the hole in the rooftop.

"Our work here is done, Jah." She used the name he was known by in the community.

He responded in kind. "Magda, Keeper of the Cup, I am certain that our time here is done. Our children are across this land and Sarah will take the cup, with Judah to protect and care for her. Our work will go on and this land will soon follow our Parent, God, in whose name we live and act."

"Is it now?"

"It is. Let it be. Magda, our children, are no longer so. They are adults and are due to return here soon. I am content. The seeds have been sown. They may feel sadness, but we have prepared them for this moment since they were born to us. The people here now know God, our Parent, known to others by many names in countless lands far away."

"Jah, have we not shown them God and one of many ways to find him? There are many routes up a mountain, and none are easy. Let us be humble. We have shown them the true way in all things, through the spirit, and not by religious rules or instructions invented by men. All people thirst for truth, understanding, their place in our universe, and the answers are there before their very eyes. It is all around them." Magda sat down on a pile of soft blankets. Her eyes were tired but her zest for life never wavered. She continued. "The people here are wonderful, and their Druids understand God better than did our own priests and Pharisees back in Judea. We are a favoured pair, Yeshua. True, we have suffered much, but such is the way. How do you define pleasure if there is no pain, cold without heat, beauty without ugliness?"

He interrupted, "Mary, my beloved, all is as One. A crack in a pot is no less perfect than the pot. The crack is nothing but perfect, as a broken pot is perfect in its brokenness. We two have known this. Opposites are of no matter what ever name you use. We are ready for this moment. Come, let us hold each other this one last time and have no sadness. Our children will understand. Let us drink from the cup and leave it, as promised, for Sarah and Judah to continue our work – the work of our Parent."

Mary retrieved the cup from its storage place, unsealed it, and raised it in offering to the heavens. Her plain beauty, her red hair now streaked with silver, shone as a beacon on a dark night. "Thank you, beloved Parent. We are ready." She took a sip and passed it to her husband.

He held it tight and felt the pain of the spear of Longinus in his side. He raised the cup. "Dear God, we are ready for this cup to pass on. We thank you for our lives and the chance to spread the eternal message of life and death and your abiding love. We have done as you asked. The people here know of you. Protect and keep them safe from harm and evil." He drank a mouthful and returned the vessel to its safe place.

They sat together in silence. Old age had forged its mark upon them. Their bodies had become frail, wrinkled, and their hair, grey. Yet their eyes shone with an everlasting youth. The time for them to leave their earthly bodies had arrived. There was no fear… only a peaceful joy. Their task was done. Magnificence shone from their eyes.

Mary looked at Yeshua as they stood facing each other, holding hands, "We, husband, are to become as one."

"Beloved, we are and will always be… one. Let us return to our Parent with universal mind and compassion for all." He kissed her forehead. She responded in kind.

Locked in an embrace of never-ending love, they were wrapped in a descending, shimmering white light, which by degrees, transformed into one of radiant gold. Behind it could be felt and heard… the flutter of wings.

They had gone beyond.

CHAPTER 17

Rome, Italy

That morning, he'd lost count of how many times he had checked through the reports on the circumstances of Bishop Vincent Fisher's death. *Ispettore* Leonardo Rizzo of the *Polizia di Stato* maintained a nagging doubt.

The thirty-nine-year-old inspector had been in the State Police for nineteen years and had always trusted his intuition. At a burly six feet in height, his unusual blue eyes gave him a rough handsomeness many women found attractive, but he had never married. He believed it would interfere with his work and not be fair on a family. He had a reputation for having explosive temper if subordinates failed in their tasks – but he was also, when needed, magnanimous and eager to praise those who truly tried. He had risen through the ranks without a university education, and because of that, he was debarred from any further promotion. With that *fait accompli* forever in front of him, he vowed that he would do what could for his subordinates to be recognised for their abilities. Men worthy of promotion who had no university education could and should be promoted beyond that barrier. He had that chip on his shoulder, but others said he was well balanced – he had chips on both shoulders. These were his driving spurs. Throughout the force, he was equally feared and respected.

He suspected there was a hidden agenda behind the bishop's death. The wounds, pathology and forensics maintained with one hundred per cent certainty, had been made by a man or men. His death was no accident, and definitely not by a wolf pack. The mutilations had been made with metal blades and hooks.

It was murder.

Additionally, the DNA analysis ruled out animal attack. There was none. He also knew that the file and findings had been passed on to the *Corpo della Gendarmeria dello Stato della Città del Vaticano* – the gendarmerie – Vatican City's police force. Exactly who had requested the file, he did not know, nor was he being told.

What he needed to know now was the bishop's purpose in the Vatican? He had made a note of exactly where the bishop had been staying and that was to be the next point of his investigation.

Thirty minutes later, Rizzo, together with his assistant officer, Angelo Florentino, had gained access to the deceased bishop's apartment. Both were wearing nitrile gloves as part of their inspection kit. A cursory look around revealed a modest setting without anything that looked helpful or interesting at first glance. He went through the wardrobe and all he could find were vestments, clerical clothing, and various black short-sleeved shirts as worn by Catholic clergy around the world. He went through every visible pocket but found nothing. His face creased up with a familiar scowl when on a search for evidence.

Next, he examined the chest of drawers. Nothing much there either, only underclothes, socks, and scarves. Right at the back of the bottom drawer was wedged a spiral bound notebook. This looks more interesting. He skimmed through it. It contained diagrams and lengthy scripts written in English and what seemed to be Latin. *I'll need an interpreter for this.* He got up and handed it to Florentino. "Bag it separately," he barked.

In a corner next to a window stood a small wooden desk, and wonder of wonders, he spotted the bishop's laptop. He proceeded to look at other items nearby – pens, pencils and what one usually expects to find on an office desk. Carefully, he bagged these up and passed them to Florentino before switching on the laptop. There appeared to be no password. Browsing through the contact file, he found names, addresses, plus email addresses of dozens of people. Most appeared to be UK based church people. His eyes landed on the name Professor Fergal Lars Christi. Next to it were the initials SOTA. Those letters also appeared beside a number of other names. There was no clue as to what they meant. *This needs to be looked into. What does SOTA mean?*

The bishop must have been an organised man. He had devised a separate section labelled 'ITALY.' In this were the names of several priests and bishops. They would all have to be interrogated. What were they doing in his list of contacts? How well did they know the bishop? Amongst them, with both a UK and Vatican address, was a Cardinal Nicholas. His name was marked with an asterisk.

The laptop was going to need more than a cursory glance.

Rizzo turned to his officer. "Florentino, bag up this laptop and let's get back to my office. We need a closer examination of the entire content of this computer. Get going now."

Later that day, Rizzo sat alone in his small but comfortable office. The walls remained bare. Not a framed picture or awards were to be seen. He had given strict instructions that he was not to be disturbed, not even if it was God himself. His subordinates knew their Inspector well, and pity on those who broke his orders.

With painstaking care, an art learnt over the years, he methodically examined each file on the laptop – even its Google history, which dealt mainly with archaeological discoveries. What he discovered was a file labelled SOTA, and in parenthesis, written in italics beneath the letters, *Society of Truth in Archaeology.*

So that's what SOTA stands for. Intriguing.

He double-clicked on the file and it opened to reveal a list of several dozen names, addresses and phone numbers – some priests and some not. Heading the list was the name of Professor Christi from the UK. Further examination revealed that this society was deeply critical of the official statements given by the Vatican Pontifical Academy of Archaeology about certain discoveries.

The society had investigated several biblical discoveries and found that some were genuine, but others were mostly fakes. Amongst these were the numerous, so-called, Tombs of Jesus ossuaries, purporting to hold the bones of Christ and his mother – even his rotting sandals. The list was long. What was highlighted in red and filled several pages of the document was an examination by the bishop, who appeared to head up the team. It was the discovery near Qumran, of extra gospels written by the apostles, Thomas and Philip. The contents were highly explosive. He could see how, if made public, it could threaten the foundations of the entire Church. Jesus did not die. He recovered and eventually fled to Britannia with his pregnant wife, Mary Magdalene, and their firstborn son. Astonishingly so, and beyond his belief, was the mention of a healing goblet or cup. Drinking from the cup healed people, it said. And that no matter how many times it was used, it never emptied. It was said to contain the blood and water from the pierced side of Christ.

Rizzo had never been a religious man and had always regarded himself as an agnostic with atheistic leanings. He was unable to accept virgin births, water changing into wine and wave walkers in the middle of a stormy sea, and any other biblical miracles. His disdain was nothing to how he regarded some of the Old Testament stories. He saw them as utterly cruel and preposterous. Yet at times, in spite of that, he often had nagging doubts. He put these down to childhood conditioning.

He leant back in his well-worn chair and let out a long low whistle. What the bishop had written in these files was potential dynamite, capable of destroying the Roman Catholic Church and its millennia-old teachings. The more he thought about it, the more it seemed the contents here held a substantial premise for a murder to occur. Someone would definitely want to prevent these finding to be made public. The possible suspects were endless.

He scoured the whole thing and then found that two days before he was murdered, the bishop was due to meet with the senior English Cardinal, Nicholas. It seems that Pope Adrian had requested the cardinal to set up a meeting between himself and the bishop. *Why would the pope do that? What does he know about this group, SOTA?*

Rizzo took a deep breath. He was running his mind around the unprecedented scenario of himself, using the law if necessary, to interview the Holy Father. *How do I arrange that? If Cardinal Nicholas sets up meetings for the pope, maybe he can persuade His Holiness to grant me an audience.*

With that thought, he began opening the files of all SOTA members. Reading through, he gathered they all had the same objective, to present the truth – warts as well. That went against the grain of the Pontifical Academy's viewpoint. The society's members, to a man, were actively involved in excavations all over the world, mostly in the Middle East. He moved the cursor to the name at the top of the list, Professor Fergal Lars Christi.

Rizzo gauged that SOTA had activities concentrated in the UK. There was a small, covert team of archaeologists located in the area where the 'legends and myths' concerning the mystical area of Glastonbury were rich in stories of Christ and Joseph of Arimathea. The hunt was to find evidence that Jesus had visited or lived in those parts, and to find the vessel that held his blood and water. Rizzo mentally registered his doubts about such an event or object. He had one other major thought. *How the hell do they get their funding? I need to meet with this Cardinal Nicholas, to set up a meeting with the pope. Maybe things will come to light.*

There's one thing Inspector Rizzo was sure of. Someone had plotted Bishop Vincent Fisher's murder because of the information he possessed. If so, it could stem from Rome or the Vatican itself. Someone from the Vatican City had ordered the file and the request had not been blocked.

He scratched hard at the back of his head, an old habit

whenever he was considering or weighing up events. This whole episode had the rich aroma of intrigue and potential cover-ups. The laptop contained important evidence, which could prove highly damaging.

Another thing sprang to mind, whoever had arranged the bishop's demise, if information about them was stored on the laptop, they had been careless by failing to remove it. He would not commit the same carelessness. The bishop's laptop would have to be placed in his safe, where he had always stored the most important evidence. Unless blown up, it was virtually 'uncrackable.' Drills were rendered useless and this was his pride and joy. He had it installed during the Berlusconi episode. Damning evidence in the safe had been protected by its thermal relocker, coupled with a glass backup version capable of resisting any thermal lance attack to gain entry. He considered the information on the laptop in the same category. It had the potential to cause a major eruption in religious circles, not just here in Italy but throughout the entire planet. It needed top class protection.

Whatever, I have to get to Pope Adrian. Maybe he can offer me something to work on.

CHAPTER 18

Three pairs of eyes staring from behind high, white, facemasks gazed down at the stone box resting in a ceramic sink. It had been washed clean and the muddy, dark yellow hue had succumbed to old-fashioned warm water and the gentle application of an electric toothbrush. It now had an almond white complexion but heavily mottled by time and water. Yet somehow, it remained superficially intact. There were no marks, initials, or diagrams. It was as plain as could be. Around the centre remained the black bitumen-sealing strip that encompassed the entire middle section. Glancing over her facemask at the others, Dr. Miriam Sinclair produced a small surgical scalpel knife. "This is it, folks. Pray to heaven that I don't damage whatever's inside, and that it welcomes our invasion."

Bending closer, she made a small nick into the strip and then gently, with a slow practised wrist movement, started slicing through the seal from one side to the other. The only audible sound was the soft snick of the knife penetrating the seal.

The atmosphere was one of tense excitement. Miriam reached her starting point and looked up at the others. "Kelvin, will you please do us the honours and remove the top section? Please, be gentle."

Kelvin nodded but was unable to hide the slight shake in his hands. Gripping the top, he gave a tender tug at the lid. To his surprise, it offered no resistance. It came away with ease.

All three gasped as the sweet aroma of honeysuckle and roses filled the air around them. It was fleeting but powerful.

"Whoa! That smelled fresh. Amazing..." Miriam whispered in awe.

All three looked stunned.

Their amazement climbed even further when they looked inside.

For several moments, nobody moved. They stared in muted astonishment at the item being protected by the box. It appeared to be a scroll of parchment or vellum. It was intact, as if it had been placed there yesterday. Miriam immediately began taking photographs of every detail.

"Nobody touch it!" Miriam demanded. "What do you suggest, Professor?"

"Well, with care and gloved up, let's take it out and unroll it. We will need a C14 test and if you like, Kelvin, I can include your tablet and say it's part of our discoveries."

"What's C14 testing?" Kelvin asked.

Miriam answered, "Radiocarbon dating, which is also referred to as carbon-14 dating, is a method for determining the age of an object containing organic material, by using the properties of radiocarbon – a radioactive isotope of carbon. It's a scientific method, and the development of radiocarbon dating has had a profound impact on archaeology. There are other exciting developments in this field, which can improve on what we are doing now. Since natural carbon deletes at a constant rate over centuries, an almost accurate date can be given to an object. To give you an example, when they carbon dated The Turin Shroud, it appeared to be just over seven hundred years old. There are, of course, counter arguments against that. Even your tablet, Kelvin, and the etchings, which are carved on limestone millions of years old, can be dated by analysing the particles in the patina decay of the script. All very complicated but leave that to us. We should be able to get an idea how old it is, and this scroll here. You okay with that?"

Kelvin looked rueful. He was scratching his head as he replied. "Yeah, if you say so. That's fine. Let's do it."

With the gentlest of hands, the professor lifted the document from out of the box. His experience had taken over. Tight lipped, he placed it on the examination table and took a deep breath. "Someone dim the lights, please."

Kelvin did as he asked.

Grasping the two ends of the scroll, Fergy made a small wrist movement and sensed no stickiness or initial obstacles. With great care, he pushed back on the bulk of the scroll. If he had the equipment, which he hadn't, he would have been able to read the entire scroll without unrolling it. He stopped and looked into the eyes of the others. "It's at times like these I wish there was a toilet close by!"

They chuckled. The tension was broken, and everyone released their breaths.

The professor continued to roll back the scroll, revealing

a light brown, coloured material. "It's a type of vellum," he said, peering closer. "Probably goat, or calf."

Miriam was recording the event with her camera.

It soon revealed some sort of writing, done with a black, inky substance. The camera continued to record every revelation.

"What on earth is this?" Fergy yelled out louder than he normally would have done. Confronting them all was what appeared to be a series of numbers and letters, as we know them from Arabic, our own system. "I've never seen anything like this before. Keep taking videos and pictures, Miriam. Don't stop. We're going to have to show the cardinal, but not everything. Pope Adrian will get them all."

Kelvin looked at the writings. "What can they mean? They look like some sort of code."

"It's that, all right," Miriam said. "I'm going to look at this in more detail. Can someone get me a large sheet of paper and a pen, please? I'm going to copy this down. It will be easier to work with than photographs. This will take a while."

Miriam took considerable time copying it all down. "This looks totally baffling. I've no idea what it's about. The lettering is definitely early medieval. I just wonder if we can break the code and read what it says… see if it's related to Kelvin's tablet. It would seem odd to me if they're not related in some way. They were in the same vicinity."

"Why all the secrecy?" Kelvin asked.

"Obviously, whoever wrote it, didn't want everybody to know what it says." She stood up and gathered her things. "Fergy, I'll take this copy back with me. Go and have these carbon dated along with Kelvin's tablet. That'll take up to a week to process. C'mon then, let's get to it!"

CHAPTER 19

I t seemed the archaeologists were behaving themselves, well... almost. Vincenzo was glad he hadn't been pulled out of bed at four thirty the previous morning. Yet, even without him watching over them, they had supplied him electronically with a file of photographs.

He sat back in his chair and drew heavily on a cheap English brand cigarette, and with an absent mind, watched the dull, grey smoke spiral upwards and away from him.

They had also informed him that they were having the items carbon dated to determine its age. When they get the results, they would let him know, and the item would be handed over with all known data.

Vincenzo browsed through the shots without any interest. It was just an old stone casket with some sort of scroll in it. It would have been more attention grabbing if there had been something on the scroll.

What he didn't know was that they had only shown him the back of the scroll and not the front where the diagram, letters and numbers were written.

With a bored sigh, he pressed 'Send' and forwarded them to the cardinal.

Cracker had complained earlier about the lack of action, although he agreed the money was an anchor for him to continue hanging around. Neither of the two men doubted that the situation would get nasty, and that time might not be far away.

* * *

The cardinal blew onto his nail file and watched as a small cloud of nail dust flew upward before disappearing into the pile of his carpet. His quarters were modest, but with unrivalled views of St. Peters and the Basilica. If on the open market, it would have cost a fortune – either as a rental or straight sale. He wiped away a trickle of perspiration from his forehead. He found the humidity of Rome oppressive. It aggravated the intermittent stabs of pain he often experienced in his deformed leg. *God is reminding me of my lack of commitment to his Holy cause. I must try harder.* Yet, in his more exalted moments, he was expectant of His grace and favour, and prayed fervently for His blessed hand to touch him even if with only the slightest brush.

With that thought, he reached for a Davidoff cigarette and placed it next to his keyboard.

Leaning forward, he activated his desktop computer and went straight to his Gmail inbox. There it was… what he had been hoping for… an email with attachments from Father Vincenzo. *I hope this is something good.*

After reading Vincenzo's message, he understood that more information would be forthcoming once tests had been conducted. *Good news.* The artefact had been found in a small lake close to Glastonbury, and it appeared to be ancient. *That could be significant.* The first of the images was displayed on the screen. He forgot his muses and leant forward, zooming the images to their greatest extent. The clarity of the photographs were excellent.

The casket looked old and the scroll, more so.

That's odd... there seems to be no writing on it. What can it be? He opened all the attachments. *No matter what, everything hints at a mystery.*

He began to imagine further discoveries of greater importance – such as the never emptying cup.

How wondrous it would be to find a cup holding the blood and water from the body of Christ. A cup that heals the sick and dying. If it never emptied like they say, then it could be used until the end of time. That would cause a religious upheaval bigger than the universe itself. Scientifically, it is impossible, but He is beyond such restrictions. For Him, there are no impossibilities. To have such an item will transform my movement and the Catholic Church will be rid of false liberals... and that includes His Hereticalness, Pope Adrian.

His thoughts were reinforced as he recalled the news of a creeping movement led by the pontiff himself, which aimed to steer women into the priesthood. By God, there had even been a pagan Amazonian ceremony held on the lawns of the Vatican, and some priests were observed to have joined in. Even worse, ninety-five-year-old Italian journalist, Eugenio Scalfari, recently caused shock among Catholics when he attributed to Pope Adrian the statement that 'Jesus of Nazareth was not God nor divine at all.' *This pope has to go!*

As his blood pressure rose, he reached for the cigarette again, lit it, and took a massive puff before exhaling the blue coloured smoke from his nostrils.

Just then, the unmistakeable ringtone of his cell phone blasted out a chorus from his favourite work, John Henry Maunder's cantata, *Olivet to Calvary*. The short burst was the chorus – '*Hosanna to the Prince who comes, to free a race oppressed.*'

A quick glance at the screen revealed a number not recognised. "Who can that be?" he muttered out loud. His number was only given to his most trusted colleagues and inner members.

He answered in his most reverential voice. "Cardinal Nicholas speaking. How may I help you?" The short sharp reply startled him.

"Cardinale Nicholas, *sono Inspettore Rizzo della Polizia di Stato.*"

The cardinal understood – Inspector Rizzo from the State Police. "Inspector, my Italian is not great. May you speak in English, please?"

"*Si.* Yes, I will speak in English."

"Thanks and may God bless you. Is there something I can help you with?"

Rizzo felt himself cringe at what he perceived as a phoney stance of humility. He had had years of experience spotting such things. *Pass me the bucket, please!*

Nicholas continued. "Before you speak, Inspector, may I ask how you got my number?"

Rizzo's reply was immediate. "No, you may not, Cardinal. That's my business, and that is what the government pays me for. The first thing I need is to see you in person and I don't mean tomorrow or next week. I mean now. I have a number of questions I wish to ask you in person, concerning the death of the English bishop, Vincent Fisher. Are you at your address near the Vatican?"

The cardinal could only answer, "Yes, I am." His mind whirled in confusion. *How did he know where I am?*

"I'll be with you in thirty minutes." He terminated the call.

For a brief instant, the cardinal felt a twinge of anxiety. *How did the Inspector get his number and address, and why did he want to talk about the dead bishop? I thought that was over and done with.* He turned to his desktop, acknowledged Vincenzo's message, and switched off. He would contact him again after the Inspector's visit.

This is getting too close to home. I hope it's simply routine work.

Precisely thirty minutes later, the intercom buzzed, and the CCTV camera swivelled around and revealed the six-foot rugged frame of a sour faced Inspector Rizzo. He was holding a small leather briefcase and a prominent ID tag hung from his neck.

"Come on in, Inspector." Nicholas adopted his calm and serene posture, a manner he had found useful when conducting awkward confessionals throughout his long career. He clicked a switch and the doors to his rooms opened. He lit another cigarette. *I might just need this.*

Inspector Leonardo Rizzo strode in with authority and extended his hand toward the cardinal. Kissing rings was not on his list of protocols. There was a slight hesitation before the cardinal stood, and for good effect, he leant on his stick more than usual. He reached out and shook the man's hand.

"Thank you for seeing me, Cardinal, and I'm sorry if I have

disrupted your plans, but I believe murder investigations take precedent over all else. Especially when a bishop was the victim."

"Please be seated, Inspector." He gestured toward a small coffee table and ambled to sit at one end. His half-filled ashtray was close by on the table. "Murder, you say?" He feigned surprise. "I thought the reports said he was decimated by wolves?"

Rizzo's successes often arose from his ability to never be gentle when interviewing somebody – no matter who they were. "Cardinal, I don't make small talk. Neither do I beat about the bush, as you English say. The forensic and pathological reports clearly indicate the work of human hands in the bishop's death. There were no traces of animal DNA but only those of unknown human beings. Strange, don't you think?"

"I'm no expert on such matters, Inspector, but I must agree with you... quite strange... and shocking also! If that is true, who could have done such a thing?"

Rizzo snapped, "There are no 'ifs' about it, Cardinal. It was murder. How well did you know the bishop?" Rizzo's casual question came across like a throw away stick of dynamite. The cardinal's eye shift was almost unnoticeable, but it was enough to show Rizzo he was unsettled.

"Hardly at all, Inspector. I met him once or twice in the past. If I recall, he's one of the new breeds of liberal priests and bishops."

"Odd that you say that, Cardinal, because we know that you brokered a meeting between him and the pope himself. Saying you hardly knew him doesn't quite ring true, does it? Why didn't you mention that rather important fact?"

Rizzo's aggressive manner caused bursts of pain to stab

at Cardinal Nicholas's deformed leg. Stretching his thin lips, he grimaced at the suddenness of it. He paused to inhale on his cigarette "Of course I remember that situation." He had to think quickly. "As the meeting never took place, it didn't seem important to mention." He tried a benevolent smile.

Rizzo's eyes flashed with danger as he leant forward and jabbed his index finger hard on the table. "Yet you still say you hardly knew him. Surely setting up a meeting with the pontiff would have required several exchanges between you and the bishop, what with all the arrangements required for such a meeting."

"Inspector, I have set up many meetings for people with the pope. It was part of my brief as head of the Congregation for the Causes of Saints and other offices. It was Pope Adrian who approached me, so I can only assume that it had something to do with a discovery."

"So, what you are saying is that you don't know what the meeting was to be about?"

The Cardinal lied. "No, I do not. The pope has many meetings with different people, daily almost."

Rizzo said nothing. For some reason, he wanted the man in front of him to sweat a little. He stared him squarely in the eye for an almost unacceptable length of time. "You say you hardly knew him, but would you know if he had any enemies?"

"Inspector, as I hardly knew him, how could I possibly know that?"

Rizzo ignored his reply. "Another question, Cardinal. Do you know who ordered all our police reports and investigation files to be sent to the Vatican? Was it you?" Rizzo saw Nicholas's genuine look of surprise. *Now that shook him. I wonder why since he has expressed so little interest in this matter.*

The cardinal's reply sounded choked, as if something nasty had lodged in his throat. "No, it was not I, Inspector. Why would I want to see such things? I have no idea at all. Why are you treating me as a suspect of some sort?"

The cardinal's face had whitened by a degree or two.

Rizzo could see that the cardinal's discomfort over the revelation concerning the police files was genuine. Why should that worry him?

"Rest assured, Cardinal, it's normal procedure and nothing more – especially in cases like this. We must leave no stone unturned." He fiddled with his mobile phone, pretending to read something. He wanted to make the cardinal squirm for a few more minutes.

"One more thing, Cardinal. You said you fixed meetings between various parties and the pope. I'd like you to call His Holiness right now and arrange a meeting between him and myself. I'll not be put off or side-lined, mind you. I will sit and wait here until it's sorted. I have time. From what I hear, he's quite accessible, and will be more so when you tell him what I'm here for." Rizzo allowed a pause then spat out his next words. "Do I make myself clear?" He banged the table with a curled fist for added effect.

The cardinal visibly jerked back in amazement. Nobody had ever addressed him like that before, and clearly, the forceful Inspector was not a man who feared anybody's rank or privilege. "I... I'll see what I can do," he stammered before standing up and reaching for a small, red, leather address book. "Pope Adrian has several private phone numbers, depending on his location. Let me try this one." His bony finger jabbed at a number, as he squinted to read it.

Rizzo stood and as he did, he appeared to stumble, and in doing so, sent the ashtray crashing to the floor. The contents dislodged and scattered into a small heap on the carpet.

"Eminence, I'm so sorry." Rizzo immediately apologised before bending down to pick up the contents.

Hidden in one hand, he had a small pair of tweezers and a small plastic envelope the size of a credit card. In one rapid movement, a largish butt was grabbed by the tweezers and fed into the envelope. He closed his fist and placed the envelope back into his pocket. The whole episode happened in the blink of an eye.

The cardinal seemed not to hear. He was too busy talking on the phone to have noticed.

The Inspector turned to look out of the window with a wry smile on his face, as he watched humanity outside jostling for space with countless pigeons.

"*Ispettore,*" the cardinal raised his voice. "You have incredible luck. I have the Holy Father on the phone. He will speak with you. Please be quick."

CHAPTER 20

Miriam had spent hours bent low over the enlarged photographs of the scroll and its cryptic diagram of letters and numbers. She was looking for a vowel pattern – a e i o u. There should be a repetitive order – either by number or letter – but that didn't appear to be the case at all. A pattern didn't exist.

The circle was divided into eight equal segments by four lines. She decided to number them as lines one to four – starting with the north to south line, followed by line two which ran east to west. Line three would be the one that ran north east to south west – leaving line four, running north west and to south east. She tried making sense of it one line at a time. Starting with line one. If she could decipher one line, then the others would be a cakewalk. The scroll appeared old, and back then, complex codes barely existed. It was only a matter of time…

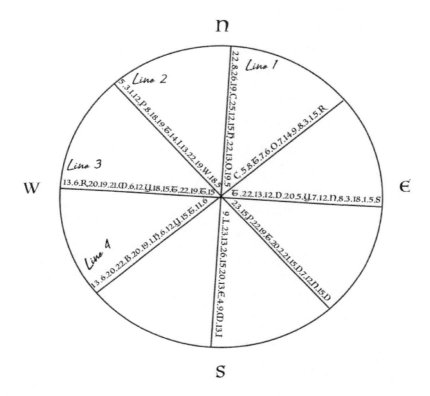

She leant back on her chair clasping her third mug of coffee. *What language can this be written in? English?* Kelvin's tablet was in Aramaic, written from right to left as was Hebrew. *Unless I can reveal a couple of words, this is going to be difficult.*

At that moment, Fergy walked in. "Hey, Miriam, how's it going?" He pointed at the piles of paper around her.

"It's not. I'm no closer than I was when I first started. It's a mystery."

"Carbon dating looks like a walk in the park compared to this. Everything is readable. This looks like back to front double Dutch to me." He waved his hand over her scribbles.

She sat bolt upright, slopping coffee out of her mug. "Say that again, will you?" Her eyes shone with anticipation. "Go on, say it."

Confused, Fergy repeated what he said. "This looks like back to front double Dutch to me. Okay with that?"

"You may have hit the nail on its head. Wait, don't go yet. I want to try something." She tore out an A1 sheet of art paper from her folder. "Let's try this on line one."

Fergy poured himself a cup of coffee and grabbed a seat beside her.

In two straight lines, one below the other, Miriam wrote down the alphabet, from A to Z. Then beneath the letters, she wrote the corresponding numbers – 1 to 26. She then drew a red line under the numbers. Where letter A was, she inverted the number sequence and started with 26, going all the way down to 1.

A	B	C	D	E	F	G	Ħ	I	J	K	L	M
1	2	3	4	5	6	7	8	9	10	11	12	13
26	25	24	23	22	21	20	19	18	17	16	15	14

N	O	P	Q	R	S	Ŧ	U	V	W	X	Y	Z
14	15	16	17	18	19	20	21	22	23	24	25	26
13	12	11	10	9	8	7	6	5	4	3	2	1

"Now look at line one and its letters and numbers." She held it to the light so he could get a better view. "There are twenty-eight in all, divided into two groups. The first half of line one is: 22.8.26.19.C.25.12.15.H.22.13.O.19.5. Using this grid, we will substitute the number with the corresponding letter, and vice versa. Let's try it on the first five numbers and see if it works." She wrote down the translation.

22.8.26.19 = V H Z S and then the letter C.

"That makes no sense at all... but look, if I use the reversed numbering sequence, I get E S A H then the letter C. Reverse the word and I get CHASE."

Miriam sat back and stretched her aching back. She could see that Fergy looked sceptical but was certain he'll be a believer soon. "I see what's happening here, Fergy. It's a sequence of reverse and counter reverse. Back to front and front to back, and then reverse the word again. I guarantee it. Much of Hebrew code was written in a similar fashion. We probably have the first recorded use of it in English. If that first word is indeed CHASE, it would be the last word in the sentence, overall. The next word will be written backwards but this time in a normal sequence. Let's see if I'm correct." She picked up her pen again. "The only real problem is that the words will have no space in between. I'll have to figure out the reversal order. It may take some time but then we'd have a pattern to work with!" She was aglow with excitement. If she was right, it would be a significant breakthrough.

She continued with the numbers on line one and the word HOLY came up quickly.

25.12.15.H = Y L O and the letter H.

With her theory proven, the entire line was deciphered in no time.

22.8.26.19.C.25.12.15.H.22.13.O.19.5.

9.L.23.13.26.15.20.13.E.4.9.M.13.I

ESAHCYLOHENOSEILDNALGNEDIMNI

She handed it over to Fergy. "Get going, Professor, and make sense of that."

He looked at it and turned to her with a wide smile. "Miriam, you've cracked it. You should be working in GCHQ (Government Communications Headquarters). What you have here is CHASE HOLY ONE LIES ENGLAND MID IN. Reverse it and you have… *In mid England lies one Holy Chase.*"

"Rubbish! A child could do it, it's so simple. The letters mark the first or last in the given word, but all in duplicitous reverse sequence."

"You've lost me there, Miriam. Carry on though."

"Remember, most people in ancient times were illiterate. It wouldn't mean a thing to someone who doesn't know codes. Somebody working at GCHQ would fall over laughing at it. It's hardly The Enigma Code, is it?"

"You did well there, and you know it. Now get to it and do the other lines. I'll unravel the word structure."

She moved on to line two and repeated the process.

5.3.1.12.P.8.18.19.T.14.I.13.22.19.W.18.5.

23.15.P.22.19.T.20.2.21.15.D.7.12.N.15.D

ECALPSIHTNINEHWREWOPEHTTBUODTONOD

"Fergy, I'm done with the second line, see what you make of it." She handed the paper to the professor.

"Simple. PLACE THIS IN WHEN POWER THE DOUBT NOT DO. Shift it around and you have… *Do not doubt the power when in this place.*"

She gave a thumbs up sign, busy with the next translation – line three.

"It's beginning to make sense. What's the next line?"

She was already matching the numbers with the letters on the grid. After a few minutes, she was done.

13.6.R.20.19.21.M.6.12.Y.18.15.T.22.19.T.15.

T.22.13.12.D.20.5.Y.7.12.N.8.3.18.1.5.S

NURTSUMUOYROTEHTOTENODTEYTONHCRAES

"Fergy, this is what it came out as." She handed him the

paper with the deciphered code.

The professor stared at it for a few seconds and had it written down and placed in sensible array in no time.

"It says:

RUN MUST YOU TOR THE TO DONE YET NOT SEARCH.

Search not yet done to the Tor you must run," he read out loud. "The Tor! This is getting more interesting."

Miriam gave him a big smile. "Now for the last line."

Fergy stood up and went to the coffee pot to refill their cups. *I wonder what the last line will say.* He was extremely pleased with how well this was all turning out.

Miriam gave a shout, "That's it. All done!" She dropped her pen on the table

13.6.20.22.B.20.19.1.H.6.12.Y.15.T.11.6.

C.5.8.T.7.6.O.7.14.9.8.3.1.5.R

NUGEBTSAHUOYOTPUCEHTTUOGNIHCAER

BEGUN HAST YOU TO CUP THE OUT REACHING.

Fergy returned with her coffee and stared at the last line. He sat down and took the pen, and after a few seconds, he said, "Wow... listen to this. It says... *Reaching out the cup to you hast begun.* I've combined the translated lines. Here's what it says." He read the entire stanza in a measured tone.

In mid England lies one Holy Chase
Do not doubt the power when in this place
Search not yet done, to the Tor you must run
Reaching out, the Cup to you hast begun

For a moment, a silence fell between them, bound by mutual looks of amazement.

"That's astonishing," Miriam gasped. "It's full of clues."

"It's not specific but do remember Kelvin's script on the tablet. I think they're incredibly similar in their references. What did his verse say exactly?"

"I have it right here in my notes… hang on." Miriam rumbled through various notebooks before pulling one out. "Here it is." She opened up the correct page and recited the lines.

Before my Parent you can only kneel
From whose eternal cup you may heal
Then seek the glass beneath the skies
The grave wherein the hidden secret lies

The professor could barely contain his excitement. "They couldn't have been written by the same hand. The scroll is considerably younger than Kelvin's tablet – which is in Aramaic – and it's written in Middle English. Yet the suggestions in both are pointing in the same direction."

"I see that," Miriam agreed.

"Both mention the cup, and a place or grave that holds a secret. Kelvin might know where this place could be."

The professor poked his pen at the scroll verse. "The scroll verse gets a little more specific. It mentions the cup in a way that seems to give it character. It wants to be found. *Reaching out, the Cup to you hast begun.* That's intriguing." The professor's research antennae were glowing bright. "The verses sound like clues to a quest."

"You're forgetting something." A quiet voice behind them caused them both to spin about. It was a pensive looking Kelvin. In their excitement, they had not heard him enter the room.

"Jesus, Kelvin, you gave me a scare! We didn't hear you." Miriam brushed aside hair hanging across her face.

"Knock louder next time, Kelvin." Fergy looked annoyed. He had never liked creepy surprises. "Anyway, what are we missing?" His question was laced with the hint of a challenge.

"Look," Kelvin began, sounding assured and confident. He indicated the third line of the scroll. *'Search not yet done, to the Tor you must run.'* It couldn't be plainer. We must search around the Tor itself. That's what the scroll is telling us. Hell, you two, the place is rife with Arthurian tales – Excalibur, The Lady of the Lake, Camelot, the Holy Grail and many more. Doesn't that connect with you?" Kelvin sounded passionate and enthusiastic.

"I don't disagree with you, Kelvin. I was just about to point that out before you surprised us," Fergy spoke evenly. "It's a mystical place, but not one of those legends have been proven. They're no more than legends… fairy tales, I guess, to keep the mysticism of this location alive. Stories like these are, at best, metaphors for wishful thinking and a sense of ancient identity. Like Druids being the real Brits." Fergy gave a smug smile and grinned at Kelvin.

Kelvin didn't flinch nor back down. "What you say may be right, but you can't prove them wrong either. So my tablet, the stone casket, and the scroll, are phoney, made-up metaphorical artefacts, are they?"

Before Fergy could reply, the Waltzing Matilda ringtone on his cell phone cut through the air.

Fergy put his finger to his lips and then answered, turning his back to them as he did. His responses could be heard clearly. It had to be the laboratory.

"It is? That's brilliant… Really? … That's not hard to believe… Are you certain?... Sorry, I didn't mean to be rude."

Kelvin and Miriam each had raised eyebrows.

The conversation continued. "Wow, as old as that…

Thanks for letting me know… I'll be over soon… Bye for now."

He disconnected the call and turned to face them. "That was most illuminating." His eyes shone like lighthouse beacons. "It was the lab, and they've finished their examination of both your tablet Kelvin, and the box and scroll."

"What did they have to say?" Kelvin looked anxious. Miriam gripped his arm.

"Firstly, the tablet is made of limestone. The fascinating thing is… the limestone is several millions of years old. It reveals much about what this place must have looked like back then. Do you know how limestone is created? Ocean-dwelling organisms such as oysters, clams, mussels, and coral use calcium carbonate found in seawater to create their shells and bones. The water pressure compacts the sediment, creating limestone. There must have been seas here once. That's your tablet. The Aramaic script, due to the remaining patina around the carvings or chippings, has been dated to around eighteen hundred to two thousand three hundred years old. What it was doing around here, totally out of place, is something we must investigate further. It almost dovetails into what the bishop and SOTA were beginning to believe."

"Astonishing and very important to our work." Miriam looked animated. "And the box and scroll?"

"The box," Fergy continued, "is made of ancient rock found around these parts. There are chip marks from a sharp instrument found in one or two places around the lid. The bitumen seal has no part in the ID process, as it is as old as Kelvin's tablet. The scroll is of fine vellum, calf, or goat. That was not totally identifiable. The composition of the ink used is a common one of that period – iron gall – and was applied using a very thin brush. It was used from the early twelfth century right up until the eighteenth century. These inks were widely thought to be the best type of ink." Fergy stopped and looked at them both. "Well? That's a brief summary of what I was told."

"Where do we go from here? Back to the caves?" Miriam shrugged.

"I think we should go back to the Tor. That's what the scroll suggested... *To the Tor you must run.*" Kelvin pointed out towards its imposing presence.

"I can't see the point in that," the professor said. "Every bit of that place has been examined, excavated, and sifted through for centuries. There's nothing left to find."

"That's what they said about the pyramids and they're still finding amazing discoveries. Fergy, I think Kelvin's right," Miriam said. "We've been given a direct clue. We shouldn't ignore it."

"But that message was written in the twelfth century."

"That doesn't matter. When it was written is not important. It's trying to tell us something."

"Okay, where do you suggest we start?"

She glanced at Kelvin and pointed to the Tor. "St. Michael's?"

"Whoa there a moment, will you? There's another issue here. How much do we tell Vincenzo and the cardinal? I've been thinking about that and I've had a change of mind. We should tell him everything. I will be forwarding all findings direct to Pope Adrian anyway. He's not going to miss out. If the cardinal then withholds our information from the pope, he will know for certain the man's dodgy, with his own secret agenda, and not to be trusted. We have our own copies and records so I'm going to send everything over to Vincenzo and see what happens from there."

"Excellent," Miriam replied. "That should clinch it one way or another. The cardinal has no idea of your direct contact with the Vatican. It must stay that way."

"That's sound," Kelvin agreed. "At least this pope is from the twenty-first century, and not the days of the Inquisition. But before we go further, there's something I need to ask you."

"Fire away." The professor leant forward. "What's that?"

"In two days, it will be November the first. It's an important day for our grove. We call it *The Eye of the Sun*, which registers the change of the season. I'd like you to join us." He smiled and extended his arms in invitation. "Let me briefly explain. This is known as Samhuinn, and it only happens from October thirty first to November second. It is a time of no-time and should not be confused with the solstice. Celtic society was well organised. Everyone knew their place. But to allow that order to be psychologically comfortable, the Celts knew there had to be a time when order and structure were abolished – and a crazy, few days of mayhem took over. Its echoes remain today throughout the world. Samhuinn was a planned event. Time was set aside for the three days of this festival, and people did crazy things – men dressed as women and women as men, is one example." Kelvin became more animated. "There will only be a few of us and I would be honoured with your presence. There will be no need to join in, rest assured. You can simply observe. It's not so different from today's Halloween." Kelvin paused and glanced at them both. "I sense you are intrigued."

Miriam was. Without saying a word, she felt a distinct shift in her psyche. A strange fluttering sensation passed through her. Kelvin's words were familiar, but she didn't know how or why.

Kelvin continued. "The veil between this world and the World of the Ancestors is drawn aside on these nights, and for those who are prepared, journeys can be made in safety to the 'other side'. The Druid rites, therefore, were concerned with making contact with the spirits of the departed, who were perceived as sources of guidance and inspiration – rather than as sources of dread. The dark moon, the time when no moon can be seen in the sky, was the phase of the moon which ruled this time, because it represents a time in which our mortal sight needs to be obscured in order for us to see into the other worlds." He paused. "All a load of nonsense eh?"

"Not so," the professor said with a smile. "Contrary to what you may think, I have great respect for ancient rites, rituals and beliefs. They keep us in touch with the real world and not the world of smart phones and AI devices. Long may these ancient ceremonies continue. Having said that… when are we going to the Tor? I feel that we should do it after attending Kelvin's event. Meanwhile, I'm off to the lab to collect the findings. I will pass them all on to Vincenzo before sending my report to the pope. Who's coming?"

"Not me." Kelvin stood up and prepared to leave. "I need to make preparations. I call you later."

A noticeably quiet Miriam followed Fergy out.

CHAPTER 21

F ather Vincenzo brushed the croissant crumbs from his cassock and took a large mouthful of an Italian Bardolino red wine. He glanced at the wall clock; it was ten thirty in the morning. He had never understood the English rule on when you should drink or not drink. As far as he was concerned, there were twenty-four hours in a day and any one of them was a candidate.

Leaning back into the sofa, he enjoyed the prospect of a lazy day. Professor Christi had delivered a new batch of documents and photographs of their recent discoveries. He couldn't ask for more. Well… not quite. He hadn't been given the artefacts, having been told they were required for further examination and reference. Once finished, they could be handed over to him. He had no reason to believe otherwise. The team appeared upfront and open. *Perhaps I was wrong about them,* he thought. Yet, he was never one to underestimate another. That's why Cracker was there to keep an eye on all their activities, morning, noon, and night. If circumstances became awkward, the man would enjoy employing some of his techniques.

He gave the report a swift perusal. Most of it was couched in the language of science, which he had little understanding of. Nevertheless, the cardinal would be pleased to receive it. He would know what to do with it.

With haste, he forwarded the report to the cardinal, eager to continue his day.

* * *

The soft electronic ping on his computer alerted him to an incoming message. Cardinal Nicholas was busy preparing an address for his society meeting.

He paused what he was writing. *This could be of importance.* He spent some time scouring the laboratory reports and the carbon dating evidence. It was firm and substantial, but nowhere near enough. The photographs were of excellent quality and both the tablet and the casket with its scroll were excellently presented. The verses made for intriguing but preposterous reading, hinting of the existence of a cup that may have been used by Jesus or The Magdalene. They alluded to a secret burial place somewhere in England, but where?

The story, he felt, was only just beginning.

The cardinal thought deeply about what was going on. There was a dichotomy. If this story were found to be true, his own society would look stupid. What was more important to him was to recover and hold the cup, should it exist. With that in his hands, he could twist and turn any religious society in the world to his agenda, and that included the Catholic

Church. The traditional, ultra conservative points of the Catholic faith could be strengthened, as God could be shown as having led him and his movement to make this startling discovery. It did not mean the abandonment of traditional beliefs. Played properly, it could only strengthen his own agendas and propel him to the leading position in the church. The severe practices and elements of his beliefs and of the society's would hold sway as the one true way – the one true belief as deigned by God, with him, Cardinal Nicholas, leading the way. No one will be able to oppose or contradict him then.

At that moment, he experienced an overwhelming feeling of gratitude and reassurance. God was holding his hand.

His next thought was how much of this information should be wired to the pope, who was paying for the mission after all. He snickered at the thought. Unknowingly, His Holiness was paying for his own demise.

Too little response might lead to a cancellation of the project. That should not be allowed to happen. This time, he would send him everything. It was just enough to keep his interest bubbling and yet, gave little away.

* * *

It was Sunday, just before one o'clock. The pope had just given his speech about the dangers of overpopulating God's planet. He had spoken longer than usual and he knew it was a theme that would cause heated debate in the corridors of power, and churches across the world. Following this, he gave the *Angelus* and ended with a blessing for the faithful flock below, in various languages, and the Apostolic Blessing at the end of his prayer.

It was with some weariness that he wandered back into

his private quarters. Of late, he had been aware of an increasing tiredness about his work. He knew he was regarded with high suspicion in various circles, ever since he had given his opinions on liberty, freedom of expression, and sexual choices. His approval of the 'Rainbow Flag' had offended many of the diehard brigades and had enthused just as many liberals. He reasoned with himself, *I'm not here to win a popularity contest. Only to spread Christ's humanity and love of all living things. They can carve on my resting place, 'Here lies a man who tried with all his might to do Christ's work.' That simple adage would make me happy.*

He sat at his desk. As was customary, plates with a few simple snacks had been prepared for him: Varied pizza slices, *Pizza al Taaglio, Panino Rapini,* a bread sandwich with *Rapini* – a small version of broccoli. Following without fail was a cream-filled croissant, *Cornetti con Panna.* His weariness had diluted his appetite. For a reason he could only guess at, he felt ashamed of his tastes in food and the fine white wines condensing around the best Italian wine glasses to be found. A vivid picture of Christ entered his mind. The breaking of simple, unleavened bread and a plain chalice of wood or metal holding unpretentious wine... made the luxury he was in feel like a travesty.

He pushed the fare to one side. "God, give me strength," was all he could utter. He switched on his computer to access the world's news. He noticed the email from Cardinal Nicholas. "Ah," he said out loud. "I hope this is good news." The cardinal didn't say much. He alluded to the findings and further tests on the discovered objects. He mentioned the two poems, without giving his own comments. The only exciting addition was the confirmation of the inscribed Aramaic on Kelvin Stallybrass's tablet. He knew this anyway. Such was his faith. This small detail only reinforced his theory. He would check

his mailbox later to see if the team had anything else to offer…
and to see if the cardinal was concealing anything.

He pressed his internal buzzer for the attendants to take
away the uneaten food and wine. The man looked surprised
at the remains. Breaking with normal protocol, he asked if
something was wrong with the food or was His Holiness unwell.

The pope responded with kindness. "Thank you for your
concerns. All is well. Nothing that sleep will not cure. There
is no need to worry."

The man pushed his trolley from the room, bowed low
and left. Without realising it, Pope Adrian had closed his eyes
and dropped into the dark gulp of an aching sleep.

* * *

He had a good view of the floodlit frontage of the hotel and
everybody who came and went. The whole thing was one big
bore. He had his instructions from Vincenzo and that was
good enough, but if these guys didn't get stroppy what was
the point of him being there at all? All the sitting around reminded him of a time when he was in Belmarsh High Security
Prison, doing time for a failed armed robbery attempt on a
famous West End jewellery shop. Two men were savagely
beaten, and Cracker and his two accomplices were unable to
escape. He got ten years for that. Since his release, he had remained one step ahead of the law and had not been rearrested
for many of his other misdemeanours. He had led a hard life,
forever in trouble with the law and authorities and in and out
of jail. He had two maxims in life – strike first and never say
sorry or apologise. That was for snowflakes and sheep shaggers.

He had learnt the hard way.

CHAPTER 22

He spotted them from the concealment of his hotel window. It was the two smart gits. They were being picked up in a camper van, which had other 'weirdoes' in it. That included the barman of the hotel. They're probably going back to that place, with the trees, stones, and water, where he had first seen them.

Time for some fun.

He packed his gun and headed down to his vehicle.

His thoughts proved to be correct. They were headed to the same location. He was now off his leash and determined to have some action.

The van came to a halt close to where he had parked previously. He counted seven people disembarking from the vehicle. His incredulity scale soared. The first to come out was the barman, dressed in a flowing, earth-coloured robe of some sort, with a headpiece, complete with some kind of badge. In his hand was a long staff, not unlike a shepherd's crook. The others came out, but they were dressed in white robes that were similarly cut. Last out, but in their normal attire, came the professor and his woman. They were positioned in the middle of the column as they set out in single file through the undergrowth and trees.

Cracker followed at a discreet distance. *Aren't these people the crackpot Druids who turn up at Stonehenge every year? Jesus, this a new one for me.* He listened hard but not a word was being spoken. The column moved in silence. They soon came to a stop and Cracker recognised it as the place he had previously been to with Vincenzo. He crouched low, not too far away, but close enough to see and hear what was going on. He felt the comforting weight of his pistol pressing against his ribs. *This could be fun.* A smirk crossed his face.

* * *

The six stood close, their clasped hands forming a semicircle. On his own and at the centre, stood Kelvin or Iseldir – as he would call himself this day. His arms were raised high and held the staff. His prayers or incantations were inaudible, although his followers seemed to be muttering in unison. Above them arose the noonday sun. Both Fergy and Miriam were guest observers and not required to participate. The incantations to Mother Nature came to a stop, leaving only Iseldir's clear and powerful voice echoing around the grove and across the waters. The other Druids bowed their heads.

Miriam did so, too. It all seemed so familiar to her. She had no difficulty following or understanding it.

Iseldir intoned in a voice that rang around the trees. "In early winter, the skies become darker and the smell of fresh snow fills the air. Take a few minutes to think about the fact that even if the skies are cold and dark, it is only temporary, because the sun will return to us after the winter solstice. See the grey skies overhead preparing the way for the bright sun soon to come. See the grey skies overhead, preparing the way for the world to awake once more.

See the grey skies overhead, preparing the way of the longest night of the year.

See the grey skies overhead, preparing the way for the sun to finally return, bringing with it light and warmth."

He banged his staff hard on the ground three times. Then, without any warning, the ear-splitting sound of a howling wolf close by filled the entire area. It was immediately followed by a savage bout of snarling and shrieks.

Everyone jumped as they looked around with wild eyes. Their expressions reflected concern and fear.

"What the hell was that?" yelled the professor, putting a protective arm around Miriam. "It sounds as if the bishop's wolves have emigrated!"

The others tightened their semicircle and Kelvin yelled out. "There are no wild animals or wolves around here. This is some kind of prank! Come out, whoever you are!"

He got a response. The crack of three rapid gunshots echoed around the grove. The bullets seemed to be aimed at the trees as large splinters fell from them. Every one of them dived to the ground, pressed flat and not daring to look up.

Howling, snarling, and gunshots followed more maniacal laughter.

Cracker's party piece, learnt from a magician in jail, worked as always – without fail. He couldn't resist it. With that, he ducked low, keeping out of view while he blasted off three more shots. But this time, much closer at them and into the sand, spraying them with plumes of dirt and shale. He knew it would be a while before they moved. He pushed his bulldog face over the edge to look. Then, stooping low, he headed back to his vehicle.

I right enjoyed that. What a laugh. That's worth a few drinks tonight!

It was a few minutes before the prostrate figures dared lift their heads. Whoever it was had gone.

"Who and what the hell was that?" Iseldir was fuming.

"It's not every day you get shot at even if just for fun. I think I know who it was," Miriam said as she brushed off the dirt from her clothes.

"Who?" Kelvin demanded.

"That man who was with Vincenzo when we were here last. He was wearing a pink T-shirt then. His name is Cracker. I swear I saw that as he slipped away. He's a pathological screwball and where he's concerned, his personal elevator never reaches the top floors… if you get my meaning."

"Perfectly. What are we going to do about it? Do we report it to the police?"

"I don't want them snooping around here," Fergy warned.

"What about my comrades, bards, and ovates here? They look pretty shaken."

"Aren't we all?" Fergy said. "We all need to think about this and it's not a decision we make in the heat of the moment. We need to get back to the hotel, clean up and meet in the bar later. We can discuss it then. Yes, I agree, it's serious and throws considerable doubt on the credibility of our esteemed Eminence, Cardinal *dodgy* Nicholas. The pope will hear of this." He paused. "Any objections to leaving now?"

There were none.

"Let's go then."

In single file, they made their way back to the vehicle.

CHAPTER 23

Miriam was quiet on the short journey back to Wells. What conversation there was remained taut, and an atmosphere akin to a dead man walking hung around them. Thirty minutes later, they disembarked, but Kelvin's acolytes declined to join in. They promised they would not inform the police unless otherwise asked.

Within minutes, Miriam was back in the warmth and safety of her room. Without hesitation, she stripped off her hiking clothes and underwear and leapt into the joys of a hot shower.

Bliss.

Standing still, she allowed the water to send its gentle cascade over her tilted head and down her back and breasts. She held this pose as part of Kelvin's words again infiltrated into her meditative consciousness.

"In early winter, the skies become darker and the smell of fresh

snow fills the air. Take a few minutes to think about the fact that even if the skies are cold and dark, it is only temporary, because the sun will return to us after the winter solstice. See the grey skies overhead, preparing the way for the bright sun soon to come. See the grey skies overhead, preparing the way for the world to awake once more.

See the grey skies overhead, preparing the way of the longest night of the year.

See the grey skies overhead, preparing the way for the sun to finally return, bringing with it light and warmth."

She knew them by heart. It seemed as if she had heard them many times in the past. She closed her eyes and the only sound to be heard was the comforting pitter-patter of water, its background hiss, and the drips onto the mint green, ceramic tiled flooring.

The words continued running through her mind and she knew she did not want them to cease. Another image began to form. She was unable to grasp what it was.

Don't try, just let it be. It will come to you.

She did just that.

It resonated femininity, kindness, warmth, and fearlessness. Miriam was transfixed. She no longer felt or heard the shower water. Another sound, of wind blowing across her naked body, replaced the noise of water… and her vision was fixed on the image in her mind. It would not materialize. She was trying too hard.

She released her anxiety and relaxed. The image fluttered. For a moment it looked like a woman, who appeared to be carrying something. The vision vanished almost as soon as it had appeared. The noise of the water once more filled her mind.

She placed her hands over her ears and switched off the

shower.

What was that? This project is getting to me.

With haste, she dried herself with a towel and dressed in jeans and a roll necked, vermillion red jumper. She had chosen that tint because it was identical to that used in the murals of ancient Pompeii. Fitting, she had thought, for an archaeologist.

As she straightened up, the imagery from her shower remained with her. She was happy about that, but it startled her. She remembered feeling odd the first time she had entered Kelvin's sacred spot. It was almost as if there was nothing about the place she did not know. There was something happening here, and her scientific self found it hard to accept... but it was real. It had happened, and she could still feel and sense it. It was, she thought, more powerful than the howling wolf or gunshots.

She turned her thoughts to Kelvin. *What of him?* She now realised that she had sensed something about him ever since they had first met. Sitting in the sofa, she glanced at her watch. There was plenty of time. She let her mind freewheel. As she did, images of Kelvin appeared in her mind.

The freewheeling continued.

The images looked blurred as they flicked by, frame by frame in what seemed to be a historical succession of close group related Gestalts. She thought this from her training. The Gestalt law of proximity states that objects or shapes that are close to one another appear to form groups. Even if the shapes, sizes, and objects are radically different, they will appear as a group if they are close. That was what was happening in her mind. She perceived Kelvin through a time frame as a druid, an ovate and bard. This wasn't just the present day. The line of images, like snapshot photos, appeared to stretch back infinitely. He never looked the same, but her inner being knew it was him. She began to resist. It was out of this world and she didn't understand what was happening to her.

She started gasping for breath as she struggled to regain her equilibrium. "Stop! Stop, please stop!" Miriam stood up abruptly and her hands clutched around her head, shaking it in anger.

"What's going on? Why is this happening?"

Her breaths began to settle as she regained control and normality once more.

She rushed over to the mini bar and heaved it open. She hadn't been drinking, but she was going to now, and before heading to meet Fergy and Kelvin in the bar. She poured the miniature scotch into a glass tumbler and downed the lot in one long double gulp.

Twenty seconds later, she felt as if her stomach had been set alight. With her senses reeling and in overload, she headed down to the bar to find the other two.

* * *

Kelvin and Fergy were in deep conversation when she hurried in. Her cheeks felt hot, but she didn't waste time. "Mine's a large scotch, please, if you are ordering, Fergy."

He looked surprised. "Hey, what's got into you? You okay? You look flustered."

"I'm fine," she snapped. "I thought we were here to discuss today's events, not my health."

Fergy looked perplexed. "Okay, don't bite my head off." He ordered a large scotch and it was soon delivered and placed in front of her.

"Miriam, what I thought we should do is inform the pope

about what happened. We leave the police out of this as that could put a hold on our activities for a while. This is what I have written and Kelvin's happy about it.

After reading it through, she replied. "If you do that and the pope takes action, Cardinal Nicholas will know that we have told him, and his and our cover will be blown away."

"Ah! I missed that. I could ask the pope not to reveal anything, but just so that he's aware of what's happening over here. I also want to inform him that we have a consignment of hi-tech equipment due to arrive tomorrow. That we're hopeful we'd discover more evidence of whether Christ and his family actually lived around here. If all goes wonderfully well, we may even find this mythical cup." He looked at both of them. "Are we agreed then?"

They both nodded.

"Good. I'll send it now." He spent a minute on his android phone to review his email. "There. He should be receiving it any moment now."

There was a momentary silence as each of them focused on their drinks. Fergal was about to speak when the ring tones of his cell phone started up. He glanced at the screen. "It's the university. I'll answer it over there." He stood and walked out of earshot.

Miriam was aware of the silence between her and Kelvin. She had never been alone with him before. Looking up at him, she saw he was staring directly at her. With a bemused look, she asked, "Why are you staring at me like that, my good druid friend?"

"Sorry, I don't mean to be rude." A somber expression wandered across his face. "I need to say something."

How odd, Miriam thought. *I know what he's about to say.* "Say what's on your mind then." Her words snapped out too fast as she attempted to conceal her deeper perspective.

"You know, don't you?" His deep voice cut through and undermined her effort to block what she knew he was referring to. "Miriam, we don't have much time, so don't try to hide what I know you saw."

"You know what I saw? How could you? What are you talking about?" Her response gave her away. It was too late to retract.

"Never mind how I know, but what you saw from this time, stretching back into the distant past… is true. You saw it only dimly. It will become clearer. I have waited so long for this to happen." Kelvin paused, never taking his eyes off her.

A weird feeling of humility and wonderment passed through her. She stared up at him in open-mouthed astonishment. The tears in his eyes were soft and had a magnificence about them.

"It has happened to me many times, and I always knew there was someone else who sees what I have seen."

"But…" She stopped short and went silent as Fergy strode back into view.

He noticed the silence. "Hey, are you two holding a séance?" Fergy's breezy tones broke the spell. "That was the Uni. Equipment's arriving early first thing tomorrow, and then to the Tor we must go!"

CHAPTER 24

Inspector Rizzo produced his police badge and ID card and the door was opened by a uniformed Swiss Guard to allow him in. He was ushered into a palatial waiting room area, in which nobody was waiting. He was directed to sit on a velvet covered armchair seat. He did, and feeling unsettled by the grandiose surroundings, he prepared to wait. Glancing again at his watch, he noted that he was fifteen minutes early. Throughout his life, he had always been an 'in-time' person and had never been late for an appointment. It was a fact he took pride in, and could never understand lateness, other than it being the hallmark of a disorganized and even disrespectful individual.

The air around him, in contrast to the oppressive Roman humidity outside, felt refreshingly cool. The atmosphere was enhanced by the black and white, diagonally tiled marble floor. To his right, a staircase with gold ormolu rails and an elaborately carved bannister wound its way upwards in a seemingly never-ending spiral. *It's like a fancy version of Jacob's Ladder ascending into the heavens.* He laughed at the thought in silence. The whole structure was overlooked by awesome paintings, in frames that one alone, would be worth well beyond ten years of his total yearly salary. Lifting his eyes, he could see the entire domed ceiling was decorated with a heavenly scene – replete with angels in poses so favoured by early artists. Centrally placed was the imposing figure of a judgmental Christ ushering the good souls to his right and the wretched failures to his left side. Rizzo could only guess at their inevitable and horrendous fate.

If Rizzo was planning to deliberate on the morality of the scene, he was cut short by the sharp rap of polished leather shoes issuing a clipping sound, but out of synchronicity, down the stairs. He didn't need a second glance. It was Cardinal Nicholas with his characteristic limp and walking cane.

With a condescending smile on his paper-thin lips, he strode forward as best he could with his hand outstretched. *"Ispettore, sono così felice rivedert."*

Rizzo gave an inward jolt. He wasn't happy to see the cardinal again. The only time that should happen is when he pulled him in for further questioning. He shook the cardinal's hand without enthusiasm. "Thank you," he replied in English, "and I appreciate the opportunity of being able to speak to His Holiness."

"It's all arranged and you two will have total privacy. This way, Inspector."

Feeling like a bemused schoolboy in an ice cream parlour, Rizzo dutifully followed the long, out of rhythm strides of the lanky cardinal. Sweeping through various anterooms and corridors, they approached a pair of massive ornate doors, richly imbued with gold decorative scrolls and swirls. On each side of them stood two impassive looking Swiss Guards holding long pikes. They didn't fool Rizzo. He knew from personal experience that beneath the finery, each packed concealed but devastating automatic weaponry.

As they drew close to the guards, the cardinal paused, gave the guards a polite nod, turned to his right, walked a few yards further on, and then turned to face a blank wall. "We are here, Inspector."

Rizzo creased his brows in bafflement. "We are?" There was nothing there.

Nicholas ran his hand down a thin wooden strip that reached from floor to ceiling. He paused and appeared to apply pressure.

A voice answered almost from nowhere. "*Come posso aiutare?*"

"It is Cardinal Nicholas," he replied in English. "Thank you for your offer of help. I have here Inspector Rizzo from The *Polizia di Stato*. He is expected by His Holiness."

"*Un momento per favore.*"

Rizzo looked inquiringly as an audible click from somewhere sounded and the thin strip appeared to move sideways, revealing a concealed opening with cameras and audio communication devices. They seemed to be ignored as the door swung open and a disembodied voice spoke. "*Prego entra.*"

"Inspector, His Holiness is waiting. A Swiss guard will be with you at all times. The Holy Father never sees anybody alone. I will take my leave of you." He bowed slightly, turned, and limped away.

"*Grazie.*" Rizzo took a deep breath and walked in.

He was surprised to find himself in a smallish room, which

appeared to be humbly furnished as opposed to the opulence outside. At the far end, behind a window, Pope Adrian was seated at a desk. There was a broad smile on his face. He stood and extended his ringed hand. Without realising, Rizzo did as thousands had done before him. He knelt and kissed the Fisherman's ring. It was something he had sworn he would never do.

Pope Adrian turned to the Swiss Guard. "Will you please go? If you must, wait outside the door."

The guard stammered. "But this is unheard of, Your Holiness. My strict instructions…"

"I am in charge of all matters here. So please leave or I may have to report your refusal to obey my order."

The guard bowed his head and scuttled away.

Pope Adrian turned to Rizzo. "There are matters that don't mind being overheard and some that do. This is one of them, I suspect. Please be seated, Inspector." The pontiff's voice was kind and soothing to hear. "It is not often we get calls from the police. How may we help you?"

Rizzo felt a flutter in his stomach he couldn't remember last experiencing… *butterflies.* "Your Holiness, thank you for seeing me. I'm here for a number of reasons. The first is that I am investigating the death of the English Bishop, Vincent Fisher. No doubt you know all about this?"

The pope nodded.

"Then you have an idea that we do not think it was accidental."

There was no change of expression from the pope.

"Somebody here, in the Vatican, requested all the police evidence – forensic and otherwise. My superior, against all protocol, felt obliged to agree to that request. For some secret reason, I have not been informed who made the request and why." He paused.

Pope Adrian remained calm. "Inspector, it was I."

"It was you?" Rizzo was taken aback.

"Don't look so surprised, Inspector. I know my action seems out of character, but I, for one, never believed the wolf attack."

Rizzo was amazed. But he was never gentle in his interrogations, no matter who they were. The pope was no exception, and he let his annoyance show. "But, really, Your Holiness." Rizzo's voice was short, sharp, and unhappy. "Nobody should have access to those files. They are highly confidential. Sightings by unauthorised personnel have the potential of undermining our work and investigations. Frankly, I am astonished that you requested for them and even more so that you were allowed access."

Pope Adrian raised his hand in a conciliatory manner. "Don't be too angry, Inspector. I apologise for what to you might seem a gross act of interference. I meant no harm. It is a long story. Let me explain and maybe you will understand why I took this most unusual action. But first, allow me to ask you a question."

Rizzo, still with the faint traces of a glower on his face, nodded.

"Are you a man of God?"

Rizzo's immediate thought superseded all others. *What the hell has that got to do with it?* He supressed a sigh. "I'm not a religious man, Your Holiness. I have no idea if God exists or not. Organised religions say they have the answers, but after all, there is no concrete evidence. It is for the believers and those who have faith in such stories. For me, it's shaky ground."

Pope Adrian relaxed. A wry smile lit up his face. "Inspector, a quote from the Psalms on faith: *'Your word is a lamp to my feet and a light to my path.'* We all have our roads to tread and yours, Inspector, is a fair answer. I see you are a man of plain speaking, and with that is often found honesty. I respect your comment."

He stopped for a moment to prod and wriggle his right ear vigorously with his index finger.

Rizzo realised Pope Adrian had a hearing problem and was adjusting a concealed hearing aid.

"Inspector, let me start from the beginning and explain to you everything I know. It will save you hosts of questions. Please take notes or recordings, whatever you normally do. The first part of this story may seem irrelevant to your inquiry, but you will soon see it is not, and why I asked for the forensic and police reports."

Rizzo started writing the time and date, and the usual details he included in police investigations. He also produced a pocket recorder and let it run for a few seconds before speaking. "Interview with His Holiness, Pope Adrian at a location within the Vatican – March 30, 2020. Present are two persons only: myself, Inspector Leonardo Rizzo of the *Polizzia di Stato*, and Pope Adrian." He turned to the pope. "Please acknowledge out loud that this is correct, Your Holiness."

Pope Adrian acknowledged. His voice was firm and steady. With Rizzo's assent, he began to talk. He explained his background and how he rose to the highest rank in Christendom. From there, he began to speak of doubts he had about certain aspects of Catholic beliefs and social positioning in a modern society. He named many.

Rizzo remained impassive.

In particular, he was dubious about the veneration of objects like The Shroud of Turin, which he said had clearly been defined by carbon dating and other disciplines, as early medieval. With not only this relic, but many other finds and discoveries, the Vatican's archaeological unit, The Pontifical Academy, had deliberately supressed evidence and closed ranks and doors on any investigations that could puncture holes in any biblical relics or beliefs. "That is dishonest, is it not, Inspector?"

Rizzo could only agree.

The pope leant forward a little and his voice descended into that of a conspiratorial whisper. "To correct this imbalance, I formed a secret alternative archaeological society – SOTA, the Society of Truth in Archaeology. Before you ask, here is a folio and information on all our members." He pushed a file across to a thankful Rizzo. "You will see that Bishop Vincent Fisher, like myself, a progressive and liberal Catholic, headed up the group and reported his finds to me."

Rizzo nodded again as he flicked through the portfolio. His detective's brain was already finding possibilities re: the bishop's murder. *A conflict of interests with possible murderous results.*

"What I'm to tell you next, as far as I know, only a handful of others are aware of. Please do not speak of it unless your criminal investigations compel you to do so."

"As best I can, Your Holiness." Rizzo was warming to Pope Adrian. What he heard next shook him. He was given an account of the further writings of Thomas and Philip found by SOTA. Close to Qumran, where the Dead Sea Scrolls were originally discovered.

"Contained in these writings are two separate accounts. Both are almost identical and both, astonishingly, tell how Jesus survived his crucifixion. They also state that with Mary Magdalene, his wife, they fled to France, and the two disciples

were with them during their journey. Later, without the apostles, the family travelled on to Britain. They had one young
son and another child not yet born. The Magdalene supposedly had in her possession a cup containing Christ's water
and blood, which she used to heal the sick and dying. It was
said that no matter how many times she used it, the cup remained full. SOTA was attempting to locate the truth of this
story, and principally, for evidence that the family lived in
Britain." He looked up at a wide-eyed Rizzo.

"Farfetched eh, Inspector? If any of it is true, then the
Catholic Church would be in difficulties. Imagine the tantalising prospect of such an artefact... and its implications."

"Some story, Your Holiness." Rizzo chewed the top end
of his cheap biro. "I can see all manner of possibilities here. I
will need to see more people, especially those on your list of
SOTA members. My obvious question, Your Holiness, is why
anyone would want to slaughter a bishop because he and his
group were looking for evidence?"

"I was hoping you might have been able to answer that
question by now, Inspector. I have no idea. I believe I have
enemies in various places within our Church. Obviously, in
most churches, there are differences of opinions, but none that
would warrant an execution... I hope. If any of SOTA's finds
are made public, or discovered to be true, then our Church
would face difficult times indeed. Some people would prevent this from happening, I have no doubt. If, however, this
miraculous cup was found and authenticated, then the opposite effect could ensue. Do I make myself clear, Inspector?"

"Perfectly, Your Holiness. I see the horns of a dilemma
here. Tell me, did the bishop have any known enemies?"

"None that I know of."

"What role does Cardinal Nicholas play in all this?"

"Cardinal Nicholas, as you know, now heads up the group. Between you and I, a poor choice on my part."

Rizzo raised an eyebrow.

"I have my informants. In my position, it would be foolish not to. I have since discovered he is suspected of leading a society of ultra-right-wing clergies. They have a Latin identity, *Ordinis Sancti et Sanctae Crucis et Gladio* or The Order of the Holy Cross and Sword. I have here, and don't ask me how it's in my possession, a sample of their headed notepaper for your investigations." He slid the sheet across to Rizzo.

The point the pope had made about them being a possible source of inquiry was not lost on Rizzo. *Highly significant*, was his first thought.

Pope Adrian paused to take a sip of water. He had begun to perspire.

"Our cardinal has sent an overseer to monitor what the British team is doing – a priest by the name of Father Vincenzo. The archaeological team are well suited for the task, and apparently, know the locations well. I have therefore formed a clandestine alliance with their team leader, Professor Fergal Lars Christi, who, whilst supplying the cardinal with progress reports, also informs me directly about all of their discoveries. The cardinal is required to share all details of the excavations to me, but I am aware that he could possibly supress information. Through the professor, I would know what has been found, and if the cardinal is being less than forthcoming."

God, thought Rizzo, *this place is a hive of intrigue and suspicions. So much for sweet, peaceful religion.*

"You don't trust the cardinal?"

"Since my discovery of his possible involvement in a secret society... no, I do not. The team have had two astonishing discoveries that could authenticate the truth of what Philip and Thomas wrote of." He pushed a bulky folder over to Rizzo. "It's all in there. Their discovery is remarkable and strongly indicates that some of this story may be true. Read it at your leisure, Inspector. I found it breathtaking."

Pope Adrian reached out for the large tissue box strategically placed on his desk, pulled out three and mopped his damp brow. He continued. "There is just one other disturbing development. My latest report from the British team reveals that the archaeologists were indirectly attacked whilst researching in the location of where Jesus was alleged to have lived. It seemed more of a warning or a prank than a deliberate attempt to harm."

"That, Holy Father, should be a matter for the UK police. We can't get involved at this stage. Would you in any way suspect that the cardinal could be involved in that?"

"No. As you know, Inspector, he is here in Rome. I do not know what to say."

Rizzo's knew what the pope was telling him had propelled the case forward several notches. *Could the murder and the UK shooting be linked?*

"Your Holiness, I need not remind you what forensics found on and around the remains of the bishop."

Pope Adrian nodded, made the sign of the cross, and momentarily bowed his head.

"Just between you and me, there were unidentified DNA samples found on the bishop's remains, and as you now know, none were animal. They were identified as human. Now, don't be shocked, but I managed to obtain a sample of DNA from a cigarette stub discarded by Cardinal Nicholas. To my astonishment, Your Holiness, it was a partial match." Rizzo's information cut the air like a lightning bolt.

"What!" Pope Adrian's face paled

Rizzo continued. "With today's technologies, partial matches are not reliable, nor a guarantee of involvement, nor are they evidence of any foul play. I believe the two had met prior to the bishop's death. They could have had conversations. That could explain the presence of the cardinal's DNA on Bishop Fisher."

"Why did you feel it necessary to secretly obtain a sample of the cardinal's DNA? I'm sure that if you had asked, he would have obliged." Pope Adrian looked agitated.

I will have to allow him his naivety. "Holy Father, murder investigations are like a game of poker. You never give anything away unless you wish to wrong foot an opponent. I've worked in crime for most of my working life, and we don't often do things like politely ask for samples. That gives too much away. It's often best if the person concerned knows nothing of what we are doing. Nobody is above suspicion. We operate a dragnet that becomes tighter and tighter as time passes, expelling the innocent one by one until only the guilty remain."

Pope Adrian pulled another handful of tissues and once more mopped his brow.

"So, Inspector, you are saying that our cardinal is a suspect?" He raised an eyebrow, leant back into his upholstered chair, and again fiddled with the hearing aid.

"Until we find the murderer, Holy Father, everyone connected to the bishop is a suspect."

"Inspector, I wish you to find whoever was responsible for this dreadful act as swiftly as possible. I find it hard to believe that a cardinal of our church could possibly be a suspect. From your remarks, I must consider myself included on your suspect list. Would you like a sample of my DNA or have you

170

acquired it already?"

The pope's gentle but pointed sarcasm was not lost on Rizzo. *He says he finds it hard to believe, but he believes in a God he's never seen or makes any sense at all.* He gave a short chuckle. "I think we can safely say, Holy Father, that you are ruled out of our lines of inquiry."

"What next, Inspector? I believe Cardinal Nicholas will be making frequent trips to the UK to gauge progress. You would like to be kept informed?"

Rizzo's liking for Pope Adrian grew a little more. "Why not? That would be most welcome. There is one thing, Your Holiness… should I need to speak to you again, I would prefer that only you and I know of it. Can this be done?"

"Of course. Firstly, give me your contact details." Pope Adrian opened a teak desk drawer and pulled out a dark leather wallet. Inside were a number of small envelopes. He handed one to Rizzo. "The information in there is highly confidential. It contains where and how I may be contacted. It is identical to the information I provided Professor Fergal Lars Christi."

CHAPTER 25

Something had happened. It was inexplicable and beyond scientific reasoning. Such things were not allowed, dismissed as fantasy and wishful thinking. To talk of such things would cause her to be a laughingstock in her field and in the same loony league as the presenters of the TV documentary programme, *Ancient Aliens.* That, she could not allow to happen.

She had never previously given much thought to Kelvin. She had guessed that there was something deep and different about hm. She felt a closeness, but what it was remained indefinable. He was simply a fellow diver, a weirdo sort of Druid, and the finder of a very startling tablet.

Miriam could not explain what he seemed to know about her. Her vision had been indistinct, but he said it would become clearer. How did he know all these things? *There has to be an explanation.*

He had known, without being told, that something had happened to her. It was an experience that had the potential of changing her life. Her vision caused her sleepless nights as she attempted to recreate the experience, although deep inside, she knew that would not work.

She didn't know what to do next. Should she share this with Fergy, or indeed, anybody else? *Hell! It's deeply personal and it's my truth and nobody else's.* That thought didn't include Kelvin, who already knew.

Miriam got dressed at speed. She wanted another chance to talk with Kelvin, but that would have to wait until later. Today, the hi-tech equipment would arrive. Who knows what they find using it? Fergy would be in his element, that's for sure. There was nothing he enjoyed more than using sophisticated equipment. It saved them so much time and labour.

SOTA, via the professor, had already gained permission to use it. Having the pope's personal signature to the request was an amazing door opener, and a bonus few excavations ever got.

They had all agreed to meet at the bottom of the Tor where the equipment was to be delivered. She drove over to Glastonbury in the Land Rover and could see the goods had already arrived. There were a few people moving around and she spotted the professor making notes on a large clipboard.

He looked up as she revved the engine before switching off. With a cheery wave, he strode over, brimming with excitement and enthusiasm. "Hi Toots! You won't believe the gear we've got here. Absolutely stunning!" He gave an expansive wave at an array of expensive and sophisticated looking equipment. "We've also got some extra help from a few archaeology students, keen to see how this all works. By the way, I let Vincenzo know what we're doing, as late as possible. So if he wants to turn up, that's up to him. C'mon, let me show you what we've got."

She clambered out of the vehicle and was surprised to see Kelvin standing close by. He gave her a polite nod and a quiet smile.

"Now, just look at this," Fergy gushed. "We have everything we need here and more." Like a child with a new toy, he pulled her along the array of equipment. "Look at this!" He pointed to the first in the row. "These are infra-red, thermo-imaging cameras that employ virtual reality shots of what's beneath us. They use a magnetometer GPS system. When we link these up with the laser scanning drone... *Presto!* a hidden world is revealed. The drone pictures are then stitched together electronically to form a composite image. So we'll know almost precisely what we're looking at." He beamed. "With these, they have recently discovered more ancient carvings of huge historical interest, and written centuries BC in Egypt, close to the pyramids. They operate by recording data as a 3D print. With this stuff, we could cover the entire complex in a week rather than several months, and that is without doing any 'dig and hope' style digging. No Indiana Jones, his hat or his whip around here." He was unable to prevent himself from laughing. He was almost ecstatic.

Miriam pulled him to a stop in front of the last piece of equipment. "Gosh! A LIDAR scanner. How did you manage that?"

Fergy turned to Kelvin and the two students who were walking in close attendance. "This is our ace card, Kelvin. LIDAR stands for Light Detection and Ranging. It uses laser technology to map the contours of surfaces. It basically involves shooting millions of laser beams at a surface, such as the surface of the ground or the vertical face of an excavated wall. Then it calculates how long it takes for the laser beam to bounce back. This thing is revolutionising our work. There have been some amazing discoveries using this system. Bournemouth University located sixteen roundhouses that were part of Duropolis, a home settlement for part of the Celtic Durotriges tribe. They dated the find from the first century BC. That location, dear listeners, is not too far from where we're standing right now. They could be significant to the work we're doing here. Again, this equipment has, within the last few weeks, discovered several Knights Templar treasure tunnels buried directly beneath Acre and the city of Jerusalem. So, we're keeping our fingers crossed that we might be so similarly fortunate."

"What exactly are we looking for?" one of the students asked.

The professor paused. "I wish I knew." He wasn't giving too much away.

Pulling away from the group, Miriam looked up to St. Michaels, perched on the Tor's summit. "Well, before we do anything, I want to go up there. I haven't done so since I was kid. Anyone care to join?"

"Not me," Fergy grimaced. "Too much climbing."

"I'll go alone then. Won't be long." She set off at a pace. She somehow wished that Kelvin had volunteered. She thought they had much to say that hadn't as yet been said. He had decided to help with the setting up of the equipment.

* * *

An early frost had begun to evaporate under the weak rays of a feeble lemony sun. The air was clear and the sky already a spotless blue. It wasn't warm. She looked around and wondered whether she could see a *Fata Morgana*. The low-lying damp ground could produce a visual effect known by that name when the Tor appears to rise out of the mist. This optical phenomenon occurs when rays of light are strongly bent as they pass through air layers of different temperatures, in a steep thermal inversion where an atmospheric duct has formed. She remembered that the Italian term Fata Morgana was derived from the name of Morgan le Fay, a powerful sorceress in Arthurian and Holy Grail legend.

She looked hard, but it didn't appear.

Moving upwards without effort, Miriam used the well-trodden walkway to the top which so many before her had used. Already, childhood recollections arose in her mind. She could clearly hear and see her mum and dad larking around and playing silly games with her. It seemed as if it was only yesterday.

She marvelled at how the power of the human brain and mind could so easily conjure up such memories. *What on earth are thoughts made of? That notion spawned the question, what is the nature of reality?*

She pressed on. Such was her absorption she barely noticed the rigours of the climb or that her breathing had become quicker as she neared the summit.

For a moment, she paused to take in the view that unfolded around her. Its panoramic extent was breath taking. Its expanse reminded her of T S Elliot's words, so eloquently expressed in his poem, 'The Love Song of J. Alfred Prufrock.'

'When the evening is spread out against the sky / Like a patient etherized upon a table.'

She knew the history and background of the church well.

Remains of a fifth century fort had been found on the Tor,

and remnants of a very early church. In 1275, an earthquake had shaken the original St. Michael's Church and destroyed the building. A second church, built in the 1360s, survived until the Dissolution of the Monasteries in 1539. What was left of the fifteenth century St. Michael's Tower were restored in modern times and the structure now stands on the Tor.

Excavations on the Tor revealed Neolithic flint tools and Roman artefacts, indicating some use of the Tor since very ancient times. The terracing on the side of the hill, if man-made, suggest they could date from Neolithic times. She had researched some of the Celtic mythology and what part this mystical place played in iron-age lives

The Tor, she discovered, seemed to have been called by the early Britons as *Ynys yr Afalon* meaning, 'The Isle of Avalon.' Some believed – including the twelfth and thirteenth century writer, Gerald of Wales – that it was the Avalon of Arthurian legend. Miriam wasn't even convinced that Arthur was a real historical figure. The Tor has been associated with the name Avalon, and with King Arthur, since the alleged discovery of his and Queen Guinevere's neatly labelled coffins in 1191. *Too neat by far,* she thought. It was more likely to have been an early medieval hoax or a put-up event to perpetuate the legend and lore of the locality.

She also discovered that Author Christopher L. Hodapp had asserted in his book, *The Templar Code for Dummies*, that Glastonbury Tor is one of the possible locations of the Holy Grail, because it is close to the monastery that housed the Nanteos Cup. At first, she had thought that the Nanteos cup could be the cup they're looking for. Not so. The Nanteos Cup was a medieval wood mazer bowl. It was on view and held for many years at Nanteos Mansion, Rhydyfelin, in Wales. It is now on display at the National Library of Wales

Like so many medieval relics, their provenance had never been proven, or to have any of the attributes accorded to them. The Nanteos Cup was said to have a supernatural ability to heal those who drank from it, not unlike the one they were seeking. It was said by many believers that the Nanteos Cup had been made from a piece of the True Cross. Miriam couldn't but help wonder how many of these True Crosses were in existence?

By the early twentieth century, the Nanteos Cup had become a Holy Grail candidate – one of hundreds in Europe. In her research, she had been unable to locate any evidence that it healed the sick.

Is our research heading into the waste bins of myth and wishful thinking like all these others?

Be that as it may, as she gazed around, there was no doubt in her mind that the place was special. Since she could remember, she had felt a strange sensation whenever she looked at pictures of the Tor or viewed it from afar.

Her encounter with Kelvin and that vision nagged away in the background. It wouldn't go away. If anything, it was growing stronger the closer she drew to the summit. Directly in front of her stood the towering open roofed remains of St. Michaels. She looked around and could see she was alone. For a moment, she felt reluctant to step inside. The opening beckoned to her to enter. One hesitant step followed another, and she was inside. Her gaze was fixed on the open roof and the bright light streaming down, bathing her in a golden glow of sunshine.

All went quiet.

Silence.

Stillness.

Then she heard them…

Voices.

They were speaking a language not spoken in these times, but she understood it clearly. They were talking of livestock and of food. Others were speaking of fortifying the Tor with terraces to protect the community from raiders and enemies. There were the sounds of children playing and of women talking and preparing meals.

The aroma of food cooking.

Of ashy smoke arising.

It was then she saw them. They were moving all around her but did not acknowledge her.

She could reach out and touch them, but they glided through her. She felt no fear, only wonderment and a deep irrevocable sense of belonging. Their clothes were bright and colourful. The men had long fair hair, coloured and embroidered belted tunic shirts, with trousers called *bracae*. Around their shoulders were cloaks, striped or tartan in design, with the separate checks close together and in various colours. The women who congregated in groups wore floor-length skirts or dresses made of wool or linen and shawls or cloaks. They were colourful and made from the dyes of vegetables and berries.

Miriam saw all this in a flash, and in seconds that seemed to stretch for hours, the vision faded.

She was left breathless, in a wondrous confusion. *What is going on with me?*

There was no way of knowing. She savagely shook her head several times from left to right, as if that would bring her to her senses. But it didn't. The memory was as strong as any she had ever had. *Who were they? It was if I knew them all.*

In her confusion, she rushed out through the furthest exit and into the morning sun again. Taking several deep breaths she stared down to where the team were located. They were all there. She could make out the tall figure of Fergy and the others close by. Heading in their direction, she could see Vincenzo's red pickup truck heading their way.

She felt reassured that she wasn't going mad. Everything was as it should be.

Get a grip, Miriam. It wasn't real. These stories are getting to you.

Her rationale, however, was unable to explain why her nostrils were full of the aroma of smoke and food cooking.

CHAPTER 26

In a packed private conference room of the Kolbe Hotel in Rome, away from possible interventions, Cardinal Nicholas, looking composed, sat in a chair mounted on an elevated dais. The chair resembled a burnished throne. Golden rods entwined with classical style vines swirled around the tall headrest, atop of which a pensive Cupidon gazed to the heavens.

The cardinal twirled his episcopal ring tightly around the third finger of his right hand. The ring was the one bestowed on him by the pope. Usually, he wore no other. At secret meetings like these, he discarded that rule and wore another ring on his left hand – a fat, gold and black, onyx cygnet ring. It was his to wear as the acknowledged head of *Ordinus Sancti et Sanctae Crucis et Gladio.* The Order of the Holy Cross and Sword.

He turned his head from right to left to survey his audience.

There were over one hundred members from across the globe, comprised of priests, bishops, and cardinals. All were dressed in their full ceremonial attire of scarlet and black, and some wore full red cloaks. Each commanded their own bands of substantial domestic followers.

The room was darkened and only Cardinal Nicholas was clearly visible. From his viewpoint though, he could see them all clearly. He was dressed as they were. He gave them all a measured and lengthy gaze. This technique had always mesmerised members. Their attentions were riveted on him. He knew that a theatrical performance always had the potential to galvanise devotion. He simply stared at them en masse and said nothing for another full minute He then began to speak, in slow, measured, and articulate terms. The longer the speech, the faster the delivery.

"My Brothers, once more our devoted ranks meet to discuss and defend our sacred faith. We last met two months ago, here in these very rooms, and declared our intention, and to promote our blessed movement, *Ordinus Sancti et Sanctae Crucis et Gladio*. Our resolve was as stone and now it has grown, hardened as steel and iron. Each day, our glorious Order gathers, and strengthens little by little. Soon, it will grow to envelop the earth. Do not doubt it. If you do, then you may get up and leave this holy meeting." As he expected, nobody did.

"We are witnessing our glorious church, which you all helped hold up, being desecrated by one who came in the night like a murdering thief – His Hereticalness, The Antichrist, our false pope, so named Adrian. Through him and his followers, our Church is in danger of becoming invisible, lost in a mish mash of anti-biblical expressions and anti-God tolerances that can only bring us ruin. You know them all. I do not have to list them. I want you all, here at this moment, to run them through your minds right now."

The cardinal had begun to sweat as he sensed his methodical, oratorical skills having the desired effect. He let over a silent minute run by before picking up the verbal link.

"We can make our Church visible once more like a beacon on a far and distant hill, a guiding light for lost souls."

He liked to use flowery similes and metaphors.

"Our world is sinking into a well of darkness and I am disturbed by the foreshadowing of liberalism, promiscuity, and all propelled by the wings of so-called science – a science controlled by Satan." He stood, ignoring the awkwardness of his misshapen leg, and raised both arms to the air. His speech was accelerating. "And what do we say of the future? Must we tolerate the satanic teachings of other faiths and religions?" He paused for dramatic effect. "Must we?!" His bony fist smashed onto the tabletop as he delivered his question. His voice ascended octaves. "Our visible church built this world and we must not let the light go out. Those who oppose us must perish as God and His Son Jesus Christ so aptly willed. The snake who lies curled in his dark pit must have his venomous head removed, for if not, he is preparing to devour us! The evil reptile must be slaughtered and all those who wind their way around him and his false satanic ideas. I am prepared to die for our God-given Church, and I am willing, if needs require, to shed blood to maintain it! Do you agree?"

A thunderous roar of approval answered him.

Excited spittle and phlegmy droplets sprayed from his mouth. He continued in this manner for ten more minutes, by which time his audience were on their feet, clapping adoringly and cheering furiously. He knew that if he asked them all to strip naked and stand on their heads, they would have done so.

"Now, my true followers of Christ, I have prepared for you all a folio. When you are alone and away from here, I wish you to study it. In this, you will find an agenda and a 'Plan of Action'."

What he didn't tell them was that they would also discover comprehensive details about the search for the never empty cup. That would soon be up for more discussion.

"Please read it and then send me your opinions. I would like your replies within fourteen days." He nodded and took a sip of water, closed his eyes, and wiped his brow with a red, silk handkerchief. *That went well!*

There then followed a series of statements and reactions to his performance from the gathered conclave. All were in favour, and to a man, a defiant militant tone had set in amongst them.

It was time to end the proceedings. What was now bothering him was a note that had been passed to him by his personal assistant, Francesca De Luca. A quick scan had caused his brow to wrinkle. He needed to read it in more detail when he was alone.

He stood and raised his hands for quiet. "Brothers, it is time to bring our sacred meeting to a close. Please listen to my prayer." After a minutes' silence, he prayed aloud. "Oh great Christ, we thank thee for your guiding hand and light as we meditate on your will and wishes. Your lighted candle will not dim. There will be no shadow. For with us and protected by our holy ranks, it can only grow brighter."

The meeting came to a close and a galaxy plus of glassy eyed cardinals and priests made their ways back to their residencies. Cardinal Nicholas knew there would be a substantial reaction to what the portfolio contained. That was exactly what he wanted.

One hour later, in his own rooms, he had more time to read through the message passed to him. A chill went through him the more he read. It contained information that had somehow leaked from the pope's secretariat. That a certain Inspector Rizzo was independently investigating the murder of Bishop Vincent Fisher, and for some reason, he figured in a list of suspects. There were no reasons given as to why this might be so. It was disturbing. *Could the pope be party to it in any way? What did it mean?* The pope, who seemed to be playing his cards close to his chest, had made no mention. *Did he know more than he was letting on?*

He sat back in his chair and rubbed at his damaged leg. Something had to be done and done quickly. Rizzo was proving to be an obstacle, and as such, he would have to be overcome. He had become an ulcerous nuisance. To his mind sprang a medical expression he knew of. It went, 'If in doubt, cut it out.'

The cardinal was never slow to act fast when he needed to. Thinking hard for several minutes, he reached out for the phone to make a very unusual call.

CHAPTER 27

T he students appeared baffled. "How does this stuff work?"

The professor was in his element, and like a child in a sweet shop. Words poured from him like a waterfall, accompanied by frequent hand gestures. There was nothing he enjoyed more than to share his knowledge. He began to explain.

"The principle behind LIDAR is really quite simple. Shine a small light at a surface and measure the time it takes to return to its source. When you shine a torch on a surface, what you are actually seeing is the light being reflected and returned to your retina. Light travels amazingly fast – just shy of 300,000 kilometres per second, 186,000 miles per second, or 0.3 metres per nanosecond. Turning a light on appears to be instantaneous, but of course, it's not!" He clapped his hands loudly together for emphasis.

He continued. "The equipment requires measuring, and

it needs to operate extremely fast. Only with the advancements in modern computing technology had this become possible. The actual calculation for measuring how far a returning light photon has travelled to and from an object is quite simple." He paused with a smile of enjoyment. "I won't go into that, as you will get too much baffling information. Basically, the LIDAR instrument fires rapid pulses of laser light at a surface – some at up to 150,000 pulses per second. A sensor on the instrument measures the amount of time it takes for each pulse to bounce back. Light moves at a constant and known speed, so the LIDAR instrument can calculate the distance between itself and the target with high accuracy. By repeating this in quick succession, the instrument builds up a complex 'map' of the surface it's measuring. With airborne LIDAR, using our drone, other data must be collected to ensure accuracy. As the sensor is moving, height, location and orientation of the instrument must be included to determine the position of the laser pulse at the time of sending and the time of return. This extra information is crucial to the data's integrity. With ground-based LIDAR, a single GPS location can be added for each location where the instrument is set up."

He smiled affably at his listeners. "Are you both any the wiser?"

There was no response. "Any questions?" He received two looks of confusion and shaking heads. He laughed. "Fine then, let's get this gear set up."

* * *

In the midst of their activities, Father Vincenzo's arrival in the pickup truck went unnoticed. He leapt out and was back in his sporting tracksuit and trainers. Around his neck hung his inevitable camera. He had travelled alone. He made his way across to Fergal and the others, "*Buongiorno figli miei!*"

The professor looked up. He didn't see himself as one of Vincenzo's children. His reply was offhand. "Oh, hi Father. What do you want this time?"

A flicker of a scowl crossed Vincenzo's face. The offhandness was not lost on hm. "I come to see what you do and to take pictures for the cardinal." He pointed to the equipment scattered around. "What is all this for?"

In exasperation, the professor straightened up from tightening a cable to an output unit. "I'm sure, Father, that if I took the time, which I don't have, you would still not understand. Basically, it's hi-tech geological surveying equipment, which can perform miracles. But sadly not the wave-walking variety you're used to."

Behind him, he heard Kelvin giggle.

The professor's jibe went unheeded.

"What is it that you look for? More writings, more relics, another box? Hey, Professor, where is the box and scroll?"

"One thing at a time, Father. The box and scroll are still at the laboratory for research. These things take time. As for what are we doing here, we are searching for tunnels that may go back to the Celtic time we are researching. There we may find evidence, one way or the other, that could show how Christianity got here so early. You, I am thinking, need to pray that we won't find any." He smirked. "Now, take as many photographs as you wish, Father, and send them to the cardinal. Should we find anything, you will be the first to know." He gave the priest a condescending smile and resumed what he was doing.

Vincenzo wasted no time and took several pictures of the

location and the equipment, and of everybody at the site. It didn't take long, and when he had finished, he leant back casually on the pickup truck and lit up a cigarette. There wasn't much else he could do until they began to dig... if they ever did.

* * *

Miriam began to help unload and assemble what was needed. But the events of the last forty-eight hours had caused a disorienting effect on her mood. She desperately wanted to talk about what had happened on the Tor to Kelvin, as she was uncertain that Fergy would be sympathetic or even be derisory. She searched for Kelvin, but he was engrossed in assembling the drone and its components. She would have to wait.

The professor had done his homework and later that day, she had provided him with geological and geophysical information on the structure of the Tor. In her research, she was not surprised to discover that Glastonbury was rumoured to have several long-lost tunnels – exactly the type of evidence they were looking for. Most was said to be attached to the nearby Abbey. Legend stated that one ran from the Abbey to the 'George and Dragon' – the local pub! Francis Bligh Bond discovered another tunnel in 1918. It started from the south of a cellar in the town's main street and led to the Abbey. A third story was of a large underground passage in a field south of Abbey, which has never been found. This was something worth looking at. The entire location was rife in rumours and legends of hidden tunnels and escape routes. If anything was to be found, it would be nothing short of a miracle.

She discovered, eerily so, an earlier 9/11 event that had occurred around the Tor centuries before the New York tragedy.

It gave her goose bumps.

On Sept 11, 1275, an earthquake shook and brought down the wooden Church of St. Michael. Some of the people of the time said it was the fairies' doing. The church was rebuilt again, but it didn't last. All that's left of it is the tower that was added in the 1360s. By whatever means, the Tor had success-fully turned its church into the pagan symbol of an upstand-ing tower.

The stones from the rubble of this church, originally said to be part of King Arthur's fort, were then used to build the Abbey. With the dissolution of the monasteries in 1539, the Abbey was reduced to a stone quarry. People then used those stones for local building works.

After Henry the VIII's dissolution of the monasteries, there was a grim episode when Richard Whiting, the Abbey's last abbot, was dragged up the Tor on hurdles, and hung, drawn and quartered there, before being beheaded. Treasures – gold and silver – were sent to swell Henry the VIII's coffers in London. There was a good chance he didn't get it all.

There are stories about secret tunnels radiating in many directions from the Abbey, one of which links directly with the Tor. There remains local geological evidence of this. Some of the Abbey's assets may have found their way into these tunnels, and legends say it could still be there. Legends main-tained that when the secret treasure is found again, it would herald a new age of peace and happiness. This treasure may not be the old booty from the Abbey though.

That drew her mind back to the verse on Kelvin's tablet and that written on the scroll in the box. Could they be con-nected to the ancient tales and lore?

There were stories about monks who found these tunnels who had returned 'insane' or 'unable to speak.' Maybe something in the experience unhinged their sheltered, monastic minds. Their accounts sounded so weird they were dismissed as crazy.

Another theory surmised that destroying the monks' credibility could have been a wily ploy to keep certain things quiet. She didn't doubt the possibility of other tunnels under the Abbey and the Tor. Secrets were always intriguing, and she knew Fergy would enjoy her thoughts on the whole thing.

CHAPTER 28

Rome, Italy

I nspector Rizzo, in his small apartment on the *Via del Boccacio* in the *Centro Storico* district of Rome, lay in bed. The sun, already warm and inviting, was telling him it was time to get up. That was the last thing he wanted to do. He had spent half the early hours analysing the Bishop Vincent Fisher case. He had thought of his conversations with Pope Adrian and the strange presence of partial DNA samples from Cardinal Nicholas found on the remains of the dead bishop. He was missing something, and he didn't know what.

A sudden burst of pain reminded him that he was not a well man. It always manifested when he was lying down and about to get out of bed. A year back, he had been diagnosed with a form of cancer. It had been treated successfully, but the end result was infrequent but recurring bouts of painful cystitis. There was no time to lose… lying in bed was not good. He jumped out and with an urgent, heated rush, made a dash to the toilet.

Slow, but burning relief.

It was annoying. He never knew when it would appear. Thirty minutes later, his bodily function back to normal, he was showered and dressed. Clutching his case file, he made his way for his usual coffee at the *Antico Caffè Greco.* It was a place favoured by writers. It had become his second office and there was always a table reserved for him at his favourite place by the window.

Stepping outside, the sun blasted down, and the noise of Rome's traffic filled his ears. He set out on the ten-minute stroll. The streets were awash with tourists with their cameras and guidebooks. Mixing with them were the inevitable pigeons and the odd, armed policeman. Since the terrorist attacks of the 1980s and early 2000s throughout Italy, the police no longer took chances now and were frequently armed and ready. Rizzo fully approved.

His policeman's instincts were never far away. He became aware of a vague sensation that he was being followed. Casually, he turned his head, as if to look across the road, but there was no one to be seen. He was alone.

He walked into the coffee bar, and Giovanni, his *barista* and old-time friend, greeted him and ushered him to his favourite seat. Unlike most customers who drank their coffee standing, Rizzo preferred to sit and pay the extra cost. Besides, he needed to do some work.

Once he had ordered, he set about reading his reports and notes. It wasn't long before the *I'm being watched* sensation crept back into his mind. He looked up, but there was nothing unusual to be seen. *I've been in this job too long,* he thought. Not long after he had settled into his notes, he noticed somebody he had not seen in the cafe before, sitting not far away. He found himself analysing the man. Again, his old police training never gave up. He began to mentally examine the man, taking note of important details.

The man certainly didn't look Italian. A lightweight, casual, khaki-style bomber jacket hung beside him on his chair. He had a shaven head and there were tattoos down both his forearms. He had to be English. The English newspaper he was reading dismissed any doubts. He looked pugnacious, jowly, like an angry bulldog trying to spit out a mouthful of wasp. Long, plump legs, wearing faded denims and large, heavy, brown boots were spread wide beneath his table. A cold beer straight from the bottle was being gulped down his thick throat.

That man looks dangerous – could be ex-military. Another thought crossed his mind. *O forse un ex prigioniero criminal!* The thought of the man possibly being an ex-convict had all the hallmarks of truth about it. Everything about him ticked all the boxes. One of the things Rizzo knew for sure was that criminals the world over often have similarities in manner, body language and attitude. His prospect displayed them all.

For a brief moment, the man put down his newspaper and looked across to where Rizzo sat. Rizzo caught his eye and they stared at each other. Rizzo felt mutual tension between them, and watched as the man turned his gaze away, clenched his fist, and began to crack his finger knuckles.

Rizzo recognised a subliminal message when it appeared. He recognized danger. *Is that man after me in some way… or am I becoming paranoid?* He decided the atmosphere had become heavy. It was time to leave. He paid at the *cassa* and began his walk to his nearby office. Every so often, he stopped to look in a shop window. The man was a short distance away from him, also looking in a shop window.

Rizzo was now fully alert.

* * *

Thirty-six hours earlier, a diminutive young priest, Father Angelo Xavier, stood in the *Sala Arrivi* – the Arrivals Hall of the Leonardo da Vinci airport, thirty kilometres from Rome. In his hands, he held up a bright, yellow and black cardboard sign. On it was simply written the name, Mr. Cracker.

He didn't have long to wait. A burly, thickset, shaven-headed man carrying a large holdall bag soon confronted him. Father Xavier spoke good English. He had an idea that the man in front of him would be limited in his choice of languages. He was correct in that assumption. Mr. Cracker had always had trouble in sounding his *th* and frequently they would sound like an *f*. Speaking another language was as an anathema to him. *All too poofy and gay* had always been his opinion of other languages.

Once the introductions had been made and identities confirmed, the young priest led him to the parking area.

"Where are you taking me?" Cracker growled as they clambered into the cardinal's aging black Lancia Ypsilon car.

"We are going close to the Vatican where Cardinal Nicholas will be expecting you. But first, I will drop you at your hotel and I will wait for you to check in before driving you over there."

Cracker grunted.

Father Xavier couldn't help but wonder what on earth the cardinal was doing entertaining this brutish looking man.

The traffic jammed journey continued in silence. It would

take them over an hour to get to the hotel. Cracker took little interest in the culture and vivacity of the ancient city they were diving through. Thoughts and memories of his life, as they frequently did, opened up his memory banks. He never thought about much else.

Childhood had been a tough experience. His father, who wasn't around much, was an alcoholic. When he did show up, his mother, a co-dependent drinker, would endure regular beatings as he, even as a small boy, did. At school, he had been the local tough guy. In imitation of his father, he would set about other boys as his father set about him. He never took any notice of school lessons and spent most his time dodging school and spending days in amusement arcades. He soon learnt to steal and that offered him things the other idiots at school would find hard to get. Crime seemed a good way of life. One that fitted in well with his ambitions of running a large gang of crooks.

It didn't work out that way. The hated authorities and police always managed to catch up with him. He spent much time in young offenders' institutes before graduating to adult prisons. He was forever in and out of them. He recalled many of his skirmishes and fights using any weapon that came to hand. It hadn't been long before he discovered firearms. He fell in love with them. They had become an essential part of his persona. One bonus he got from all this was that amongst the criminal fraternity, he was respected and regarded as a person not to interfere with or cross in any way. He rarely refused an assignment. One firm rule he had, though – he would have nothing to do with drugs.

Father Xavier's voice cut through his thoughts. *"Signore* Cracker, we are at your hotel."

The Vatican Style Hotel was by Rome's standards, an

inexpensive three-star hotel which offered views of St. Peter's Basilica from some rooms.

"Please check in, *Signore,* and I shall wait for you here. Please, not to be long for police and parking not good here."

Cracker nodded. "I won't be long, squire." This was his first foreign mission and it didn't excite him in the slightest. Father Vincenzo, back in the UK, had seemed put out that the cardinal had asked only for him. *The job must be important.* The thought made him feel good.

CHAPTER 29

He inhaled deeply before watching the blue grey smoke plume from his nostril. The gradual swirls began to vanish like forgiven sins at a confessional. The cardinal was in an affable mood. He had received good reports from both Vincenzo and the professor. Everything was going to plan and dovetailed neatly into what the deceased bishop would have planned. They were looking for tunnels, and that was excellent, nothing like secret tunnels and hidden clues to engender positive interest from all concerned.

So far so good.

In his secret heart, he hoped the excavations attempting to prove the legend that Christ and his so-called family ever existed in Britain, failed. This secret venture was so typical of Pope Adrian, who had little regard for the scriptures and tenets of the Catholic Church. It seemed to him that the pope lived in a naive world of wishful thinking. It was too fanciful for belief and could only be built on a fragile pyramid of evidence – only too easy to invalidate.

The cup, if discovered, empty or not, would be a different matter. Exercised properly, the artifact could be used to turn the whole story about its healing powers as true – and he knew just how to exploit it. The pope would have no part in it. With that artefact in his hands, Pope Adrian and his liberal visions of where the church should be heading would be annihilated overnight. The old ways would return in all their glory.

God be praised. He took a quick glance at his antique, Gothic-style, Italian long case clock standing in the corner. Father Xavier was running late.

But he didn't have long to wait. There was a sharp rap on his apartment door.

From behind the door, Father Xavier heard the cardinal's tobacco enriched voice call out.

"Entare."

He did. Pushing open the door he walked in, followed by the bullish figure of Cracker.

"Ah." Nicholas stood and moved over to them both. "Thank you, Father. I'll call you later to take Mr. Cracker back to his hotel." He took note that Xavier could be ideal material for his clandestine order.

The young priest gave a perfunctory nod at both men and left the room.

"How nice to see you again, Mr. Cracker. Please take a seat. I trust you had a good journey and the hotel is to your liking?" He gave a condescending smile.

Cracker's response was terse. He dispensed with courteous etiquette. "The trip was fine but the hotel's dingy. How long am I there?"

"That will be up to you, as you will soon see, Mr. Cracker. Dingy it may be, but far more preferable to a prison cell... don't you think?"

Cracker didn't miss the veiled threat. "What's that supposed to mean?"

Before answering, the Cardinal took a hefty sip of his Napoleon Brandy. He made no offer to share any. He licked his lips. "It means that I did more checks on you to make certain you were the man we need for the mission we have in mind. With your record, I'm certain you fit the bill wonderfully. Let me see now... you have served prison sentences for grievous bodily harm, manslaughter, actual bodily harm, robbery and the list goes on." Nicholas allowed himself a smile.

"So you know more things about me now, than you did before. You didn't drag me all the way here just to tell me that, did you? Stop pissing about and tell me what you want from me?"

The cardinal took a deep breath. *He's as smooth talking as ever.* He fumbled for another cigarette. "Cigarette, Mr. Cracker?" His raspy voice sounded more croaky than usual as he offered the packet.

Cracker shook his head. "Gave that up years ago."

Probably the one sensible thing he's done in his life. The cardinal took a deep lungful of smoke. He needed it. "I have here a file of information about a certain individual." He pushed it over to him. "In it you will find several photographs of this person. You will find addresses – where he lives and works, his hobbies, his habits, where he eats and drinks, etcetera."

Cracker started to open the file.

The cardinal looked alarmed. "Not in here, please, but when you get back to your hotel. Nobody is to know of this file except you and I."

"A big secret then, is it? What do you want doing then?"

"May God forgive me, but it is for his glory that this has to be done."

"Cut the crap will you and just tell me?" Anger was never far away from Cracker.

Nicholas spoke evenly and without a tremor. "We would like to see an accident happen."

Cracker's eyes hardened. "Of the fatal persuasion, I assume."

"Yes. Your assumption is correct. You have as long as you wish."

"What's in it for me?"

"All your expenses will be paid, along with anything else you have in mind. Your hotel is taken care of and you need not be concerned about a thing. Once your mission is accomplished, you will be rewarded with twenty thousand pounds – five thousand of which is in that file folder."

The faintest trace of a smile could be seen on Cracker's fleshy face.

"You will be left alone to accomplish your task. You do not need to report to us… we do not want to know any grisly details. You have never met your driver or me. In a nutshell, we have no knowledge of each other, and should there be a mishap, any attempt to say we have met or spoken will be vigorously denied. Am I clear, Mr. Cracker? Do you accept this mission?" The cardinal liked the word 'mission.' It had a religious sanctity about it.

"I understand, boss. That's a deal… say no more. I never thought I'd end up batting for Him upstairs." He pointed his finger skywards.

"Yes," Nicholas replied, unable to keep a rare spark of

amusement from his voice. "Indeed, God does move in mysterious ways." He stubbed out his cigarette and reached for the brandy. "There is one other thing…" The cardinal dug into his desk drawer and pulled out two cell phones. He handed one to Cracker. "These are *burner* cell phones. You may have seen them used in the movies or TV shows like *Breaking Bad*. I have for you a number where you can reach me, and I also have your number. Both are written on the packaging, which you will destroy back at your hotel. The numbers are temporary and totally disposable. The app allows you to remain anonymous. Once your mission is finished, you must destroy the phone. These phones were purchased in cash and has no service provider, which means that there is no record connecting you or me to the phone numbers to begin with. Do you understand this?"

"You're taking the piss again, boss. I've used them for over a year. There are only two numbers this phone recognises and that's the two you passed on to me. Correct?"

Nicholas looked surprised. "Forgive me, Mr. Cracker. I should have realised."

"Forget it. If that's it, call your driver and I'll be on my way. Expect to hear from me soon."

Nicholas pressed his desk buzzer to summon Father Xavier.

* * *

Back at the Vatican Style Hotel, Cracker stood by the window looking out at the distant view of St. Peter's. In one hand he held a cold beer, and in the other, a photograph he had extracted from the file. It was a clear facial shot of a man entering a coffee bar, and its name was clearly visible, *Antico Caffè*

Greco. Attached to this and to hosts of other material were addresses and route directions from his hotel to numerous locations. The name of the man was Inspector Leonardo Rizzo.

Holy shit! This guy's from the fuzz and he wants me to whack him. No wonder the cardinal was so bleeding cagey. It's almost an f12.

Cracker downed his drink at speed and opened another. A hit on a policeman, and an inspector at that, was something he had never encountered before. Minor dickheads were his usual fare, but this knob was senior stuff, and Nicholas, a professional 'sky pilot,' was asking him to waste him. *No wonder the contract payment was so generous.*

After a lot of thought, Cracker decided he had to know a lot more about the man, his life, his routines, and behaviour patterns. This was going to be challenging.

CHAPTER 30

Glastonbury

S everal days had passed and nothing had been discovered apart from the odd coin and pieces of ancient pottery. It was enough to confirm that the area had been inhabited centuries before, if not longer. There was a silence amongst the team as they had such high hopes, but as yet… nothing.

The LIDAR equipment was assembled and the link and cooperation with the drone was in place. The professor tested it and it worked well. It had been decided that they would work from the furthest edge of the distant and surrounding fields, before reaching the Cretan structure of the Tor itself. Fergy had said he didn't think there would be much chance of finding anything beyond a certain height.

Miriam remained silent about that. Fergy had yet to learn

of her visionary experiences. If what she had seen at the top of the Tor was real, she was sure they would find something there.

Annoyingly so, they had to endure the presence of Vincenzo who was forever poking his camera lens at everything. He was acting like a bleating lost sheep without his companion, Cracker. Where he had gone, Vincenzo wasn't saying. Not that the team cared a jot about the man.

The furthest extent of the longest field was close to Kelvin's hidden grove, the Grove of Taranus or Taran – the Bull and Thunder god, as Miriam had discovered in her researches. What was confusing her was the clash she was experiencing between science and what seemed like a world of fantasy, found only in films or books like Dan Brown's.

A shout from Fergy got her attention.

"Hey Miriam, look at this. Quick!" He was staring hard at the data displayed on the monitor. "I think we found something."

She rushed over. "What is it?"

He jabbed a finger at the display.

"What are those black lines showing?" She was pointing at a long stretch that seemed to continue beyond the monitor.

"That has to be a tunnel," Fergy's face lit up. "There has been a rumour of this existing, but nothing has ever been found. This could be it. It seems to appear from somewhere around Kelvin's grove, and if I'm not mistaken, passes beneath and across this field before reaching the base of the Tor." He turned to the students. "Activate the drone to pass in a straight line in the direction I am pointing, and let it hover at the end."

They did this and both Miriam and the professor could see the in-depth readings from both the LIDAR and drone, which fed images to a pair of linked monitors to create a virtual 3D representation of what lay beneath them.

After several minutes of careful scrutiny, Fergy let out a shout. "Bingo!" His fist punched the air. "It's a tunnel, without a doubt. Look at that!"

On the screen were the fuzzy but unmistakable signs of a long, hollow furrow about six feet high and equal in width. It seemed to stretch out in both directions without end. The highest point of the structure sat six feet below the surface.

"What are we going to do next?" Miriam asked. "We don't have enough archaeologists here for a full-scale dig."

Kelvin answered, "We need a JCB excavator."

"Don't be so bloody daft," snapped the professor. "This is an archaeology site not a road repair outfit."

"There's a simpler solution," Miriam added. "Each end must have a way in or out. That's all we need to find. With any luck, once found, we may be able to pass into it."

"Good thinking, Batman!" Fergy quipped. "Let's follow the lines to their fullest extent. There must be a beginning and an end."

"Yes. That way," Miriam continued, "if we dig down at either end, we should be able to find a way through."

Vincenzo was called over. He was shown the screens and informed about what they were planning to do. A screen printout was given to him, and he began photographing everything, ready to send the latest discovery to the cardinal who was still in Rome.

The professor didn't doubt they would all find their way to the cardinal. But how much of it would reach Pope Adrian, he couldn't say. It doesn't matter. The pope would get all the information, right down to the smallest detail, from himself.

CHAPTER 31

The Vatican

He looked down at his swollen and painful knees. The beginnings of arthritis worsened his physical discomfort. He had been kneeling for almost an hour and praying that his suspicions would be unfounded. Pope Adrian raised his eyes skywards, to the open window where he could see the rising sun blazing in a clear blue sky. In spite of his prayers, he was unable to shake off his disturbed thoughts.

All was not well in Rome and the Vatican.

Several dark clouds swept through his mind. First was Inspector Rizzo's disclosure of traces of Cardinal Nicholas's DNA found on the clothing and body of the deceased Bishop Vincent Fisher. How did that come about? It was something that Rizzo would have to discover. His next thought was more alarming. For some time now, rumours of a deeply re-actionary clique of priests, bishops and even cardinals, were escalating. This group was supposedly being fermented by no less than Cardinal Nicholas, and that this 'secret' order was becoming increasingly militant. They were dedicated to countering any liberalism within the church.

He had known of this earlier and had confided his worries to Rizzo. It was being circulated that Cardinal Nicholas was planning a revolution in the Church. That they were attempting to form a church within a church – ultimately to overthrow the God-given authority of the Vatican itself.

The cardinal rumoured involvement was of no concern to the pope. These sorts of events had happened many times in the past and had come to nothing. He knew what various priests, bishops and cardinals were saying about him, their elected pope.

"He's soft on the homosexuals, the lesbians, and the transsexuals."

"How dare he criticize the Curia? Accusing us of spiritual Alzheimer's just because his papacy is unravelling."

That had shaken the pope's confidence. It gave Rizzo's DNA discovery added impetus. Was not the dead bishop an arch liberal and enemy of reactionary Catholicism? He had headed up the clandestine archaeology society, SOTA, which the pope himself had established. Now it was being suggested that Cardinal Nicholas, the very man he had appointed to continue the research, was the head of a militant group.

He had prayed this would not be so. Part of him suggested that he should relieve the cardinal of his role in the research, but he was still hoping the rumours were unfounded.

Underlying his suspicions were two reports he had received concerning the excavations in England. There was the cardinal's report and that of Professor Christi. They did not match up. From the start, he had noticed that the cardinal's reports were scanty on detail, dismissive, and made no mention of tunnels and the attempts to unravel the meanings behind the mysterious verses. Nor did it mention any of the Celtic stories and possible legends of Jesus having lived amongst them – the very reason for the project. The cardinal had also suggested that he thought such stories were planted to assist tourism in the area. He considered such stories were mainly superstition and make believe. However, the cardinal maintained that the excavation should continue. Just to prove a point and lay to rest the absurdity of it all.

Hardly the stance Bishop Vincent would have adopted.

Despite all that, the pope could not easily accept that the cardinal's explanation was intended to deceive him.

Why is the cardinal holding back on information? Is there no hope in his heart or is it part of a militant agenda? I must ask him soon.

Many thoughts ran through his head. *I believe, as did the bishop, that there is every chance the Magdalene's cup is real. If so, mankind can be saved for eternity – if not physically, then spiritually. If discovered, I wonder if still holds any liquid. It was all an enchanting mystery.*

There were too many unanswered questions revolving around Cardinal Nicholas…

With that in mind, Pope Adrian pulled out his android smartphone equipped with the Signal encryption app. The Vatican Intelligence Service, the *Santa Alleanza,* had all but demanded he equip himself with this state-of-the-art encryption service. He had noted that Rizzo used the system too. Any message or phone call he had with Rizzo would be encrypted from end-to-end. There would be no way for anybody to eavesdrop or access the conversation. That factor gave him a sense of reassurance.

He was prepared to wager that God had no use for such devices!

* * *

Rome, Italy

It had been going on for two days. This was something new. He had never been tailed before, and he was not being paranoid. The thuggish, shaven headed man matched every step he took. He forever seemed to be in close proximity to him.

Rizzo had always been a cautious man. His job demanded it. Now, he was even more so. The worry lines on his well-worn features creased as he gazed out from his *Via del Boccacio* apartment window. He was careful to stand to one side so as not to be seen. At first glance, there was no sign of his stalker. Then he spotted him. He was seated in a café bar across the street and reading a newspaper. Rizzo doubted it was Italian. The man never looked up, and Rizzo knew it would be pointless to confront him direct. Whoever he was, someone had presumably hired him... but why? The only case he was working on was Bishop Vincent's.

All avenues in that direction had come to a dead end. No new information had emerged. The only immediate, unanswered question concerned the cardinal's DNA and two other specimens. It was inexplicable, but it was not enough to make a case out of.

As he continued to observe the man from his concealed position, a sudden but compelling thought struck him. For a fleeting second, he was ready to dismiss it... but the thought persisted.

Could the cardinal be behind this man's unwelcome attentions?
All permutations were possible.

Reaching into his desk drawer, he checked his Beretta 93R police issue firearm. It was fully loaded. He strapped it to his shoulder and put on a casual jacket. It was expected and part of Italian police officer regulations to carry this weapon at all times.

If he was being tailed, what was the point of that? Unless it was a prelude to a nasty episode of some kind. A firearm was a wise precaution.

The time had arrived to reverse the process. The hunter was to become the hunted, and Rizzo had enough experience and cunning to accomplish that. Unnerving an opponent was always an effective strategy.

He went over his plan again before moving to the door. The ringtone of his mobile phone stopped him short. He pulled it out of his pocket and was surprised to see that it was Pope Adrian. That didn't happen to anybody every day.

Ten minutes later, their conversation ended. He could not help but think the bread was beginning to bake. After the conversation, there was little doubt that Pope Adrian would have made a first-rate detective. They shared the same thoughts and suspicions. The DNA was the cohesive factor.

Stepping out of the apartment and into the sunlit street, he noticed his adversary was still seated and looking his way. It was time to put into gear his plan of action. Increasing his pace, he was amused to see the man struggling to keep with him on the other side of the road. Rounding a sharp corner, Rizzo slipped into the entrance of a small hotel.

Cracker was forced to dash across the busy road, and in doing so, he lost sight of Rizzo. He turned both left and right and behind him, but the Inspector was nowhere to be seen. He set off at a fast rate in the direction Rizzo had been heading.

Rizzo set off after him, keeping a safe distance between them. He wanted the man to glimpse him, then he would give him a wave and disappear again. The man would then know that Rizzo was on to him and effectively sabotage whatever plans he had in mind. He would have to report his initial failure to his provider. *Could that be Cardinal Nicholas?* He was starting to believe it. There was no such thing as a coincidence in his field.

Reaching a bar, Cracker stopped to look inside but there was no trace of the inspector. Rizzo watched him turn around, looking in all directions. That was when he gave him a short, sharp wave. The man saw it and appeared to freeze on the spot. His reaction was obvious. He had been rumbled. The inspector slipped away, down a short flight of steps and into an alleyway. It had been a dangerous manoeuvre for it signalled the gloves were off. Both would now be on high alert in what could be a deadly game of cat and mouse.

CHAPTER 32

Glastonbury

T he dig to reveal the tunnel had entered its third day and was proving to be a sterner task than they thought. Miriam and Kelvin plus two archaeologists from a local society were there to assist. They were operating at the furthest end of the GPR readings, and closer to the base of the Cretan maze that formed the first ring of the Tor. Back at the other end, the professor and three others made up of students and other members of the local group had set to work. Trowels, small hand shovels like coal shovels, normal sized shovels, spades, buckets, and wheelbarrows were used to clear away the loose dirt – known as 'spoil' – and take it to the spoil heap. They had also brought along mattocks, which were large hand tools used to break up hard ground. With these, there was an assortment of marker pegs, location cards and balls of high-quality string.

Vincenzo appeared to have given up wearing his priestly attire and was clad in his sweat suit. Moving from one group to another, he made constant notes and took countless pictures. Both Fergy and Miriam had similar equipment but relied extensively on the constant readouts and printouts from their equipment. Without complaint, it continued to operate tirelessly.

The location gave Miriam a chance to talk to Kelvin about her experience up at St. Michael's. She told him what she had seen – the people, their colourful clothing and the smells of cooking, smells that she had experienced for a full day after. At the end of her story, she looked hard at him. There was a look of anticipation across her face.

"Well what do you make of that? Am I going mad?" She hoped his answer would tell her she wasn't. Whatever was going on with her pulled her in two directions. She was a scientist – an academic – not given to fanciful notions.

Kelvin put down the trowel he had been using. "Of course not. Following on from your previous experience, it should be a clue to what's going on with you, and the strange power of this place. You are being called. By whom, I don't know, and the why remains a mystery. This matter is far from over and there will be more to come. I have had similar visions in the past, but your experiences and visions are particularly powerful. The reason for your presence here are being manifested through you and nobody else. You are being singled out as some type of conduit. I sense we are getting closer to something. There is more to find, of that I'm certain. I also feel that the story doesn't end here. If I'm wrong, your experience, the small things we have discovered, and those enigmatic verses become meaningless. Don't you agree? So, let's dig and allow time to reveal what has been hidden."

Miriam looked pensive. She began biting down on her lip, a childhood reaction when uncertainty presented itself. "Thanks for that, Kelvin. I honestly don't know whether to feel excited or scared. I can't find an explanation apart from what you have said. You are right. They could be nothing or they could mean something. I should let it be and see what happens."

"Yes, just let it be," He nodded and gave her a small smile. "Hand it over to the universe and it will do what is required."

"You sound mysterious."

He laughed. "I'm a Druid, remember?"

* * *

At the lake end of the tunnel dig, a few things were discovered. They had found tiling, broken clay pots, and a magnificent cluster of mud encrusted jewellery – necklaces and bracelets made from bronze, and one that looked like a gold torc. The items were Celtic for sure. One of them was a circular, twisted metal neckband. Fergy knew that chieftains, warriors, and important characters wore these, and other neckbands in a similar style often made of silver, tin, enamel, or copper.

The professor became extremely excited.

This was a significant find and of top museum quality. He rang the makeshift bell to alert the others at the far end that they had made a discovery. Within minutes, both teams were huddled together, examining the find.

This was proof positive that Celts had lived here. Their next task was to discover how old they might be. There was still no proof, however, that Jesus, Mary, and their family had lived here. That was too much to hope for at this point.

Vincenzo became animated and more voluble. He was waving his hands and arms. *"Stai indietro! Stai indietro!"* Stand back, he said. He was shouting and poking the camera lens everywhere he could. Then, he began to handle the find.

That was too much for Fergy who visibly reddened. *This mindless so called Lamb of God, was nothing but an unwanted nuisance.* The professor pushed him to one side before he could do further damage.

"Father! Get out of the way, will you? Please don't touch anything. That's an order, not a polite request! You'll have every chance to take your stupid pictures once these items have been examined and restored to a pristine condition. Right now, you're contaminating our site. Now bugger off!" Fergal couldn't care a jot that the man was a priest. He had been nothing but an aggravation since he had arrived.

"You pushed me." Vincenzo's affability melted like ice cream on a stove. His fist visibly clenched and for a moment, he looked as if he was about to punch the professor. He refrained, but his expression had hardened, and his eyes darkened with unmistakeable menace.

His chilling transformation reminded Fergy of a Mafia soldier rather than a man of God.

The veins in the priest's neck bulged big and blue. "I will not forget. You shall see." He waved his index finger at Fergy, and the hostility was not lost on everyone around him. Gone was the mild-mannered, clumsy priest.

The professor looked around at the others and they looked uneasy. Shrugging his shoulders, he turned his back on the priest. "C'mon everybody, forget it. Let's get going, please. More digging is required."

Vincenzo jumped into his pickup truck and slammed the door, before furiously revving the engine to express his anger as the truck roared out of the area.

Fergal felt troubled. The change in the priest's persona had come faster than an attack dog.

The team said nothing about the episode and resumed digging. It was not long before a student found the beginning of something that looked like a stone portal.

"Professor!" His excited shout brought Fergal rushing over.

There, in front of them both, half buried, stood a massive stone construction of some weight, extending down six feet deep. It had sidewalls that had filled with dirt and earth over the centuries. They could also see the beginnings of stone steps.

The GPR confirmed their assessment. Displayed on the monitors, there appeared to be twelve of them, and they obviously led into what was undoubtedly a tunnel. A series of distressed, but large iron rings – looking like handholds – were embedded into the left sidewall. What they were truly for, nobody could say at this point. The entrance had been partially bricked up. It would need to be carefully dismantled to open a passage through.

All work at the far end of the excavation was halted and the crew was brought down to assist with the dig at the lake end.

* * *

The professor had taken the artefacts to the university laboratory immediately. There, they would be cleaned up, identified, catalogued and C14 tested. He prepared a preliminary report for Pope Adrian, with the promise of more detailed information to follow. Fergy explained that no further Aramaic writings had been uncovered yet, but hopes were high.

He did not share his encounter with Father Vincenzo. He decided, this was not the time. They were on the verge of an important discovery and everything else could wait.

Fergal was aware that his incident with the priest would have consequences, one way or another. Trouble was brewing.

* * *

Back at the site, work on expanding the tunnel was moving along at a rapid pace. The spoil heap had grown extensively, and the digging lessened as the dirt diminished. The team had penetrated twenty yards, opened up the brickwork, and the heaps of soil had become appreciably less the further in they progressed. The tunnel had not been completely filled in. It was big enough for an adult male to walk through without bending down. It seemed well built, with properly built rock walls, and was far from being just a hole in the ground. The walls were made with evenly cut and dressed limestone bricks. This tunnel had been built with a purpose.

Flashlights and strapped helmet versions were essential. Miriam led the way. The light, the first that had shone this way for unknown centuries, scanned the damp roof and the walls. It created an eerie silence for those behind. Miriam had a distinct feeling that she was an intruder treading on sacred ground, and that they shouldn't be there. Their presence was a violation. Yet… there was nothing to see. The walls were bare. The only visible thing around was their shadows, flicking backward and forward across the walls. She began to wonder what the construction was meant for. Clearly, it was a secret route. What else would an underground tunnel beneath open fields be used for?

As far as Miriam could see, the tunnel was heading directly toward the Tor, and the route now appeared to be unobstructed. She shivered as they moved forward with care. *Where does this lead to and what are we going to find there?* She sensed the presence of Kelvin directly behind her. Of late, she had been more aware of his thoughts. Things had not been the same since the discovery of his Aramaic tablet. She had always been wary of unguarded emotions and distrusted the inexplicable. Yet, the inexplicable persisted, as if it were demanding a revelation. For certain, there was nothing romantic or sexual about her feelings. It was fuelled by an element of sameness and mutual understanding that went way beyond what she experienced with Fergy.

It was in the middle of these thoughts, because she was not paying enough attention, that Miriam lost her balance and stumbled over a projecting slab of limestone rock lying flat on the ground. Her flashlight revealed that her foot got caught in an iron ring that looked like a handle. Kelvin and a student bent to haul her up, but her foot was caught tight in the iron loop.

She yelled as Kelvin twisted her foot around and another team member heaved her ankle clear with a hefty pull. Miriam took a deep breath when she realised she was clear and uninjured. "What the hell is that? What joker put that there?" Her flashlight shone brightly on a foot sized, rusting, ancient metal ring.

"Wow, I wonder how old that is." Kelvin reached down, grabbed the ring, and twisted.

Nothing happened.

"Well, it must be there for a reason." He gave it another powerful twist. Something beneath it moved, but not enough to shift it in any way. They needed a stronger tool.

One of the team was carrying a hefty mattock – just what he had in mind. It was an invaluable hand tool, used for digging, prying, and chopping at the ground. It was similar to a pickaxe. At the end of the handle was a stout head, which combines with a vertical axe blade.

"That's perfect." Kelvin pointed at the tool. "Over here with that." Grabbing hold of the mattock, he attempted to lift the slab, but it still won't move. He moved forward for a closer inspection. "Ah! Take another look. It's a slab within a slab." He scraped the mattock head along a straight line, about an inch in from the edge, and all the way around.

Miriam bent closer with her torch. She could clearly see he was correct. Centuries of dirt and soil had disguised and sealed up the inner portion. "You're right, Kelvin. Try twisting that ring with the mattock as a lever."

Kelvin's face creased with amusement. "I'm not Archimedes. Didn't he say, *'Give me a lever long enough and a fulcrum on which to place it, and I shall move the world?'* With that in mind, this puny piece should shift. Stand back everyone and give me some room." He inserted the metal head into the loop, held the handle firmly in his grip, and heaved with all his might.

The sound of ancient metal giving up its life struggle echoed around the tunnel like a dog vomiting a bone. One last tug and the entire plinth shifted.

Silence descended on them all as quiet as the moon rising. They looked around at each other.

"Bingo." Kelvin broke the spell. "Listen… can you hear that?"

Several pairs of ears strained. Kelvin began lifting the slab. The sound became clearer.

KEN FRY

"It's running water." Miriam bent her head low as Kelvin and a student helped hoist the slab to one side.

"Miriam, quick! Shine some light down there."

A beam from her torch illuminated an area that had never seen the light of day for ages. It looked like a cavern with running water passing swiftly through it, into the direction of the Tor. It was about ten feet below the ground layer, and the gently sloping walls were of solid rock and limestone.

"The water doesn't surprise me," Kelvin said. "It's all around this area – springs and wells are common. I guess it must be coming from the Chalice Well in Glastonbury itself. But… what was this tunnel for and why the sealed entrance? It looks like it's been deliberately concealed. Why?"

"Let's take a look. As long as it's not slippery, we should be okay." Miriam made a move to begin a descent. "Kelvin you come too. You all should stay where you are and don't move in case we need you."

They all agreed.

They began the descent and upon landing, were happy to discover that the ground was firm beneath their feet. The air around them was cool and had no doubt been the same temperature for centuries.

"This must all be part of the underground tunnels and caves of the entire region. I've never seen it so extensive as this." Kelvin's flashlight shone into the gloom like a solar flare.

"Just a moment, Kelvin. Stop right there. This place was once used. Look!" She pointed to a large, flat ledge that stood proudly from the rock face. It was perfectly smooth and about five feet in height. She got more excited when she saw what was on it.

221

CHAPTER 33

They watched the stars go out one by one as the morning sun began its slow chase across the sky like a stealthy hunter. They had prepared for this moment, but emotions and sensibilities always had ways to overwhelm even the most intense of preparations. Judah, now a man, looked first to the sky and then to his beloved sister, Sarah. They had grown up together with their adored parents — Magda and Jah — as they were called, although they knew them as Mary and Yeshua.

They had known their time was upon them. All their life, they were told that there would come a time when they would return to their own Parent, God, who lived nowhere and beyond, and yet was everywhere.

This was their destiny and responsibility, and they had prepared for this over the years. They were now joint protectors of their parent's most precious secret. As Keepers, they would pass it on to the worthiest of their own kin. It would survive the ravages of time

222

and it would be a beacon of hope for all humankind.

Sadness sat in their hearts. Yet there was also a joy that surrounded them, for they could hear the soft whisperings of their parents ripple through the leaves of trees. Time and its fortitudes would never part them or their descendants. The link would never be broken. Distance would not matter. Even if they knew each other not, like magnets, they would forever be drawn.

CHAPTER 34

Rome, Italy

Cardinal Nicholas had the look of a worried man as he stubbed out his cigarette, finished off the brandy dregs in the bottom of his glass, and hurriedly limped from his apartment building. He carried his walking cane. Once more, he was wearing his mohair suit. The less like a priest or church dignitary he looked, the better. After all, it was not every day he met a convicted felon such as Cracker. They were to rendezvous in a quiet restaurant and bar the cardinal had selected. What could be more appropriate than the Roman version of London's Harry's Bar, where he had first met him? Situated on the *Via Vittorio Veneto*, it was an iconic rendezvous. It's interior, filled with plush and expensive antiques, offered the degree of privacy required.

The sources of the cardinal's worries were threefold.

Vincenzo's latest missive was an angry outburst full of hints of physical violence on the team leader, Professor Christi. The photographs he had sent back, however, looked promising. The professor could not be curtailed at this moment in time. There was too much at stake.

The second area of concern was the pope himself. Francesca De Lucca, the cardinal's PA, had whispered to him that she had heard it spoken that the pope knew about The Order of the Cross and Holy Sword. If this were so, then urgent action would be required to scotch the story once and for all.

Rizzo's recent meeting with the pope had now become more of a concern. Was the issue of the DNA discussed? If so, then it was possible both the pope and Rizzo could be drawing some unwanted conclusions. Rizzo was already on Cracker's 'to be dealt with' list. As of yet, that hadn't happened. When Rizzo was out of the way, for good, he had to think of the unthinkable next. It wouldn't be unique because it wouldn't be the first. The magnitude of such an action, however, was magnificent. He didn't dare to think of it, but the idea would not leave him alone.

His cane beat a rhythmic tattoo on the cobbles as he limped furiously to his destination.

With his mind swirling with every possibility, his thoughts were interrupted by the sight of Cracker approaching from the opposite direction. He was relieved to see that for once, Cracker looked presentable. He was wearing a dark suit with an open neck white shirt. He looked less brutal when not in his trademark T-shirt and jeans.

* * *

The grey haired, academic-looking man walked some distance

behind the cardinal. He was careful not to overtake him. His shoulders were hunched over, causing his Irish style tweed jacket to wrinkle around his lower neck. Age was catching up to him. A white goatee beard had grown straggly, which aged him a little more. Under his arm, he carried a thick, gilt-edged volume of the poetical works of Alfred Tennyson. He paused as the cardinal appeared to greet a man in a dark suit with a shiny head. They both turned into Harry's bar. The academic waited a minute before pushing through the purple tinted glass doors. He followed them inside. The interior had the aroma of expensive aftershave.

It was not long before he was ushered through an affluent, wood-panelled room, to a large, winged chair and table about twenty-five feet from where the two men were seated. He glanced up at the photographs of the rich and famous that hung from the walls. It was not often he found himself in such an imposing place. There were no other customers about. He quickly ordered sea bass and white wine.

From the corner of his eyes, he could see the two men had ordered and appeared to be having a serious conversation.

It seemed to be the opportune moment.

The academic opened up the volume of poems, which had been hollowed out. Within the hollow sat an upgraded GSM Spark audio listening device. It was his favorite spying product. All he had to do was call the SIM card inside the device using his smartphone. Once done, he could clearly listen to and record whatever he wanted within a certain range. The powerful upgraded microphone allowed him to monitor audio in real time some thirty feet away from where the equipment was placed. He called the device, adjusted his earpiece, and closed the book.

Inspector Rizzo, in disguise, now had a God-given opportunity to overhear the conversations of the cardinal and the man who had followed him – whom he now knew as Cracker. *How ironic. He went through all that trouble and here I am, yards away from him, and he doesn't have a clue.*

* * *

"I'll start from the beginning." The cardinal lifted a forkful of grilled beef into his mouth. "When you get back, do something about Vincenzo. He's threatening to do some damage to the professor who is heading up the team. It's too early for that. I need that man and his workers right now, so sort Vincenzo out in your own way. I don't care what you have to do, just do it."

"Ok, boss. I'll do it in a way he understands." Cracker smiled and picked a sliver of corn cannelloni from between his teeth. He never ate meat and had been a vegetarian for twenty years.

"Good. Now… a bigger worry," The cardinal's lifeless eyes could have come straight from the tomb. "Rizzo. What's happening there? That man's like a dog with a bone and I want him eliminated and I want it done fast. What's keeping you? He's getting too close. Him and the pope are getting too chummy, and the man's attempting to implicate me in the bishop's murder. I can't have that. There's too much at stake."

Rizzo kept his head bent low. He found it hard to believe what he was hearing. *Why should I? I've been doing this job long enough not to be amazed at anything. But here is a suspect, a cardinal for God's sake, meeting a man who he obviously sent to follow me. Now, I clearly heard him say he wants me eliminated. Accidenti! Phew! That doesn't happen often.* He had to see the pope and soon.

Cracker gulped at his overpriced beer. "Boss, he knows I'm on to him. I followed him the other day and I got spotted. No need to worry. He doesn't know me, and he won't know we're acquainted. He managed to give me the slip, but I'm getting to know his routines and habits. I'll get him soon for sure. I've got an Omega suppressor, that's a silencer if you didn't know it – the best in the business. I can take him out from seventy yards if I have to and nobody will ever know a shot has been fired."

"Please see to it and God will reward you when you pass away. Now, I have a bigger target for you. The financial reward would take care of you for the rest of your life."

"What's that?" He leant eagerly forward as a small glob of food spat from his mouth, missing the cardinal's wine glass by the narrowest of margins.

The cardinal pulled back and quickly covered his glass with his hand. "It is extremely risky and will take some planning. But if your weapon is what you say it is, then there shouldn't be a problem. There's no rush yet, but it's on the cards."

Cracker glared hard and tapped his knife blade several times on the edge of the cardinal's plate. "Stop pissing about. What's the job?"

The cardinal appeared wary as he cupped his hand across the side of his mouth, looked to his left and right, checking all was clear. He couldn't see anyone paying attention to them. "The pope may need to go to heaven."

For once, Cracker was lost for words or threats. His jaw dropped and his eyes held a look of incredulity. Not one to swear often, he eventually replied, "Fuck! You are not joking, are you?"

"Lower your voice. I have never been more serious."

Cracker's appetite had vanished, and he put down his knife and fork with unusual gentleness. He gulped heavily on his beer, pausing only to wipe a large hand across his wet lips.

Not far away, Rizzo's concealed listening device picked up every word.

It transmitted directly into Rizzo's earpiece. Rizzo didn't know who was more startled, himself or Cracker. He was eavesdropping on a potential plot to assassinate Pope Adrian. For a moment, he was spellbound with a sense of inadequacy, but then his training kicked in and he felt the reassuring comfort of the Beretta concealed around his shoulder. *This can never happen. Both of these men need constant monitoring. I'm going to need backup. I must get to the pope urgently.*

As the two men prepared to leave, their last remarks sent a chill through Rizzo. Both the cardinal and Cracker left the agenda open, agreeing to meet when it was time, and after the matter of Rizzo has been settled.

Rizzo realised it was now urgent to move the game up a few notches, and fast! He reached for his smartphone and punched out his assistant's number. Angelo Florentino was swift to answer, and a meeting for later that afternoon was arranged. Rizzo's next call involved using his and the pope's mutual Signal encryption app. The reply was immediate, and he recognised the pope's distinct accent.

CHAPTER 35

Glastonbury

S hine your torch with mine onto that slab." Miriam grabbed at Kelvin's arm and swung it in the direction she was looking at. The slab was free standing. It looked unnatural and far too smooth. It had to have been man made. "Just look at that..." She pointed to a familiar symbol.

Kelvin was taken aback. "It's another triskelion. I knew there would be another! But what's it doing here?"

"If we search long enough, we might find out. This limestone rock has been ironed out flat, almost smooth, like some kind of altar." Miriam leant forward to touch it for closer inspection. "When was the last time anybody touched this?" She smiled.

"There's more. Look at this." On top of the structure, he could see a circular indentation with a diameter of about eight to nine inches. Centrally placed was another iron ring, which seemed to open the circle. He grabbed hold of it and gave it a gentle twist in both directions. To his astonishment, he felt it shift. "Hey, it's moving."

This time, Kelvin exerted extra strength and the entire circle let out a loud, scraping sound, similar to someone treading on a cat.

"It's quite heavy." Kelvin gritted his teeth and gave it one last tug. With an unexpected *whoosh...* the cover came off cleanly. It was a perfectly formed stone circle about three inches thick. It could have been put there yesterday.

They both stood stock still... not daring to speak. The atmosphere was like a church congregation in silent prayer. In the gloom, they stared at each other, almost afraid to breathe. Without a word, Kelvin shone his flashlight on the plinth and knelt on one knee with his head bowed. Miriam could hear the soft murmur of what she imagined was a prayer. She didn't move nor peer into the now exposed pillar. She waited, and as she did so, she felt an emotion that brought tears to her eyes. She didn't know why.

After what seemed like hours but was only a few minutes, Kelvin stood and said, "C'mon, let's light up this discovery."

She gripped his arm and gave it a gentle squeeze. "I understand what you did." She didn't know what she understood exactly, but his response was totally appropriate.

"When was the last time a pair of eyes looked into this?" It was a breathtakingly illuminating moment, as all discoveries are.

With bated breath, she shone a powerful beam into the opening. It didn't look deep. She swung the beam around the entirety of the cavity.

"See anything?" Kelvin asked.

She peered long and hard before she scrambled backwards, her hand covering her mouth. "Oh my God!"

"What?"

She pointed into the plinth. "Look in there and pull out what you see."

He bent low over the aperture as she shone the torch above the opening. He stretched down to his fullest extent. "I've got something." He picked up an object and placed it next to the column and then repeated the exercise and did the same again. For a third time, he reached in. "This is the last I can see. I've got it… and out it comes."

It was Kelvin's turn to look astonished. Before him stood three inscribed stone tablets – not unlike his previous find but equally as stunning – a plain, copper-alloy stemmed chalice, embossed with a Celtic cross.

* * *

Later that day, the professor was glowing with happiness as he examined the finds. He estimated the chalice as eighth century AD and was certainly not the fabled cup of The Magdalene. This cup was empty. He got into full flow.

Miriam rolled her eyes and looked at Kelvin who only smiled.

Fergy began. "I'll get the cup carbon dated… there's a

new method available now. Why not C14? There has always been a problem with copper. When exposed to air, a natural layer of cuprite known as Cu2O covers copper surfaces. That can screw up the findings and cause possible damage. The new method is electroanalytical. It compares various corrosion products that form over long periods of time and works with only a few nanograms of material. So it causes almost no damage to the artefact. What's more, it's spot on accurate. So my guess at eighth century could be way out. I'm only going on the evidence of the Celtic cross. There weren't many of those about before that century."

"Prof," Miriam said with a drawn-out sigh, "belt up for a bit, won't you? I'm trying to concentrate here."

Fergy raised his hands upwards. "Sorry, Your Highness." But he shut up with a grin and poured out more wine for them all.

The tablets were again etched in Aramaic, but one of them, inscribed with the use of ink onto stone, was in Middle English. Miriam hadn't attempted a translation yet. She was waiting for Fergy's inevitable, irascible demand. She didn't have to wait long.

His impatience began to flourish. "This is an important discovery, but it presents as many problems as questions it could answer. We've taken lots of pics and now we need to know what it says. Get going on it, Miriam. Here's a lens, plus pens and paper. I haven't told our priestly overseer yet, but that is something we can decide on later. We'll have a drink while you are doing it."

"Charming as ever, Fergy. It'll be interesting to see how it matches up with Kelvin's original tablet." She began her examination using an eye lens, going through the words from right to left. Her first statement confirmed its authenticity as

Aramaic. It appeared to be written in straight prose and not verse. "Here's something that'll make you sit up and take notice. It appears to be signed."

"What?" The professor's surprise caused him to spill his drink.

Kelvin said nothing but gave an enigmatic smile. Miriam looked intense as she bent over the tablet surrounded by reference books and piles of paper. "Give me about an hour and I'll have this finished. I think the medieval Middle English will be more difficult than the Aramaic. I'll look at that later."

Eighty minutes later, Miriam looked up, took a long gulp on her third wine, and eyed them both. "Well, that's done. It was difficult. Many of the etched strokes seem to have faded, presumably with time. So you two, please do not interrupt me or say anything until I have finished reading it back to you. Liberties have been taken where text is obscured or broken down, but I sense my interpretation is consistent with the tenure of what was originally written. You'll find it startling, and I think it goes a long way to support Bishop Vincent's original hypothesis – that those unearthed gospels are ancillary works of the apostles, Thomas and Philip."

The message is on two tablets. She began.

Yeshua, beloved father, Mary, most beloved mother, it is thee we honour and obey. Our grief at your joining with the Parent is a sadness we must bear, but also mixed with joy. In this place, this joyful land, you're honoured and known as Jah and Magda. We sense you with us at all times. We accept your charge and your mantle. We shall travel when needed. With your blessing, our Keeper of the Cup, the never-ending blood and water of Yeshua will pour, heal, and spell your words and those of the Parent, known here as God, throughout the lands.

234

You spoke to us of nails, of wood, and your flesh hammered to-gether in pitiless horror in a land far off. A land we may never enter, which myself and Sarah feel so strongly for. Drinking from your cup cannot cure our sadness. Yet we must endure and rejoice in God's legacy and in each new cure.

The holy vessel will pass disguised through time and genera-tions. Each Keeper a descendant of you, Yeshua, and you, Mary the Magdalene, Keeper of the Cup.

Eternally, Judah and Sarah.

Three separate minds were entwined in a silence like drifting sand in a desert.

"Holy mothers!" Fergal's whispered response was heard and endorsed by the other two. His face drained of all colour. "It's unbelievable. I thought Christ's mother, Mary, had a cup – the one from the last supper, known as the Holy Grail. *That* cup is the stuff of legends. But this... this is new and would be a world shaker, Miriam."

Miriam's hands shook slightly. "This is telling a different story." Her next words came from a place she did not know. As she spoke, her eyes rolled backwards.

"Mae'n gudd, ond byth ar goll."

There was an immediate response from Kelvin. He stood straight... his eyes closed.

"Bydd i'w gael a byddwn yn dod o hyd iddo. Fy mod yn gwybod yn awr."

The professor looked baffled. "Stop! What are you two on about for God's sake?" His voice cut across the room and broke the interaction.

Kelvin appeared normal but Miriam was ashen and shaking

like a leaf. "It was a Welsh derivative, spoken by our Celtic Druids." he said. "And Miriam was saying, 'It is hidden, but never lost,' and I replied, 'It will be found, and we shall find it. That I know now.'"

Miriam appeared to have regained her senses. "But I don't even speak Welsh. This is getting spooky. What happened here?" Her scientific, rational mind had suffered a serious assault, but she refrained from saying so.

Fergal ignored the weirdness of the moment and asked, "How do you know we will find it?"

"It was an intuition, Fergal. It just seemed right. I speak Welsh, but I'm surprised that Miriam spoke it fluently. She says she had never studied the language. Mysterious, to say the least."

Miriam protested. "All I can say is that I absorb languages like a sponge. Working so closely with Celtic culture, it is not so surprising I spoke as I did. I pick up things so easily. Listen, hypothetically four thousand years old, Welsh is one of the oldest living languages in Europe. It originates from the Celtic language spoken by the ancient Britons and the tribes around here. The ancient names for the Tor and of Avalon signify that. Before the Roman invasion, Celtic languages were commonly spoken across Europe."

"If this plaque is to be believed, the implications are staggering. If it becomes common knowledge, this mission is over. Amateur diggers, the press and TV, will besiege us forever more. I'm suggesting we see what the ME version has to say first. It's a leap forward in centuries. What that tablet has to say will determine our next move. Father Vincenzo and his mentor, the cardinal, are not to know of this. The only outsider who will hear of this, at this stage, will be Pope Adrian. Agreed?"

They all agreed.

* * *

Miriam began a preliminary examination of the remaining stone tablet. She picked it up, turning it around in her hands. She knew that stone tablets, clay and wooden writing tablets, and even wax-covered wooden tablets were common writing materials of the Middle Ages. She didn't doubt the stones antiquity, easily confirmed by the laboratory. That would be easy. The ink used was another matter. Whatever was used in this tablet would have to be authenticated. The most common ink colour was black, which early in the Middle Ages, was made from carbon scraped from singed objects then mixed with gum and water. Later, black ink made from oak galls was used. It was the swellings found on oak trees where a gall wasp has laid its eggs. The composition became more refined as technology increased across the centuries. The stone she was looking at had been written on with black ink and that would have to be examined in the laboratory.

She turned her attention to the ink-written text. It was definitely written in Middle English, the language used in the Middle Ages. Geoffrey Chaucer's works, including *The Canterbury Tales*, were good examples of its usage. There were six lines of text. She copied them down and then read them out loud.

Atte chays et Chamelot sacren grund
Thilke ease whare quenes eterne cuppe kunnenn beade funden
Yette her et atte tor standen hin as defensens
Searce jette elles-hware street ant henne
Ant tyre in middle-seaxe canstow finden

THE KEEPER'S CUP

As arten opyn al ant ehes ant kepen nat blinden

Miriam felt a surge of excitement she had not known since her work on an early, unknown language discovered in Turkey. Written down, it was estimated at eighth century BC. She was now experiencing the same sensation, and all thoughts of Vincenzo and the cardinal evaporated. Her natural desire to learn and know had taken first place in her mind.

Using various textbooks, she began to translate.

I never studied the forms of ancient English, but I should be able to manage. What she noticed was that… whoever the author was, they were either badly educated or overly so. The text was an amalgamation of various ME dialects. In various places, the dialects rejected her attempts to translate it into plain, modern English.

After two hours and several drinks later, she turned around to the two men. They hardly noticed her. They were locked in a game of chess.

"Hey, you two! Attention, please. I think I've got most of what is written here. If you can tear yourselves away, I'll read it out to you." She sounded exasperated. *Men! We have the discovery of a lifetime and they're playing Chess?*

"Sorry, Miriam, you have our complete attention. Fire away!" Both men sat upright and turned towards her.

She gave them a soft glare, and began speaking slowly and with care, ensuring that the relevance of the translation would not be misunderstood.

The Chase at Camelot's sacred ground
Shows where a queen's eternal cup can be found
Yet here the Tor stands in its defence.
Seeker get elsewhere straight and hence.

And there in Middlesex ye may find
If ye open mind and eyes and keep not blind

Miriam beamed. Her audience had eyes the size of saucers.

"That's so specific. Does it say who wrote it?" Fergal looked stunned. "Middlesex! Hardly Glastonbury, is it? It's part of London now and full of noise, tube trains and technology. He spread his hands open wide. "The Chase at Camelot is where it can be found. Is this some sort of prank?"

"Well, it does say to get there and keep an open mind. I find it thrilling."

Kelvin held up both hands. "Hold on a minute, you two, let me check something on the computer." In seconds, he had accessed and navigated to the book page. He found what he was looking for. "I remember this book from some time ago. I have a copy of it somewhere at home. I'd forgotten all about it. '*London's Camelot and the Secrets of The Grail.*' Christopher Street is the author."

Both the professor and Miriam, with added interest, peered intently at the screen.

Kelvin agreed to bring it in so they can all read it. It might have information they can use. Maybe then the ME references would not appear so laughable.

CHAPTER 36

Rome, Italy

A thousand miles away, Angelo Florentino, at Inspector Rizzo's command, had started investigating Cracker. Interpol, on request, had forwarded all that was known of the man. Reading through the list of charges and imprisonments, he understood that his target was a dangerous prospect. He would be keeping a constant watch on the man and report directly back to Rizzo to determine the next steps. Rizzo was busy monitoring Cardinal Nicholas. It was tedious work, slow moving and boring. But Florentino was aware that Cracker was tracking Rizzo and it would only be a matter of time before he made an attempt on him.

* * *

The inspector took comfort in the fact that Florentino was never far away.

It was a Saturday morning. Cracker, wearing a pair of Nike trainers and sporting a grey New York Yankees baseball cap, eased himself out of his hotel and into the humidity of Rome's streets. Shielding his eyes from the sun's glare, he wore a pair of Ray-Ban sunglasses. There was another reason. He did not want to be recognised by Rizzo, who he was now attempting to locate. It was early and he guessed he would still be in his apartment.

His routine was consistent. He would first go to the coffee bar opposite Rizzo's place, and from there, keep watch. The interior looked empty. This time, he took a seat inside and ordered a large cappuccino. He felt confident in his disguise. Rolled up in his jacket pocket was another baseball cap, this one was white with a prominent red peak. It bore the name and label of the Boston Red Sox. Changing caps was a strategic move when stalking a target.

He leaned back in his chair and watched the adjacent building. *This Rizzo must think I'm stupid. He won't recognise me with this kit on. Today could be his last.* The comforting bulge of his shoulder holster added to his assurance. He kept his eyes fixed on the doorway, waiting for his prey to exit.

* * *

Angelo Florentino had been in constant contact with Rizzo. It was confirmed. Cracker's disguise had not been adequate enough. His lumbering gait was difficult to conceal. He seemed to have forgotten that he was dealing with trained police officers.

Using binoculars, Rizzo had little difficulty in recognising

Cracker in the coffee parlour, even with his baseball cap and shades. He had devised an action plan. A case file needed to be built up on both Cracker and also the cardinal. Telephoto lenses, listening devices, audio recorders, bugged phones and tracers would have to be put into place. The cardinal was a prime target and his meetings and conversations with Cracker would need to be monitored.

This morning would be a trial run.

Rizzo took several photographs of Cracker in the coffee bar. He then went to the front entrance and made himself obvious, feeling safe in the knowledge that Florentino was close by.

As I thought, he's taking the bait.

Cracker emerged within thirty seconds of Rizzo's appearance.

As arranged with Florentino, the plan was to lure Cracker to an agreed location, get more photographs of his activities, and gather as much evidence as they could. There was no doubt their quarry would follow the taxi Rizzo was about to call, but behind would be Florentino, following them.

Later in the morning, Rizzo had an appointment with the pope, and he didn't want Cracker knowing about it. To achieve this, he would have to give Cracker the slip. That would leave Florentino to continue his scrutiny.

Five minute later, Rizzo was in a taxi and heading to their agreed destination – 'The Pyramid of Gaius Cestius.'

A glance behind him confirmed both Cracker and Florentino were not far behind. *Perfect.* Five minutes away from the pyramid, Rizzo left the taxi and gave the driver instructions to go to the far side of the pyramid and wait. He would be no longer than ten minutes. He began to stroll towards the structure, a short distance away from the Protestant Cemetery.

Rizzo had always felt an enormous respect for the pyramid. Open only on a Saturday, it was a popular tourist attraction. The pyramid was built as a tomb about six to eighth century BC, for Caius Cestius, a magistrate. *An apt place to lead Cracker to.* Standing at thirty-seven metres in height, it was an impressive sight. It was built with a brick-faced concrete, which in turn was covered with slabs of white marble. In the Middle Ages, it was thought to be the tomb of Remus, and its complement the tomb of Romulus near the Vatican. Both men were hailed as the founders of ancient Rome. Later excavations proved it was not the burial place of Remus.

Every so often, Rizzo stopped walking to take a photograph of the structure. A casual look around and the baseball cap was not far behind. Florentino was well placed. Things were going to plan.

Approaching the entrance, Rizzo suddenly bent low. Taking advantage of the workman's panelled fencing, he made an urgent dash around to the other side and out of his stalker's sight. As he hoped, the taxi was waiting. He dived in, keeping his head below the windows. He then asked the startled driver to drive him to the Vatican. He was not going to miss his appointment with Pope Adrian.

* * *

The sudden disappearance of Rizzo confirmed his suspicions. Rizzo was on to him. *Where did he go?* He felt a growing confusion. *Police tactics are the same the world over. I'm being set up as some sort of patsy.*

Anger flared.

He knew another detective would be watching him. It was standard routine. Rizzo had vanished, but a second would be in close attendance. Who could it be? The front of the pyramid looked typical, with a small cluster of visitors and cameras pointing in every direction. He turned to look behind him and it was no different.

It was at that moment he spotted a man with a camera hanging from his neck, but with an exceptionally large tele-photo lens. He appeared to stop at the same time he turned around. *Rizzo's done some sort of switch. I'll move forward and stop again and see what the camera guy does.* Cracker began a cautious approach around the side of the pyramid and to-wards the rear. It was deserted. He moved to the far end and made a sudden turn around. Sure enough, the guy was there, and his camera was aimed at him.

Seeing that he may have been spotted, Florentino stepped back, out of view.

Cracker smiled. He checked his weapon, making sure the Omega suppressor was attached. He had no doubt the man was a cop.

Time for some fun.

He rounded the next corner and waited. The man swung into view and was on his own and definitely following him. Cracker lifted the pistol and fired a shot. The only sound was a soft *thwot*. The bullet cut through the woodwork close to Florentino's head. Cracker barely missed, but this time he did.

Florentino was taken by surprise, but not enough for him to reach for his Beretta. Nobody else around noticed what had happened. There had been no sound.

Cracker raced to the entrance of the tomb. It was open and still empty. He slipped inside. He'd seen the Beretta and knew what that meant. He hoped his follower wasn't calling for back up.

The interior of the burial chamber was a simple barrel-vaulted rectangular cavity. Scant traces of frescoes could be seen around the walls. Cracker wasn't on a cultural visit. Work had been going on for restoration, and in the corner, he saw a small table altar. *That'll do.* He launched himself behind it. He had a first-class view of the entrance and he would clearly see anybody coming in.

Outside, Florentino moved quickly but with care. He could not underestimate his target. The opening into the burial chamber looked dark and Cracker could be anywhere in there, ready to fire at him. He would have a clear line of fire in any direction. Florentino inched himself forward and hugged the wall to his right as close as he could. He stepped over a pile of scaffolding poles. He was now close to stepping inside and becoming a prime target. He mentally counted the number of strides needed to get inside and dive for cover. He reckoned about six. He practiced his move in his mind. His Beretta 93R could fire a volley of rounds in a sustained burst of fire. He had little reason to be afraid.

One, two, three! Florentino took the six strides at speed and dived into the open entrance. He hit the floor flat out with extended arms, his Beretta poised to fire.

Apart from his own breathing, the place was deathly quiet and there appeared to be nobody about. The tomb looked empty. His eyes adjusted to the gloom and then he glanced about and could make out the small table in the far corner. *Is he behind that table? There's nowhere else to hide in here. He must be there.* He inched himself forward his nerve ends taut and on high alert.

"I'm not there, matey. I'm right behind you."

Florentino heard the London accent and felt the gun barrel pressing into the back of his neck.

"I was behind the entrance wall." He snickered. Cracker

had learnt some Italian words, initially meant for Rizzo. This seemed like the perfect time to use it too. *"Addio maiale della polizia!"*

It was the last voice Angelo Florentino would ever hear – saying goodbye to him and calling him a police pig. A round fired and a supressed thud blasted into the back of his head.

CHAPTER 37

The white SPQR taxi, like a frightened rabbit, scuttled through the Saturday morning traffic. Rizzo had lived in the city long enough to know traffic density rarely improved. If anything, it had got worse over the years. He glanced at his watch. He would make it in time provided there would be no gridlocks in his path.

As they drove at a slow pace, he thought of the pope's quest to discover the truth of an ancient story, and the implications that would bring if found to be true. He was thankful he wouldn't be the one who had to explain *that* to billions of Catholics and Christians around the world.

Then, there was the Cardinal Nicholas problem.

The man was up to his nostrils in excrement, and the devil, Leonardo Rizzo, riding in a wave-making speedboat was heading his way. I wonder how Florentino is making out with Cracker at the pyramid. It will be interesting to get his report.

Heading directly to the Vatican, the taxi crossed the River Tiber on the Ponte Margherita and then onto Via Cola di Renzo, swerving hard to the right as it neared St Peter's Square. As usual, it was bustling with visitors and tourists. The morning sun gave short shadows and hinted at another hot day.

Rizzo called the taxi to a halt, got out, paid the driver, and headed briskly across the piazza for his appointment with Pope Adrian.

* * *

Pope Adrian was looking forward to his meeting with Inspector Rizzo. Uppermost in his mind was what was he should do with the cardinal. There was no definite proof that he was involved in the death of Bishop Vincent Fisher, although his DNA around the dead bishop was a cause for concern. Nor was there actual proof, as yet, that he was heading up a clandestine militant group. It was an issue he was planning to take up directly with the man. But first, he needed every bit of evidence before he could be confident enough to confront the cardinal with such an accusation.

On his computer was an unopened message from the SOTA group in the UK. He would examine it later.

There came a knock on the door and the *Camerlengo* announced the arrival of *Ispettore* Rizzo. He understood the meeting was of great importance and should remain private. He turned and instructed the guard to remain outside the door.

"*Entra, Ispettore.*"

Rizzo walked in briskly and the pope stood but did not offer his ring for the customary kiss. It was unnecessary.

"I hope you have interesting news, Inspector." The pope was eager to hear his report.

"I have news, but not good, Holy Father." Rizzo looked grim. He had in his hand the gilt-edged volume of Tennyson's poems, where he had hidden the listening device as he eavesdropped on the Cardinal's conversation with Cracker. He held it up for the pope to see.

"Ah Tennyson, one of my favourite poets, Inspector." The pope beamed.

"I'm going to disappoint you, Holy Father. In here is not good poetry." Rizzo opened it and revealed the recording and bugging equipment sitting neatly in the hollowed-out pages. "This a spying device. Recently, I had the opportunity to use it. I'm going to play the recording. Please brace yourself, Your Holiness. You may recognise one of the voices." Rizzo lifted it out and switched it on to loudspeaker and then pressed PLAY. Sitting back, he watched for the pope's reaction.

It didn't take long. The pope listened up to the end.

"*Santa madre di Dio!*" Pope Adrian's face had drained to the pallor of his white papal cassock. "It's Cardinal Nicholas. I can scarce believe it. We are being threatened with death! What are we to do?"

Rizzo stared hard at the pope. "Your Holiness, I suggest at this stage we do nothing."

The pope's customary calmness had evaporated, and he began twisting his hands and fingers. "This cannot be possible! A man of God! Who is he talking to?"

"I'm afraid it is possible, Your Holiness. I was there, disguised. The man he's talking to is a *Signore* Cracker, a convicted British criminal. He has been following me for several days. As yet, there is not enough evidence to take him in for questioning, as no crime or an attempt has been committed yet. The English have a saying – 'Give a man enough rope and he will hang himself.' This, I am certain, will happen. Right now, I have another man watching the cardinal's colleague, Cracker. Presumably, he's waiting for an opportune moment to strike. As he's Cardinal Nicholas's accomplice, I believe he is also the man who has been watching your archaeologists in England. The cardinal wants me out of the way because of my investigation concerning the bishop's death, which I now believe he was party to. I could detain him for further questioning, but I want him *colto con le mani nel sacco* – caught with his hands in the bag."

"We are in danger from this man, Inspector. How shall I deal with him?"

"Carry on as usual, as if you know nothing. Keep a record of anything he says if you think it relevant. If he learns of the details of our discussion here, he will certainly abandon his immediate plans. What he's doing is being done in the name of Christ and that makes him a very determined and dangerous man. If he's truly heading up a militant group, I wonder what its purpose may be? Do you have an idea, Holy Father?"

The pope sounded wary. "I can make a good guess. He wants to overthrow the Vatican and turn back the clock to the days of the Inquisition. Very well, Inspector, it will be business as usual. Feel free to call me any time and if necessary, I will contact you immediately. Do take care."

Rizzo stood, made a self-conscious bow, and left the room and a worried-looking pope.

CHAPTER 38

South West England

The team sat around a large table, which they had festooned with reams of paper, pens, books, and eBook readers. They were discussing their objective, its viability, and the relevance of the clues they had uncovered.

Fergal looked around at them all and sensed a mood of expectancy. "What we've found around here is beginning to add strength to SOTA's mission. The Aramaic is astonishing and it's authentic. Of that, there can be no doubt. Kelvin, your plaque has been carbon dated and fits the two-thousand-year slot. I suspect we will have a similar result with the other two here. The lab will be using the latest electroanalytical C14 techniques. When the tests are completed, I might tell Vincenzo… but not before. I'm still thinking about it. We need an approximation on the age of the stones first. Then I will share the news with the pope."

* * *

Miriam found herself increasingly wondering about the strange things that had been happening around her. She had an urge to abandon her scientific thinking and open her mind. Kelvin's presence had altered her perception of events. It was too much of a coincidence. If the tablets were as old as suspected, then it validated the writings of Philip and Thomas. *This was huge and could be shattering to billions of people.*

The tablets mentioned both Jah and Magda – the names the Celts gave them – but their true names were Yeshua and Magdalene, Mary. The tablets were signed by Judah and Sarah, their son and daughter. The implications gave her goose bumps. The evidence was building up, and it's not a good one for the Church. The tests on the ink had not come in yet, but she was certain it was written in the Middle Ages, around the time of the Dissolution of the Monasteries Act.

She turned to the professor. "I don't think there can be much doubt, Fergal, that there's an odd link here. The evidence is too powerful, and we must share this only with Pope Adrian. I don't trust Father Vincenzo or the cardinal with these new developments. I remember too well how he rubbished Bishop Fisher who was barely cold in his grave."

"I sent the pope an email and told him to check the address he gave me. When he does, he will find all the information he needs."

"We might know more if we went to this mysterious Chase, in Middlesex, as the verse describes." Kelvin didn't understand their hesitation. He knew they were being led there.

"Why would a secret treasure go there from here?"

"According to that book I mentioned, the Chase is located in Enfield. When Henry the VIII dissolved the monasteries in 1536, I guess who ever lived around here wanted the secret to remain so. To shift it to the other side of the country has a certain logic to it. I've made some preliminary notes and ideas. It includes relevant authors, locations, history, toponymy, early settlement, etymology, and anything else that might be connected. The author of the book suggests, Enfield Chase could be the true home of Arthurian legends – Camelot and all the other mysteries we grew up with… even the Holy Grail. Given what we have discovered, the author is not as off the wall as some have suggested. We need to examine the area before we make any other conclusions. I'll go myself if you don't mind. I have to see it for myself."

The professor seemed convinced. "Okay by me. What about you, Miriam?"

"I wouldn't mind going along. I translated the tablet after all."

"Fine, then. What's the plan, Kelvin?" Fergal turned to the Druid.

Kelvin smiled and addressed Miriam. "If we leave early tomorrow morning, I can park in Hounslow off the M4 motorway and we can catch the underground, get on the Piccadilly line, and make our way to Cockfosters at the far end. The place we are looking for is Enfield Chase, home of the Camelot Moat. It's a walk away from the station. By the way, early means I leave at four AM." He gave Miriam a smug grin.

She groaned. "OMG!"

Fergal laughed out loud. "That'll teach you!"

CHAPTER 39

H e's brown? What do you mean *brown*?" Cardinal
Nicholas sounded agitated. Cracker was on the
phone reporting the latest developments. The man
was telling him the details of how he had been following
Rizzo, and then lost him, and how he discovered that another
policeman was tailing him.

"Well, what happened?" Cardinal Nicholas demanded.
He only had so much patience to spare.

"As I said, he's 'brown bread.'"

"Brown bread?"

"Boss, wise up. It's Cockney rhyming slang for dead.
Brown bread, dead."

A gasp could be clearly heard from the other end. "What!
Don't tell me. You didn't!"

"No choice," Cracker's reply was phlegmatic. "He pulled
a shooter on me. It was him or me. I got lucky. He lost. I was

254

neither seen nor heard."

Cracker didn't mention that he had fired a first shot out in the open air.

A million scenarios pulsated through the cardinal's whirling brain. Rizzo was probably aware that someone was following and assigned the other policeman to watch Cracker. The death of his colleague would reach him. *God, he probably heard about it by now. The man would know who the killer was.*

It was too close... too close to me. Then he remembered that Rizzo didn't know of his association with Cracker. Why would he come asking questions? Nevertheless, the cardinal decided it was time to get back to the UK... at once! He needed to get Cracker there immediately where Rizzo could not easily get to him. Breathing space was what he needed. Rizzo's demise would have to take a back seat. Whatever... they couldn't be seen together.

Within ten minutes, he had arranged flights that afternoon and hoped he was early enough to jump ahead of anything Rizzo was planning.

The pain in his misshapen leg was starting up again.

* * *

Two days had passed but Pope Adrian was still shocked by Rizzo's revelations of a potential murder plot on Rizzo's life and that of his own. It was surreal. No matter how rattled he was, he would abide by the Inspector's request – mention it to nobody and carry on normally, as if he knew nothing. *It would*, he surmised, *be difficult.*

Later that afternoon, a small package he had collected from his private mailbox was sitting on his desk. He knew it came from Professor Christi. He slit it apart with his silver letter opener. He read and reread it several times. There were also several photographs.

Thoughts of the cardinal and Rizzo evaporated.

The contents held translations of both the Aramaic and Middle English discoveries and the clues they contained. Outlined were the procedures they had used and everything the team had found, and their proposed future activities.

God be praised! The story has to be true. Jah and Magda surely are Jesus and the Magdalene, and Judah and Sarah their children. Aramaic tablets in a Druid and Celtic culture says that there can only be one answer. But more proof is needed.

Of particular note was that neither Father Vincenzo nor the cardinal were yet aware of the latest findings. It would be interesting to see if they would report it to him, once they knew.

He sank to his knees and dropped into prayer.

The distinctive ringtones of his encrypted phone brought his murmurings to a halt. *It must be the Inspector.* It was.

An hour later, a grim-faced Inspector Leonardo Rizzo was sitting in front of the pope. He had informed him of the recent death of his assistant and friend, Angelo Florentino, who had been following the man named Cracker the previous day. He had been shot at point blank range in the back of his head. There was little doubt the killer was Cracker. A quick raid on his hotel revealed he had checked out the yesterday. Further checks showed he had left the country.

"God rest his soul." The disturbed pope made the sign of the cross.

Rizzo continued. "I attempted to reach Cardinal Nicholas, but it seems he is nowhere to be found. I thought it was about time I confront him with my recordings, and all the implications that it held, including his possible arrest. I spoke to

Francesca De Luca, his PA, and all she could say was he had gone away somewhere on archaeological business. She had tried ringing him, as so did I, but his phone was either switched off or he's not answering."

At that moment, the pope seemed to age by decades. He was devasted. "Things have gone far enough, Inspector. A man has been killed and there could be more, and that doesn't even include Bishop Vincent. Nicholas must be arrested."

"Yes, on suspicion of compliancy to murder. As my assistant was slaughtered on Italian soil and not on the Vatican's, any arrest must be made by us and not by the Corps Gendarmerie of Vatican City."

"I can arrange to have him defrocked but there has to be sufficient evidence to do so. Neither you nor I have that yet, Inspector."

"What exactly and how does defrocking work?" Rizzo had to be certain of every aspect to make sure any charges would have a chance of success.

Pope Adrian's mood was somber and his eyes had lost their warmness. "It's a function that may be applied on grounds of criminal conviction. Defrocking, Inspector, implies a forced laicisation for misconduct. Do we have that?"

"All we have at the moment, Holy Father, is the recording." Rizzo displayed some dismay. "It's not enough to implicate him. I have nothing else. No crime has been committed as yet, and there's a good chance the cardinal knew nothing about the murder of Florentino. It seems like an unprovoked attack by this man Cracker. The way it stands, any decent lawyer could get him off. His neck noose is tightening, though. There must be a reason why the cardinal and this Cracker both left the country. Maybe they're scared of something." He rubbed his face, thinking through the dilemma. "I have an idea," he said after a minute or two. "Your Holiness, can you give the details of all those involved in the excavations in the UK? I think I need to take a trip. In the meantime, should the cardinal show up, please call me or my colleagues in the force if I can't be reached. I'll keep you informed of all my movements."

Fifteen minutes later, Rizzo left the Vatican. His briefcase contained all the latest details of the excavation team in the UK, including Father Vincenzo. With rapid strides, he headed for his driver waiting across the Piazza. Rizzo began planning his trip to the UK.

CHAPTER 40

A t three-thirty, her alarm gave an unwelcome wake up call. *Is this really necessary?* She groaned. Even though she had gone to bed early, Miriam had found it hard to sleep. Memories of her strange visions and dreams of Celts and Druids gave her little rest. Unlike most dreams, they did not disappear once awake. Of late, they had remained with her throughout the day. It looked as if this day would be no different. She was aware, although she still resisted it, that transformations in her perceptions were forming. She didn't know the reasons and had no time to dwell on it.

She headed for the kitchen. On her way out, she stuffed a couple of bagels into her bag with a knife and a tub of cream cheese.

She met up with Kelvin as arranged and they started their long journey towards Cockfosters and then into Enfield Chase, which was located in nearby Trent Park.

"How're you feeling?" she asked Kelvin as he put his foot down on the accelerator and sped the car along the empty roads.

"Excited, there's a lot at stake here. There's supposed to be a druidic atmosphere around the place, and I can't imagine what we shall find."

"Me too. I already feel drawn to the place although I've never been there my entire life. When you spoke of it the other night, I knew I had to come. I felt the place was inviting me."

"Funny, that," Kelvin said with the concentrated look of a driver going beyond the speed limits. 'I had a similar feeling."

The dark sky had begun to surrender to the encroaching light of a new day. They barely noticed Stonehenge as they sped along the A303 towards the east. The hours passed by and the motorway approach roads were looking busier. Kelvin routed to the M25 and then onto the M4 before taking the A4 turning to Hounslow. Once there, Kelvin parked and they walked to the Tube station, both locked into their own thoughts and expectancies. There existed between them a common and as yet unspoken bond. They both felt it, but neither could define it nor mention it to the other.

The Tube journey would take about seventy-five minutes and it gave Kelvin plenty of time to relate to Miriam what he had uncovered "Miriam," Kelvin began, like an excited academic who had just made an awesome discovery.

"Iseldir," Miriam, without thinking, used his Druid name, "I'm all ears." She had to be, as the tube trains rattled noisily both over the ground and under, until it reached London city where it would be subterranean for most of the journey.

He reached into his pilot's briefcase and produced a thick

A4 folder. "This is where I have listed my findings, amongst other stuff." He flicked through his notes and found the file he wanted. The page was marked in red ink as CAMELOT. A large question mark can be seen beneath it.

"It seems local historians have been able to define the origins of the Chase from approximately the late eleventh and early twelfth century. That suits the age of our scroll and stone findings and fits perfectly with Chaucerian Middle English. The term Camelot or Camlet referred to a moat that I believe we shall see later today."

"Sounds very Arthurian, and that name – Camelot or Camlet – is definitely Celtic." Miriam pointed to his file. "Do you believe all that stuff?"

"Without a doubt." Kelvin was looking and sounding more like his Druid persona, Iseldir, by the minute. "Remains of Roman artefacts have also been found there. They're guessing it used to be a settlement or a strategically important place back then. There's loads of historical records of previous owners, from the early Middle Ages up until the present day. Accompanying these records are stories of buried treasure, hidden wells and dungeons."

"Indiana Jones is alive and well." Miriam sniggered.

"I know it sounds contrived," Kelvin said as he stared at the file, "but excavations in the twenties revealed an enormous drawbridge that seemed to have formed part of a castle, with thick, colossal walls. With that sort of information, it is highly possible that the holy cup could be buried in that place, if it exists. There's also a famed well that remains, although it's been extensively searched."

"So, are we looking for another similar well? If one existed, since that area has been thoroughly searched, they would have found it by now."

"That's what they said about Tutankhamen. I believe from my intuition, which rarely fails me, Miriam, is that there is something to be found in this place. I have a feeling that the moat could possibly hold an answer."

"I know what you mean, Mr. Druid. There has been too much of Carl Jung's synchronicity going on around us. I'm sure we'll discover the truth of that or otherwise." Miriam gave him a rueful smile. "So where are we so far? We're looking for evidence that Jesus and Magdalene lived amongst the Celts. What we have found so far goes a long way to validate that possibility. The names we have are Jah, Magda, Judah and Sarah, and of course referrals to Magdalene's miraculous cup."

The train plunged into the darkness of the underground and the lighting automatically switched amidst the rattling and noise of crossing over points.

"Yup, and that's more than anyone has ever found on that topic." Kelvin raised his voice to overcome the sound of the train as it sped along. "I've studied lots of odd things. One of them is the Celtic and Druid god of healing, Noden. Oddly enough, old maps around Chase refer to a Noden's Well. It could be significant and connected to the cup we're looking for." The sudden slowing of the train alerted them that they had reached their destination. They stood, and when the doors slid open, they stepped out onto the Cockfosters platform.

They glanced at each other.

"Our adventure begins." Miriam had a determined look in her eye. "Let's go!"

CHAPTER 41

Inspector Rizzo leaned his head back on the headrest and closed his eyes. He had had little sleep. His face was unable to conceal the sadness and guilt over of the death of Angelo Florentino. *It was me who put him in that position. I am to blame.* He attempted to console himself by thinking that dying was one of the hazards of police work. That was a creed that had been drummed into him since the first day he had joined. Yet, when it happened to someone close to you, it was a difficult thing to accept.

Flight AZ 204 was on time and the roar of the A319 blasting down the runway for take-off broke his gloom. The flight would be under three hours

With his Chief Superintendent's blessing, Inspector Leonardo Rizzo, in his business class seat, was looking forward to reaching his destination. They were arriving in London's Heathrow airport and arrive at Terminal 4 on time. From there, he had a car booked and was planning to drive himself to Wells in the county of Somerset. It had been some years since he had been in England, and that was with his previous Superintendent, when they investigated the fake wine and vinegar scam that had been going on for years. This visit was potentially more dangerous.

He knew charges against the cardinal at this stage would not succeed. The man, Cracker, who was working with the Cardinal on the UK project, was a different matter. It seemed a good bet that where the excavations were happening, there he might find one of them, or if lucky, both.

The flight was uneventful, and the inspector used the time to study road maps of the UK and the route to take down to the city of Wells. One thing he had to do when he collected his car was to make a call to an unsuspecting Professor Christi.

* * *

Fergal's mobile phone began to ring. He glanced at the time. It was nine thirty AM. Miriam's cheerful voice was a welcome distraction from his impending report to Father Vincenzo.

"Hi, Fergy! Just to let you know we've arrived safely and are about to go into Trent Park. Kelvin filled me in with masses of information. It's interesting and I certainly think we could be on to something here, but all we can do at the moment is snoop around. We need you, the others, LIDAR and the drone, to really search. How are things down there?"

"That's good to hear. We're digging at the other end of the tunnel where you started. We've got as far as we can as it appears to be bricked up. We were hoping to find a way through from the other side. I'll let you know. I was about to meet with our saintly minder and let him know a few things, but not all, as we discussed."

"Okay, Fergy. Keep cool with the priest and best of luck with the dig. I'll get back to you later."

Thirty minutes later, the professor was about to face an affronted Vincenzo.

* * *

The professor waited, as arranged, in the hotel reception area. It was a meeting he was not looking forward to. Five minutes later, an unsmiling Vincenzo arrived. He was dressed in a blue T-shirt and jeans.

He dispensed with any formal greeting. "What is it you bring?"

The professor handed him a file detailing their work on the tunnel, the triskelion, and photographs of the ink-inscribed stone, but with no translation. "Dr. Miriam has gone to London with our other assistant, to follow up some clues about a twin location of our work and see if there's a connection. I will let you know what they find."

"Where do they go? The cardinal will want to know."

"It's an extension of London called Enfield and a park known as Trent Park. It's all in the file."

"Where is this stone?"

"It's being examined at our laboratory," Fergal lied.

"I wish to see it soon. How do I know you will tell the cardinal or me what you find? You may be keeping things to sell and make money, for all I know. You pushed me, a priest. You pushed me hard. That says a lot about the sort of man you are."

Fergal ignored the insult, but he felt his anger rise. *This idiot is as thick as pig shit.* "Well that's something you will have to work out for yourself, Father. Goodbye for now." He turned to go but not before Vincenzo's hand had grabbed his arm and swung him around.

Vincenzo's face was flushed and scrunched up. Fergy was taken aback. "You give me no respect. I am a man of God, but you insult me. Where I live, you will make an apology or I can have retribution. *Capisci?*"

Fergal understood perfectly. He stared down at Vincenzo's restraining hand, grabbed it with his own and forcibly removed it. "Does the cardinal know what you are really like? I'm sure he would be most interested."

Vincenzo's echoing laugh was not what the professor expected as he strode out of the hotel. He knew instinctively that it was not going to be the last he had heard of the matter.

* * *

Back at the excavation, from the Tor end of the tunnel, the small team had unearthed a similar bricked up limestone entrance that the southern end had possessed. Fergal was certain it would lead to the other excavation site. LIDAR indicated it did just that. Even with all the activity, he remained uneasy about his encounter with Vincenzo. Surely a priest wouldn't act like that. Then again, the cardinal's direct verbal attack on the dead bishop wasn't that illuminating. *I don't understand these priests... men of God, hah!*

His phone rang again and brought him back to the present. It was a number he didn't recognise. *It could be a student.* He answered it. "Hello, Professor Christi speaking."

The Italian sounding voice surprised him. The English was good.

"Hello Professor, I am Inspector Leonardo Rizzo of the Italian State Police. I am driving down to Wells to hopefully meet with you. I'm investigating the death of Bishop Vincent Fisher in Rome. I understand from our pope that you are now in charge of archaeological operations, looking for evidence and relics. Yes?"

Fergal was taken off guard. "What? Can you repeat that?"

The voice at the other end did so. "Pope Adrian gave me all the details and I have some important matters I wish to talk to you about. May I see you tonight? I know where you are staying."

Still feeling wrong footed, Fergal found himself agreeing to the proposal. Once the phone was switched off, he continued to stare at it with surprise. The man sounded genuine, but he could easily confirm what he said. If he's for real, Inspector Rizzo would be the only other person in Rome to know of his links with Pope Adrian. For an unknown reason, he felt a flutter of excitement. *This assignment has more spikes than a porcupine.*

CHAPTER 42

T he first thing Kelvin and Miriam noticed was the tranquillity of Trent Park. In spite of its urban setting, there was something about it. Kelvin described it as spiritual. That was a word she avoided. Spiritual, as far as she was concerned, was a feeling – similar to when people spoke of miracles. She had always pointed out that science was full of tangible miracles, and with modern day technology, more so. Yet as rational and logical as she wanted to be, she was unable to dislodge an indefinable essence of something that refused to be categorised. The word 'sacred' was another she had difficulty with and here was Kelvin telling her that many people thought Camelot Moat to be a sacred site.

"Define 'sacred,' will you, Kelvin? Because I always have trouble with it."

"We're here near the well, standing at the edge of Camelot Moat, very close to it. Be quiet, close your eyes and just be still. You *will* get what sacred means then, I am sure of it. Something that is sacred is dedicated or set apart for the service or worship of a deity or deities or pertaining to something considered worthy of spiritual respect and devotion. It inspires awe or reverence among believers. Its flavour is often ascribed to objects, or places, like the one we now stand before. Go ahead, close your eyes and just feel your surroundings."

Miriam did just that. She closed her mind to all else and reached out to everything around. The smell. The feel of the wind.

"Now open your eyes. Is it not a wee bit different here?"

At the back of her mind, she understood what he was referring to. But her academic mind resisted. "Yes, I agree. But I won't be giving it reverence if that's what you're waiting for. That seems a bit primitive to me. I'm an archaeologist, Kelvin… a scientist! I believe in things that can be proven."

Kelvin gave her an enigmatic smile and nodded. "Then we'll just have to get some proof, won't we?" He continued. "I have a feeling that The Chalice Well at Glastonbury is connected to the well here at the Chase. Remember the verses telling us to get to the Chase? Doesn't it strike you as synchronistic that here we are at the Chase and in front of a well that so many regard as sacred? This is just not by chance,"

She hesitated. "I can't deny that."

"According to legend, this well was supposed to have sprung from the ground, at the place where the chalice that Jesus drank from at the Last Supper was rumoured to be located. Furthermore, the chalice is believed to have been placed into the well by Joseph of Arimathea. It's all hearsay and I'm not so certain any of it is true. They're mostly legends. My particular interest is the odd link this story has with the

Druids. The well itself is thought to have been built by them and that the water gushing from it, reddish in colour and tasting of iron, has been claimed to have magical powers."

"So, being a Druid, you've heard of these legends before? I don't believe anything without evidence. The likelihood of Jesus and Mary Magdalene's presence in the UK, though, is in the realm of possibility. The Aramaic tablets, the scroll, the triskelions, the verses, and the stones, are all validating the writings of Thomas and Philip. We just need more concrete evidence."

"Yes. We Druids have a lot of stories and legends. They're part of who we are." Kelvin started getting excited. "This link between Jesus, Magdalene, their children and the newly discovered writings of Philip and Thomas… they are potentially volcanic! And may not *just* be stories told around a campfire."

"That we have been pointed in this direction is almost unimaginable… but here we are."

"Look at the well and the tree growing beside it." Kelvin pointed to a strong looking beech tree. From its branches hung numerous scraps and small pieces of rag and cloth. "It's not just a tree."

"What?" Miriam screwed up her face.

Kelvin explained. "We Druids continued with the Celtic tradition. This well can be called a clootie well. The 'cloots' are scraps of cloth hung from trees surrounding a sacred well or spring. They were used for healing. It's a source of clean water and have been used for millennia, coinciding with ancient Druid and Celtic beliefs in spirits and nature. The Christians absorbed the culture, and nature, sprites, and local gods were replaced with a retinue of various saints. There are at least ten thousand listed. For example, there is a saint for travellers, another for cancer and so on. The setup is a disguised pantheon of pagan gods. Yep, it's good to see, even here in urban London, that the ways of nature, Celts and Druids are still in existence."

Miriam looked intrigued. "That makes this well *sacred*, huh?"

She got her answer. Kelvin had his eyes closed and his lips were moving in silent prayer. Her eyes scanned the waters of the moat. *Perhaps these waters are hiding the answers. We need our scuba gear.*

* * *

Later, they examined the woodland around the area. Miriam felt a familiarity she couldn't explain. Pushing back some low hanging branches, they came upon what looked like a clearing. Kelvin stopped and looked up at the treetops and beyond.

"This place looks like a Druid's glade." He turned a full circle to get a clear picture of what he was looking at.

"It's not," Miriam whispered.

"What?"

"It's a burial site." Miriam was uncertain how she knew this, but without a doubt, a strong sensation told her it was. Not wishing to appear unscientific, she added. "My archaeological experience tells me so. Look at the slight undulations in the ground and their length." She thought she had made up the story, but when she looked again, there *were* undulations that were almost imperceptible unless one looked hard enough. *How did I know that? I haven't even examined the ground.*

Kelvin looked. "You could be right." He walked a few paces. "Hey, what's that over there?" He pointed to an oak tree at the far end. "It appears to be some sort of shrine. And what's that at the base of the tree? A figurine?" He moved closer.

Her gaze was fixed on the small figure. As they drew closer, it appeared to shimmer in a dazzling white light that grew in size to form the shape of a bright, white-robed female figure. Around her head was a crown of hawthorn, white flowers, and red berries.

Miriam and Kelvin were transfixed. She couldn't bear to look at the apparition and closed her eyes, her head tilting back. In her mind, she heard gentle words – clear and distinct. Around her, she felt herself being embraced by an over-whelming sensation of healing love and comfort. It oscillated through every pore, blood cell, brain cell, sinew, vein, and artery of her being. It was the bliss of peace – one she had never before experienced… a state she had never known. A voice… soft, melodious, and clear, began to speak. She raised her hands to her ears. She did not want the words to escape.

Miriam, your heart is pure. You are our seeker and you draw nigh to what you search for. The Mary Magdalene, Sarah, our countless descendants… they watch over you. There are dangers for you ahead and your path will not be easy. Persevere. Walk on with your companion… never cease. You are loved.

The occurrence began to shimmer into a diminishing haze. Miriam reached out with both arms. "Wait, wait! Who are you?" There was no reply… and the next moment, the vision was gone.

She forgot where she was, who she was, and who the person standing close by could be. Her breath quickened and she gasped with every shallow breath. Only when she felt Kelvin's hand on her arm did a degree of normality return to her. With questions in her eyes, she stared at Kelvin. She was trembling.

"Did you see that, Kelvin? What just happened? Did you hear it speak? I can't believe it!" She moved closer to the tree, but the figurine had vanished.

"It's gone, Miriam. I saw her but didn't hear. Apparently, it's a known phenomenon around here. She is known as 'Our Lady of Camelot.' Many people think it's The Blessed Virgin Mary or the Holy Grail, which is why this area is considered a place of healing. Now, doesn't that tie in nicely with our own findings? With what we've found so far, I reckon it's the Magdalene and not the Blessed Virgin as many believe."

Miriam couldn't answer. Her mind was in a whirl. She mustered a shake of the head. Her hands continued to tremble. *That voice was real. I know it was.* She took three deep breaths – one for the vision, the second for acceptance (*she knew she was not imagining it*), and one for her heart (*she knew not why*).

"Iseldir," she began after a few moments of silence. "The voice told me that Mary Magdalene, Sarah and our countless ancestors watch over me, and that there are dangers around me." She looked deep into his eyes in earnest. "She said that I must walk on with my companion. Did she mean you or Fergal? Both of you are involved in this. And Kelvin… she called me by my name! Look, I'm a trained scientist and archaeologist and things like this don't happen, and if they do, there has to be some sort of non-spiritual explanation." The beating of her heart increased.

It was Kelvin's turn to look bemused. "Put like that, it is scary. I've never experienced a vision that called me by my name. What is this danger she spoke of?"

"I don't know. Maybe that man with Vincenzo, called Cracker. It could be any religious person who wouldn't want any of this revealed."

"The pair of them are dodgy, even that Cardinal Nicholas. One with a gun and the others with a holy cross and fists the size of a crusader's helmet."

Miriam shrugged and began walking back the way they came. "C'mon, let's get out of here and head back to Wells. It's too much to take in. We have a lot to talk about. I'll give Fergy a call to tell him we're heading back."

* * *

Fergal switched off his phone. He had been speaking to Miriam, who was on the way back but stuck in a ten-mile tail due to an accident on the M4 Motorway. *She seemed bothered by something. Glad they have made notes and taken pictures. Should be interesting.* He headed for the bar for a much-needed drink. There had been a lot of manual soil shifting and mattock work, but the next step would be the removal of the brick walling. There was nothing further to relay back to Father Vincenzo.

He was halfway through his cool lager when Stella, the lady behind the bar, approached him. "Professor, you have a visitor in reception. Here's his card."

Fergal took it from her well-manicured fingers. Embossed lettering on the card read: *Ispettore Leonardo Rizzo. Polizia di Stato (Roma).*

"God, I forgot all about him. Can you show him in, Stella? Thanks!"

A few minutes later, she returned, leading Inspector Rizzo to where he was seated. The man looked impressive. Fergal was immediately struck by his blue eyes, which were unusual for an Italian He was immaculately dressed as most Italians are, in a black suit complete with a white, open necked shirt. Stella introduced him and the two men shook hands. Fergal felt at ease with him. "A pleasure to meet you, Inspector. Allow me to buy you a drink. What will you have?"

Always the policeman, he replied, "Thank you, Professor. As I am staying nearby tonight and not driving, but soon to eat, I will have an *aperitivo*. A Campari and soda would be fine."

Fergal ordered the drink and went straight to the point. "Inspector, you have flown here from Rome after a talk with your Pope. I'm sure you're not here to ask about my health. I can guess what this is about. How can I help you?"

"Let me start from the beginning, Professor."

Rizzo explained he was investigating the death of Bishop Vincent Fisher, which was now a murder enquiry. Wolves did not cause his death. The lack of animal DNA and the presence of human DNA scrapped that theory. Next, he spoke of his conversation with Pope Adrian. "Professor, let me reassure you that the work you are undertaking for the pope and SOTA is safe with me, and unless required in court, it will remain secret. I have promised that to the Holy Father. I'm not sure if you know that the pope has expressed his concerns about the cardinal, who he suspects of heading a breakaway militant group comprised of clergies."

Fergal leant forward with interest. It was the first time he'd heard about this militant group. He suspected the Inspector was about to tell him more.

He was right.

Rizzo shared how he had managed to eavesdrop on a conversation between the cardinal and the man named Cracker.

Fergal's eyes widened. "What!" His astonished expression said it all. "He's the man with Vincenzo! Are you saying

Cardinal Nicholas has contracted this Cracker to kill you and the pope? Pope Adrian?"

"Not only that, Professor. We have strong evidence that this man Cracker shot dead my assistant and friend. I was his intended target. I'm closing in on the bishop's murderer, of that I'm certain." He pushed a photograph across to Fergal. Do you recognise this man? Is it the same man you mentioned?" "This was taken by me as he had been following me for days. I have here a European Arrest Warrant for his custody and extradition back to Italy."

Fergal stared at it. "Without a doubt, that's him, and as I said, he's been assisting Father Vincenzo, who I report my findings to. The priest is here acting as the cardinal's agent. We haven't seen this Cracker or the cardinal for some time. They seem to have vanished. What about the cardinal? Are you going to arrest him?"

"I know of this Vincenzo from the information the pope gave me. As for the cardinal, there is not enough evidence and there is no further proof he has committed a crime, but that will come, I am certain. Where can I find the priest, Vincenzo?"

Fergal wrote down Vincenzo's phone number and the name of the hotel he was staying at. "Here... I think you might find this helpful Inspector. I have to mention that I've had an encounter with this priest, and he did not act priestly at all. On the contrary."

"*Grazie professore, grazie.* You have been most helpful. Do not worry. I will call him tonight and surprise him." He grinned.

Fergal then wrote down his own details and those of his team.

Once he was alone again, Fergal took stock of their conversation and all that he had learnt. He didn't doubt there was to be a lot more action to come.

CHAPTER 43

Father Vincenzo felt a niggling unease. Two things bothered him. On a personal level, he disliked the professor and wanted nothing more than to punch his face in. Men like that he had disliked all his life. *Typical of university idiots who sat around talking big all day long, and always getting others to do their dirty work.* He vowed. *I will take the smirk off his face, the bastardo arrogante! I can't wait.*

His other concern was the news that Cardinal Nicholas, on an earlier phone call, had told him Cracker had gunned down a police officer and had fled Italy. He guessed he would find his way back to Wells. The cardinal couldn't afford to be seen associating with a wanted man and nor could Vincenzo. He didn't doubt that Cracker would find his way to him. *What then? Caution will be needed.*

A phone call ten minutes later added a third concern. One he least expected. This one was he knew, major. A voice speaking perfect colloquial Italian jolted him.

"*Padre Vincenzo, questo è l'Ispettore Rizzo della Polizia di Stato Italiana.*"

Vincenzo felt hot all of a sudden. *How did he find me?* Their conversation was in Italian. "Yes, Inspector, this is Father Vincenzo." He had to think quickly and not give anything away. "What on earth can I do for you? Has one of my colleagues died?" He attempted to convey concern.

"Not so, Father. I am in England looking for a man who seems to be a close acquaintance of yours."

Vincenzo's brain struggled for a reply. *He must be looking for Cracker. But how could he have known my phone number? Only the cardinal and the dig team know of it.*

"Who are you looking for? This is most unusual. I know a lot of people."

"Father, I am not discussing this on the phone. I am in Wells and I know where you are staying. I shall be about ten minutes and I expect to see you when I arrive. *Arrivederci.*" The inspector's tone was abrupt and far from friendly.

Vincenzo felt a tremor pass through him like an electric shock. The Inspector's knowledge and presence was baffling and highly worrying. There was little time to prepare, and the only thing he knew he could do was to play innocent and ignorant.

Vincenzo, to create the right impression, changed into his clerical cassock – complete with a crucifix and a rosary around his wrist. He made his way down to the reception lounge. The last thing he wanted was a detective snooping around his room. He didn't have to wait long, and a tall man soon walked in. Vincenzo knew it was him. He had *police* written all over him.

* * *

Rizzo spotted him at once. He didn't like what he saw. Coming towards him was an unsavoury looking individual clad in priestly attire. *Un lupo in veste di agnello.* "A wolf in sheep's clothing, if I ever saw one," he muttered to himself.

Vincenzo offered a half smile and held out his hand. *"Ispettore Rizzo?"* He asked.

"Yes, that's me, Father. Thank you for seeing me at such short notice." Without asking, Rizzo sat in a comfortable chair and indicated to Vincenzo to be seated. It was a simple trick to let someone know who was in charge.

Vincenzo looked wrong footed, but he sat down.

Rizzo produced his police ID and laid it down in front of Vincenzo. "Before you ask, Father, I know you must be wondering how I know of you. That's police information and will not be divulged, nor form part of this conversation. I'll get to the point. You have an association with a man I am seeking, a Mr. Daniel Cracker. He is wanted on suspicion for the murder of a police detective back in Rome a short time ago. How do you know this man? What was he doing here?" Rizzo's face had a hard look as he bent forward and opened up his notebook. "Take your time and think carefully before you reply."

Rizzo calculated that Vincenzo was not used to being roughly interrogated. His estimation was correct.

Vincenzo was tense and he couldn't help fidgeting as he wracked his brain for a reply.

"Inspector. I do not know about Mr. Cracker. I have only met him a few times."

Liar.

"He seemed a pleasant man. He was sent to me by Cardinal Nicholas to assist in the recovery and protection of any items our excavations discovered. A week ago, he said he had business to see to and would return later. I have not seen him since."

"You are sweating, Father. Shall I open the window for you?" Rizzo knew the man was uncertain of what to say. "It seems most strange, Father, that an eminent cardinal should use a known criminal to work with you on what I understand is a sensitive project. Did you know that he was a criminal?"

Vincenzo didn't answer for a short moment. Rizzo let him sweat in the cold silence. Eventually, he replied, "I know nothing. You best ask the cardinal."

"We've tried that, but he seems to have vanished too. Where he is, we have no idea. Would you have anything to say on that, Father? When did you last see him or speak to him?"

"No. I cannot know or speak about what our cardinal says or does. You best find him and ask him. I have not spoken with him for some time now."

"Are you sure about that, Father?"

"Are you suggesting I know more than I am telling you?" Vincenzo was sounding annoyed.

"*Buon Dio!*" Rizzo suddenly exclaimed, and the priest flinched. "What a thing to think of. Of course not, Father. We just have to explore all avenues to get to our objective. I am sure you can understand that." He closed his notebook. "Well, that will do for now, Father. I may wish to speak with you further and I know where to find you. Should you decide to go somewhere for a few days, I will need to know. Here is my card with my phone number. Am I being clear?" Rizzo gave a condescending smile and handed him the card.

Without looking at it, the priest placed it in his pocket. "Of course." His reply was strained, like a man lying at a job interview.

Rizzo stood and without thanking or shaking hands, he muttered, *"Buona note Padre,"* and strode from the hotel. He knew a liar when he met one and this priest was as bent as a foetus in a womb.

CHAPTER 44

Miriam lapsed into silence and she noted that Kelvin had a similar inclination. She was unable to shake off her experience at the Chase. Her previous dreams and visions were all connected with it and there seemed to be no room for doubt. What disturbed her most was that they were so real, but there was no scientific explanation that could be attributed to them. That voice rang clearly in her head and mind. She recalled every word and it hadn't been her imagination.

Kelvin had witnessed the apparition, a Mary-like figure. *Mary who? Mary, The Blessed Virgin Mother? Mary Magdalene?* She had never been *religious* in the accepted sense. What she believed was strictly a personal affair, and she kept well away from male organised, hierarchal structures. She had always viewed organised religion as a male dominated construction, designed to keep women in their place – behind a kitchen sink or in bed.

God was always referred to as a man. That had forever grated with her. Man was the product of a woman, a union of male and female. There was no dominant partner in the act of creation. These thoughts she had harboured since the age of twelve.

She thought of Karl Marx stating: *'Religion is the opium of the people. Religion is the sigh of the oppressed creature, the heart of a heartless world, and the soul of soulless conditions...'* She had a small sympathy for that grand viewpoint but never fully subscribed to it. There had always been stirrings deep within her that rejected that belvedere, but to define what those feelings were, she had never been able.

Her visions now confirmed in her an inner struggle manifested in a female form, both physically and vocally. She could not deny it.

Miriam felt a metamorphic twinge in her power of analysis. Somehow, things were not going to be the same again with her. Science and spirituality, and she didn't mean organised religion, were not going to be the same again. She never liked the word 'spirituality.' It had resounded with a wooliness used by those who disliked scientific explanations. Now she understood, and it didn't need an explanation. It was okay. She glanced across at Kelvin who was absorbed with his driving.

Without looking at her, he spoke with a quiet voice. "Better now? Don't fight it. I know it's inexplicable, but it doesn't need a reason or an explanation. It just is."

"I think I understand it better. Anyway, how do you know what I'm thinking?"

Kelvin grinned. "That doesn't need an explanation either.

You keep forgetting I'm a Druid. Remember?"

"How could I forget? This gets weirder by the minute. I don't know how I'm to explain this to Fergy."

"Only do it when you are ready."

"How is it you understand without even batting an eyelid? It seems odd, and don't take this the wrong way, Mr. Iseldir." She paused to gather her thoughts so she could carefully phrase the next bit of what she was about to say. "Ever since I've got to know you, strange things have happened that never normally occur in my life. In a strange way, I feel I've known you forever, way beyond my lifetime. That can't possibly have any truth to it, yet you're never surprised at the odd things that have happened to me. It's almost as if you were a part of them. I truly don't understand."

"You will. If it's any consolation, my own thoughts aren't dissimilar to yours. That feeling of having known me forever is no different from what I think of you. Nothing romantic, I assure you, but just a solid understanding of you and how you feel."

Miriam smiled. "Has this search for a mystical, biblical cup somehow opened up channels we never knew existed?"

"You, Miriam, are now finding out. I've known all my life, that there's something beyond this plane that we cannot see. Be easy with it and it will unfold like a flower in the sunlight. Never try and force it. If you do, nothing will happen except frustration and annoyance." Kelvin swung the car along the A303 route, back past Stonehenge. "Look, my ancient home." He muttered and gave it a silent prayer and a nod of his head.

She suspected he wasn't joking.

* * *

Later that evening, they arrived back safely and found the professor waiting for them. Three large scotches were ordered, and they began to relate the events of the day and what promising signs they had found.

Fergal held up his hand. "Whoa there, just a moment. There's something I have to tell you." He informed them of Inspector Rizzo visit and how Cracker was wanted for suspected murder in Italy. The case had possible implications for Cardinal Nicholas, which were highly unsavoury. The pope had been informed.

"No wonder we haven't seen Mr. Cracker. That's amazing and frightening too." Miriam shuddered.

"Don't worry, I don't think we'll be seeing him again, and Inspector Rizzo will be around for some while yet. I will carry on normally until instructed otherwise. Now, your turn. What happened at Enfield? Let's see what you got."

The professor looked at all the photographs and notes. He looked hungry for more. "These look great and you've done a lot of work and research. I can't wait to go there with the proper equipment. That moat looks ready for me to jump right in and see if I can find another casket of some sort. The name Camelot is to say the least, intriguing. I never knew of it."

Miriam had opened up her phone and was speaking to the Council for British Archaeology, of which she was a member. She was in luck. There existed an agreement with the Borough of Enfield. Provided notification was given, with responsible work and appropriate safety measures, limited excavations would be permitted.

Fergy agreed to submit the proposals to the correct person first thing in the morning. Miriam didn't think there would be any problems considering their mentor was Pope

KEN FRY

Adrian, from Vatican City – worldwide spiritual leader of an estimated one point two billion Roman Catholics.

The three planned to meet at the Tor end of the tunnel and open up the existing brickwork tomorrow morning.

Miriam looked at Fergal and knew she would be unable to relate her experience to him. She understood well that he would attempt to analyse it and ultimately dismiss the experience. It could wait for another time. She was certain there would be more to add to her story. She no longer felt afraid of it but was looking forward and hoping for the next one.

The following morning, Miriam, Fergal, Kelvin, and the other members all assembled at the Tor end of the tunnel. The limestone brickwork was fully exposed. They began to hack and prise at the stonework. Piece by piece, it surrendered to the team's steel and sweat. It wasn't long before a large gap appeared in the brickwork and they were able to peer through. With a suitable flashlight, it was possible to see what lay inside.

Nothing.

Blackness.

Fifteen minutes more of measured blows from pickaxe and mattock and the way was clear. Daylight flooded in on a darkness that had never seen the light of day for centuries. With the added aid of powerful flashlights, the interior became visible to the naked eye. It was clear that the tunnel was connected to the other end of the tunnel they had previously cleared. They made their way into the cool interior. A short stretch onward, they saw the shape of a square block of stone.

"Bring that light over here." The professor's excitement was palpable.

As the light shone on the object, his excitement increased.

"Look at that!" He pointed to the top of the stone. On it stood two of what looked like granite crucifixes. They were mounted on both sides of yet another stone tablet, similar to the others they had found.

"Don't touch anything!" Miriam was surprised at the strength of her voice. "This looks important. Stand back everyone." She pulled on latex gloves and asked for photographs from all angles and ranges to be taken.

The cold silence was interrupted by the sound of camera shutters and the faint noise of flashes illuminating the site. She and the professor closely examined the find. After a while, Miriam was holding the tablet, careful not to contaminate it in any way, and Fergal the two small crucifixes. With care, they carried them out into the sunlight. There was an air of exhilaration amongst the archaeologists. "Miriam, I think you have more translating to do. Is it in Aramaic again?" Fergal eyed the stone in her hand.

"It is," she replied. "I'll get these items back to my wheels so I can have a closer look."

From a secluded and unseen vantage point, Vincenzo, with his 16 x 50 high-powered binoculars, saw clearly what was happening. He could see their delighted faces and quite clearly two stone crosses and a plaque of some sort they were all staring at. He could make out vague writing on it, but it was too far to read. He didn't doubt the possibility of the find being kept from him. This needed to be reported to the cardinal. *The time is coming when I will have to take things into my own hands.*

At the thought of that, a surge of adrenalin swept through him.

* * *

Several hours later, the finds had been gently washed down in warm water, using both a dentist toothpick and a soft toothbrush to remove mud, dirt, and debris, before being placed on a drying tray. The etched markings now stood out, clear enough to read.

"Can you read that now?" Fergy looked eager, rubbing his hands together like a kid in a toyshop.

Miriam took out a foolscap folder, a lens, and began copying the script from right to left. "It's amazing. It's so clear. If our previous assumptions are correct, this script could be in the two-thousand-year range or thereabouts."

"What's it saying?" Kelvin broke his silence, looking and sounding solemn in the presence of the tablet.

After thirty minutes, she looked up. "That's about it. It's done. This is what I can make of it. Hope you're ready for this. It's shaken me somewhat."

Both Kelvin and Fergy gave her a reassuring hug.

She gave a small gulp and read the translation in a loud clear voice.

"I, Sarah, daughter of Magda and Yeshua, ask all thee that art unwell that ye will drink from this, their cup. So brothers and sisters, weep not that they are no longer with us. Be not distressed nor doubt, for their grace will be with you for all time. You should praise their greatness for they unite us as one and make us true human beings."

Miriam's voice broke at the end and she began to weep.

Fergy jumped up. "Why are you crying? You've done a great job."

Her sobs worsened. She managed to stutter, "Tell him, Kelvin. Tell him, please."

"Tell me what?" It was Fergy's turn to look baffled as he turned to Kelvin.

"Something happened at the Chase. Sit down, Fergy, and I'll explain, and you will see the connections Miriam's been having. She didn't want to tell you as she thought you would dismiss it all as nonsense."

Kelvin began a lengthy and detailed explanation of all the things that had been happening to her recently, culminating with the vision at the Chase. When he finished, he gazed around at them both. A powerful silence filled the cabin.

"Miriam, I'm so sorry." Fergal meant it. "I admit that things have got to me a bit around here. I've never been on a mission as weird as this one. I'm beginning to understand the pope's motives and all those involved. These are powerful visions, Miriam, and I know you wouldn't invent them. I'll talk with you later. That tablet is amazing in what it says. It mentions Jesus, Mary Magdalene and implies that Sarah was their daughter. It mentions a cup, which surely is the one we are searching for. So where is it?"

Kelvin answered. "It's either at the Chase or here somewhere. In the Druid tradition, the story of a healing cup is told, brought by travellers from far away, but at some place in time… it disappeared. I think it was here, but with the Dissolution of the Monasteries by King Henry the VIII, sometimes referred to as the Suppression of the Monasteries, it could have been hidden away, maybe in the tunnels between 1536 and 1541 – possibly by the Druids."

"Clearly, if your analysis is correct, Kelvin," the professor said, "then Mary Magdalene did not spend thirty solitary contemplative years in a cave at Saint-Baume near Marseille in France. There are those who believe that and there are shrines to testify to it. What we have found here debunks so much legend and myth. The discovery of The Gospel of Mary begins to make sense. If accepted, it would turn the Church on its head several times over. Holy crap! Think of it! It is possible and more than likely that they have descendants living amongst us this very day." His eyes were alight with his passion for discovery. "Wow! These are remarkable finds. I will inform Pope Adrian immediately before I pass this over to Vincenzo. I won't hide it and then we can't be accused of anything. No doubt, information will find its way to the vanished cardinal."

"Vanished? Where to? If there are no charges against him, why vanish?" Miriam looked puzzled.

In the middle of an explanation, Fergal's phone began ringing. It was from the Enfield Borough Council. A few minutes later, he hung up. "Good news, everyone. We can start a dig in three days' time. Subject to safety regulations and provided we return the area to its previous state when we're finished. That call for drinks all round. Let's do it guys!"

Miriam looked across to Kelvin and mouthed the word, "Thank you."

"You're more than welcome," he replied with a smile.

CHAPTER 45

He needed some space and time. Too many possibilities and scenarios were passing through his mind. At times, he felt a mild panic attack creeping up on him, but he was able to supress it. Direct action was the obvious answer, but with Cracker a wanted man, he could no longer rely on him. He could not take the risk of being seen or associated with him in any way. He was to be denied, if needs be, as Simon Peter had done so at the arrest of Jesus Christ. Right now, he had no idea where he was. That left him only one choice. Father Vincenzo. He thought about it in more detail and warmed to the idea. It was not such a bad choice. If apprehended, as a priest, any suspicion would be hard to believe. He'd have to be caught red handed for any charges to stick. *Besides, I have a sneaky feeling he might enjoy my propositions.* The world, for Cardinal Nicholas, began to glow once more and his heart soared… soared just a little.

With a feeling of relief he made the decision to book into another hotel in the area and make contact with Vincenzo. He did not wish anybody to know where he would be staying. It became important to change into discreet, secular clothing. His cardinal's attire was too conspicuous and would only be worn again at the next assembly of The Order of the Holy Cross and Sword. This was scheduled in one week's time – but not in Rome – in Firenze, Florence.

His net was spreading. Discreetly, he made a booking for a week at the George & Pilgrim hotel situated at the start of the High Street in Glastonbury. He needed to contact Vincenzo as soon as possible. The last person he thought he wanted to see was Cracker.

Once checked in, he barely noticed the delights the hotel had to offer, and that included his four-poster bed. He went to the bar and ordered a Vodka Martini. With all that was happening, he reasoned that God wouldn't mind the odd indulgence. After all, he was working for Him and his beloved Son. Once the drink arrived and he had taken a swallow, he made the call to Vincenzo.

Vincenzo sounded relieved to hear from him. "Where are you, Cardinal?"

"I'm not saying right now. I wanted to talk to you about Cracker."

"I thought you might. I've already heard."

"You've already heard? Heard what? Who from?"

"It seems, Cardinal, he shot dead a policeman in Rome not so long ago and hasn't been seen since. A policeman, Inspector Rizzo from the *Polizia di Stato* in Rome, is here. He has a European Arrest Warrant for him. He's staying in Wells and trying to find Cracker. He seems to know of our connection with him. He was very suspicious and is looking for you as well."

The cardinal knocked his drink over. He thought he was going to be sick. His trip back to the UK, in just a few seconds, seemed like the worst move he had made in the whole business. "Vincenzo, how does he know all this? It puts us in a dangerous position."

"He would not tell me. I asked him but he refused to say."

The Cardinal put his hand to his forehead. "This is disastrous. He must not know I am here under any circumstances. If Cracker should appear, you don't have to be too careful in letting Rizzo know. It's him he's after, not me. If he finds him, he may be happy with that and leave."

"Cardinal, the man Cracker killed was close to Rizzo it seems. He is not happy."

"Okay, Father. There are other things I want to discuss with you urgently. You don't mind some lively action, I believe."

"I enjoy it," his reply was immediate and reassuring.

"I'll call you tomorrow to arrange a meeting. How are the excavations going? Any finds?"

"You have everything they give me, apart from what I saw them find this morning. They have not told me yet. I watched them through my binoculars. They all got excited and hurried away. It looked like a crucifix and a *placca*."

"You mean a plaque, I think. Let's see if they tell you about it unless they are trying to keep it for themselves and claim a handsome reward."

"Cardinal, I have sent you a report. They are going to another place near London. It is in my report. I cannot recall the name."

"I haven't looked at it yet but will do so tonight. That will do for now, Father. Remember, you know nothing, nor do you know where I am or have spoken to me since I was in Rome. *Capisce?"*

"Si, capisco."

The cardinal powered down his phone. He couldn't stop himself from glancing around the bar area. To see Rizzo staring at him wouldn't have surprised him. *For him to be here means he must know of the excavations. I must not be seen. Meeting with Vincenzo is my priority. At least nobody knows where I am yet.*

Without thinking further, he ordered another drink.

* * *

Daniel Cracker experienced a sense of relief now that he was back in England. He had little idea where he should go from here. He had attempted to call Cardinal Nicholas but there was never a reply. There was no choice but to go back to him and then proceed to one of his favourite East London haunts, 'The Blind Beggar' pub. It was made famous by East End gangster Ronnie Kray's murder of George Cornell at the bar in 1966, in a gangland dispute. Cracker felt at home there, but anyone looking for him would know that's where he could be found. He made the decision to head back to Somerset instead. He had a bulging wallet of cash and credit cards, so there would be no financial difficulties. Easy access to Vincenzo in Wells was required, but not too close. His destination wasn't difficult. It had to be Glastonbury.

CHAPTER 46

P ope Adrian had been surveying the view across the *Piazza San Pietro*. He usually never tired of it. His gaze embraced the numerous colonnades, and the one hundred and forty Bernini studio statues that gazed upon both earth and sky. Forever in his view was Emperor Caligula's Egyptian obelisk, which drew visitors from all across the world.

This morning, his thoughts and feelings strayed away from his contemplative pleasures. They had a worrying edge. He had not heard from either Inspector Rizzo or Cardinal Nicholas, with whom he had to behave as if everything was normal. There was something else. His secret informers had hinted at a possible meeting of The Order of the Holy Cross and Sword next week, rumoured to be held in the city of Florence. *The forces of reaction are gathering strength and it can only be a matter of time before they will abandon secrecy and become a viable force. God Forbid!*

He couldn't stop thinking that of late, his prayers were confused – and that would not do for a pope. He had begun to wonder if God was punishing him for harbouring secret doubts about the Immaculate Conception, the various miracles, and other Christian concepts. He came to the conclusion that if he thought that, then he was no different from the far-right conservatives within the conclave and other places across the world.

NO, he would steer the course he had planned, and if successful, he would guide the church into modern, sane, clear, liberal, and open waters, where men and women would be on equal terms and footings. Patriarchy and matriarchy would cease to exist.

He prayed silently for the courage to push ahead. He paused a moment, inhaled deeply and then remembered he had not opened the package from Professor Christi in England. A few swift slices with the papal letter opener and the contents were revealed.

Whenever the professor's reports arrived, he experienced a tremor of excitement, and he hoped that this would be no different.

It wasn't. It was more so.

There were clear photographs of all they had found, complete with Miriam's translation and the possibility of the cup's location at The Chase in Enfield, a London Borough. Early medieval records believed that the area could be part of Arthurian legends – Camelot and the Holy Grail. The names on the previous files had astonished him and this was equally so.

The Aramaic was astounding and posed what would be uncomfortable questions for many. It appeared to have been written by Sarah, the alleged daughter of Yeshua and Mary

Magdalene. He felt close to tears, more so when he read the account of Kelvin and Miriam's encounter with the female entity wearing a hawthorn crown at the Camelot Moat, close to the clootie tree. *Could she be the Magdalene or Mother Mary?* His mind began to race. He read through further and the professor's own personal analysis was most interesting as he outlined Miriam's reactions and experiences to the mission generally. He didn't disagree that if this became public knowledge and with the finding of the additional writings of Philip and Thomas, it could bring many people to stop and think. That alone could cause a major upheaval in the Church. *This will need careful thinking.* He concluded that should this magical vessel be discovered then that would seal the matter. Much would depend on the result of their excavations. He wished he could go and see for himself, but his papal duties here took precedence.

In his excitement, he had forgotten about his secular troubles, until the ring tone of his cell phone brought him to a stop. He looked at that screen and knew it was the inspector.

Rizzo was never great on formalities, and quickly told the pope what he was up to.

"Holy Father, I've spoken with both Professor Christi and Father Vincenzo. Neither have seen or heard from Mr. Cracker or Cardinal Nicholas. However, I suspect Vincenzo is being economical with the truth. To a certain extent, he has lied. I am watching him closely and am staying at a hotel nearby. Where he goes, so will I. If you see or hear from the cardinal would you please inform me? It would be of considerable help. I suspect he is around somewhere and most eager to see how much advantage he can get from your SOTA work here. The professor is a likeable man and he has agreed to cooperate with me fully."

"Of course, Inspector. I heard a rumour that there is to be a meeting next week of the secret society he is said to run. I hear it may be held in Florence. I will keep you informed. I am almost certain he will be there."

"Thank you, Your Holiness. I will check that out and will speak to you again when I know more. *Arrivederci.*"

* * *

Using his laptop, Cracker checked hotel availability in Glastonbury. There wasn't much to choose from, and none was what he fancied at all. He opted for one, gave it a call and booked himself in for several nights. The George & Pilgrim looked like the best out of a mediocre selection. From here, he would call Vincenzo and devise a plan of action. If there was anything of ancient value found in the excavation, it could fetch big money in the antiques markets. A solid gold goblet would set him up for life, especially if some biblical story could be hung around it. He had to steer clear of the police, especially those in Italy. He doubted he could ever go back there. He had to wonder what had become of the cardinal and the detective, Rizzo. He hadn't spoken to the cardinal since he left for the UK. Cracker knew he needed to lie low for a while.

Once he'd checked into his room and unpacked, he decided it was time for a decent drink and headed downstairs to the bar. Dressed in a denim jacket, and brushed velvet trousers and loafers, he felt relaxed and comfortable. He ordered a large Tequila and soda. The pressure was off. It was in these more relaxed moments, especially with a few drinks inside of him, that he would question his motives and the implications of murdering people. He didn't give a toss about the religious side and burning in hell bit. What he did find himself thinking of was the consequences of his actions on those intimately connected with his victims – the wives, their children, and companions, even their pets. He reckoned he'd done about six altogether. This was him, at his most maudlin. In these rare moments he would feel a degree of remorse... only a small degree, mind you.

He shouldn't have been following me anyway. What else was I to do? Maybe I shouldn't have done it, but it's done now and what's done can't be undone.

He took a large gulp of his drink and savoured the taste and warmth spreading through his mind and body. Pulling out his phone, he decided to ring Vincenzo. It was then he saw a familiar figure seated at the far end of the complex, dressed in a black, rolled neck sweater and grey slacks. Next to him, his walking cane was propped up against the table. He stood to get a better view. Without a doubt it was him and not wearing his priestly robes.

He picked up his tequila, took another mouthful, before advancing across to the seated cardinal, who was absorbed in writing notes. Cracker moved in closer. The cardinal had not seen him yet.

"What's a holy man like you doing in a place like this and drinking cocktails?"

The cardinal visibly gave a start and his head gave an upward lurch. He found himself staring into the smirking face of Daniel Cracker.

For a moment, as recognition registered, there was a look of astonishment followed by disbelief. "Cr...Cracker?" he stuttered.

"I'm not easily forgotten, old fruit. Let me guess now... you're checking up on your holy brother, Mr. Vincenzo, or you're hiding from either the long arm of the Vatican or that detective Rizzo, or even all three. What's it to be?"

Nicholas's surprise was short, and he regained his composure with speed. "Mr. Cracker, you'd better sit down and quick. There are things you need to know right now before you say another word."

The smirk remained. Sitting down, Cracker pushed his glass forward. "Before you start, I'd like another one of this."

The glass got refilled and the cardinal revealed all that had happened since they left Rome, and details of Rizzo. It was Cracker's turn to appear shocked, when Nicholas mentioned that the inspector was in nearby Wells, had located Vincenzo, and was asking questions as to where he and Cracker might be.

Cracker's words spat out with fury "Holy mothers!"

This was what he wanted to avoid. He didn't know how the inspector knew so much, but he was starting to connect the people involved. *This is not good. The man is hunting me.* he wondered again if he should have murdered that policeman following him.

"See it another way, Daniel. It's a God-given opportunity given to us to complete the mission." Nicholas's words poured out like honey squeezed from a plastic bottle. "You know the area and your way around. Rizzo doesn't. I don't want Rizzo to know we are both here at this hotel. The implications would be disastrous for us. With Vincenzo's help, you should be able to devise a plan, locate the inspector, and finish the job. Do that and there will be a bonus for you."

Cracker wasn't entirely stupid. He sensed a desperation emanating from the cardinal. He wanted the job done and done quickly before the inspector discovered more.

"How much bonus?"

"Two thousand sterling."

Cracker gave the cardinal his hard look. "Make it five or no job will be done."

Nicholas noticeably gulped as the suggestion of a white pallor drifted across his bony face. The pause was not long. "Agreed. Five thousand it is but not a penny more. Now, we both have to contact Vincenzo urgently. Let's leave it at that. I want to make one thing clear. Keep away from me, for obvious reasons. I will contact you whenever needed. Understood?"

"Understood, boss." Cracker stood and moved back to his original seat.

Ninety minutes later, a meeting between all three had been arranged.

CHAPTER 47

The entire team and all their equipment, including scuba diving gear, stood within an area that was roped and taped off – the well, the glade and the entirety of Camelot Moat. As he didn't want another confrontation, Fergy had got Miriam to give Vincenzo the full details of where they were going. It was up to him to come along with them or wait for their report on return. It could take up to a week or more depending on what was found… if anything. Vincenzo elected to remain at his hotel but required daily reports. He couldn't tell her that he had other meetings planned.

* * *

The professor read and reread Miriam's translations of all the Aramaic and Middle English verses and writings. Once he had surveyed the area, he sensed that they were in the correct place.

"Miriam, what can I say?" He sounded apologetic. "You were right, this place has an atmosphere. I can't quantify it, but there is definitely something here. It's almost spooky."

"Speak to Kelvin. He'll tell you it's the Druid connection."

Kelvin pointed towards the well. "Look, Fergal there's a clootie tree next to the well." He indicated the tree with branches from which were hanging strips of cloth – some of which must have been there for some time. "It's an old Celtic and Druid healing practice. Let me explain. An offering of silver, a coin, or whatever, is dropped into the well. The cloth is then made wet and applied to the part of your body that needs healing. With a prayer given, the strip is then hung on a branch. As it deteriorates over time, so will the bad condition of that person who hung it there. They are still common in Celtic areas here and in Europe."

"Not quite up to the qualities of the cup we're looking for, eh Kelvin?" Fergal retorted with a smirk on his face.

Kelvin was on the defensive. "Maybe not, but it works, believe me. I've tried it in the past."

Miriam came to the rescue. "I think we should scan in the area of the burial ground before we try the moat." She was aware that she was allowing herself to be guided by her natural instincts. She was now beginning to trust them much as her scientific inclinations. She didn't want to sound weird in front of Fergy or the other archaeologists, but she could feel the pull of the place and had become aware of a soft repetitive whispering in her mind. It had been communicating with her since they had arrived.

Be still, listen and you will see. You will know, and you draw close.

She kept this to herself but would talk of it later with Kelvin. *What does it mean, be still, listen, see?* She had no idea and moved off to assist in setting up the LIDAR.

The professor had decided they wouldn't be able to use it in conjunction with the drone over the waters of Camelot Moat. The problem was water penetration. The majority of topographic LIDAR sensors used a wavelength in the infrared – typically in the 1550 nanometer range, which theirs did. They needed a wavelength that wasn't absorbed rapidly by water. That they didn't have that equipment. Scuba diving was more fun anyway, even if the water was not deep and muddy looking.

After a series of adjustments, they were ready for the initial passes across the ground. Miriam knew that the elongated mounds, twenty in all, were burial mounds. Fergy disagreed. He said they were ancient medieval ridges and troughs that had been ploughed up in the Middle Ages for crops. They retained their structure since they have not been ploughed since. The ridges helped increase soil depth and drainage. Obviously, previous excavations had left them alone.

She didn't doubt her intuition. She knew enough about excavations, although Fergy's knowledgeable observation was also right. A week ago, she would have agreed with him. Things had changed around her dramatically since that time, and when they had embarked on this mission. She felt compelled to trust her newfound instincts. It was as if she was dowsing, and the metal rods were in a mad spin.

She watched as Fergal made several lengthy passes over the entire area on and around the mounds and out beyond. All that was needed was now to process the information. Once the data was accessed and interpreted, what was beneath the soil could be analysed and accurately interpreted.

This was not a quick task but would definitely save them hours of unnecessary digging.

* * *

Kelvin and the others headed off for Camelot Moat. It was more out of curiosity than work. There was no doubting the spiritual pull he felt for the place. It was equal to what he experienced in his Grove of Taranus back at Glastonbury. He sensed that somewhere in this place they would find what they were looking for, or at least a strong clue.

He was soon standing on the banks of Camelot Moat. It was situated on the northern side of the park, accessible only by a solitary crossing point. It was an isle – and roughly square in shape. The entire area had a chequered history. For Kelvin, the well, the clootie tree and the moat, were dripping with Druid influence. The name Camelot was pure Arthurian and that couldn't have happened by accident. All around were groves and small shrines people had erected. Some were older and others had been made recently. All had been left with decorative items and ornaments. It pleased him to realise that the old ways still survived. Clearly, the place generated a wide-ranging spiritual impact.

Miriam, he knew, was blessed. She had had a vision of the White Lady. Some would say she was possibly Guinevere, or the Blessed Virgin Mary. Miriam had said she had never ever heard of the White Lady before, never having encountered it in her work. There were Arthurian stories that suggest that the White Lady could only be Guinevere, King Arthur's wife, and lover of his first knight, Sir Lancelot. Miriam had assumed that the vision was the Mother Mary. Kelvin liked to think that she was correct. It fitted in well with what the SOTA enterprise was about.

He had a small shift in his view of the Catholic Church. Because of what Fergal had said about Pope Adrian, he found himself thinking that there could be some hope for mankind if the great man was allowed to implement changes to various dogma, entrenched views, and agendas. He also knew that would be a dangerous task for the pope.

He stared long and hard into the dark waters and found himself drifting into some other realm of being. In front of his mind appeared a simple wooden or metal goblet, nothing special, but old... well used... inviting and comforting. It belonged to nobody but was owned by everybody.

In one swift stroke of time, for Iseldir... there was nothing and there was everything. He saw, he knew, the ancients had not been wrong. He was not a part of the universe... he was the universe. Organised religions or belief structures were not needed. Creation was wrapped in compassion and loving-kindness. What he had suspected since he had met Miriam and the professor flooded through him. He was connected to her. In what way, he could not say nor understand. He felt it strongly and she had hinted at it. They had admitted that they felt a connection with each other, but the origins of that insight they had been unable to elucidate. That wasn't that important, although he understood that something would eventually transpire. He resolved there and then to remain quiet about it until she raised the possibility.

He opened his eyes, and all was as it had been when they had first arrived. Thoughts and temperaments were normal. He stood silent, deep in thought. He was used to this and he felt no fear or confusion. In his sacred grove, he had experienced the same many times. They emanated from the *one original source* that was nameless – and he refused to attempt a name. It did not need a label of any sort. It was, is, always had been and always will be. He would talk to Miriam and even Fergy if he cared to listen.

* * *

LIDAR had revealed what looked like rectangular formations about five feet or so beneath the surface. Fergal began agreeing with Miriam – they looked like some sort of burial place. They decided to open up the first one and see.

With care, they gently uncovered the earth and soil, which was rich and fertile. The soil was sifted through, but nothing was found. Eventually, they came to where LIDAR had pinpointed the shape. It quickly opened up. A rich, unpleasant, and musty smell locked in over centuries, greeted the diggers who backed off quickly. What was revealed was a skeleton laid flat out, surrounded by various artefacts – some resembling weapons and body decorations, others were pots and domestic items.

"I knew I was right," Miriam exclaimed. "This find is precious! I wonder why previous digs had not unearthed this before. Just look at that…"

Using soft brushed, the team began busily removing centuries of dirt and damp. The finds were in remarkable condition.

The professor knelt down at the exposed remains. He became quiet and Miriam could see what he was looking at. It was a dirty but small metal slab, which was resting on the skeleton's rib cage. He brushed at it very gently.

"I think it's gold. Whoever this was, he or she must have been somebody of rank. They wouldn't be buried with what I'm certain is a gold piece and all these other items otherwise.

Can you hand me the bucket, please?"

She passed it over full of lukewarm soapy water. With careful strokes, he began brushing away the grime and dirt. He peered at it intently "No doubt about it. It's gold all right, and there appears to be an inscription on it. Here, have a look."

She took it from him, got out her eyeglass and examined what was written. In spite of its age, it had not suffered across the centuries and remained legible.

"Amazing," she said at first. "It's written in italic Latin. Someone must have done this for him or her unless this person was literate. Normally, only the Druids had that skill at the time. Perhaps, he was a Druid?" She explained further. "Although the Celts didn't have their own writing system, Celtic-language inscriptions in Latin or Greek alphabets have been found on Celtic sites all around Europe. Contrarily to popular beliefs, Celtic languages were still spoken after the Roman conquest. It's interesting that italic inscriptions can be traced back to the first century and BC periods, known as Paleohispanic. This in Latin and is simple to read. It says, *"Non diu vixit. Ei calicem me servavit."*

She looked at Fergal. "You haven't a clue, have you?"

He shook his head. "Not a clue."

"Brace yourself, Fergy." She translated loud and clear. "*I lived long. Her cup saved me.*"

There was a lengthy pause.

"Bloody hell!" was all he could say. The implications couldn't be clearer.

Be still, listen and you will see. You will know, and you draw close.

The words resounded yet again in her head. Once more, she covered her ears.

"You ok, Miriam? You look as if you've seen a ghost."

"Both seen and heard. She is speaking to me. *We are close.*"

"Well, she hasn't been speaking to me. What did your good fairy have to say this time?"

"No, she wouldn't, but I understand what's been happening around Miriam." Kelvin's voice cut across them both.

They had not seen or heard him arrive. They had no time to show him their find. It was as if he couldn't see it or couldn't care less.

"I've been to the Camelot Moat. I've seen it in a different way. Fergy, you may have trouble believing this, but I know Miriam won't find it so difficult after everything that's happened. Back at the moat, I had the strangest experience. Whatever you think, it was my experience and nobody else's. So, believe what you may. I was standing, staring into the waters and somehow, I got transfixed. Amazingly, in my mind, the entire universe seemed to open up to me. It all had to with what we are doing here. The Lady in White could be one or one of two or even three women. Of that, I am convinced. I'd like to talk about it all at dinner tonight."

"Fine by me," Fergal agreed, but couldn't prevent himself from rolling his eyes. *Did they have to be so dramatic about it?* "Look at what we found." He handed over the gold slab. "Yes, it's gold. Miriam will tell you what the inscription says."

She read it out to him, and his reaction was as theirs. Astonishment.

"What the hell is happening around here? How many more weird things and occurrences are going to appear?"

The professor stared at them both. "It gets stranger. I thought I'd save the next discovery for last, while you're both here."

Miriam and Kelvin looked at each other. Miriam exclaimed,

"What, there's more?"

"This." Fergy held out a tattered but reasonably preserved leather pouch. It bore the stain of years, and soil and dirt, which he had carefully brushed off. "It was under the skull and protected somehow. Open it and look." He handed it to them. "Handle it gently."

Miriam reached out, her hands shaking a little. She handled it with professional care and gently eased it open. The contents spilled into her palm. Her jaw dropped and she felt a rush all over her being.

In her hand were three long, rusted, and venomous looking nails. The heads of which were bent and misshapen.

"No! My god... it couldn't be," was all she could say.

CHAPTER 48

The cardinal gave instructions to both Vincenzo and Cracker. They were to meet away from their hotel. He needed the meeting before getting back to Florence for his rally. He had made bookings for an evening meal at the Crossways Hotel and Inn, in the ancient nearby town of Shepton Mallet. He chose it with a certain sense of irony. The town once had a prison which was believed to be haunted. The prison closed a few years back. The hotel was far away enough to be out of Inspector Rizzo's sights.

Vincenzo had with him a printout of the professor's previous discoveries, but it all seemed like *torta nei cielo* – or to use the English expression, 'pie in the sky.' When he left his hotel, he had not been inclined to inform Rizzo of his evening plans as he had been instructed to.

Emerging stealthily from his hotel, and dressed in secular attire, he stepped out, stealing glances in every direction.

There was no sign of the inspector. Cautiously, he made his way to his pickup truck. Satisfied there was nobody about, he fired up and began the four miles plus journey to the Crossways Hotel.

It should be an interesting evening. At last, some action appears to be on the way.

* * *

Unseen, and standing from his hotel window, one hundred yards from Vincenzo's, there was a smile on the face of Inspector Rizzo. He stared through his high-powered binoculars at the departing truck. There was no rush. He had guessed that Vincenzo would not be telling him of his movements. The magnetic, car-tracking device he had lodged under the rear wheel arch of the truck took good care of that situation. He could locate him when he wanted, anywhere he went. The device automatically started reporting its location and Vincenzo's speed. GPS live software transmitted all he needed to know, direct to his smartphone. It didn't take long, and his phone showed him that the priest's vehicle had stopped. He checked the coordinates and decided to drive across to the town of Shepton Mallet.

I don't have to be a mind reader to know whom he might be meeting.

Ten minutes later, complete with his cell phone and loaded Beretta, he set off to the town. He had one major observation. He would be unable to arrest Cracker unless he had UK police assistance and written authority. In the sequence of events, this was one point he had overlooked. He would have to explain it to the UK police very quickly or nothing would be achieved. Red tape was the same the world over. He would need their assistance. He arrived in Shepton Mallet without a fuss, and the GPS was registering the exact location of the meeting – The Crossways Inn and Hotel. The red pickup truck was clearly visible in the car park. Rizzo had nothing else to go on. He was alone, with no backup, and the worst thing that could happen is that he would be seen. That would blow the entire operation. He moved slowly to the bar entrance, opened the door and peered in. They were not in the bar. It was a good guess they had moved to the dining area. A quick glance confirmed his guess was correct. Sitting in the far corner, he recognised all three engaged in earnest conversation. Ah! *Vorrei poter essere una mosca sul muro.* At times like this, he wished he could be a fly on the wall. It was not to be. This had to be approached in stages.

He ordered a beer and out of sight, he slid into a corner seat. It could be a long wait. He wanted to discover where Cracker was staying. From there, he could coordinate his arrest warrant with legal and physical back up from the UK judiciary. Cracker could be detained in a UK jail until the paperwork came through. He could then be extradited legally.

* * *

The cardinal was in an explosive mood. He reasoned that timing was of the utmost importance.

"You two, I have to be back in Italy in a few days' time, so our timing has to be coordinated in every respect. I am not to be seen with you. I will leave here without you. Cracker, keep close to Father Vincenzo, but not at your hotels. Rizzo is somewhere around here, and this is your big chance to complete your job. I want it done quickly. I'm certain he suspects me of being connected with Bishop Fisher's death. That won't do. God has plans for me and this is His work I am entrusting to you." He glared intently at the two men.

Cracker looked faintly embarrassed. Doing God's work was not how he saw it. He looked across at Vincenzo. "We need to lure him somehow, but not at the hotel. Father, you must set the trap. Alert me and I will do what is required. What about that place, the glade where those archaeologists were last? Get him there with some story and I'll be waiting for him."

"Leave it to me," Vincenzo said, "and I'll do what is necessary. Ok?"

"Fine, Father, but don't take too long. I'd like it done some time in the next seven days.

Vincenzo shrugged. "He's watching me closely. I think I know how to do this. We both have guns, and this should not be too difficult, yes? This is what we will do..."

They bent close together as he outlined his plan.

* * *

Forty-three minutes later, Inspector Rizzo ducked his head low behind a menu folder as he watched all three get up and leave. Vincenzo was the least of his concerns. He knew where he was lodging. What he wanted was to know where Cracker was staying. That would be useful. He was expecting the police and judiciary permission any day soon. With that in hand and a small backup team, getting to Cracker would be simple.

He waited a moment before getting into his car and watched all three drive off in their separate vehicles. Cracker was the last of the three. He followed them. Driving through Wells, he watched Vincenzo parking at his hotel and Cracker was a short distance behind the cardinal. They were both heading for Glastonbury.

Once in the town, Rizzo was surprised to see both cars come to a halt some distance from each other. He could see Cardinal Nicholas disembark from his vehicle and head into the George & Pilgrim hotel.

His surprise continued as after a few minutes, Cracker emerged from his car and entered the same hotel. *They are obviously playing a 'we are not connected game.' Clever, but now I know. It makes life much easier for me.*

Rizzo sat there for an hour and nobody left. This was definitely where they were both staying. He turned his car about and headed back to his own hotel. This was going better than he had had expected. Once apprehended, Cracker would be imprisoned until the arrest warrant process was completed.

CHAPTER 49

His encrypted smartphone bleeped twice. He looked at it. Pope Adrian felt a small flutter of excitement touch his heart. Messages from his SOTA team in the UK had, of late, the enjoyable effect of lifting his morale and general well-being. Their discoveries were intriguing and provided a rare excitement in his round of religious duties and dictates. He checked the backup on his desktop and the exact configuration was there. He opened it up. The first thing he did was read it through. Professor Christi's message was precise and direct. It made a quick summary of the events that had led them to their location in London's outskirts – and the significance and symbolism behind names, locations and Arthurian legends concerning such things as the Holy Grail. The message spared nothing. It told of Miriam and Kelvin's experiences, and how Miriam, as a scientist, had a few issues in the beginning, but now accepted them as something beyond science.

The Pope paused his reading and sat back in his chair with a deep breath. He didn't doubt the experiences they were having. It was for him, not unexpected, but part of a gathering body of events and evidence that were moving into his orbit of beliefs and suspicions. He carried on reading. He was astonished when he came to the part about the skeleton and the gold inscription. *It clearly states that a healing cup had prolonged his life.* More tantalizing evidence… and finally, God be praised… three nails!

He looked at several photographs attached to the message. He enlarged them to maximum. There were shots of the skeleton and the skull, all taken from various angles. There were more photographs of the gold plaque and the nails, clear and unequivocal, including the Latin inscription, '*Non diu vixit. El calicem me servavit.*' Miriam's translation accompanied it. *I lived long. Her cup saved me.*

The nails from Christ's flesh was said to have been extracted by Joseph of Arimathea. The tale of Jesus and the Magdalene living in the UK, and the healing cup, had grown stronger as the team discovered more. But this! Three nails! *This cannot all be coincidence.*

What Pope Adrian saw – the gold plaque, the nails, and the dilapidated leather purse, gave rise to an inevitable question… *Could the skeleton be the remains of Joseph of Arimathea?*

The pope's eyes filled with tears and wonderment.

Here was a serious case that required further investigation. He knew he would have support from various quarters, but again he knew there existed an even stronger faction of deeply conservative diehards within the Church, who wouldn't have looked out of place as the scheming Pharisees in Jesus's time.

Across his middle-aged face, a grimace appeared. For one

unexpected moment, his vision blurred, and a sudden sharp pain erupted through his stomach and bowels. It went as quickly as it had appeared.

"*Devono essere le sardine e le acciughe che ho mangiato a colazione.*" His stomach gave another short burst. *It definitely must be the sardines and anchovies I had for breakfast.* He noticed he was breathing faster than usual.

He observed it for a moment and decided it made him uncomfortable. Pressing the buzzer beneath his desk, he summoned his chamberlain. He would ask him to call his doctor just to check and make certain nothing was amiss. As the leader of the world's Catholics, he had sworn that he would entrust his health to his doctors, who he knew were guided by God. Whilst he took his health seriously, it seemed of little matter at that moment... the Holy Father was full of SOTA's discoveries. They were sensational. All that was needed was the final prize – the blessed cup itself. The world would be turned upside down.

He made a silent prayer to God that it should be found for the good of all men and the approaching end of days.

His overwhelming euphoria was interrupted by thoughts of Cardinal Nicholas. He had received no messages from Inspector Rizzo, and his instructions were for the pope to carry on with him as usual. He knew he might find that difficult, but it would have to be done.

The intercom buzzed. The doctor had arrived.

CHAPTER 50

The Waltzing Matilda ring tone of his cell phone reminded the professor that he was in the real world. Vincenzo's sing song English voice left no doubt who it was. His demanding tone ensured he was never going to be friends with him. His call was terse and to the point.

"Professor Christi, what have you found today?"

Fergal had decided to tell him everything except for the implications of the find. He doubted whether Vincenzo had the imagination to make the connections. That would be up to the cardinal. He told him of a skeleton, a gold plaque, its Latin inscription, and a bag of rusty nails.

The mention of gold got Vincenzo's attention faster than the hounds of hell. "Gold! I must see it. What does the inscription say?"

Fergal read out the Latin but offered no translation.

"Do nothing but keep it safe. I must tell Cardinal Nicholas.

He will understand what it says. He will want to examine it. I will call him."

"No problem, Father. What about the old nails?" Fergal knew what his response would be.

"Not too worried about those sorts of things, but the gold plaque is interesting. Keep them safe and I will let you know what he says."

The professor agreed, and Miriam, who was listening in, agreed with a nod of her head.

"Will do, Father. Catch me later." He turned to Miriam. "What surprises me is that neither of those two slime balls know anything of the rules and regulations we archaeologists are required to adhere to. Perhaps we should have informed them. They should know that we are not allowed to keep or make cash out of anything we find. Every single thing an archaeologist finds must be recorded. Whilst on site, we field archaeologists carefully clean, label and number all finds, and then they are examined by specialists. The gold we have discovered, the rusted nails, the inscriptions, and parchments work, will be carefully conserved. Any environmental evidence, such as residues from containers, seeds and pollen are separated and analysed in a laboratory. Once reports have been produced for all the finds on site, the physical evidence is sent to an archive, usually at a local or regional museum, where they will be made available for future study. Exceptional finds are usually put on display in a major museum. What will happen to our finds, we will have to wait and see. Those two creeps think they can take them away. Not a chance in hell."

"What of the pope? He's funding all this. Does he get a claim?"

"I don't know the answer to that one, Miriam. This is unprecedented. We'll have to wait and see."

* * *

He had three phone calls to make – one was to Cracker, the other to Cardinal Nicholas, and the final one to Rizzo. He called Cracker first.

"They've found gold. They are going to let me look when they get back."

"Do we snitch it?" Cracker was way ahead of himself.

"Not yet. We have a few other things to consider, like Rizzo and that professor and his woman."

"Okay, let's do Rizzo. How do we do it?"

"I'll get him to that lake place the professor and his friends went to. You will be there and we both have guns. Should be easy. I'll try for tomorrow and I will let you know, of course. Be ready."

His next call was to the cardinal.

Cardinal Nicholas answered the phone. His tone was guarded.

"Father Vincenzo, good news, I trust?"

"*Si eminenza*. They have found a gold tablet with an inscription that they are cleaning it. They will send me photographs of it and you will understand what it says." He made no mention of the rusty nails. "I have other news for you. Our plans are prepared and ready to act upon tomorrow. This time tomorrow, my Cardinal, your wishes will have been carried out and your fears will have vanished like a bad dream. God be praised!"

"God be praised! Indeed, Christ be praised!"

By the tone of the cardinal's voice, Vincenzo needed only to imagine the great joy he must be feeling.

Before his next call, he sat back in his chair and thought carefully about how he was to go about it. It had to be believable and enticing. He knew the Inspector was no fool. After about half an hour, he had worked it through. With some trepidation, he dialled Rizzo's number.

* * *

The caller's name came as no real surprise to Inspector Rizzo. He knew his presence in the area was unnerving for Vincenzo, Cardinal Nicholas, and Daniel Cracker. He was forcing their hand. Not for one moment did he doubt there would be trouble on its way. *They must all know where I am and have a good idea what I'm here for.*

He answered this phone. "Father Vincenzo, this is Inspector Rizzo speaking. What can I do for you?"

Vincenzo's voice had a nervous edge to it. "Inspector, glad you are there. I have discovered some interesting information concerning the man Cracker, who you are looking for."

"Oh yes? And what might that be?" The inspector was unable to conceal a wry smile. They had no idea that he knew where they all were, and their plans for him. He would go along with them up to a point, and then things would get unpleasant.

"As you may know, we are conducting an important archaeological exploration around here, to discover the truth in a story that Christ once lived in these areas. Do you know that story? Well, Inspector, we have located a site near a small lake nearby where items have been found. The man, this Cracker, was in Italy a short while back, and we know he got to hear of this. Such items, I heard there's gold, would be most valuable

323

on the open market. Yes?"

Rizzo held back. Vincenzo's story was ridiculous, and full of holes, but he went along with it. Cleary the cardinal was up to his eyeballs in the plot. *I need some information from Professor Christi and the pope himself, possibly.*

"Do you know what was found?"

"Gold bars, I hear." Vincenzo lied.

Rizzo knew a separate dig was being conducted in the outer London area, and a long distance from Glastonbury environs. A simple call to the professor would confirm if the priest was telling the truth. Pretending he knew nothing, he asked, "Where are these items being discovered?"

"As I said earlier, Inspector, in a lakeside glade not far from here. Exciting, eh?"

Nice try, Vincenzo, but so obvious. "That's amazing, Father. When do I get to look and what of Cracker?"

"Let's go tomorrow," Vincenzo replied. "The man, Cracker... I don't know where he is exactly, but he knows of this gold and will find it soon enough."

Rizzo's eyes narrowed and his brain made a quick calculation. He proceeded to wrong foot Vincenzo. "Can't make it tomorrow, Father, so you'd better sit on the pope's gold bars."

What Rizzo wasn't saying was that he was expecting the arrest warrant to be acted upon soon, courtesy of the UK police. When everything was in place, then that was the time to make a move.

He continued. "Father, from what I know, archaeology finds are not allowed out of the country. It's illegal. There has to be a full examination of any artifact discovered. Such things could end up in a museum."

There was a pause. The inspector could almost hear Vincenzo's brain whirling around.

"What do you suggest, Inspector?"

"I'll call you very soon, Father. There are a few things I must do beforehand." He disconnected the call. *He's setting up a hit, an ambush, and he's doing it very badly. That would upset his first plan. It's now my turn to put my plan into operation. I bet he's now calling both the cardinal and Cracker.*

Rizzo sent a call off to the professor. He had a list of questions to put to him. The phone answered almost at once. Ten minutes later, he had the response he expected. He knew everything that had been found and the incredible possibilities that it posed. There had been no cup as yet, but much circumstantial evidence. Vincenzo's lies confirmed that the priest was planning to assassinate him, and no doubt with the help of Cracker. The cardinal's bugged conversation in the restaurant gave total credence to the theory. He decided to leave the trip to the lake for a while. He needed the cooperation of the police and a plan had to be worked out. It was going to be his way, and not Vincenzo's.

CHAPTER 51

In her hotel room, the whisperings in her head would not abate. Dr. Miriam Sinclair had abandoned her reliance on science. There were things and events that were clearly beyond logical explanation. Since the finding of the skeleton, the gold inscribed artefact, and the nails, she thought nothing could be the same again. An image had been forming directly in her mind's eye. It persisted. Daily. At times, hourly.

At first, she didn't realise what was happening. The voice sounded like a faint hiss, almost as if it was demanding her attention. It soon changed into a soft murmur. She found herself stopping work and straining her ears to hear what it was saying. Initially, she was unable to make out what she thought she was hearing. As the hours passed, she had abandoned any attempt to logically define what was happening. She simply opened up to it. Finally, with clarity, she heard what was being said. It was a shock to her that the voice was speaking in Aramaic. She recognised it at once. The passage was from Matthew's gospel.

"You are close. Ask and it will be given to you, seek and you will find, knock, and it will be opened to you."

Her hands clasped around her head. "Who are you?" she shouted at no one.

Then the shape of a woman manifested before her. She was in white and her entire appearance shimmered. Her features were unrecognisable. Gold ornaments hung from her wrists.

Her voice echoed in Miriam's mind. *"I am Ganna. I am the Banduri of the Durotriges people..."*

Miriam shook her head in disbelief. The female figure was introducing herself as the Druid High Priestess of the Celtic Durotriges, who formed the communities over two thousand years ago.

The voice continued. *"I am sent by she, whom you saw before. You are almost there, but you are uncertain. What you seek is before you and is found from where you came. Trust in Iseldir, but he can only travel so far. You have both been led this way and given paths to follow. Trust in he who was taken from that cross, and in her whose vessel captured his essence. Listen to your heart, not your brain. Your heart never lies."*

For a fleeting moment, Miriam glimpsed what looked like a cup before her. She reached out for it, but it evaporated in a soft, golden light that also faded away. A faint whisper arose in her head...

"We have waited so long. Go back from where you came. You are worthy and through the doors you must go. Your light shines brighter, and your time here is done. The way has been shown. It is now known and glows clear and true. Trust it."

The vision appeared to shimmer once more before it

vanished in a diminishing pinpoint of light.

Miriam fell to her knees. Something, she knew, hovered around her – intimate, knowable, so familiar. She didn't dare, didn't want, to question it. Control came back to her and everything seemed so clear. There was a connection between all the events that had surrounded her mind. She ran them through her head, one by one. Always in the back of them was Kelvin, or Iseldir, as he was named. But the Celtic title was becoming more appropriate as events unfolded. Somehow there existed a connection with the Magdalene. She now perceived the motives behind Cardinal Nicholas and his unpleasant aides. The cup was the prize. If found, and he gained possession of it, there would be a world in crisis. The words of her earlier vision became clearer. There was danger around. She needed to speak with both Fergal and Kelvin. There would be no holding back.

CHAPTER 52

The cardinal sat in his chair, staring at his phone. Vincenzo had told him of their plan to eliminate Rizzo. He had plenty of time to think it through. Rizzo's impending murder now seemed brushed with uncertainty. If he survived, it would be the end of them all. He didn't doubt that the inspector had been in touch with the UK police regarding Cracker. The man was no fool. It was only a matter of time before they caught up with Cracker for murdering the policeman in Rome. That had been a stupid mistake. It had put his entire plan into jeopardy. How near the archaeologists were in finding the supposed cup, didn't seem so remote. They had uncovered some interesting and intriguing material… but not enough. If found, and only if it worked, would religious history have to be rewritten.

It's ridiculous to even imagine such a thing existed, let alone still containing fluid. Blood and water. Ludicrous! It's the pope's

*money and I'm in charge of it. That's a joke! The man threatens our
God-given church and all it has ever stood for, the one and only true
faith! But he won't be around much longer. One thing's for certain,
Pope Adrian will not know of the gold slab. I hear his health is not
good.*

The Cardinal reflected on a secret he had recently been
harbouring. He had friends and supporters in the Papal
household. The most useful to carry out his plans were the
chefs and cooks in the papal kitchens. He had two supporters
he knew he could rely on.

He had orchestrated the slow murder of the Pope by poi-
son, in varying stages over a period of time.

From the papal private gardens, he had seen some rare
and dangerous plants growing, of which he had some
knowledge. One of them was as toxic as it was beautiful… the
Castor Bean. Known for producing castor oil, it was harmless
in that processed form. But the leaves and especially the seeds
of the plant contained the powerful toxin ricin. It was one of
the most poisonous plants in the world. One or two seeds
would kill a child, and up to six to eight would kill an adult.
A bean here or there, perhaps two or three, would have unpleasant effects, and there would be no discernible cause of
sickness. Administered correctly, there would be severe
vomiting, breathing problems, diarrhea, and seizures. A fatal
dose would have to wait. *There is no known antidote.* The poi-
son, he learnt, was used in 1978 to assassinate a journalist
named Markov who spoke out against the Bulgarian government. He was jabbed in the leg with the tip of an umbrella. All
very innocent. Several assassination attempts had been made
worldwide using the seeds. They were mailed to various USA
politicians in failed terrorism activities.

No need to get Cracker to finish him off. He, the cardinal

himself, was managing well enough. Of late, the pope had been experiencing stomach problems. His doctors, he had heard, secretly suspected an ulcer or at worse, colon or bowel cancer, but nothing was proof positive.

He smiled.

The more he thought about it the more he realised it was not a wise move to be seen in the company of Vincenzo or especially Cracker.

After some serious thought, he put a call out to Vincenzo. The priest answered the phone.

"Father, it's your cardinal speaking. Listen carefully. It's not wise for us to be seen together, so I'm off to Florence in the morning. You are to maintain contact with Cracker and work on your plan to dispose of Rizzo. When it's done, report back to me in Rome or Florence. I'll let you know where I am. I don't think he knows I'm here and it must stay that way. Understood?"

"*Capisco.*" Vincenzo understood perfectly. "It will be done, Eminence."

The cardinal put down the phone and breathed a sigh of relief. As far as he knew, his little problem was sorted. *Now all that remains is for me to get back to Italy.*

* * *

Rizzo slammed his phone down with barely controlled annoyance and frustration. He had been speaking to the UK police. There had been a serious delay in processing the paperwork for the arrest warrant due to a mistake in the EU documentation. It could take another week or more to put it straight. Never a patient man, he found the delay unacceptable, but there was nothing he could do about it. He had two options. The first is to sit it out and wait, or take up Vincenzo's 'guided tour' offer to the hidden lake, which was an obvious bait to lure him in. If he accepted that, what would he do when he got there? He could be shot and killed, or he could shoot and injure or kill one or both of the assassins. How could he explain that away to the police?

There was also the cardinal to consider. If played correctly, all three could be netted in one go. Sitting about doing nothing was the least attractive of his options. The situation needed serious thought. The more he thought about it, the more he was attracted to the deadlier option. He needed some clarification.

With that in mind, he decided to call Professor Christi.

CHAPTER 53

T hey stood facing the moat. Kelvin looked across to Miriam. "You don't have to tell me, Miriam. You saw something or somebody again, didn't you? I can tell from your face and body language. You don't have to hide it. Who was it?"

Miriam blanched. "How can you possibly know that I saw?"

"Let's say I'm pretty good at spotting things like that."

"You are right. It wasn't the same woman. She called herself Ganna."

It was Kelvin's turn to look surprised. "Ganna, no less! A famed Druid priestess. Now, that is impressive. What did she say?"

"It was odd... she spoke in Aramaic. How could she do that and why in that language?"

"I would have thought putting together what we have

found should be answer enough."

"The Jesus Mary thing and their family?"

"Exactly. She must have learnt the language from somewhere. I have to say the Aramaic language sounds hauntingly familiar to me."

"Hey, we're talking as if this whole thing was real."

"Isn't it? You believed in it a while back. Tell me, what did she say?"

Miriam explained what the woman said. She added at the end, "I need to speak to Fergy."

* * *

The LIDAR had performed remarkably well. The graves, previously declared as agricultural furrows, had been a major discovery and an upset for the established archaeological wise men. The professor thought about what they had achieved. It was uncanny that in such a short time, they had found more in a few days than previous excavations – which took months – had failed to achieve.

He thought about the conversations he just had with both Miriam and Kelvin. He still thought it was imaginative rubbish. But it was so unlike Miriam. She had always been scientific, level-headed, and never prone to mysterious, imaginative wanderings. This mission was turning out to be like no other he had been on. The more he thought upon it, the more he felt she had experienced something that neither of them had previous knowledge of.

He considered Kelvin's role. He had always been passive in such discussions and only ventured an opinion when asked. He certainly had no part in her visions. However, he had never scoffed at Miriam's tales and understood what she was going through. Something he knew he was lacking. Miriam didn't even want to tell him about her experiences at first. But he told Kelvin. He felt the brittle touch of jealousy. That had never happened before.

They had informed him it was time to go back. The moat was a series of large ditches and she said it wasn't worth looking at. The tunnel they had uncovered at Glastonbury was of more interest. Oddly, he found himself agreeing with her. There was no scientific reason why, only a nagging prompt in the back of his mind.

The Aramaic language should never be where it was, thousands of miles from its homeland. However, here it was in England, and in most mysterious circumstances. How? Not only was it in written form but spoken in Miriam's visions. He believed her now. For those who chose to hear and see, it was a clarion call.

Overriding all this, he wondered what Pope Adrian thought of it all. It was breathtaking for him, no doubt. Cardinal Nicholas and Father Vincenzo were not seekers of the truth. They were opportunists and would seize the best moment to use it all to their advantage. Fergal knew the pope could be in danger from many quarters.

He agreed to terminate the Enfield mission for the time being and return back to the West Country. He called out to them both.

"You two are right. God knows why I've reached that conclusion, but we are returning back to the Tor." At that moment, his phone rang. He checked the screen. It was Inspector Rizzo.

"Inspector?"

"Professor, I have a dilemma."

Before Fergal could reply, Rizzo explained the warranty

problem, and asked if they had seen any of his suspects. Then added, "Did you discover anything new?"

"We did. Gold and old nails, and in very unusual circumstances. We are on our way back with it. We have already informed Vincenzo who is busting his gut to get a look."

"Excellent. I need to speak closer with you. Before you show him, I need to see you first. Agreed?"

"Okay, Inspector. I'll call you on my return." Fergal paused. It was not every day he was asked to help a policeman. "I'll do what I can, but it won't be much. Talk later."

CHAPTER 54

Glastonbury

T he professor called Rizzo as promised. They were now fully updated with each other's concerns and have shared the information they possessed. They agreed to keep Vincenzo in the dark, to a great extent. The priest was still unaware of the team's early return and that Fergal was in communication with Rizzo. It would remain that way as long as possible.

Fergal was respectful of Miriam's call to return and the importance of the work they had started at the far end of the tunnel. He had noticed the discernible change in Miriam's attitude and behaviour. She had become quieter and her usual chatter had ceased. When she did speak, it was positive, curt, and to the point. It was so unlike her. She was different now from the Miriam he knew.

It became darker the further they moved into the tunnel. The walls were a mixture of soil, dirt, and surprisingly, polished stonework. Without asking, and out of character, Miriam gave a direct order. "Bring in and wire up the generators. We need more light here."

Fergal raised an eyebrow but said nothing. *There's no doubt she's acting differently.*

The equipment was wheeled in and wired up, and powerful lighting illuminated the complex like it had never witnessed before. Never ever.

Fergal stood straight. The structure they were in was over seven feet in height. Running his hand over the limestone walls, he was surprised to see and feel how smooth they were, and the perfectly aligned jointing and fitting. It was the work of skilled craftsmen.

The initial tunnel appeared to be a series of chambers and passageways, just as the LIDAR had hinted at earlier. A series of rock carved rooms led forward to reveal amazing chairs and tables, roughly carved and hewn from the rock and stone. Fergal gasped. Miriam said nothing, as she remained stock still with Kelvin standing alongside her.

* * *

For what felt like an eternity, a thought swirled in her mind. I know this place. The recollection wouldn't leave her. She closed her eyes, but the thought persisted.

Fergal gave voice to what they were all thinking. "This place was used for something. Looks like a stone age pub straight from the 'Flintstones.'"

The quip raised a laugh amongst them all.

Miriam didn't respond. She remained expressionless.

He carried on. "It looks like a secret meeting place, a witch's coven or a Druid connection."

"No chance the Druids had a hand in this, Fergy." Kelvin looked offended. "Druids hold everything in the open, in contact with the natural world. This place is not natural."

Miriam suddenly said, "The doors are ahead. Follow me." Her voice was commanding and gave no room for argument.

"Doors? What doors?" Fergal looked puzzled, but found himself obeying her, and following behind Kelvin and the others.

They came to a point where the tunnel suddenly widened.

"Oh my god!" Fergal was lost for words.

There, at the widest part of the opening… were two large doors – aged by time but perfectly preserved in the constant cool temperature.

Miriam stood still and perfectly straight. She said nothing but pointed to the clearly visible symbol spanning the double doors.

The party was struck into silence. All they could do was stand and stare.

Miriam clasped Kelvin's arm. She recalled the voice of Ganna in her head: *We have waited so long. Go back from where you came. You are worthy. Through the doors you may go. Your light shines brighter and your time here is done. The way has been shown.*

A sense of peace descended upon her and she was happy just to be there.

The professor's voice broke the spell. He spoke in an excited but hushed whisper. "I know what this is. It's the

Portuguese Cross, the Templar's symbol for the Order of Christ! What's a Portuguese cross doing here in an English tunnel beneath Glastonbury Tor? I'm trying to get my head around this. The Order was ruthlessly annihilated in 1312 by the then Pope Clement V. They eventually fled to Portugal, and King Denis of Portugal refused the pope's commands and gave them refuge. It was rumoured that they brought with them much wealth – secret and sacred objects. Their military zeal and love of Christ was legendary. They survived and are still around today, I hear."

"This is the door she told me of." Miriam stood transfixed.

"Your vision voice?" Fergal sounded irritated. It was not easy to change a lifetime's opinion overnight. "Well, let's get it open." He moved toward the door.

"No, you do not!" Miriam turned and blocked the door with her body, her arms spread out. Kelvin turned with her and stood beside her.

Fergal came to a sudden and bewildered halt. "What?" Without waiting, he ducked behind their arms and pushed at the doors. They refused to open. Other team members came to his assistance, but the doors refused to budge.

For a moment, both Kelvin and Miriam looked annoyed. Their command had been ignored. Their anger soon turned to amusement. Fergal was straining and searching for a way to prise open the doors.

"Move over, Fergal."

As frustrated as he was, Fergal found himself obeying her once again.

She shook her head at him. "You have no idea at times, have you?" Inwardly, she felt as if her entire mind and body were experiencing a complete transformation. So many mysteries and unanswered questions were falling into place.

He stepped back with a puzzled look on his face. Miriam moved closer to the door and again, Kelvin followed beside her. As everyone looked on, silence filled the area. She nodded at Kelvin, before uttering a prayer to the woman she had first seen.

I am here. Allow Ganna's words to be true.

A few minutes passed and all that could be heard was the encompassing silence. Then, without a sound, both doors moved inward and began to open.

The way was clear.

CHAPTER 55

A few hours had passed since Pope Adrian had finished his *pausa prenzo* – his daily lunch break. It was his customary fare – a dish of pasta, a second of fresh fish, and a side dish with cheese followed by several cups of coffee. Of late, he thought his digestive system was getting to complain too much. He'd been experiencing severe stomach cramps, nausea, sweaty breathlessness, and diarrhoea. He didn't know what to put it down to. It frequently attacked after meals. He began to suspect, as the doctors had suggested, that he had developed an ulcer – probably caused by his concerns over SOTA and the situation revolving around Cardinal Nicholas.

The inspector had not been able to produce any further evidence of the cardinal's role in the murder of Bishop Fisher, although he had damning material on the cardinal's role in a plot to dispose of Rizzo.

Obeying Rizzo's request, he could only marvel at the workings of the police, but he had carried on with the cardinal, pretending there was nothing amiss. Cardinal Nicholas had reappeared and said he'd been in England checking out the SOTA activities. He had nothing to report except that he was off to Florence for a private engagement. Pope Adrian knew for certain what that was. It was a secret rally of the cardinal's supporters. Their agenda, he knew was the ultimate overthrow of his papacy, and a return to a medieval structure of Catholic beliefs and actions.

In the midst of these thoughts, another crippling surge of pain sent him scurrying to the bathroom. The half-digested remains of his lunch disappeared down the toilet. He stood bent over the bowl as a dripping cold sweat broke out across his entire body. Minutes later, he stood upright, wiped his face clean, and staggered back into his main room. His hands were trembling, but the pain was beginning to subside. His smartphone was ringing, and the screen showed Rizzo's name. He took a deep breath as he quickly assessed his body.

"Inspector Rizzo. What can I do for you?" The last wisps of pain had evaporated.

Rizzo related his conversation with the professor and the on-going situation regarding Cracker. "At the moment, Holy Father, I am powerless. All I can do is watch and wait. You may be receiving good news from SOTA soon. I see they have been remarkably busy and excited. I will keep in contact and if I have more information on Cardinal Nicholas, I will let you know immediately."

"May God bless and keep you safe." The pope spoke quickly and thought, *me also*, as another burst of pain stretched itself around his stomach. He placed his phone down and made a mental note to summons his doctor the following day.

* * *

Rizzo was not good at doing nothing. He had run and rerun the circumstances concerning Vincenzo and Cracker. He decided to set up his own plan and lure both men into playing their hand. In doing so, they would risk being exposed and arrested by the UK police. All he had to do was stay alive and uninjured. He had one major advantage… he knew what they had planned and discussed. It was risky, but if successful, he would get closer to implicating and arresting the cardinal. He picked up his phone and with a determined stance and voice, called Father Vincenzo.

He promptly answered. "Inspector, I was just thinking of you."

I bet you were. "I'd like to take you up on your offer of showing me the place where the finds are being made. To see what is causing such interest could be helpful in my investigations."

The silence was lengthy, and Rizzo was not going to break it. He thought he could hear Vincenzo's brain doing somersaults.

Vincenzo replied, "Of course, Inspector. I have a couple of matters I must attend to but let me call you back later today and perhaps, we can arrange something for tomorrow. Yes?"

"I look forward to it, Father. I'll except your call later." *That will give him time to call Cracker.*

Later that evening, Rizzo received his call. Vincenzo was not so available.

"Inspector, I have to make my reports tomorrow and check on the excavations, and that may take a while. After that, we can make firm arrangements. That is ok?"

"I await your call, Father." He replied sourly.

He expected trouble and guessed a trap was being fixed. But he was as ready as he could be for it. He set about his next task. He unpacked his Beretta, before expertly dismantling it. He ensured all parts were functioning and smooth running. It was standard Italian police procedure. There would be less chances of the gun jamming or misfiring. The anticipated meeting would be interesting.

CHAPTER 56

T
he gloom of centuries flooded from the exposed area. Everyone present gaped, expecting riches to be revealed. But before them, there was only an all-embracing, womblike darkness, punctuated by what seemed like the sound of rushing water.

"Lights, please." The professor broke the spell.

Two sets of generator powered arc lights were wheeled over, until they shone brightly into the forgotten area. The brightness cast shadows of them all across the perfectly smooth walls, where fiery torches had once hung.

Everyone was frozen, waiting to see what the lights would uncover.

A beam of light cut through the central area and a square shaped room revealed itself. Fergal did a quick assessment. The area covered about fifty square metres and every surface, including the floor, was completely smooth. He checked his thermometer. The temperature stood at ten degrees centi-grade and must have remained that way since it had been constructed. A thousand thoughts rushed through his mind. The Portuguese Templar symbol on the door would indicate that it was these knights who had constructed this remarkable edifice. *But how and why?*

The lighting was wheeled closer and began to pan slowly around the entire structure.

Miriam and Kelvin had not moved. They stood motion-less, wrapped in their own all-knowing quietness.

The lights continued its exploration and swung down to the far end. There before them stood a grey coloured block of limestone the size of a park bench, but taller at chest height. The lighting pivoted on to it, first to the right and then to the left. Clearly visible were numerous stave-like indentations. There was no doubt they were runic. Intermingled with these were undeniable etched crucifixes.

When all the lights picked it out, it was unremarkable. What stood on it was not. That caused a gasp all around.

"Nobody move!" Miriam's command echoed around the chamber as she spread out her arms wide in both directions. It had the desired effect. Not a foot moved and that included Fergal.

She approached with care. Kelvin remained where he stood, spreading his own arms out wide as she moved for-ward. The closer she got the clearer it became.

Three metres off, and she was able to see what had riveted everybody's attention. In front of her stood an oblong glass container, each side held in place by what looked like gold struts on each corner angle. It measured about eighteen inches in height and about twelve inches both in width and depth. The glass surround was blemished and covered in the dust and detritus of centuries passed. She could not see what it contained, but whatever it was, it was an object of veneration.

The voices of both Ganna and the lady in white returned to her mind. She could not prevent it nor was she surprised. She both welcomed and wanted them. As the seconds ticked by, the more she understood what was happening around her. Everything was falling into place.

A dawning certainty, without rules and guidelines, began to envelope and soften her cemented science. Her logic began its inevitable collapse.

She found herself resisting until the end, but it was useless. She surrendered.

You are near… You draw close.

An intensely personal experience began to transcend all that she had ever learnt. She felt she was going beyond… on a never-ending journey. There was nothing to know, nothing to learn. It was all so simple, and it had been staring her in the face from the time she was born. Only at this moment, after all these years, was she able to see it. Her memory took her back across the centuries and it was only then she knew from where she came.

She moved closer and reached out to touch the glass. Her head rolled back and a well of laughter erupted from her which soon became a bubbling sob.

Not a sound came from the team behind her. Transfixed, puzzled, and for a reason they did not know… they were awestruck.

Kelvin remained as a tree with arms that did not tire – outstretched, forbidding anyone to approach. Nobody dared.

Her hand rubbed gently at the tarnished glass surface. She knew what she would find there. Disconnected biblical quotes rippled through her mind. Religion had never been part of her make up, but she could remember various parts of the Bible.

My cup runneth over. Drink ye all of it.

What lay beneath the glass slowly came into view. It had the shape and size of a goblet made of wood, perfectly pre-served. It appeared to have a tight lid screwed on the top. Without any thought or consideration, Miriam found herself kneeling in front of it. It seemed the natural thing she should do. She bent her head. There was little need to speak. Her thoughts were all that was required.

I have found you. Once more we are together.

She reached for it, but the image appeared to shimmer in a golden glaze before it faded from view.

The professor moved forward.

"Not yet," Kelvin commanded, thrusting himself physi-cally to block Fergal's movement. "She is not yet with us. I will tell you when. Stand back, please." He sounded as if he was in some other unknown place.

Without a word, Fergal moved back to where he had been standing.

Neither he nor any team member heard or saw the portly priest hidden behind a jutting promontory of smooth rock. In his hands was his usual camera, complete with a large zoom lens.

After several minutes had passed, Miriam stood up and turned around. Nothing about her had changed. She was as she was always been. A smile crossed her face and she slowly walked toward Kelvin who had lowered his arms. Looking directly at Fergal, she said in a quiet voice. "I am home. None of you are to disturb what is here. I will explain everything later. Now please, move away and we will close these ancient doors. They will only open for me and Iseldir and nobody else, no matter who you are and how hard you try. So, let us go back and I will tell you what I now know."

"What the hell are you on about?" Fergal bristled with anger, but he found himself doing as she asked, as did the others. They all moved away.

The zoom lens had captured it all on video and an incredulous Vincenzo scuttled off before he could be spotted. This changed everything.

CHAPTER 57

P ope Adrian's CT and MRI scans had come back as negative, but the pains continued and had become worse. Exploratory surgery had been suggested but he had refused this. If it didn't improve soon, he would agree to it, but it had to become unbearable. Amidst this, the professor's latest communiqué had given him a surge of religious joy, akin to his first ever religious experience of the Magdalene when on a retreat in the Dolomite Mountains many years back. A few nuisance pains would not stop him from enjoying SOTA's latest finds. What he had found most intriguing was the professor's description of the circumstances of the discovery and his partner's strange reaction to it. She had seen something that the others had or were prevented from seeing.

He dearly wished he could be there with them but was totally unable to do so in his condition.

He was now sure Cardinal Nicholas had been lying to

him. Comparing his report with those of his SOTA team, it was clear he was not being honest and had a devious intent. He wished Inspector Rizzo could find something that would allow him to make a move against the cardinal before he could do more damage.

* * *

"What are you saying?" Cardinal Nicholas bellowed into his phone. "Are you sure of this?

"I saw it all with my own eyes, Your Eminence." Vincenzo was beside himself that he carried such revelatory news. "The doors had a large red cross painted on them and when they were opened, they found what looked like an altar on which stood a glass case of some sort. What was in it, only the woman saw, and she prevented anybody else from seeing. Nobody was able to open the doors apart from her. It was *fantastico da vedere!*"

"You have photographs?"

"*Si.* I have a video and am sending it now."

"Excellent. What about Rizzo?"

"He wants to see the glade and Cracker will do the rest when he falls into the trap. It is very close."

"Do it quick! Very quick. Understood, Father? We must end this problem once and for all. With this new discovery, nothing can stand in my way."

"*Si, Inteso Cardinale.*"

* * *

Minutes later, the Cardinal was watching the video from Vincenzo. He saw the ancient room, the doors, and Miriam and the other team members.

This is unbelievable. Those doors are centuries old and what is that cross doing there!

He took in a large lungful of air and blew it back out fast. He peered closer, especially at the footage showing Kelvin with his outstretched arms and Miriam kneeling behind him in some sort of prayer posture before what looked like a glass dome. He felt a surge of emotions – a mixture of thrilled excitement, incredulity, rapidly followed by an overwhelming rush of doubt and disbelief.

If this is what they have been looking for, I must see it and have it. If the Doctor woman is the only one who can access it then we must get to her first and persuade her to allow us in.

His thought processes went into overdrive. Somehow, Cracker had to dispose of Rizzo and then set to work on the woman. Everything now hinged on his two men to make this happen.

CHAPTER 58

Rizzo was fully prepared. He had agreed to accompany Vincenzo to the grove and had examined all the possible scenarios. Daniel Cracker and his gun would be waiting for him, and possibly that of Vincenzo's. It was obvious that the trap had been set.

He drove a distance behind Vincenzo's pickup truck, having refused the offer of being driven to the spot. That would only pose more difficulties and potential dangers. It was best to remain alone and that gave him a degree of control. He noticed nothing of the journey and kept his eyes fixed firmly on the truck up front. He had not been able to work out why he was doing this, but the inaction was more than he could bear. Whatever they were planning, if he survived, they would have no place to hide. The truth would be out.

It was not long before Vincenzo began to slow down. He pulled into the side of a small layby with a hard to see track that meandered into the bushes and trees. Within seconds, he was out of the pickup truck, wearing his tracksuit and walking towards Rizzo, who was himself clambering from his vehicle.

As he did, he noticed a silver SUV style Vitara parked and partially hidden by the undergrowth. *That could be Cracker,* was the first thought that came into his head.

"It is not far, Inspector. Please follow me. Okay?" Vincenzo sounded tense. "You will be surprised at what you see."

"Okay." Rizzo grunted as he felt his blood begin to rise and the first drops of perspiration slid down his back. He wasn't going to be ambushed. He knew he was taking a risk, a huge risk, but something had to be done to force the issue and reveal what he wanted to know most. The cardinal's role in the murder of Bishop Fisher was the prime directive in all the events that had followed since. Vincenzo's shoulder holster had not gone unnoticed. His bulky form offered a sneaky glimpse of it through the lining of the tracksuit's material.

Vincenzo, beginning to puff, was not in good physical shape and the inspector had no problem keeping pace with him. He followed close. If there was to be an attack, he didn't want to be isolated. Keeping the priest close by could be helpful in a firefight. He kept his eyes wide open, constantly scanning ahead, and both left and right.

Several minutes passed. The going got tougher as the undergrowth and trees increased in density. Sunlight filtered down between the trees like an intermittent strobe. If there was going to be an attack, these conditions would suit it perfectly.

He was right.

Up ahead, he caught sight of a figure darting behind a

small mound behind a tree. Rizzo didn't hesitate. With one huge shove into Vincenzo's back, he sent the unprepared priest sprawling flat out into the dirt. He himself sidestepped off the track and did a low shoulder roll behind a large oak tree, before he stood upright with his Beretta fully loaded and pointing in the direction of where he had seen the figure. He didn't have to wait long. There came a deathly crack – a sharp sound that filled the woods as a hand sized slice of bark and timber split two inches away from his ear.

"Gesù Cristo!" Rizzo ducked down to the thickest part of the trunk and let off a shot in the direction of the hidden figure. He guessed Cracker would be taken by surprise by his reaction. Three more shots peppering the oak tree confirmed his guess. From the top of his vision, Rizzo could see the priest still lying flat on the ground. He hadn't attempted to move. He was directly in the line of fire. The figure was out of sight but if he attempted to change his position, Rizzo would see him at once.

Two more bullets thudded into the oak, and if it hadn't been there, Rizzo would have lost his face. Cracker was a fine shot, but so was Inspector Rizzo. Somehow, Rizzo had to keep him firing until he ran out of ammunition. Also, Vincenzo was armed. He had to disable one or both of them quickly.

He saw Vincenzo begin to wriggle belly first across the track.

Rizzo's first shot exploded close to the priest's outstretched arm. "Do not move, Vincenzo. If you do, my next shot will be into your leg.

The priest froze like a block of ice as another shot spattered up the dirt next to his other arm. He didn't move an inch. Rizzo's command needed no further deciphering.

The main objective was Cracker, still hidden and as vulnerable as himself. Crouched low, Rizzo's heart hammered twice as fast as normal in his chest. It caused sensations in his mind and body, akin to a charge of high voltage electricity. Adrenaline flowed through him like a waterfall. This was a unique situation. Never before had he been hunted, and it was not an experience he would recommend. He let fly a barrage of shots and as he did, he did another shoulder roll toward a closer tree. He hoped his move had not been spotted. In his new position, he now had a better view of both men. They had not noticed him move.

Cracker's attention was still fixed on his former position. Vincenzo was motionless and face downwards in the earth. For once in his career, Rizzo was not sure what to do. It was only at this moment that he truly appreciated the desperate situation he had placed himself in. Killing or wounding his assailants would take a lot of explaining to do. The best thing would be to get the hell out of the place. He himself would be more valuable alive then dead.

Vincenzo's real agenda was now exposed, and Cracker identified. Looming over it all was the figure of Pope Adrian and the future of his Church. The evil nemesis of Cardinal Nicholas embraced them all. Rizzo's hands were tied until his paperwork was ready. When that happened, he could make his move and have the backing of the UK police force.

He had now let the enemy know he was on to them. Killing or wounding them could make the situation worse. Surveillance and containment of some sort was the only solution for now.

He watched as Cracker fired another shot at the tree. It would be only too easy to shoot him dead from where he was in his hidden position. The temptation was huge as he raised his gun and took aim. *No! He and Vincenzo have to be arrested and convicted for their crimes in Italy, and I can't achieve that on my own. Once there, the cardinal will be next. Time to get out of here. Leave Vincenzo to worry and sweat about what will happen next.*

Rizzo took a deep breath and with great care, he lowered his weapon, crouched low and moved slowly behind Cracker. He could have taken him easily, but this was not the way. Soon, he had completed a full circle and was out of sight and back on the track, heading back to his car. He needed to change hotels fast and get in touch with the SOTA team and Pope Adrian. Events were approaching a head of steam. His disappearance would have an unsettling effect on the two men.

With that thought, Inspector Rizzo's foot hit the gas pedal and he U-turned the vehicle and drove back at top speed. He had to get away fast.

CHAPTER 59

The rally at Florence had gone well, better than expected, in fact. His movement was attracting more
and more followers. Underscoring this, the cardinal's
elation at what SOTA had discovered had been replaced by a
mixture of wonder and dread. Vincenzo's description of the
event and his video had given Nicholas a profound shock. *Has
the cup been found?* If so, the results will cause shockwaves
throughout the religious world once the discovery was revealed. He could almost imagine the mayhem that would ensue. *This is not the way I have planned things.* Only after he had
the chance to evaluate the find and confirm what it truly was,
could he determine his next move.

His mobile phone rang. It was Vincenzo.

"He what?" the cardinal exploded.

"*Si*, Your Eminence. He got away. We didn't realise he
would be armed. It was as if he knew. He had me pinned

down but was hidden from Cracker. Then he disappeared and his car was gone. What do I do?"

The alarm in the priest's tone was not lost on the cardinal, who for once was at a loss for words. "Where's Cracker?"

"He must have got back to his hotel. He doesn't think that the Inspector recognised him. There was little chance of that. If Rizzo makes any charges, I can only deny them and say I knew nothing about what happened or who the shooter was."

"Do you know where Rizzo is now?"

"No idea, Cardinal."

There was a long pause before the cardinal spoke again. "I don't think we have seen the last of him. Tell me did anyone else see you?"

"There was no one else, I'm certain."

"For your sake, Father, I hope that's true. Get hold of Cracker somehow and forget about Rizzo for the moment. What we need to do right now is take possession of that arte-fact, whatever it is. This is highly important. The fate of the Church will be in your hands." *God forbid,* he thought. "Cracker will have to abduct that woman and force their hand in surrendering the find. If you can avoid direct involvement, do that. Once you have it, I may have to return to collect it personally. I'll make use of my special envoy diplomatic sta-tus, together with my Vatican passport. This will ensure I will not be searched. Keep in touch, constantly. Understood?"

The enormity of Cardinal Nicholas's command was not lost on Vincenzo. "Yes. It is understood.

* * *

The setting sun was causing a glare problem as it began its dip to darken the streets of Rome and those of Vatican City.

In the gathering gloom, behind shaded windows, sat an agitated Pope Adrian. His nervous excitement was a mixture of concern and religious fervour. Yet the now acute stabbing pains attacking his stomach and digestive systems tempered these lofty appraisals. There were fluctuations of nausea, vomiting, sweating plus both wet and dry heaves.

Something was seriously wrong with him.

In his heart, he only wished to concentrate on the implications of the SOTA find and those of Dr. Miriam Sinclair, but his physical condition was preventing him from fully concentrating. Added to this, he had decided to confront Cardinal Nicholas about lapses in his reports when compared to those he had received from the professor. Then there was the strange behaviour of Father Vincenzo.

Are these men of God?

Irrespective of Rizzo's requests, it was time to take off the gloves and get tough. Reports of the cardinal's secret rally in Florence had also reached him. The matter could spin out of control. The cardinal had been unreachable and out of contact. That was not unusual but now times were different and major issues were at stake.

A stifling burst of stomach cramp caused him to bend double. His pains were becoming worse and he had only eaten boiled fish, bread and drank a glass of wine. His blood test results had returned as negative, and what was ailing him remained a mystery. His worry was increasing.

It couldn't be the food. There had to be another cause. What he didn't know was what he should deal with first. Whilst in total power, he had never felt so alone. There was nobody he could truly confide in. Rizzo and Professor Christi were, at this time, the only two people he could trust, and they were not immediately to hand.

THE KEEPER'S CUP

He moved across his chamber to face the large wooden
crucifix hanging from the wall and knelt to begin a fervent
prayer.

CHAPTER 60

I want to know precisely what went on in there with you two and I'm not going to be fobbed off." The professor was beyond annoyance. He was fuming.

The three sat around a table in a nearby pub, away from the cosy hotel atmosphere and where they were not known or recognised. He stared hard at them both. He was not going to be side stepped.

"Remember, I set this project up, and I have every right to know what's going on. I demand an answer or the whole project will be closed down and closed down right now. So talk!" His clenched fist on the table was there for both to see.

She had known him most of her life and had never seen him look so serious and upset. She gazed at Kelvin. "Kelvin, Fergy is right. We have no reason to hide anything we know from him. Can you start, please, and I will say what I know when it's the right moment."

Kelvin agreed.

He began with his own thoughts and feelings and the stunning synchronicity of what had brought them together.

Fergy began to interrupt him. "But what…"

Kelvin raised his palm outright. "Please do not interrupt, Fergy. I need to say it all so that the find may make some sense to us all. "I've had many dreams and visitations of late and Miriam figured in them before I even knew her. That is in this life. From the moment I saw her, I felt that we were related in some way across millennia and centuries. I know, without asking, that she feels the same. Do you not, Miriam?"

Miriam's eyes grew moist and she nodded vigorously. "There's no science present here, Fergy. I feel as if I've lived through a thousand lives and more."

"I can see that," he snapped. "It sounds like a fairy story. There's no way you could be related. Feelings are emotional, and in my book, not to be trusted."

Kelvin ignored the jibe. He then related all the episodes that Miriam had encountered since the project commenced that were in many ways related to his own visions. He said all he could and didn't miss a thing. When he was done, a strange silence hovered around them.

The professor still looked puzzled. "Okay, what about the door? What was that about?"

"I knew it wouldn't open for you." Miriam said. "Don't ask me how I knew but I did, and I knew it would open for me with Kelvin's help. He knew that too."

Kelvin nodded his agreement.

"I won't go into that," Fergy continued. "What I want to know is what you saw on that altar piece."

Her voice descended to a whisper. "What I saw vanished… but it was a cup of sorts, with a lid and seemingly made of wood. It was more felt than seen."

"The same for me," Kelvin added.

Their answers irritated him more. "What are you two on about? Why were you kneeling like you were in church and why did you prevent us from getting closer, Kelvin? More felt than seen? You *must* have seen something. You just never do those sorts of things, Miriam, all the time I have known you."

"I know, but it was the right thing to do. The story behind our mission I now know as true. Every part of it, as I'm sure Kelvin does also." She looked hopefully in his direction.

"It is true, Fergy." Kelvin grasped his arm. "Believe us. There are things science can never explain. What is behind that glass is what we have come to look for. I know it with complete certainty. What I am about to tell you I have never revealed to a living soul, but it seems I must. Stories passed down to me from an ancient succession of Druid lineage, of which I am the present incumbent, talk of a cup and its Keeper. She was named Magda – the name we have seen written in that stone. They mention a chieftain, Arthwys and his woman Brianna, who was healed when she drank from a cup."

Fergal looked bemused. "So, you're saying that whatever is inside that glass cage is this so-called healing cup?"

Miriam interjected. "I've not heard that story before, but it seems so familiar, almost as if I have always known it." She paused, raised her head and tears filled her eyes. "Judah and Sarah…" She was unable to finish her sentence.

"It's not the time, Miriam." Across Kelvin's face, for but a brief moment, an expression of deep and profound wisdom flickered.

Fergal looked around uncertain of what to say or do. Events had moved away from his understanding. He felt awkward. "More wine, anybody?"

Miriam took his cue. "Look, will you excuse me for a moment? I have to pay the local shop for the wine I brought and some groceries the other day. If I don't pay, they could get grumpy. Won't be long. You two have a chat while I'm gone. There are a few things I'm sure you need to sort out. See you soon. Don't go away." She gave a sharp turn and headed out of the door.

There was an awkward silence between the two men. Their viewpoints were poles apart. Fergal broke the silence. "Let me start from a point I am familiar with. You mentioned a Druidic lineage. Are all these traditions passed down orally? Why weren't they written down? It could all be a case of Chinese whispers. Over time, and from person to person, the story gets distorted far beyond the original truth."

Kelvin shrugged. "The Romans put paid to that. We were seen as a threat so they systematically killed off whom they could, and all our records were destroyed. The Christian elements around got blended in with pagan rites to form the religion we know today. You must know that."

"I know this. What about those runes and crucifixes on that altar? How do you explain that?"

"This is not difficult, Fergy. It seems clear, based on what we have found, that Christianity appeared here long before the rest of Britain. The story of Yeshua, Mary Magdalene, their children, Judah, and Sarah, if true, which I now think it is, was clearly the prime cause. The story of Arthwys I have held dear. I don't doubt that Miriam feels a bond with all this and the stories of Sarah. Their essence is as one, as is mine with her. Tracing her lineage back would be an interesting exercise. I sense we are both descendants of that time and people. During that time, many Celts and Druids were converted. The pantheon of Celtic Gods, the similar rituals and prayers were adopted and woven around Christ, his Mother Mary, and the Magdalene. The ideas were similar, but the old ways were never abandoned or totally absorbed. They just changed clothes. I am living proof of that. Miriam is extraordinary. She has experienced a direct link, proof positive of her connection with those times and Sarah."

"Whoa there, Kelvin. Are you serious?" The professor's eyes were wide open almost as much as his jaw. "You're actually suggesting she is a direct descendant of Mary Magdalene? No one is ever going to believe that! You've made a lot of wild suggestions there. Fantasies are made up of that sort of material." Fergal took a huge intake of breath, shook his head, downed a large mouthful from his glass and stared incredulously back at Kelvin.

There was a long silence between them and neither attempted to speak. Fergal was first to break the impasse.

"Kelvin, what I'm going to say next may surprise you."

"What's that?" Kelvin looked wary.

"I'm keeping an open mind about all this. Something about it all doesn't make scientific sense. Part of me rejects what you are saying as wishful and fanciful thinking – emotional hogwash. It's a hope that you and Miriam want desperately to be true. Yet part of me won't reject it entirely. There are clearly too many inexplicable occurrences, discoveries – or as you would say, synchronicity. The changes in Miriam are profound. Believe me, I've known her all my life and have never seen her like this, ever. She would have been the first to reject such theories as nonsense. She never does things lightly. In my own way, I trust and love her. For her to behave so, is I think, significant."

Kelvin visibly softened. He held out his hand and shook

it with Fergal's. "Thank you, Fergy. I am surprised and moved that you can admit the possibility. No more need be said. I respect you so much for your admission."

He looked at his watch. "Where's she got to?"

Kelvin leant back and relaxed. "She is probably giving us time to talk, don't you think?"

The professor took another drink. "She's a clever lady. I'll give her another ten minutes. If she hasn't arrived, I'll give her a call. Tell me, Kelvin... if we find more startling evidence, what do you think the Catholic Church, the Pope and etcetera are going to make of it all?"

"They'll panic, I guess. It will all be locked away in deep secret vaults."

"Exactly what I was thinking. I do really need to examine that altar and the glass structure and whatever may be inside it."

Kelvin shook his head. "I think only Miriam can agree to that. Let's ask when she gets back."

The professor accepted Kelvins strange statement without dissent. They sat back and waited.

CHAPTER 61

I nspector Rizzo awoke with a start. A shooting pain across his operation scar put paid to any further sleep. It was something he was told he would experience for the rest of his life. But it was a small price to pay for living.

For a moment, he felt confused. His surroundings were different. Then he recalled he had changed hotels. He was now at the Crossways Hotel in Shepton Mallet. He had to change hotels fast to avoid Cracker and Vincenzo. His life would not have been safe, so he had checked out and was certain he hadn't been noticed. It took a few moments to clear his head and decide what to do.

He had to pressure his UK counterparts to speed up proceedings and report the attack on himself by an unidentified person – he had a suspect and an accomplice. The need to contact the professor was almost as paramount.

He checked his Beretta. It was loaded and he had an extra three full magazines. *"Ciò dovrebbe tenere a bada la feccia."* This should keep the scum at bay. The thought was reassuring.

His mobile started to ring. He recognised his police phone number on the screen. Sostituto Commissario Romano was calling him. Romano was the Senior Inspector of the *Polizia di Stato* and in charge of all events. His voice was slow and calm.

"Leonardo, I have news for you. Applying the latest DNA techniques from the US, forensics have discovered things which will concern you. We may need you back here. Your reports are extremely thorough. One of the three people you're observing is back here in Rome – Cardinal Nicholas. A full imprint of DNA has now been translated, found on the chest of the dead Bishop Fisher. It matched Cardinal Nicholas's DNA exactly. Alongside it, we have confirmed the other DNA from our old records. It was identified as Father Vincenzo's, his aide. You need to see these findings and I will email them over to you promptly. Be prepared to be called back from England. The whereabouts of the Cardinal is unknown right now, as his phone is not being used. We suspect he has a burner phone or two, but he can't hide forever. He has a large following in his Order of the Holy Cross and Sword. That might prove a problem and he could use it as a hiding place. We don't want to act immediately. We need your full input first before we do. We have also placed him on every airport passport control list. Diplomatic immunity will be waived. This was authorised by the Vatican, by Pope Adrian himself."

Rizzo punched the air with delight! *Breakthrough!* With their DNA confirmed, the charges could now be bundled and thrown at the suspects.

"*Commissario*, this is what I have been waiting for. The

two men here are highly dangerous and one, Daniel Cracker, used me as target practice. But as you can hear, I have survived. The paperwork should be ready in the next few days. I will have allocated UK escorts and when that is done, the two can be arrested and brought back to Italy and from there, we can find and arrest the cardinal. Wonderful news!"

No sooner had he switched off when his phone rang again. It was a no number call.

Who could it be? He picked up the call.

It was Professor Christi.

"I was about to call you, Professor. What can I do for you?"

The professor sounded panicked. He spoke rapidly. "Inspector, where are you? I need you here urgently. There's been a nasty development."

"What's that?"

"It's Dr Miriam. She's been kidnapped!"

"What!"

"Yes! You heard right. She managed to get a message to me before she was cut off. She sounded terrified. We need your help urgently. Where are you?"

Rizzo paused briefly. Kidnappings were not new to him. He had been part of the team investigating the abduction of seventy-four-year-old Anna Maria Valdata, the wife of a construction billionaire. Kidnappings had long been part of Italy's crime network. Such cases had to be carefully handled. Nervous kidnappers could easily snap and kill their victim. "Take it easy, Professor. I've changed hotels. I'm at the Crossways Hotel and Inn in Shepton Mallet. Give me thirty minutes to get to you. Say nothing to anybody and do nothing. I'm on my way." He shut down the phone.

Rizzo's brain whirled. There were only two suspects on

his list.

Twenty minutes later, he screeched his car into the nearest and nearby Cathedral car park alongside The Green, a short walk to the hotel as it did not have its own. Ignoring the receptionist and her attempts to address him, he strode swiftly into the lounge area and spotted both men in a far corner. They had seen him approaching and both stood up and greeted him with very white and serious faces.

Rizzo wasted no time. "Tell me everything you know and why haven't you contacted your police?"

"We don't know where she is. We haven't called the police as yet but wanted your advice and opinion first. Miriam is the key to our latest find. Without her, we cannot even open the door."

Rizzo looked baffled." What are you on about, Professor? You will have to do better than that. Explain please."

Fergal looked over to Kelvin. "Tell him all, Kelvin. You'll do better than me."

"Sit down, Inspector. This may take a while and try not to interrupt."

Kelvin began and started from the first day he had met both of them. He related everything he knew – the discoveries, the mystical events, the altercations with Vincenzo, the wolf sounds and not least of all, the Templar emblem on the doors that only she and himself were able to open. He moved on to the mysterious glass case and told the Inspector what it might be, and the effect it had on them all. "That's about it, Inspector. Any thoughts?"

Rizzo ran his hand through his dark hair. His blue eyes appeared dilated and there was an intense expression on his face. *"Tutto sta inizando adare unsenso adesso!"* he muttered with his head bent low. He looked up at them both. "It's all beginning to make sense now. Let me explain. Pope Adrian, SOTA, Bishop Vincent and you and your team, are being used as tools by Cardinal Nicholas. His quest is to topple the Vatican with the help of his reactionary order of followers. If the miraculous cup you say you've found is truly authentic, Nicholas wouldn't hesitate to use it to overthrow the entire Catholic Church, and as holder of the cup, proclaim his own doctrine as the one true faith. He's now employing Father Vincenzo and the murderer, Daniel Cracker, to make sure what you find goes to him. There is little doubt from the latest DNA findings I have just received that both he and Vincenzo were part of the murder plot to dispose of the bishop. The pope, I fear, is also in his sights. Now, you must show me the place you found the doors. Undoubtedly, she will be taken there to get hold of the discovery. Somehow, Vincenzo and Cracker heard of your find and what happened when the doors and the altar were discovered. Somebody could have been watching. Is there any other reason why she would be kidnapped, and do you have any idea where she might be?"

"None at all to both questions. My bet is one of the numerous caves around here."

"No time to lose. I hope we are not too late. Let's go to tunnel where you found those doors." Rizzo, followed by the two men, turned and headed for the exit.

373

CHAPTER 62

C ardinal Nicholas answered his phone. It was Father Vincenzo who spoke rapidly and was in an excitable mood.

"My Cardinal, I have important news. Cracker has the woman and she is being held in a cave nearby, where I saw the archaeologists. She does not know I am involved, and she will lead Cracker to what she was praying to, which is I think, the cup. We shall take it and when we have it in our possession, I shall tell you so you can return here. As for Inspector Rizzo, our little episode has scared him off and he appears to have vanished, hopefully back to Rome. Good news, eh Cardinal?"

"It's getting better," the cardinal approved. "It would have been more so if Rizzo had been dealt with. I don't fancy having him back here poking his nose into what I'm doing.

Let's hope you can achieve this task. A whole new faith hangs on your success. God will bless your endeavours, I swear it."

* * *

The thick, plastic, cable handcuff ties held her wrists securely in front of her body, while her legs were tied together with rope. She found it difficult to wake up and move. There was a strange taste lingering in her mouth. Miriam struggled to recall events that led her to be where she was. It was hazy. She remembered paying the shopkeeper, stepping outside, and then a heavy arm from behind her, without warning, went around her neck and a large sweet-smelling cloth covered her mouth. She hadn't seen the attacker nor had time to scream out. She now felt confused. Doing a quick mental search of her body, everything seemed to be intact. She had not been violated. Looking around her, she could see filtered light above her head, coming through a gap in the roof structure. She realised she was in a cave. She had no idea which one but was convinced it had to be close to where they had discovered the doors.

Cognition crept in.

It has to be the discovery. News has somehow got out… it must have! I'm being held like this because of it.

Oddly, she realised she was experiencing neither fear nor panic. All would be resolved. She had no idea how, but she sensed an unusual assurance around her like she had never felt before. She didn't have to question it, nor did she have any idea of how it would unfold. It just would.

The approaching sound of footsteps broke her thoughts. She knew at once who it was… Cracker. He had made no attempt to conceal his face, which wore a triumphant smirk.

"'Allo darling! So you're awake. That makes things easier. We need to talk, don't we?" He crouched low in front of her, clutching a pistol with a large silencer attached to the barrel. He tapped it on her forehead. "You're not going to be a silly girl, are you? I think you know what we want, don't you?"

"We? Who's *we*? That priest and the cardinal, I'm guessing."

He gave a sneer. "I'm not here to discuss. I'm here to get results. I'm going to untie your legs. If you attempt to run, I'll put a bullet into them. I rarely miss. Understood?"

"Understood." Her reply had a defiant contempt to it.

"Good. When I'm done, I'll lead you out of here and you will then take me to your dig and show me what you found and hand it over to me. If any of your friends turn up and attempt to interfere, bullets will fly, and people could die. I might also just smash your little trophy. You wouldn't want that, would you?"

"They have no idea where I am. But if you have to harm anybody, make it me and nobody else."

"Very noble. I can't promise anything. We will have to wait and see, won't we?" He pulled roughly on the rope knots and freed her legs. The handcuffs remained. Hauling her to her feet, he turned her around towards the opening and pushed her forward

"Any noise from you and I'll end up gagging you. Now get going."

His car was parked outside. Opening the boot, he shoved her hard inside and onto a soft rubber mat. She made no sound but closed her eyes.

"Don't worry. It's a short ride. I know where you were working, and I guess that's the place. Yes?"

Miriam managed a short nod.

"Good." He slammed down the lid and started the engine. Fifteen minutes later, Miriam felt the car slow and come to a halt.

Within minutes, Cracker hauled her out and the sudden influx of light dazzled her. She could make out that there were no other vehicles about. It was deserted.

"In we go, sweetheart." Still carrying the gun, he propelled her to the steps into the tunnel and immediately spotted the lights and generators. "Now look at those... just what I need!"

He fired up the generator and the whole place was flooded with light. His gaze scanned the entire chamber. Miriam stood motionless and made no sound.

"This is right weird. I've never seen anything like it. Now, where are these doors?" He grabbed her by an arm.

Her first thought was, *how does he know about the doors? Vincenzo must have seen us and told him. It couldn't be anybody else.* She said nothing. They had only to walk into the next chamber and he would see them. She turned and ducked through a narrow stone arch and walked into the chamber, and there in front of her, illuminated by the floodlights, were the doors with the Templar's Portuguese Cross emblazoned on them. Cracker walked behind her. Once in front of the doors, she moved to one side.

"This is what you wanted to see, I believe."

"Too right, my lovely. Let's get 'em open." He pulled hard on the doors, but nothing moved. Next, he tried pushing, kicking, and rattling them – but got the same result... nothing. Breathing hard, he stood back and glowered. "You opened them before, so now you try."

How did he know that? Vincenzo for certain! Miriam refused to move or try.

He grabbed her by the shoulder and put the gun to her head. "Do it!" His face was a blaze of menace. She knew what he was capable of. He thrust his face inches from hers and the words spat out through the odour of his sour breath. "Do it now or I will kill you."

Miriam felt her heart lurch and her stomach turn. She knew he meant it.

"You had better do it, Doctor. He means what he says."

The unexpected voice of Father Giuseppe Vincenzo startled her. She swung around and there he was, dressed in his *Athletica Vaticana* sweat suit and also brandishing a pistol. The pretence and secrecy was over.

For a moment, words failed her. She managed to gasp out, "I always thought there was something unpleasant about you. Now I know for sure. You call yourself a man of God! What rubbish!" Her cheeks reddened with fury. *May the Magdalene, Sarah, and all her descendants protect our team and save this treasure.*

Vincenzo smiled and waved his gun skyward. "It is God's will and we are his warriors. Soon, the whole earth will know of us and there will be a great transformation across all nations. Do as Daniel asks or you and your boyfriends will perish. Do it now, please!"

Cracker gave her head a sharp jerking prod with the barrel of the gun.

Miriam pulled away, faced the doors and walked towards them – at the same time, she said a silent prayer. In front of them, she stopped and stared up at the Templar's Portuguese Cross. Placing her extended palm on the ancient woodwork, she knew exactly what would happen. How she knew this, she had no idea. The knowledge had always been with her, but she had buried it with science. Her hand remained motionless for a moment before she gave the gentlest of pushes.

Silently and slowly, the doors swung open. The chamber was exactly as she remembered it.

Both men stared hard into the half-light. At the far end of the chamber, the altar was visible with the glass structure on its top surface. Vincenzo, pushing Miriam in front of him, headed towards it followed by Cracker. The glass case was as she had left it. The shadowy outlines of some sort of cup or chalice could be made out.

The priest made a grab at it together with Cracker. Both had their hands around it. Miriam did nothing but stood and watched. She knew what would happen.

The glass container refused to budge. The two men pushed and heaved but the container would not yield.

"What's that inside it?" Cracker asked the priest.

"It's a drinking vessel of some kind. That's what we want, not this. Stand back."

Vincenzo stood back and aimed his pistol at it and blasted off an ear shattering shot the noise of which echoed around the chamber. Miriam was unable to cover her ears.

Nothing happened. The glass remained intact.

Vincenzo, with a puzzled expression, turned and looked at Cracker. "You try."

Cracker aimed and blasted several rounds without missing. His bullets hit the glass directly, but again… nothing happened.

It did not crack, shatter, or break.

It looked no different. His bullets merely ricocheted around the chamber, causing flinty splinters of rock to fly off in all directions.

"What the fuck!" Cracker yelled out. "That's not possible!"

Vincenzo fired off more rounds, but again the same result.

Miriam, white faced, had crouched low to avoid being hit by the flinty shrapnel flying about.

Vincenzo turned to her "You stand up and move over here." He waved the pistol at her. She moved slowly to an upright position.

Her voice was low and deep like a war requiem. "You should not have done that. The vessel is sacred and is thousands of years old." An agonised glow shone from her eyes.

"We don't give a shit, lady. Now, you seem to be able to do strange things. It's your turn now. You try and remove whatever's inside it. Get moving!"

"No, I will not."

A sharp slap from the back of Vincenzo's hand sent her head reeling. Another sent her head in the opposite direction.

She made no sound.

"Stop that!" a voice bellowed out across the chamber.

Both Vincenzo and Cracker swung around with their guns pointed at the figures of both Kelvin and the professor rushing towards them. The sight of the guns stopped them in their rush. They froze to a halt.

"One more step and she gets it." Cracker had placed the barrel of his gun against her head.

"Do not do it!" Fergal roared and his entire body shook with fear at what might happen.

"It's okay, Fergy. I'm going to do what he asks." She twisted her head around. "I can't do it with that jammed into my head. Lower it and let me try."

Vincenzo's gun remained pointed at Fergal and Kelvin, as Cracker, with his coarse burger-like hands, dragged her roughly forward toward the altar.

In her mind arose a certainty. *Something wonderful is going to happen.* What, when, or where... she didn't know. She sensed both Kelvin and Fergy's fears and concerns but knew she could not reach them mentally or physically. Cracker's voice, harsh like cement cracking, broke her thoughts.

"It's in front of you. Now lift it open."

As he spoke, a soft glow emanated from inside the glass and he could no longer see what's inside. The glow was obscuring. It grew stronger. A yellowy gold colour was filling the case, disguising what it contained.

Miriam remained impassive. *I have returned.* Her heart sang.

Cracker reeled back as his arm covered his eyes. "Holy shit! What is it?" He yelled to Vincenzo. "Over here, quick. You gotta see this!"

The glow began to spread outwards. Miriam remained motionless, transfixed in awe-like rapture.

Vincenzo shouted to his two captives, "Don't move, you two. If you do, I will shoot." To emphasise his point he raised his pistol and fired a warning shot up to the roof. Great clumps of dirt and rocky splinters spat outwards.

Both Fergal and Kelvin ducked low as the priest turned and moved across to Cracker.

The glow was increasing and spreading.

Kelvin signalled the professor who gave a quick nod. They both understood. In one swift movement, and with a deafening roar, they rushed at Vincenzo and Cracker.

It was a bad move.

There was the loud bang of a pistol firing. Kelvin was struck and fell with an agonised groan to the ground. He was motionless. Fergal dived flat and covered his head. Two shots exploded close to his body. Then, he heard other shots coming from behind. He didn't dare look. They sounded different. There came a pain-filled yell and through the gaps in his fingers, Fergal saw Vincenzo drop like a stone, clutching his stomach. He had taken a gut shot and was in immediate agony, writhing like a snake on the ground.

Fergal didn't dare move. Cracker was still standing, armed and dangerous. It was then he heard the unmistakeable Italian voice of Inspector Rizzo. His Beretta was in his hands.

"Drop your weapon, Cracker. There are four armed policemen with me. I now have extradition papers to take you back to Italy along with the priest, if he lives. You are both under arrest."

The golden glow had grown and now surrounded Miriam like a protective shield. Cracker made to grab her, but not knowing why, he was unable to touch her. She had somehow become unreachable. In a few swift moments, he knew he had no chance. Two other men were on the deck badly injured, and he could make out the shadowy shapes of the armed police.

Rizzo shouted out. "You are under arrest for the murder of Assistant Police Inspector Angelo Florentino and various other charges. Father Vincenzo faces similar charges for the murder of Bishop Vincent Fisher. Now, drop your gun. These police are trained to kill. I only have to say the word and they will shoot you dead. I promise! Now drop it! This is my last warning."

Cracker appeared uncertain. His arms gradually rose upward as he let the gun drop. "I surrender. Don't shoot." The police and Rizzo rushed up and immediately handcuffed him. Cracker looked at Miriam. "I don't believe this is happening. What and who are you?"

The chamber echoed as she spoke with the profound timbre of past millennia… that had never nor would not die. "Something wonderful is going to happen." Her wrist ties dropped away. "Everyone, please move back and remain where you are and watch. Do not worry for the injured… they will live."

Everyone felt compelled to obey. All eyes were trained on her as she moved to the glass case. The glow began a more powerful shimmering as she placed her hands on it.

Awed expectancy hovered in the air.

Not a voice spoke as with care and gentleness, she opened the glass case. It moved with welcoming ease – without resistance. Cracker could not accept it.

Reaching inside, Miriam pulled out a plain wooden chalice with a tight-fitting lid and held it aloft.

The professor gaped at the unbelievable scene. It was the source of the glow around them.

She started walking toward Kelvin.

He had taken a bullet through his left wrist and lower body. Blood was pumping from the wounds. His voice croaked with pain. "You have it. You've waited such a long time to see and touch it once more."

She spoke softly, close to his ear. "My brother, Iseldir, indeed it has. Now drink for another is wounded here. He drank deeply, and a brief but violent shudder passed through him. Within seconds, his pain started to fade. He looked at his wrist and his side. The wounds had closed, and all bleeding had ceased. All that remained was a small scar. He pulled himself up to stand, as if he had never been wounded.

Astonishment was on the faces of all present, including Cracker.

Miriam turned next to the prone but still writhing body

of Vincenzo, who continued to groan and call out loudly for his Mother not to let him die.

"Mamma, mamma, per favore, aiutami. Non lasciarmi morire!"

The entire front of his body had formed a spreading, darkening, red pool of blood that seemed endless. She knelt beside him and again spoke in a low whisper. "Did you ever believe your vocation, Father? Perhaps now… you will. Look, for here is the man you wounded, Iseldir, our beloved Druid and a member of my family. He is well again as you will be. Be still and drink from this cup." She stared into frightened and incredulous eyes as she lifted it to his lips and poured.

He gave an agonised but small convulsion. The pain was leaving him, and the internal damage began its repair. She gazed down at him. The potentially fatal wound was healing rapidly. "You are going to have much time to reflect on this, Father. Inspector Rizzo will be charging you with complicity in the murder of Bishop Fisher. Now stand up and know that physically, you are as you were… if not better. I can do no more for you." She placed the lid back on the cup.

Father Vincenzo was dumbfounded, and for once in his life, ashamed. With disbelief written all over him, he got to his feet.

The cup's contents had not diminished.

Miriam returned it to the glass case. The glow faded away and as it did, it vanished. All that remained was a stupefied silence from those present. One policeman moved forward and handcuffed Vincenzo.

At the same time, Rizzo did a strange thing, so unlike his normal character. He moved forward, and clasping Miriam's hands, he bent his head low and said, "I have seen many things in my life, but what you just did is the most remarkable of them all. I am much moved. *Era Cristo come.* It was… Christ like."

CHAPTER 63

Two prisoners alighted from Alitalia Boeing. They had arrived at the Leonardo da Vinci – Fiumicino airport, thirty-five kilometres from Rome. A dozen armed Italian police immediately met them. Their British counterparts willingly handed the prisoners over. Inspector Rizzo remained in charge and supervised their transport, future charges, and interrogation at the main police HQ in the Via di S. Vitale.

Two issues were on Rizzo's priority list. He had heard that the pope was seriously ill, and his doctors were unable to locate the cause of his demise. There had now been a breakthrough. Utilising the latest methods from a cutting-edge research laboratory, and using a medical assay, a form of analysis was done on his food and various swabs were taken. They provided clear evidence of adulterated food, and the swabs used to wipe surfaces had levels of contamination. It was ricin. Using a few drops of a mixture of reagents, the test pieces emitted light. The higher the luminescence, the greater the concentrations of ricin.

Pope Adrian was being slowly poisoned. As a policeman, Rizzo had never been far from suspecting foul play. He now had proof. Only the two cooks got anywhere close to the pope's food. He immediately ordered the kitchens to be shut down and off limits to all, apart from forensics and laboratory scientists. There was little doubt that Cardinal Nicholas was the prime motivator.

Rizzo could not help thinking of Pope John Paul I and his short reign of thirty-three days in 1978. His death was mysterious. No post-mortem was carried out and the exact cause has never been known. It was announced that he had suffered a heart attack in bed. Rizzo had always thought that was a tad too convenient. As Pope John I was a man of liberal views many die-hard cardinals and priests opposed him. Conspiracy theories of murder were rife. Pope Adrian's condition sounded similar to those theories. Cardinal Nicholas was leading an ever-growing band of followers – not only in Rome, but across the globe – and his rhetoric of late had become increasingly unpleasant.

The cardinal had made a rare error, as most criminals do. He had switched on his phone and made a call to Vincenzo's cell phone, which was being held by Rizzo's unit. From this, the experts in the Communications Department had managed to trace his exact location. Using a method called triangulation and a tracker app, they had located his hiding place. This method was an illegal procedure and can only be used by permitted agencies, such as the police.

The cardinal was about to get a visit, but first Rizzo needed to inform the Holy See, Pope Adrian. He was still capable of coherent speech and reasoning. The two cooks had been arrested and vigorously interrogated. They were close to a full confession but had not yet succumbed.

* * *

Wrapped in a large blanket, Pope Adrian was seated in a comfortable wing-backed chair. He looked gaunt, pale, and frail. The dynamic light of his once penetrating gaze had gone and was now replaced by a dull flicker.

Rizzo was shocked at his condition. He managed to bow low and kissed the Fisherman's Ring which was now too loose on his extended and trembling hand.

Pope Adrian spoke first. His voice matched the tremor in his arm. "It's always a pleasure to meet you, Inspector. I am certain you are thinking how dreadful I look. Have no worry. Since my food has been changed, I am feeling much better and improving daily. What news do you have? I have not been able to read any of my emails or messages from SOTA. What of my errant cardinal?"

"It's a long story, Your Holiness. Make yourself comfortable and I'll start from the beginning." Rizzo told it all and his part in it. He saw the pope's interest spark. He got to the events and miraculous healings in the tunnel. The light returned to the pope's eyes like a blazing fire.

"*Un momento per favore, ispettore, puoi ripetere?!*" He attempted to stand but it was too much for him.

Rizzo did as he was asked and repeated what he had witnessed and the effect it had on himself and the others.

Pope Adrian began to weep.

Rizzo, without being asked, arose and placed his arm around the pope. "It is true, Holy Father. I saw with my own eyes."

"I believe you, Inspector. I wish with all my heart I could have seen it for myself. You are indeed most favoured. What of the cup and the woman, Miriam?"

"I don't know," Rizzo replied. "It was most strange, mystical almost, and we were all transfixed. We felt powerless and were content to do as she asked. The cup seems to have gone, evaporated before our eyes. Father Vincenzo and the man Cracker are now in the Italian police's hands, and I have come here to apprehend and arrest Cardinal Nicholas. I know where he is. Do I have your blessing?"

"You will arrest him with or without my blessing," the pope replied, "but you have it anyway." He paused. "I just wish, hope, and pray, that you will all be well and safe – and that before I leave this world, I wish with all my heart that I have seen the cup and the lady named Miriam. I am deeply moved by what you have told me. Happiness fills me. Everything I've believed is true. Will the world ever know? Keep me informed, Inspector... and thank you. But one more thing before you leave..." The pope had the trace of a smile on his face.

"Yes, Holy Father?"

"Are you now attending mass?" Pope Adrian asked, and at the same time, he embraced an embarrassed Inspector Rizzo.

"Yes, I have been to mass three times this week." He bent his head to cover the slight blush that raced across his cheeks.

"I thought you might. You were meant to."

Rizzo, for once uncomfortable, bowed low and left. He had a destination to go to.

CHAPTER 64

The room was quiet… tense as a taut wire. The professor was troubled and bewildered. He saw himself as a stranger amongst people whom he had regarded as good friends. He now felt like somebody excluded, blackballed from a private club. He looked at both Miriam and Kelvin and couldn't deny the closeness of their relationship. He had heard her clearly refer to him as her brother and a member of her family.

What the hell was she going on about? I've known her all her life and Kelvin Stallybrass is certainly not her brother, nor a member of her family. This is just too bloody weird.

"Fergy, I know what you are thinking, and it's not weird." Miriam reached out and placed her hand on his arm. "Perhaps you should be named Thomas."

Fergy snapped. "Can you read my mind now?"

She knew it was unusual for Fergy to be angry with her, but there was little she could say to take that away. "I don't know, Fergy. Impressions and feelings appear in my heart and mind. They seem so true, and as if I have known them all my life. Not just this life, but others, going back thousands of years. What you saw and heard in the tunnel was as true as us here sitting together. If you can't believe it, I understand that, but there has been a seismic shift in my mind and body that I can't deny. Science could not take it away from me."

Kelvin joined in. "It's true, Fergy. I have felt the same as Miriam. We both independently experienced the same visions. Call them archetypes if you wish, but they did happen. In some strange as yet unknowable way, we are related. Not as lovers, or husband and wife, but as brother and sister. We both experienced the same thoughts and feelings. It's hard for anyone to believe or understand, but it's there and I can't deny it. I feel my Celtic roots as if they were only yesterday, and the presence of Jah and Magda as they are written on the stones and parchments we found. We were meant to find them."

"Okay." Fergy's tone had softened. "I saw something as did those present in that tunnel. It went beyond immediate explanation. I agree, it was startling, amazing, and beyond belief for anybody who had not seen it with their own eyes. I agree there is much I do not understand nor can accept." He rubbed his face before he asked, "What now of SOTA, the doors, the glass container, and the cup thing that was inside it?" He looked questioningly at them both, hoping they could come up with an answer.

Miriam gave a smile. "They are safe. They may not remain here for much longer. We should all remember that whether we like it or not, this quest had been given to Pope

Adrian and not to us. We are in some way beholden to him for the honour of what we have discovered. I would like to meet him one day, as I'm sure you both do." She squeezed Fergy's arm.

There was a long pause and the tense silence returned, its vibrations affecting the three of them.

The professor stood and what he said was unexpected. "I've had enough of all this. I'm quitting. This project is, as far as I'm concerned, finished. I'm packing and I shall be leaving tomorrow to go back home and my studies, where I can feel normal once more... away from all this mystical mumbo jumbo."

He turned and slammed the door as he left. Both were surprised at his stance but neither made any attempt to say anything to stop him.

Fergal strode away, and for the first time in his life, he understood the depth of feeling he had, and had always had for her. It was being taken away from him.

CHAPTER 65

Rome, Italy

The unexpected rain had turned the cobbled road surfaces into a gleaming and slippery prospect for both pedestrians and vehicles. The police had sealed off a section of the surrounding streets, known as the *sampietrini* or the 'little Saint Peters' – close to the medieval renaissance building, the *Villa Farnesina* in the bohemian *Trastevere* area of Rome. Tourists and all other people and transport came to a stop. Inspector Rizzo had assured them it would not be for long. Integrated police work, with the help of modern technology, were able to pinpoint the exact location of Cardinal Nicholas.

The doorway to the hidden apartment was down another small alleyway. Two armed policemen stood guarding both ends. There was no other way in or out.

Rizzo wanted to confront the cardinal personally. As he approached the bright yellow door, it wasn't difficult to notice the CCTV camera mounted on the upper ridge support. His visit would not be unexpected. Using the brass knocker, he rapped hard on the wood.

Silence.

He tried several times more and rang the doorbell persistently.

Nothing.

From his raincoat pocket, he produced a short, compact crowbar. Wedging it into the doorframe where the latch was mounted, he gave three hefty heaves and splitting the wood, the door cracked wide open.

He was in.

In front of him was a short flight of stairs leading up to a living area. He hesitated to gain his bearings. He was about to proceed upwards when a very English voice bellowed from the upper floor.

"Do come up, Inspector Rizzo. I have been expecting you."

Rizzo responded. "I'm fully armed and on my way up. Do not try anything stupid. I warn you... cardinal or not."

"Have no fear, Inspector. I shall not harm you in any way. I need to know much from you. Please, come up."

Rizzo was taking no chances. He bounded up the stairs with his Beretta in his right hand. Upon entering a large room, he immediately adopted a Weaver stance, firing position. He was not prepared for what he saw.

At the far end of the room, standing as straight as his crooked leg allowed and next to a large desk was the cardinal.

He was stark naked.

On the floor around his feet were his priestly vestments –

his zucchetto, his scarlet garments, including his cassock, mozzetta, biretta and white rochet.

"Please come no closer, Inspector. I was expecting you. I heard that Father Vincenzo had been arrested along with a Mr. Cracker, I believe. As you can see, I have defrocked myself. It saves the Vatican the bother." He swept his arm around the pile of clothes.

Rizzo felt too startled to move. This was not what he had anticipated. "What are you playing at, Cardinal? I'm here to arrest you for compliancy in the murder of Bishop Vincent Fisher and the attempted murder of Pope Adrian."

"Oh dear! Is that Antichrist still alive? What a pity. He must be as strong as an ox. After this silly little episode is over, Inspector, I would not be appointing a lawyer to represent me. What I want to know, please, is if the miraculous cup was ever found."

Rizzo, still in a firing position gave a brief nod. "It was and I saw it work. Astonishing to see. Sadly, you never will."

"Yes, I'm fully aware of that. I would have liked to have seen it. It would have done wonders for my Holy Cross and Sword Order and the true faith."

"Get dressed, will you?" Rizzo snapped at him and with his gun, gestured for the cardinal to move. "Be quick about it."

"Oh I don't think so, Mr. Policeman. My story ends here."

The cardinal leant forward slightly and picked up a large hypodermic syringe. Before Rizzo could react, he had plunged it into a large vein in his own arm and began to press the plunger.

"Neat liquid ricin, Inspector. Twenty milligrams in this one. You need only two to kill you by injection. It won't take long."

"Don't do it!" Rizzo shouted as he rushed at the doomed man. He grabbed for his arm but already, the cardinal's eyes had rolled back, the empty needle still hanging from his arm. He gradually sunk to the floor.

Using his phone, Rizzo yelled for the guards to get an emergency ambulance, but he knew Cardinal Nicholas wouldn't live another hour. The dose had been massive.

God damn it! Damn it! Rizzo clenched his fists and thumped the table. In front of him, writhing in agony, the whitened form of Cardinal Nicholas was going through his final death throes.

It was over minutes before the ambulance arrived.

Rizzo watched the body being removed. If he felt anything at all... he felt cheated.

CHAPTER 66

Two years later...

H ardly a day went by when the professor did not think of the events surrounding Miriam and the cup. They would forever stay in his mind. He had refused monetary reward from the pope's SOTA unit and all invites to meet with the Holy Father.

Miriam, who at first wanted to meet the Holy Father, now declined to do so. She did not want any of the organised religions hanging their hats on her and her discoveries. He had felt the same way. They had shared everything with the pope electronically and had sent him written accounts of what they'd personally experienced – emotionally, mentally, and spiritually.

Pope Adrian had replied and said their finds and the events surrounding them had contributed to his recovery, which was now complete. He expressed sorrow at not being able to meet Miriam or to have set eyes on the blessed artefact. The truth of the chalice, he realised, was not his to announce. It would stir transformations in humanity in its own quiet way. There was no rush.

The universe was almost fourteen billion years old... a mere week in God's design. He felt a new burst of hope and joy. Overall, mankind was not yet ready. They would be, long after he had passed away. In the meantime, he was content and supremely happy. The struggle had not been in vain.

Rizzo had maintained contact and had shown interest in their work. He and Fergy had become friends. The events surrounding SOTA and its mission had caused a dramatic change in his belief system.

At first, Fergal had felt bitterness and anger, but time had smoothed away the rawness. Much of the angst and sadness had been softened by the amount of work he was undertaking as the new CEO of the OxCam Archaeological Unit. Under his auspices, they had discovered two ancient British encampments close to the City of Bath – one dating back from the Bronze Age and the other from the early Celtic periods. In one way, he had wished he hadn't found that. It reminded him of Druids and the presence of Kelvin.

Fergal had various other assignments in the UK. His home country was rich in undiscovered sites from the earliest days of recorded history. He had made numerous finds of importance, but none would ever match the Templar doors and Miriam's performance with the cup.

It was not long after that episode, he remembered, that she announced she was giving up her academic work and taking a sabbatical to investigate the scientific validity of numerous spiritual and biblical events, mainly in Europe and the

Middle East. Some days before that announcement and after Rizzo's departure back to Rome, they had both revisited the site of the Templar doors.

As they approached, she had spoken to him. "You go on and push them open."

"But I thought only you and the Druid could open them?" He had replied and recalled being unable to prevent his sarcasm.

His omission of Kelvin's name went without comment. "No longer," she replied. "Don't ask me how I know, I just do. Go on… push."

He leant forward and gave a tentative shove. The door swung open with ease. He looked puzzled. "What has changed?"

She gave no answer but walked in with him close by. "Look." She pointed to the area where the stone altar and glass case had stood. They were gone. All there was to see was a blank space.

He had gasped. "What in God's name has happened here? How on earth could that be moved from this place and by who? I don't believe it!" A frantic scour around began.

There was nothing to see.

He looked hard at Miriam. "I think you know something about this. Tell me."

"I don't know where it went, any more than you do. What I sense is that no earthly person came in here and removed it. It is where it belongs, but not in this place."

"More mumbo jumbo. How are we going to explain this?" The professor sounded exasperated.

Miriam had looked thoughtful, as if she were choosing her words. "Fergy, sit on that rock over there for a moment." She pointed to a large flat protuberance.

He sat. "Well?"

She had sat close to him and reached out for his hand. He looked surprised.

"Fergy, since we started this, so many strange things have happened around us – not counting murderers, dodgy cardinals and a sick pope. One of the most amazing is my connection with Kelvin. Yes, I believe that we were brother and sister once, related to Jah and Magda. I know you do not believe that, but just a little bit would please me so much. Can you do that for me?"

He looked into her eyes. "I will keep an open mind, I promise you."

"Thank you." She moved her head and kissed him on his cheek.

He bent his head low.

She continued. "As for the cup you saw in that case, it will never leave me. I don't possess it, but now I know it is always with me, metaphorically speaking. It will appear when it is called or needs to. Kelvin knows that and he will never be far from me, as it guides him as it does me. I have plans, which I will tell you in a few days."

Her departure hurt him more than he could have ever imagined. As he had expected, the years rolled by and he received no news of her or where she had gone. Miriam, Kelvin, and the cup had vanished – as if they had never existed.

He missed her so much.

CHAPTER 67

Many years later...
St. Maximin la Sainte Baume
Var, South France
July 2nd, Feast day of St. Mary Magdalene

A tall man with silvery flowing hair walked slowly up the long meandering slope. Beside him, a woman with auburn tresses, beginning to grey, walked in step with him. Around them were countless lesser paths heading in all directions, through thick woods and forests. The air was fresh, cool, and clear. The only sounds breaking the hushed silence was that of birds calling and the gentle sounds of rainwater dripping from the trees after a recent shower. They were over halfway through the ninety-minute hike to the top. Their destination was a mountain cave, now a hidden monastery – the grotto and Sanctuary of Mary

Magdalene. Its guardians were Dominican monks and had been since the late thirteenth century.

Both walked in silence.

They reached the approaches and could see the one hundred and fifty steps leading up to the oak door entrance to the huge cave.

The man spoke. "This place was used by the Celts centuries before Christians absorbed it into this setting."

"I know, Iseldir," Miriam whispered to keep the sanctity of the place intact. "Pilgrims have been coming here since the fifth century."

"Miriam," Kelvin continued. "The people here believe the Magdalene lived here for thirty years before she died, but we know differently, do we not?"

Seconds passed and she didn't reply. Miriam was gripped by the reverential atmosphere of the place – the candles, the lingering incense, the darkened stone walls and roof. It was a place of intense spirituality "We do know but nobody here would believe us. The cup was with us for a time, although in one sense... we never had it. It was hers and always will be. It appears when I ask it to, and that's the way it has been for over two millennia... and that's how it will always be. Who our children will be, we will never know, but they will always find each other as we had found each other, as those that came before us had found each other. The mystery is vast and knows no dogma or religion."

"I know that is true. I'm sad to think that these people believe she used to dwell in this place." Iseldir sounded distant. "But it doesn't matter. She is here in every way, physically or not. What matters is the love and inspiration such legends generate across time. The truth prevails and is assisted by such wonderful folktales. Do you remember your old friend

Fergal? I wonder what he would make of all this?"

She laughed. "Fergy never breaks a promise, and the last one I heard from him was that he would keep an open mind. Who knows? I have hope."

Ω

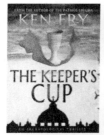  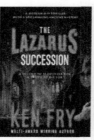 

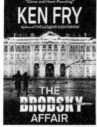   

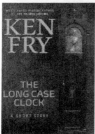 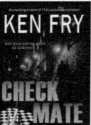  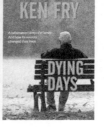

ABOUT THE AUTHOR

Bestselling, and multi-award-winning British author, **Ken Fry,** holds a university master's degree in Literature and has travelled around the world.

He has extensive knowledge of the Art world. This he acquired while working as a Publisher in a major UK publishing house, a wholly owned subsidary of the HEARST Corp of the USA. In his thirteen years with the company, he worked within the Fine Arts and Antiques division of the organisation and controlled four major international titles.

He is now retired and devotes his full time to writing. He lives in the UK and shares his home with 'Dickens' his Shetland Sheepdog.

WEBSITE - www.booksbykenfry.com
AMAZON - http://author.to/booksbykenfry
TWITTER - @kenfry10

Printed in Great Britain
by Amazon